To: Elyse

The Unveiling

Enjoy!

Dennis Gilmour

www.theunveilingbook.com

This book is a work of fiction. Names, places, characters, incidents, and organizations either are created from the author's imagination or are used fictitiously. Any resemblance to actual events, locales, organizations, or any person, living or dead, is completely coincidental.

Library and Archives Canada Cataloguing in Publication

Gilmour, Dennis, 1969-
The unveiling / by Dennis Gilmour.

ISBN 978-0-9784144-0-5

I. Title.

PS8613.I5U58 2009 C813'.6 C2008-907748-2

WritePharma Parable Publishing
#36 – 11245 – 31 Ave.
Edmonton, Alberta
T6J 3V5

780-934-7778
dennis@theunveilingbook.com

Cover artwork by Brent Orenchuk of www.misplacednewt.com

Printed in China

Chapter 1

The digital readout on the DVD player indicated 3:55PM, only five more minutes before the time scheduled for the special telecast. Valerie Saunderson and her children, Nick and Stephanie, clung to each other on the living room sofa and watched the TV. They were as still as statues, as their senses of sight and hearing strained to funnel every bit of information into their minds and make sense of it, as if they tried hard enough they'd come up with an answer for all of this madness.

When Valerie had first heard the news several hours ago, she had doubled over from the shock of the words, her head spun, her heart pounded. She'd since reclaimed some composure for the sake of the children but didn't feel much better. The knot in her stomach clenched tighter. She tried to be strong and reassured Nick and Stephanie with words of comfort but all the while struggled to control her own emotions.

Reports had poured in all day about unprovoked attacks on individuals worldwide by close associates and family members or sometimes complete strangers. The attackers had no coherent explanation for their actions and it was mostly being written off as stress. And then suddenly people just disappeared! The latest count put the number of people who had vanished in the millions. Some experts were speculating a time distortion might have flung people into a different space-time continuum. Some had other theories but nobody knew for sure. The affected people were from every country on earth—young, old, rich, poor, famous, unknown, black, white.

The reports kept pouring in so fast they couldn't tally accurate figures fast enough. One reporter speculated that by the time they were done counting the world's population, perhaps as many as a half a billion would be reported as missing.

The reporter also speculated that perhaps the disappearances were due to some new secret weapon that had malfunctioned in the growing tensions in the Middle East. It had only been several years since Iran had proven to the world that they had the nuclear bomb by a test detonation on their own soil. The United States had immediately tried to push a resolution through the United Nations and called for severe sanctions and threatened force if noncompliant, but Russia and China had vetoed the resolution, tabling a motion instead for an intensive diplomatic effort and tough sanctions, though far less crippling to Iran than what America had wanted. At this the U.S. had threatened unilateral invasion of the Muslim country, but Russia and China had boldly sided with Iran, promising full-scale war if she tried, gambling the U.S. would back down—which she did. Israel was similarly constrained by the same bellicose retaliatory war talk from the two communist nuclear powers.

So years dragged by peppered with talks, sanctions, periodic threats of war from the United States and Israel, more talks, U.N. resolutions…but no real action. America's colossal failure in the war on terror, especially the debacle known as the Iraq war, pretty much guaranteed that the world no longer trusted America's leadership on the international scene and the U.S. was pretty much hated universally, exceptions only amongst most of her English speaking brother-nations and Israel. The rest of the world seemed determined to band together to prevent another Iraq situation, and the U.S. just couldn't muster enough support to risk lone military action against Iran, which only served to embolden the Muslim country into openly continuing nuclear tests.

Now, just last week, Iran announced that it was finally ready to use the arsenal of nuclear weapons that it had been stockpiling. Iran held the world hostage, as it set a one week deadline for Israel to agree in principle to vacate the Holy Land and relocate elsewhere or face nuclear annihilation. Most of the Arab countries quickly united around Iran's leadership and formed a fragile coalition, but Israel refused to be intimidated, openly admitting what the world always suspected. The Jewish nation also had an arsenal of nuclear weapons and would fully retaliate against any strike. The rest of the world tried to mediate through the United Nations, but as Iran's one week ultimatum neared without even a hint of resolution, the situation seemed to quickly spiral out of control, as the major world powers took sides.

The U.S., Britain, Canada and most other English-speaking nations stood firm behind Israel while Russia, China, and Europe sided with the Arab coalition. The U.S. increased military alertness to Defcon One, Maximum Force Readiness, and Russia countered. Both nations promised full release of their nuclear arsenals in support of their respective partners in the Middle East and in defense of their homelands.

People all over the world started to panic and Marshall law had to be implemented virtually worldwide. Even Valerie's hometown of Star City, Louisiana had seen an increase in some looting and a strict curfew had been implemented. The town's population was only about seven thousand, mostly employed in the oil and gas industry, usually a docile town of mostly middle class working families where everybody knew each other, reasonable average people trying to deal with the sudden stress of the world situation.

Valerie's husband, Jeff Saunderson, a pharmacist at one of the local drugstores, had told her of the massive increase in use of anti-anxiety medication and anti-depressants over the past week.

Valerie had also eventually succumbed to the pressure to medicate and suddenly felt the need to do so again. She rose from the sofa and went to the washroom.

She opened the cabinet and retrieved the prescription vial from Armstrong's Pharmacy for the anti-anxiety medication Valium 10mg. The doctor had initially given her Ativan but it hadn't been potent enough. She went back and insisted on something stronger and longer acting. The directions said three times a day as needed, but she found herself taking as much as six a day. As she opened the vial and put the round blue pill in her hand, she recoiled a bit from her frazzled look in the mirror, bags under her deep blue eyes, shoulder length flame red hair matted and sticking to the sides of her head from nervous sweat, looking more like the unkempt mane of a wild lion than the hair of a late thirties mother of two. She poured a glass of water and swallowed the pill before trying to put on a comforting face for the kids and returning to the sofa.

Pressure had seemed to lift somewhat when all of the leaders in the growing world conflict suddenly inexplicably agreed to a meeting at a secret locale for discussions. But it was several days past Iran's deadline and the tension in the world was palpable. Everybody felt like something was going to happen soon, but nobody expected that that something would be millions suddenly disappearing worldwide. Valerie agreed the most likely explanation was that some new secret U.S. or Russian weapon had misfired. They were likely the only two powers with the capability to make such a device. Otherwise a targeted strike would have only affected one country or group of countries in the conflict. But the disappearances seemed to be totally random.

So far only a handful of people from Star City were unaccounted for. Word had been leaked to the press that the special telecast from the world leaders would explain everything. Valerie had grabbed the first opportunity she could to check with her husband, Jeff. She called the drugstore and was very glad to hear his voice, quaking though it was. She learned that he had been one of the victims of an unprovoked attack by a longtime customer. Jeff said he was coming home early to be with them, and she hoped he'd make it in time for the telecast from the leaders of the world.

Valerie held her children tightly, not saying much, waiting. She clenched her teeth in a vain attempt to remain patient and willed the time to pass quicker. Stay calm, she reminded herself. All her questions would soon be answered. They'd promised.

It was all she could do to contain herself, but finally it occurred.

The TV screen suddenly went blank.

After a few seconds the picture came back. It showed the president sitting at a long table with various world leaders. Valerie recognized leaders from Canada, Russia, Europe, and several other nations. A tall handsome man with short black hair sat in the center. He was wearing a sharp looking gray suit.

Mesmerized by the TV screen, they watched the President of the United States get up and stand behind a podium filled with clusters of microphones and wires. The camera zoomed in on him.

"Good evening ladies and gentlemen of the world," the president said. Flashes of light and clicking noises danced around his head as reporters took pictures. "While I speak, this message is being simultaneously broadcast world-wide on all channels and translated into all languages." There was a slight pause before he continued. "As most of you undoubtedly know, we are here to discuss the world situation and very strange events that have occurred lately. We won't explain it ourselves, for our special guest is far more capable. We only ask that you try to listen to everything with an open mind before you react."

There were several seconds of silence as he looked at his prepared speech, presumably reading a line or two, and shuffled some papers around. Then he looked up. “Ladies and gentlemen of the world, for many years mankind has seriously pondered the possibility of intelligent beings, other than humans, in the universe. But today we have undeniable proof of the existence of extraterrestrial life.”

The president turned slightly and faced the man at the center of the table. “I—along with the rest of these world leaders as representatives of the governments of earth and the human race—would like to formally introduce you, the citizens of the world, to Khur-ak, the Balazon, and leader of the Balazon race of beings.”

A stunned moment of silence fell over the press room.

“Is he serious?” Nick asked. “Is our president really that brain dead that he thinks a man in a gray suit is alien?”

A gasp of incredulity filled the press room, as crowds of reporters jockeyed for position in front of Khur-ak. Random clicking noises filled the air as camera flashes streaked across Khur-ak’s face like strobe-lights.

“Just wait and see what they say,” Valerie said.

At fourteen years of age, Nick liked calling everybody brain dead. But Valerie couldn’t help worrying that this was real and that the aliens were intent on conquering the world. The president wouldn’t say something like that if he couldn’t prove it. Perhaps the broadcast was to formally declare earth’s surrender. On the other hand, the president didn’t seem to be apprehensive about Khur-ak’s presence. His speech, tone of voice, and manner seemed to convey a positive outlook.

The president began again after a suitable moment of silence. He explained that the aliens had a message to bring humans about God many might not welcome—perhaps even causing world-wide uncertainty about everything people thought they had known to the point where humans might collapse as a race of intelligent beings.

However after much deliberation, the leaders had decided the world needed to know, as the world situation was becoming untenable anyway. He also tried to reassure the viewers with the revelation that the aliens had helped all parties in the nuclear showdown to agree to an immediate stand down of all military readiness and that further help would be forthcoming. He then talked for a few minutes about the Balazons and the benefits to mankind of contact with them, such as enormous leaps forward in science, technology, and medicine. As he started to close, a reporter jumped in with a question.

"We will answer all questions in due time," the president said. "Please be patient. There are many things we would like to say, but we have agreed to limit ourselves so Khur-ak himself can give a special introduction. I would like to close by assuring everyone listening that the Balazons are a benevolent race of beings who have my utmost trust. They are not—I repeat—are not out to harm anyone and there is absolutely no reason to fear or mistrust them. Please stay calm. We will soon address all of your questions."

When it looked as if the president were about to sit down, another reporter started to ask questions but the president insisted on patience until the end of the session. He sat down and for the next forty minutes each member of the international delegation got up and said a few words at the podium. Mostly they expressed their appreciation of the aliens' help and affirmed their belief in the goodwill of the Balazons.

"This is boring," Nick sighed as he rolled his eyes. "I want to see this guy prove he really is an ET. How much longer are these politicians gonna keep babbling?"

Valerie wasn't so eager. The longer the leaders talked the safer she felt. As long as humans directed and controlled the program, the aliens could not be thought of as bad. If the creatures willingly submitted to a well-controlled, well-thought-out human plan of revealing themselves on a familiar household device, she figured they must be courteous enough to allow humans freedom in other areas of life.

Stephanie didn't seem too optimistic either. She turned to her mother and asked, "Mom, are the aliens friendly?"

Valerie imagined her face must be pale; she sweat and licked her lips. She hoped her physical appearance didn't give away her true feelings. After she paused for a moment, Valerie took a deep breath and tried to talk in a soothing voice but it still sounded shaky. "It appears they are friendly."

It was the best she could do. She wanted to comfort her children but didn't want to lie either. When it looked as if Stephanie might ask some more difficult questions, Valerie said, "Khur-ak is going to talk now. Let's see what he has to say."

Stephanie reluctantly turned her head to see more.

"It's about time," Nick blurted out. "I was beginning to wonder how much longer we had to listen to this stupid preamble."

The camera zoomed in on Khur-ak's face as reporters snapped photos. "People of earth, I bid you greetings in the name of the Balazon race."

"He speaks English!" Valerie said with amazement.

"I am communicating to you telepathically. My thoughts can travel the wavelengths of the transmission you are receiving and your mind can interpret them as verbal communication. My mouth movements will even appear to coincide with the words of your native tongue."

"Cool," Nick said.

"Quiet!" Valerie commanded. "I don't want to miss anything."

Nick defiantly huffed once and then made sure he kept silent.

"I come from a planet called Nerovan, many light years away. I am the leader of an innumerable multitude of beings like myself. We have many natural abilities humans do not possess. At will, we can selectively bend light rays and phase shift our bodies' molecules to become invisible and untouchable. We have an existence that never ceases—what you call immortality—and have been influential on earth in our wraith-like forms for millions of years: studying, observing, and guiding mankind's development as best we could.

"We can also assume human form, which I am doing now so as not to unduly frighten you. But in order to prove my legitimacy, I will now cause some objects in your vicinity to levitate."

The unoccupied love seat in the corner of the room started to rise. Stephanie screamed and Valerie had to grab her and hold her tight.

"Ok," Nick said. "I'll accept that as proof."

Khur-ak took a deep breath as if he intended to ramble off a whole list of statistics but abruptly stopped short and closed his eyes for several seconds. "I am sensing a massive tide of thought-fear pulsating throughout my body. Please, we mean you no harm. Though we are highly evolved compared to yourselves, you need not fear us. Our minds are so advanced we could destroy this planet with a mere thought if we so desired but we will not. Does this not demonstrate we are sincere? Why would a superior enemy come to you peacefully?"

Khur-ak closed his eyes again, took a deep breath and held it, as if analyzing the aroma of some fine fragrance. Then he opened his eyes. "I can sense many are still suspicious. Let me tell you more about ourselves. Without need of mechanical devices, we travel the universe in search of life with the potential to evolve into higher forms such as ourselves. Once found, we help such life overcome the obstacles to their development so they can ultimately reach their objective—total freedom from physical constraints, what you call a spiritual existence or immortality. This is the highest form to which any race can evolve. With the attainment of such development came freedom, peace, and joy I can't even begin to express."

Khur-ak stopped speaking and his face took on a contorted expression. "Oh, how I wish I could make you fully understand the joy we too experience helping other life-forms attain their awesome potential. You see, we discovered your planet millions of years ago when the dinosaurs reigned supreme. Upon using our abilities to look into the future, we predicted a ninety-six percent chance the dinosaurs would continue to dominate the planet and cause the extinction of many species, including the rudimentary beginnings of man—the ape. But the dinosaurs had no evolutionary potential and wouldn't develop higher consciousness. So we destroyed them by redirecting a large meteorite to hit the earth, which hurled dirt and debris into the upper atmosphere, blocked the sun, destroyed plant and animal life, and lowered the global temperature. But as we predicted, numerous warm-blooded mammals, including the ape, survived the harsh climate. Many eons later, you evolved sentience and entered the *dark stage*."

Khur-ak turned his face violently to his left side as if some invisible foe had struck him. "I have just felt the pain of your rejection. In time I hope to make you understand. The dark stage is that evolutionary period which we have found intelligent beings inevitably go through as they slowly evolve beyond their bestial natures and progress towards the fullness of virtual godhood. But they must battle against their animalistic tendencies during this time, a predisposition towards violence, selfishness, intolerance, and hatred. It is a time marked by wars, lying, stealing, cruelty, greed, and many other forms of what is generally termed 'evil.' The conduct of the evolving race becomes so reprehensible that in virtually all cases they eventually destroy themselves. My people, the Balazons, were a rare exception to survive."

Khur-ak stared into the camera and shifted his eyes back and forth as if searching for some understanding from his viewers. "One of the principal ways we helped you was to implant a conscience-bubble into every human born, a type of mind implant that tries to make one believe in 'God,' right and wrong, and life after death in a good place such as 'heaven' or a bad place such as 'hell,' based upon one's behavior in this present life. Many humans believe they have no religious tendencies whatsoever, as the implant exerts a very subtle effect on their minds; yet it is usually a sufficient hindrance, for most evolving beings, to inhibit unrestrained reprobate actions."

Khur-ak stopped talking and stared at the camera hopefully. Then he added softly, "Now do you understand? We chose not to openly reveal ourselves to mankind at large until humans had progressed intellectually to the point you have. Most will soon be ready to accept that there is no such thing as God. We are, in fact, the closest thing you will find in the universe to the Almighty."

Khur-ak gasped and jerked backwards in his chair. After a few seconds, he regained his composure. "Unfortunately, many people are presently unable to accept this. I sense many are hurt, confused, and feel betrayed by their belief systems. But I hope the majority will accept us in time. Please let us help you. We have prepared a way to make this possible."

Khur-ak leaned forward and, with as much earnestness as he could muster, said, "We are prepared to counsel privately each and every individual on the face of this planet. This is not difficult for us to do, for our kind count in the billions. If you are living in one of the poorer countries of the world, starving and diseased, we can help with that too. At this very moment, Balazon representatives are amongst all individuals on the face of the earth—cloaked and phased, of course."

Valerie slowly turned her head right and left but didn't see anything out of the ordinary. A cold shiver crawled up her spine, and her stomach started to ache. She didn't like the thought of one of *them* in her house.

"Neat, man," Nick said and jumped up. "Show yourself, spaceman! I want to get a better look at you!" He ran excitedly around the living room, as if he hoped to get the first glimpse of the Balazon if he decided to show himself.

"Sit down!" Valerie commanded and grabbed her son.

"Don't you dare show yourself either," she said to the empty air. "I don't even want you in my house! Get out of here! Now!"

Nick, Stephanie, and Valerie froze, senses of sight and sound straining above the TV, searching for any sign of a Balazon. After a few minutes, Valerie looked at Nick. "Don't do that again."

"Aw, mom. Why can't we? We might as well talk to one. They're here anyway."

Valerie didn't care. She might not be able to make them leave her house, but she certainly didn't want to talk to one personally.

They took their places in front of the TV and continued to listen.

"Our representatives will not show themselves if you don't wish to see them. If you feel more comfortable with the TV, I will continue to inform you about us through this medium alone. However, I can sense innumerable specific questions from your minds. I cannot possibly answer them all on air. I encourage you to simply ask the Balazon to show himself and he can give you the individual attention you need. At any point in the discussion, you can ask him to leave and he will obey your request immediately."

He continued to talk, explaining more about themselves and their reasons for unveiling to the world.

Valerie began to feel rather silly. Nick and Khur-ak were right. The Balazon was in their midst anyway, so she might as well talk to him. If the Balazon had wanted to do her family any harm, he certainly could have done it by now, and she had many questions she wanted answered; they still hadn't explained why so many people had disappeared. She couldn't totally shake the nagging fears from her mind, but after several more minutes of deep contemplation, she decided to do it. She was working up her nerve when Nick turned and pleadingly looked at her.

"Please can we talk to one, mom?" he begged. "What harm could it do?"

"OK."

"OK?" Nick said as he raised his eyebrows. He looked surprised but certainly didn't argue.

"I don't think I want to," Stephanie said. "I'm scared."

Valerie had to hold Nick's younger sister and comfort her. "It's going to be fine. I'll make sure nothing bad happens." They sat on the couch, Valerie in the middle, children on either side. They held the remote control together and pushed the *Off* button, a symbolic gesture of their unanimous decision to initiate personal communication. Then Valerie gave the invitation.

Chapter 2

Star City, 7 hours before the unveiling

Jeff Saunderson drove his Honda Prelude to work slowly so as to avoid attention from the military vehicles tasked with keeping order in one small town in one big nation that seemed to be loosing its grip on normalcy, as nuclear conflict over a small plot of land in the Middle East seemed destined to consume the world in an atomic fireball. His workplace was only several blocks away and he usually liked to walk for the exercise. But with the world situation as tentative as it was lately, he figured it was safer to drive. Some looting and assaults had already taken place, proving the police presence was there for a reason.

He parked in the designated employee area and entered Armstrong's Pharmacy. The pharmacist-owner, Allan Armstrong, greeted him in the dispensary with his usual somber look of late. Allan was very much into world politics but a rather pessimistic personality, and he didn't hold out much hope for a solution to the world situation. Jeff was more positive. He believed the emergency secret talks with the world leaders would prove something out soon.

"Do you mind if I go home early?" Jeff asked. "I want to be home with Valerie and the kids for the special worldwide telecast at four o'clock"

"That's fine, Jeff," Allan said. "I'm closing the store early anyway. I want to be home too. I think everyone in the world is going to be glued to the tube so there's no use having the store open."

"It's not the end of the world as we know it. I believe something will work out."

Allan grimaced as he left the dispensary and mumbled, "I hope you're right."

It was just a few minutes past nine and no customers were in the store yet, so Jeff slipped away to the staff room to grab a coffee. He poured himself a steaming hot cup and tasted it, nice and strong, just the way he liked it. He returned to the dispensary and was greeted by several customers with prescriptions for the latest trend, anti-anxiety medications and anti-depressants. He filled the prescriptions, counseled the patients, and plodded along the rest of the day, doing his best to do his job and not think too much about all the madness in the world of late. The pace was brisk, a bit busier than normal, which was good and helped the hours pass more quickly. The sooner his shift ended the better, as he was anxious to get home and watch the special broadcast.

Allan relieved him for a quick lunch, and when Jeff returned to the dispensary, it was a little past one o'clock. Clarence Althouse came up to the counter, a longtime and very good customer.

"I need another month's supply of everything," Clarence said.

"Sure," Jeff said and pulled up Mr. Althouse's file on his computer.

"And this too." Clarence placed a new prescription on the counter. Jeff went and picked it up and read the name Zyprexa 5mg and the Latin abbreviations for 30 tabs and to take 1 tablet daily. "I've been a little strange lately and the doctor said this would help."

Jeff nodded with understanding and tried to appear soothing. "Many people have been having problems coping lately." However, beneath his professional demeanor, Jeff couldn't help but be a bit shocked. Zyprexa was an anti-psychotic and Clarence had always seemed the most level headed person he had ever met. The brain was a mysterious organ to be sure, and the stress of late was definitely producing strange fallout among people, but Clarence was the last person he would have picked to lose touch with reality.

Clarence fidgeted with his hands in his pockets and started to say something but then stopped. Jeff had known Clarence for years and had counseled him on many personal issues. He could tell Clarence wanted to say something else.

"Is there anything else I can do for you?" Jeff asked. "Anything else you'd like to talk about? I'm not very busy right now and we can go around the corner to the semi-private counseling area?"

"Thanks, yes, I'd like that."

Jeff went around the corner to the half-enclosed counseling counter. Clarence met him on the other side and came up close to his face and whispered in low tones. "I was admitted to the hospital a few days ago. The doctor said I had a psychotic episode with hallucinations but I still can't believe it was all in my head."

Jeff nodded his head. "It's a stressful world situation right now, a lot of uncertainty. You have nothing to feel ashamed about—"

"You don't understand! I don't think I was hallucinating. I know what I'm about to say sounds goofy but—" Clarence shook his head, obviously reluctant to say more. Jeff prodded him a bit and finally Clarence let it out. "I was abducted by aliens… at least I think I was. I mean I have a memory of it, but the doctor says I can't trust my perceptions."

Jeff thought he was prepared for anything Clarence might say, but still found himself momentarily taken off guard. He hadn't expected that. "Please, tell me more," he said in a soothing professional manner.

"Not like in the movies. You know, the short grey beings with big eyes. These guys were like tall skinny versions of humans, with bald heads, and made out of something like pure light. I tried to touch one and my hand went right through it. They took me aboard their spacecraft and started zapping me with electrodes. The pain was excruciating but I couldn't move or scream. One of them said, 'This one is going to kill you,' but before he could zap me, another alien started fighting with him. I don't remember much after that but what I do remember is so vivid in my mind…"

"Psychotic episodes always seem very real but they're not." Jeff paused and waited for Clarence to counter with something else, but Clarence just stared at him. His face slowly took on a contorted expression and he snarled. Jeff sensed an aura come over Clarence that he couldn't explain, something eerie and foreboding that instilled an instinctive fear in Jeff.

Clarence's face twitched and he snarled again, like he was fighting himself, and Jeff feared Clarence might be having another psychotic episode right in front of him. "If aliens unveil and say there is no God, do not believe it," Clarence said in a raspy voice.

"Excuse me?"

"Sacrifices must be made to prevent the unveiling. Prepare to die human."

The attack came suddenly, from the left and right, Jeff only having a blurred impression of Clarence's arms but feeling repeated blows across his face. Jeff instinctively threw his hands up and blocked Clarence's arms. He pushed Clarence back and ran into the dispensary to grab the phone so he could activate the emergency pager system.

From his new vantage point sprawled on the floor, Clarence snarled as he rose, eyes fixed on Jeff. Then he leapt bodily into the air, covered the few feet between them in seconds, grabbed Jeff's collar with one arm and struggled for the phone receiver with the other.

Jeff kicked Clarence in the gut and knocked him to the floor again, granting him the precious seconds he needed to dial the store pager number and screamed into the telephone receiver. “Help! Code Red! Pharmacist being attacked!”

Clarence was back up on his feet but Jeff slipped past him and out the side dispensary door. Jeff’s heart was pounding as he rounded the corner and made for the staff room, where he was sure several male staff members would be able to help him subdue Clarence. But Clarence was too fast, quickly came behind Jeff and grabbed him by the neck before he even made it past the cough and cold section. They tumbled together into the shelves, knocking bottles and boxes over themselves as they wrestled to the floor. Plastic bottles of cough syrups broke open as they rolled over and over, each roll staining the floor and their clothes with colorful mixtures of purple and blue.

Clarence wrapped his hands around Jeff’s neck and began choking him. Jeff tried to pry Clarence’s hands off but his grip was too strong. He couldn’t breathe and started seeing stars and black spots. He felt as though he would black out soon. But suddenly, he was free. He opened his eyes to see a young woman standing over him with a confident smile on her face.

“My name is Monica,” she said. “Everything is going to be alright. He won’t harm you now.”

Jeff was stunned at how this young woman had seemed to save him so quickly and easily. His eyes had been closed so he hadn’t seen a thing but Clarence now on the floor, docile and merely mumbled some obscenities.

“How did you do that?” Jeff asked as he coughed and breathed in deeply.

“Your friends are coming,” she said. “They will help you. I must go now.” Then she simply disappeared before his very eyes.

Jeff wondered if he was now having a psychotic break and had imagined the whole thing.

Allan and several others came running out of the staff room.

"Are you ok?" Allan asked. "What happened?"

"I think so. That customer just attacked me for no reason." As Jeff pointed at his attacker, two male staff members went over and picked Clarence up and held him firmly. They were young, strong stock boys, about 16 and 17 years of age.

"Take him to the staff room and hold him," Allan ordered, and his staff complied. Allan helped Jeff to his feet and led him to the staff room where he covered him in a blanket, poured him a cup of coffee and said, "Take as much time as you need to rest. I'll cover you for the rest of the day. Just go home, Jeff." Then Allan made two calls, one to the police and one for an ambulance for Jeff and left to cover the dispensary.

The police arrived within minutes. The officers questioned Clarence, who still seemed dazed and confused about the whole incident but started to come to his senses.

"I'm so sorry Jeff," Clarence said. "The aliens took over my body. It wasn't me!"

The officers didn't waste much more time trying to question Clarence. As soon as he started babbling about aliens, they seemed to close their minds to further inquiry.

"He obviously needs medical assessment," one officer said to Jeff, as the other handcuffed Clarence and took him away. Jeff nodded but felt rather hypocritical, as he knew the officers would probably refer him to medical assessment too if they heard him say a young woman named Monica single-handedly rescued him and then disappeared right before his very eyes. He wasn't sure they would be wrong to do so either.

Jeff agreed to the police request for a written statement, but didn't offer details about Clarence's recent medical history. Such information was confidential and would have to be obtained later through proper legal means if needed for defense. However, given Clarence's recent psychotic episode, Jeff felt certain no charges would stand up in court. He couldn't see himself laying charges anyway.

Jeff was just glad it was over.

Allan's voice boomed over the pager system and indicated Jeff had a call on line one, and Jeff went into Allan's office to pick up the phone. It was Valerie. They exchanged strange stories, she telling him about millions of people disappearing all over the world, and he telling her about his strange attack. At least he knew he wasn't crazy now, seeing as how disappearing people suddenly became a common occurrence, but he didn't buy Valerie's explanation that the cause must have been a misfire from some new super-weapon. Monica had said she had to leave and then did so. Her disappearance was volitional.

He began to desire some of those Valium pills that Valerie had been taking lately.

"When are you coming home?" Valerie asked.

"Just as soon as the ambulance guys clear me. But I feel fine. I'm sure it won't be long."

"Get home as soon as you can. I'll feel better watching the four o'clock telecast with you."

Jeff confirmed he'd be home as soon as he could and hung up the phone.

Chapter 3

A bright light flashed. Valerie instinctively shielded her eyes as a gush of warm air pelted her body. Dancing stars of every color replaced her vision, the kind produced if one squeezes one's eyes together too hard and too long. She started to get frightened and wondered if she and the kids had done the right thing by requesting that a Balazon show itself.

Soon the light display faded. When she dropped her hands, she saw a being that was semi-transparent, whitish-yellow, taller than an average human, with skinny body and extremities and long fingers. Its head was narrow and the face, though similar to a human's, had stumps for ears, slightly larger eyes and no hair. It also seemed to have female facial features.

Nick and Stephanie stared at the Balazon.

"My name is Acin-om," it said. "How may I assist you?"

Stunned and unable to speak, Valerie stared at the Balazon too for several seconds. Then she hypnotically said, "Please sit down."

"Thank you," Acin-om said and sat in a leather chair across from the couch.

All four were speechless. Even Nick seemed to be too overwhelmed for words.

After a while, Acin-om spoke. "I am neither female nor male."

"Um...what was that?" Valerie said as if snapping out of a daydream.

"I am neither female nor male. You were wondering what sex I was."

"Oh...I'm sorry." Valerie looked away, slightly embarrassed.

"No need to apologize. You simply do not understand my people cannot sexually reproduce. We can only duplicate ourselves by helping other beings evolve to a higher plane of existence. That is why we are so concerned for you humans. You are like our children, so to speak."

"Yes," Valerie said slowly, trying to remember the words Khurak had used. "I guess this mind implant of yours didn't work as well as you thought."

"No," Acin-om admitted. "People used their creative imaginations to add to what they sensed from the implant and developed all types of religious systems, everything from the ancient beliefs in the Egyptian, Roman, and Greek gods to the more modern philosophies of Buddhism, Confucianism, Daoism, Hinduism, Islam, Jainism, and Sikhism. These religions are often violently opposed to each other. Others are extreme and cruel, even involving rape, torture, and burning of babies on altars."

"Are you saying Christianity is merely another human attempt at explaining God?" Valerie asked. She had never been a diehard believer anyway, but the thought was still a little disheartening—sort of like when she was younger and woke up to catch her mother putting a quarter under her pillow, glad she finally knew the truth about the tooth-fairy but sad her mother had lied. She would have preferred to remain ignorant until she had grown up and out of simple beliefs on her own.

"Not exactly," Acin-om countered. "Christianity is not merely a human invention, for we have expended a personal effort in creating it. We had to come up with some way to try and curtail your wild imaginations from totally corrupting what we were trying to do. So we decided to try to create a more vivid depiction of what God might be like if he did exist. We guided the development of a nation called Israel and inspired various individuals such as Moses to write down the

Scriptures, giving more appropriate definitions of God, his laws, principles for living, and worship ceremonies."

"Wow!" Nick suddenly said. He had been uncharacteristically quiet for several minutes. "You inspired the Bible."

"Yes," Acin-om said. "We had hoped Israel would influence other nations to worship and obey the types of directives we had given them."

"I guess the plan didn't work too well," Nick said.

Valerie thought Nick must be referring to the centuries of moral depravity the Bible writers had recorded the Israelites had done.

"No," Acin-om replied. "We have found humans to be exceptionally rebellious, self-centered, and self-seeking."

"But how did you inspire people to write and do all those things?" Nick asked. "I didn't know they had pencils or paper when Adam and Eve were alive."

Acin-om smiled. "They didn't. The events recorded in the Bible weren't written as they happened. In fact, there were no organized Scriptures until Khur-ak appeared to and instructed Moses what to write in the first five books of the Old Testament around 1400 BC. Previous to that, any knowledge of our involvement with humans was passed on to others by oral tradition because for the first few thousand years we were mainly involved in people's lives in a very secretive way—influencing them subconsciously through the conscience-bubble and inflicting guilt if they disobeyed. But, as I said, it was quite difficult to control people reliably and consistently through these means alone, for they simply didn't listen very well, and the promptings of the mind implant were subject to human interpretations and feelings. You needed more definite guidance.

"So we carefully thought through the best way to appear to humans physically and influence them further—by pretending to be God. In the case of other Old Testament writings, Khur-ak again appeared and talked to some of the authors. At other times we spoke through prophets, dreams, visions, or disguised as angels. Rarely would we appear visibly because you were not ready for such a thing. We were usually either revered or feared—neither of which we wanted for we are merely the same type of creature as yourselves, but much older."

"Just a minute," Valerie said. "This doesn't make sense. Whether humans revered you or feared you, either way they would obey you. Why didn't you just appear to people physically and command them to behave with civility." Valerie realized she sounded like a doubter, but inside, started to feel less and less like one. She simply desired to understand.

"We considered it, but our future forecasts showed there was virtually a one hundred percent chance such action would have led to man's extinction around 1000 AD."

Valerie wrinkled her left eyebrow up in a thoughtful pose. "Are your forecasts always right?"

"No."

"Then how could you be sure it wouldn't work?"

"We couldn't, but we weren't willing to take the chance. From our observations of human nature, we believed the forecasts were correct in this instance."

"Why?"

"Because, as you humans are fond of saying, familiarity breeds contempt. If we were constantly visible, commanding everyone to obey us, it wouldn't be long before the novelty of our existence would wear off and people would start openly challenging us. We have observed that humans have an exceptional hatred of domination and have a strong desire to govern themselves. If we had tried to rule this world with an iron hand, pretending to be gods, it would work for awhile, but eventually people would rebel, forcing us to either destroy everyone, or leave—of course we would have chosen the latter. Once gone, any possible influence a belief in God might have once had would be minimal. People would realize they could rebel against us 'gods' and triumph, and they would assume the same would hold true after death. Your extinction would then be pretty much a certainty.

"Instead, we decided a form of human self-government, built on basic laws and principles of a mysterious 'God' would be best. We had observed that this, combined with a conscience, and the fear of what will happen to oneself after death, was the best possible behavioral control mechanism for humans."

"I see," Valerie said with a bit of resentment swelling up in her voice. She was beginning to dislike the realization that the Balazons had subtly manipulated humans for thousands of years.

"The ancient world was a very sensuous and violent place; the reason you didn't destroy yourselves long ago was because you simply didn't have the technological capability to do so. We looked ahead to this present time and saw the danger of a human race with a lack of more precisely defined moral guidance. So, before we appeared to Moses, we took our time and carefully thought through every contingency that came to mind, ironing out all the little details and deciding exactly what we wanted to do with this idea of 'God.' For the past several thousand years, we have more or less accomplished our objectives. There was some inevitable divergence from the road we wanted to lead you, but for the most part, we have been able to deal with them."

"Then what did you do?" Nick asked.

"We created the idea of a loving but just God, the perfect balance between love and forgiveness for repentant sinners on the one hand, yet vengeful dispenser of horrible punishment for evildoers on the other. But we knew humans needed something more authoritative than just another set of sacred writings to get them to listen. We saw that even though we might give you written laws such as the Ten Commandments, humans nevertheless wouldn't fully understand or obey them. You needed a powerful human personality to live life as an expression of these ideals and explain them to you."

Acin-om paused before continuing, as if expecting a reaction of some sort. "Khur-ak decided that when he felt the time was right, he would take on human form and try to authoritatively pound home the necessity for commitment to such things as love, forgiveness, good thoughts and actions, and in the process, die in such a dramatic way that humans would know a higher power loved everyone dearly. Khur-ak would try to do away with strict obedience to the external laws we had given humans earlier as a rough guide, and try to inspire people to live deeper lives of true goodness. In order to lend credence to the Scriptures and to prepare people for his arrival, right from the first few pages of the Bible we dropped hints, clues, and prophecies of Khur-ak's imminent appearance; we manipulated events to make sure these and all other prophecies came true. Even the religious festivals we instructed Moses to initiate, such as Passover, and the animal sacrificial system for sins, were types and shadows of our leader's future role in human affairs."

Valerie's mouth dropped open, and her eyes widened. She understood the implication.

"I don't get it," Nick said.

Acin-om said plainly, "Khur-ak took on human form, born of the Virgin Mary, and became the Biblically prophesied Messiah: Jesus Christ."

Now they both stared at Acin-om. The Balazon waited for a few seconds to let everything sink in before continuing. "Starting life as a human baby, he had no recollection of his life as Khur-ak, or of his mission on earth. Slowly, throughout his life, his memory returned and we revealed ourselves to him personally to explain things further. By the time Khur-ak, or Jesus Christ if you will, reached the age of thirty, he was fully aware of who he was and what he must do. To lend validity to his message, we performed many signs and miracles for him from behind the scenes: healing the sick, raising the dead, feeding the poor and hungry, and the biggest one of all—coming back from the dead himself. These things seem supernatural to humans, but to us they are relatively simple to do. Ever since then, we have recruited and helped humans from behind the scenes to propagate the message Khur-ak came to bring. We couldn't do this openly ourselves or it would have destroyed the illusion of mystery, and a few sharp individuals might have figured us out. Throughout your history, we have limited our supernatural interventions for the same reason."

"You tricked everyone," Valerie said, half-sounding offended. She was increasingly finding the idea of being lied to and manipulated insulting. For approximately two thousand years, one of the great faiths of the world, and the founding religion of many of the free-world democracies, was one big *lie*.

Acin-om nodded her head in understanding. "I sense you are feeling uneasy. What we did, we felt we had to do in order to ultimately help mankind. A short-term illusion back then could potentially yield attainment of so much more than a human being could ever have desired on earth. It all depends on whether or not you humans will accept us.

"At first, if necessary, Khur-ak had intended on going through with the original plan, which was to fulfill Bible prophecy about Jesus Christ coming back to set up the Kingdom of God. We made the prophecies concerning the timing of his second coming specific, yet vague enough, as to be able to be applied to any generation since he ascended into the sky in front of many witnesses; we had hoped the threat of Jesus' possible second coming at any moment to judge the world would coerce people into obeying their conscience-bubbles and the laws and principles set forth in the Bible. But if it didn't, Khur-ak would have come at the last possible moment, when humans were about to destroy themselves. Our leader would then have pretended to be God and forcefully established a peaceful and fair new world order. We had hoped Khur-ak would be able to reign until humans had evolved beyond the need for such tricks.

"However, the desire to govern yourself is even stronger than we had first thought. Our forecasts gave us good reason to believe humans would not accept Khur-ak's rule, but that we'd have a better chance if we unveiled. To psychologically prepare you for this day, for decades we have slowly tried to validate the reality of extra-terrestrial life by mysterious personal and public appearances of UFOs and aliens. Humans naturally built on these themes in literature and broadcast media to better prepare you for our unveiling."

Valerie thought about this for awhile. Sometimes even friends and relatives had deceived her before in life, and she had gotten over it—their motives hadn't even been pure. Her ninth grade "friend" Lisa had told her Scott, Valerie's boyfriend at the time, was philandering, which led to their breakup. Later she had found out Lisa had lied so she could date Scott.

She remembered what she had said when Stephanie was very young and kept playing in the streets despite repeated warnings to the contrary. She had intentionally lied to her daughter, trying to frighten her into obeying, by saying the boogie man liked to kidnap children who played in the streets. It worked. At least until she was old enough to question her mom about this doctrine, Stephanie never played in the streets again. By then she understood why her mother had lied—and forgave her. Valerie's motives had been pure, though her method had not been totally honest. But it was justified under the circumstances, for love had motivated her to lie.

Valerie suddenly felt like a five-year old. She was beginning to understand how much these Balazons really cared for the world, realizing all the trouble, time, and effort it must have taken to get humans this far. She quickly cast away any childish resentment and embraced the parental care of Acin-om and her kind.

"I'm sorry," Valerie finally said. "I know you were trying to help. I shouldn't feel resentful."

"That's OK," Acin-om replied. "I just wish everyone in the world could be as open and accepting of us as you are. Then we will be able to help everyone to have a better life now and ultimately immortality."

However, there were still some important questions to be answered. "Why did so many people vanish? And why did you attack my husband?"

"Because of a Balazon named Xsalma," Acin-om answered immediately. "It's always difficult to decide when to reveal the truth about ourselves to an evolving civilization. For instance, we unveiled to the Gerutniks of the Spiral Belt Galaxy during the eight thousandth year of their dark stage, but they were still too immature, and ended up destroying themselves with nuclear weapons. Some Balazons began to have severe doubts that humans were ready for the unveiling, and their leader, Xsalma, started a movement to prevent it. In an effort to force Khur-ak to reverse his decision, for years now Xsalma and his small band of supporters have been terrorizing humans in all sorts of strange ways."

"I don't understand how scaring us could cause your leader to change his mind," Nick said.

"Xsalma hoped Khur-ak wouldn't unveil if the world was afraid of us, so has been sowing fear of aliens for decades, almost as long as

Khur-ak has been trying to allay people's fears of extra-terrestrial life."

"Ah," Nick said. "That explains why there have been so many negative accounts associated with UFOs over the years. Cattle mutilations and such."

"Yes," Valerie said. "I remember watching a documentary detailing the alien abduction phenomenon, where people are brought on board a spaceship and terrorized, and assaulted, subjected to experiments, had mysterious objects implanted in their brains, pregnancies inexplicably terminated as fetuses disappear. Really strange stuff."

"Yes, these types of incidents originated from Xsalma," Acin-om said. "But Khur-ak sanctioned most of the more benign accounts to prepare you for open contact— mysterious lights in the skies, UFOs toying with fighter jets, crop circles, and such."

Valerie shook her head in disbelief. "How can such obviously advanced and capable beings as you fail to come to some sort of agreement about open contact before now? I mean, UFOs and alien abductions have been reported since before I was even born!"

"Actually, it has been a very short period of time from our perspective. On our plane of existence, we experience time differently than you do. As a rough analogy, you could say 1000 years from your perspective only feels like one day in our perception of time. Since we only started intense UFO activity shortly after World War Two, it has been a very short span of time to us."

"Wow," Nick said. "So all these decades of mysterious UFO encounters from our perception of time, converted into your time, would be about..." Nick tilted his head to one side somewhat, and his eyes rose to stare at the ceiling. "Hmmm, let's see, I'm usually pretty good with math in my head..."

"A little under two hours from our perspective," Acin-om said, saving Nick the bother of the calculation.

"Right, I was just about to say that."

"As the moment of our unveiling drew near, Xsalma's followers began intensifying their efforts and started assaulting people at random, but especially concentrated on those who were socially influential: newspaper and TV reporters, politicians, movie stars, and powerful businessmen. They even attacked Jeff because of a potential connection to somebody important."

"So to you guys a million years of your working with humanity would seem like a little under 3 years work seems to me," Nick said, obviously still fascinated with the time differential calculations.

Valerie ignored Nick's obsessive comment and tried to imagine who Acin-om was referring to. Then it hit her. "Of course! Jeff's friend, Brian Ferster."

"Precisely. He could've turned people against us if he'd used his investigative television program to do a report on the danger of our kind."

"I'm sure Jeff would've called him too," Valerie said as she slowly took in everything Acin-om said. She paused for a few more seconds. "But how could Brian do an expose on the Balazons who hadn't yet shown themselves?"

"He couldn't, but Xsalma had hoped to make our leader reluctant to go through with the unveiling by making sure it would be difficult to win people's trust if he did."

Valerie nodded her head. "His plan may work yet. Humans can be very unforgiving. What exactly did Xsalma do to all those people who disappeared?"

Acin-om looked at the floor, seemingly ashamed to answer. "Since their initial attempts were relatively unsuccessful at reversing Khur-ak's decision, Xsalma and his followers increased their efforts further: they randomly vaporized a total of about a half a billion people all over the world. But you must understand! Xsalma did care, even though it may seem he showed it in an inappropriate way. He believed killing millions of people now could save your entire race if it prevented the unveiling.

"Besides, our future forecasts showed a high probability that nuclear war would ensue in the Middle East standoff, which would have resulted in even more deaths than what he did. Xsalma believed some would survive a nuclear war, so better to delay open contact. Khur-ak thought it more likely your entire race would be obliterated. The data from our future forecasts was inconclusive, so not very helpful either. It was a difficult decision, but Khur-ak gambled that it was less dangerous to unveil now."

"What's so dangerous about showing yourselves?" Nick asked with childlike innocence.

"Many humans would rather die than welcome us as friends. Many will be suspicious, thinking us horrible invaders out to kill them, especially after what Xsalma did. Many others may be tempted to live hedonistic lifestyles because they no longer need fear death. But you must control yourselves or you may not reach the exultation stage. Unfortunately, the only way of controlling some would be to destroy them, which we do not want to do."

"What's the exultation stage," Valerie asked.

"If a race of beings can survive long enough, they will enter exultation—the final stage I am now in and always will be: immortality."

Valerie thought about this for a moment. The story made sense, and a part of her really wanted to believe Acin-om. Her dad had been a preacher while he was still alive, and had always told her humans were the only intelligent life in the universe. Valerie silently disagreed, although she didn't say anything verbally; she didn't think anything in the Bible contradicted at least the possibility. The narrow-mindedness her father seemed to exude on this point probably fueled her mild discontent with religion over the years. She never wanted to become as close-minded to scientific possibilities as her dad had always appeared to be. She never wanted to be accused of checking her brains at the door just because she had a belief in a God. Now to see undeniable proof of alien life before her eyes was something extraordinarily exciting.

As an adult, Valerie still went to church the odd time, more for social contacts and to make friends though. She had long since had too many questions about religion to take it all too seriously, and tried to encourage her kids to think for themselves and find their own path about faith.

"It still seems a rather extreme way to try and 'help' us," Valerie said. "Could Xsalma think of no better solution?"

Acin-om looked down at the floor with seeming regret, then up again. "You must understand. Occasionally some Balazons disagree with our leader about how best to serve an evolving civilization. Xsalma was bound by the highest law, love, to act as he thought best. In cases such as these, we must appeal to the Council, a board of super-beings that live in the center of the universe.

"The Council members are made up of exultation entities who have willingly merged their very essences into one mass of collective energy; they are very powerful and wise, and all Balazons willingly submit to their judgments. I, or any of my kind, can join the Council after 100 million years of service and experience in the field as an exultation worker. Most of us aspire to join the Council someday. It's the highest form of office in the universe."

Acin-om shrugged. "Anyway, we took the conflict to the Council to consider the matter and a ruling was to come down before four o'clock, the time scheduled for the unveiling. Though we were confident the Council would rule against Xsalma, we had to respect his right to do as he deemed right. Until then, Khur-ak sent me to guard Jeff. I appeared to him as a human female named Monica and preserved his life on several occasions."

"I see," Valerie said.

"We hope to prove our sincerity. It was a calculated risk to reveal our existence after what Xsalma did, but we knew it was very important we do something soon."

"With your help, our odds of surviving are better?" Valerie asked.

"Much better, but there are still risks. There is an all too real possibility humans will reject us and force us to leave. If that were to happen, mankind is almost certain to become extinct. Without our help, this world conflict will likely spiral into something like your two world wars, and threaten your entire existence."

Valerie nodded in agreement, considering the logic and wisdom of all of Acin-om's words up to this point. It was a lot to take in.

Chapter 4

Jeff tore off another piece of his shirt to replace the one already stained completely red with blood. He dropped the crimson rag to the ground and put the fresh one on his left shoulder, wincing with the sharp pain but holding it tightly to stop the bleeding, wondering how he could have been so careless. Societal programmed respect for authority, he supposed. If Monica hadn't helped him, he never would have known that they weren't who they claimed to be.

He forced his reluctant feet to walk the final steps to his destination, a dark blue house at the end of Mulberry Street. He was very tired; head spinning, needed to sit down. Darryl had better be home. He rang the doorbell and waited.

It opened to reveal a man with broad shoulders, about three inches shorter than Jeff, dark hair and mustache. "Oh my God!" Darryl shouted, eyes wide with surprise. He immediately led Jeff inside to sit on the couch. "What happened to you?"

"I don't understand it all myself, but it has something to do with the disappearance of all those people."

Darryl ran into the kitchen and came back with a white box. He quickly took out a disinfectant bottle, scissors, and opened a package of gauze pads. "Looks like the bullet went clean through the muscle. All I can do is bandage you up."

Jeff nodded his approval.

"So tell me how it happened," Darryl said.

"I was driving home for the special telecast when a black car forced me over to the side of the road. Two guys in black suits jumped out and flashed badges in my face. Claimed to be FBI agents. They tried to get me into their car but I knew something was up and bolted. They shot me."

Jeff didn't bother to add that a mysterious woman named Monica was in that same car and alerted him to the danger of the situation, or that she used her supernatural powers to help him earlier at the pharmacy. He didn't dare mention that the supposed FBI agents had transformed into some sort of light beings right before his eyes, and attacked him. Darryl would probably think he was crazy, and Jeff wasn't entirely certain he would be far off there. But it had happened!

The last thing he remembered seeing was Monica battling the two supposed FBI agents, who now appeared like alien beings, with something like a sword but it glowed yellow like the sun. Then Monica had just waved her hand and somehow Jeff found himself within several blocks of Darryl's place, a friend who worked for the ambulance service. He had been confused and disoriented, and when he checked his watch, Jeff noticed that time had seemed to jump ahead several hours past the special telecast time. He had no recollection of what might have happened during the missing time, or even if he was missing time. Perhaps Monica's transportation "magic" just produced a side effect of pushing one forward in time.

"I know it sounds crazy," Jeff said, "but this is the second time today I've been attacked for no reason. Why, a customer I've known for years just suddenly turned on me. It just doesn't make any sense!"

"Yes is does, Jeff. The Balazons have explained all that."

"What do you mean?"

"You have to hear it for yourself." Within a few minutes, Darryl had finished bandaging Jeff's shoulder and said, "Come downstairs. I'll show you."

Darryl led the way downstairs, but by the time they reached the last step, Jeff's heart started to pound with the fear of not knowing what to expect next. Darryl sat down but Jeff stood at the last step and didn't move.

The man talking on the TV called himself Khur-ak and claimed to be an alien. He said his kind were the "gods" humans had always worshipped. Every so often, he would pause and invite viewers to ask a Balazon representative to appear. Jeff reluctantly sat down beside Darryl, and despite himself, became engrossed in the words of explanation from Khur-ak. He lost track of time until Darryl jarred him back to reality with a foolish suggestion.

"I'd like to ask one of their representatives to appear. I was about to do it when you rang my doorbell."

"Don't," Jeff said. "They're killers."

"But it wasn't malicious. You'll understand after you hear it for yourself. Here, I'll rewind it for you." Darryl pushed a button on his satellite remote control, and the picture started to reverse rapidly. Darryl had a later model digital video recorder satellite system that automatically taped live broadcasts, but it didn't mark specific start points and had to be manually rewound. "It was about an hour ago, so here should be good." Darryl hit play again. Khur-ak was talking about a Balazon named Xsalma. "Here's where he talks about why people vanished and others were attacked."

Jeff listened intently for the next few minutes.

Of course. It made perfect sense. He had nothing to fear from the Balazons and should be welcoming them with open arms. But he couldn't shake the fear. The fancy explanations the aliens were spinning to justify their immoral behavior brought back memories of the kind of explanations his cult leader had used to rationalize abusing Jeff so many years ago.

Jeff stared questioningly into a distant nothing, rubbing and occasionally clenching his flame-scarred forearm, scarred with the remnants of self-inflicted punishment. The pain his past cultic rituals had caused him reached a depth far greater than his cold appearance portrayed, and he felt his facial muscles tense and harden as he remembered the past.

It had been more than ten years earlier that Jeff had first believed in God. He had read books about God before, thought about Him occasionally, but usually ignored such things. However something, or someone, kept pulling him back, and he would occasionally read a Christian book, the Bible, or watch a gospel TV program.

Some of the preachers on TV seemed so phony to him back then, and many were. "Oh...oh...I feel God talking to me right now!" they would say. "His Holy Spirit is telling me to tell you to call in to the prayer counselors for your healing, whether it be physical, financial, or emotional. God has got a miracle waiting for you!" Usually by this time they would be pounding their fists and screaming into the camera, but they would get very serious when they started to talk again.

"And when you call or write, don't forget to make a $100 gift or more on your favorite credit card. We take checks; however, we will withhold miracles until your money is in our account. If you want any of our tapes or books, send $1000 for each one to our ministry at the address on your screen. We need your help to stay on the air so we can keep begging you for money. After all, I have many expenses such as my mansion and acreage just outside town, my Rolls Royce, Ferrari, and Jaguar, all my household servants, my wife's extravagant clothing bills, my private jet... and remember God loves you, but we don't: we want your money."

Of course they never actually said that, but Jeff was intelligent enough to read between the lines. Even so, before they made their pitch for money, they would usually talk about sin and the necessity of repentance. Some of the things they said would convict Jeff deeply, even though they were obvious phonies. But mostly he ignored any inclinations to believe in God—until the day he read a Christian book.

Jeff didn't remember the author, the title, or even much of the contents, but he did remember one particular analogy. The author explained the limitless intricacies of a car: spark plugs, distributor cap, radiator, pistons, cylinders, carburetor, and the delicate interplay of these parts with the oil, fuel lines, and electrical wires. Then he described the complex intricacies of the human body: heart, lungs, brain, kidneys, liver, pancreas, and the delicate interplay of these organs with the blood vessels, capillaries, and neurons.

The author asked his readers to consider the vast amount of human effort and intelligence that went into the planning and construction of a car. Next the author asked some penetrating questions. How much more awesome and intricate was the technological marvel of the human body? How much greater was the intelligence of the Being who constructed man? Could there be any doubt a Creator existed? There was no longer any doubt in Jeff's mind.

The only question Jeff wanted answered was what kind of Creator He, or She, or it was. He'd read further, understood and accepted Jesus Christ's sacrifice on a cross for his sins, and had started an earnest search for knowledge about his Maker. He read the Bible hungrily in those days. Every word was like food and water for his malnourished soul, and he desired others to eat and drink the same sweet fulfillment he experienced daily. Life had been so much simpler back then. Things had been black or white, right or wrong. One either did things the way Jeff believed God wanted them done or one didn't do anything at all. There could be no compromise.

Jeff's spiritual hunger led him to become involved with a group claiming to have all the answers. They seemed so knowledgeable and wonderful at first, especially the leader, so kind and loving and accepting, an affirming presence Jeff had never had when growing up. Jeff came to think of the leader as the father he had never had. His real dad was an alcoholic, and a cold, angry, and distant man, who used to beat him regularly. He got addicted to the emotional love high from the group and figured they must definitely be the "one true faith". However, eventually, it slowly got to the point where if Jeff disagreed with them—especially their illustrious leader, godlier than the Creator Himself—it was obviously satanic influence and he had to repent or risk the loss of salvation and face eternal damnation. The leader's patience started to wane and Jeff learned it was psychologically safer to acquiesce.

Over time, the leader somehow gradually become his "dad", cold and distant, verbally and emotionally abusive, but by then Jeff was hooked. He had as much difficulty setting boundaries with the leader as he had had with his dad when growing up. In later years, Jeff's counselor helped him understand that the reason he had been susceptible to the cult was that Jeff had come to associate the leader with his father. The same childhood fear Jeff had of abuse and beatings were psychologically transferred to the leader, but now magnified by the deep seated fear that somehow the leader had the power to hurt him with eternal damnation. No wonder he was afraid; he obeyed every command…for a while anyway.

Jeff later learned the definition of their type of organization: cult. In those days, the group brainwashed him to walk, talk, breathe, witness, sleep, and think like the rest of the group. The leader did not allow him to watch TV, to listen to the radio, drink alcohol, take any kind of medication, eat meat, or observe traditional holidays such as Easter and Christmas—the list of strict arbitrary rules and regulations was virtually endless. The only literature he was allowed to read was that which dealt with the teachings of the group. He gave the cult his money, possessions, time, and energy. He gave himself totally over to "God" and completely ignored the small voice in his mind that said, ever so softly, *No*.

The small voice was Satanic! He would not yield! He would stand steadfastly and resist faithfully! However, the small voice would not stop. The voice said *it* was the truth and begged to be listened to.

Concerned friends and family tried to help him regain his sense of identity. Jeff had been warned of them. "Satan has blinded the hearts and minds of everyone but us," the leader told him. "Don't let family and friends deceive you!"

Valerie was violently opposed to the cult. To his new-found friends, it was obvious a demon possessed her. He was instructed he would have to leave his family or risk eternal damnation. This edict was too much. He loved his family dearly and couldn't bear to leave them, so refused to do so. The leader had seemed surprised at Jeff's stance, the first time Jeff had really showed some backbone against the man. Then things really got strange.

The leader showed Jeff a secret interpretation of the scriptures that "proved" the only other option was to undergo a painful ritual to ensure his own and his family's salvation. A little physical pain Jeff figured he could endure, but leaving his family was out of the question. So he went along. The ritual was long and grueling, involving physical endurance tests, cutting himself, group sex with several female cult members, and burning his forearm with a torch. The cuts had long since healed but the scarred forearm was Jeff's constant reminder to always think for himself in the future. The leader periodically kept pressuring Jeff to leave his family, and repeated the ritual upon Jeff's refusal, each incident bringing Jeff closer to the now obvious conclusion: the guy was crazy.

Jeff almost had a nervous breakdown but eventually faced his fears. Valerie, also a Christian, was free to live as she pleased, and family and friends were free—but he felt he had to obey his religious leader or suffer eternally in hell. His leader was either right or wrong. He had to know the real truth. In later years, Jeff's counselor helped him realize the leader's rituals were attempts to take back power that Jeff was challenging by his refusal to abandon his family.

The real breakthrough came when Jeff confessed the group sex thing to Valerie. Jeff had felt so guilty confessing, but she was totally forgiving and understanding. She had such compassion for what he was going through, and said she would just be glad if she could have him back. He realized again why he loved her so much, and how she reflected more the character of a loving God than the leader ever could. After some more serious self examination and support from Valerie's church friends, Jeff realized he indeed didn't have to blindly obey some human being and left the group. For awhile, he tried instead to just follow his own heart and understanding of the Bible. Over time though, Jeff came to the conclusion that God was just too mysterious for him to ever figure out. He eventually put all this faith stuff out of his mind.

The previous intricacies in creation that seemed to so strongly convince him that God existed were now simply relegated to mysteries everybody had to learn to live with. God would have to appear to Jeff and say, "Touch me, I'm real." Until such time, Jeff determined not to bother torturing his mind with trying to figure out what "God" wanted.

Not long after, Jeff found himself openly making fun of not only Christians, but all faiths. Anyone who believed in *a* "God" was fair game, including his wife. Fortunately, his wife's Christianity was easy to live with. She didn't even go to church very often. Only occasionally, when teaching their children morals, would she talk about God. If that was the worst she did, Jeff could live with it.

"Let's ask one to appear," Darryl said, breaking Jeff's train of thought by reiterating his most stupid suggestion.

"I've got to get going," Jeff said and stood up. "Thanks for everything but I'm not staying around if you're going to do that. I don't want to talk to one personally."

As Jeff walked up the stairs, he heard Darryl give the invitation. Even with his back turned, a bright flash consumed his vision and he felt a warmth come over him. He resisted the urge to turn around and hurried up the stairs.

"I am Durzak. How may I assist you?" Jeff heard the alien say in a surprisingly human sounding voice.

Jeff closed the basement door. He had much to think about on the way home.

Chapter 5

Valerie was fast becoming convinced of Acin-om's sincerity. One of the biggest barriers to her own acceptance of the Balazons had been understanding the reasons why the aliens attacked her husband and others, and why the aliens had caused the disappearance of so many people. Now that she understood the details about Xsalma's motivations, her apprehension was beginning to melt away like butter on warm toast. However, when she looked at Stephanie, she saw a little girl who seemed frightened. Valerie reached for her daughter's hand, held it, and smiled comfortingly at her.

Stephanie was rigid.

"Would we really have destroyed ourselves in a nuclear world war three without your help?" Nick asked.

"We think so," Acin-om said. "Our forecasts aren't perfect, as the future is always changing and hard to predict, but the odds didn't look good. Now that we are out in the open, we can do more to help mankind, but if the world rejects our aid and forces us to leave, the odds won't be much better than to have just let the nuclear war go forward."

"Why would anyone want you to leave?" Nick asked.

"Some people will not trust us," Acin-om said. "Many fear what they don't understand."

Nick shrugged his shoulders indifferently as if to say he didn't care what other small minded people did. Then a new thought seemed to hit him, and he said excitedly, "You mentioned something earlier about not being male or female. Then why do you look like a female?"

"Before I entered the exultation stage I, too, was a simple physical creature such as you. In that primitive form, I was a female. When one changes from mortal to immortal, one retains some of the external characteristics of their former life."

"Wow," Nick said slowly. "It must be wonderful."

"How long has mankind been in the dark stage?" Valerie asked.

"Since shortly after humans reached sentient status—approximately six thousand years ago."

"How long does it last?" Valerie asked.

"Millions of years."

"Oh," Valerie said and looked again towards her daughter, noticing a more frazzled look than before; no mere hand holding would suffice this time. She reached over and pulled her daughter in close. "What's wrong, sweetheart? You haven't said anything the whole time. There's no need to be afraid. Ask Acin-om any questions you wish—it's like having God in your living room. Anything you could possibly desire to know, she will have the answer."

Valerie looked at Acin-om and said," I hope you don't mind if I call you by a female pronoun. I know it's not totally accurate, but that's how I see you."

"Not at all," Acin-om said.

"She's not God!" Stephanie said, pointing an accusing finger at the alien. She looked up at her mom. "What about all those Sunday school lessons? What about everything I've been taught? You told me we were going to live forever in heaven when we died. How do I know what's true anymore!?"

Valerie thought about this carefully for several seconds, understanding and regretting the disservice she may have done her children by not expressing her own doubts about religion a little more forcefully as they were growing up. She felt guilt start to creep over her, but forced it back with the fact Nick had turned out different. He seemed to adjust instantly to the Balazons' presence, so it couldn't be all her fault.

Nick had never cared much about religion. He seemed to emulate some of Valerie's skepticism. He used to tease Stephanie with some of the difficult philosophical questions like how it doesn't make sense that a loving God would torture people in hell forever. It just seemed to make Stephanie stronger in the end though. She developed a good relationship with her youth pastor, who helped ground her with answers to these difficult questions. It wasn't long before Stephanie could skillfully defend herself against Nick's attacks and quote more of the Bible than either one of them.

"Give it up, sis," Nick said. "Reality is sitting right in front of you. We can finally get some intelligent answers to the really big questions of life without having to listen to you quote scripture all the time."

Stephanie's face visibly soured, but she ignored Nick's insult. "How can you be the perfect God that I worship?" Stephanie asked. "You admit to making mistakes and Xsalma started a rebellion of sorts. That is not my idea of perfection."

"It depends on how one perceives 'perfect'," Acin-om said. "Yes our kind makes mistakes and has conflicts occasionally, but our motivations and heart attitudes are pure love: that is perfection. We don't have to be motivated by ideas of rewards and punishments, but are self-motivated by love always, even if we disagree sometimes on how best to express it. It will always be difficult for you to fully comprehend our existence until you share it. It is pure joy, but you must experience it to fully understand."

"Yeah, Stephanie's idea of perfect is primitive and influenced by religious dogma," Nick said. "Your conscience-bubble mind implant has done a really good job brainwashing her."

"It affects you too, Nick. You are just not consciously aware of it. It exerts a very subtle yet powerful effect on every human being, mostly on a deep subconscious level. You have to understand that the conscience-bubble broadcasts a certain standard message to every person's mind, but we have to inject specific messages into each individual's thoughts to optimize influence over that person's actions. We've known everyone intimately who has ever lived, and we have always customized our hidden interactions with people on an individual basis to moderate their actions."

Nick's left eyebrow crocked into an inquisitive gesture. "Give us an example of how you might use these techniques to prevent a rapist from hurting someone."

"Well, we can't always prevent it because people choose to go against our influence all the time. It pains us to see you hurt one another, and we feel terrible manipulating people, but we mostly have to let bad things happen for the greater good of the survival of your species. But to answer your question, we would typically try to induce fear of temporal consequences like getting caught and going to jail. This is the conscious influence. Then we would subliminally suggest to his subconscious that if he can be brought to justice in this life, it follows that God will justly punish him in the afterlife, and therefore he is in danger of eternal damnation. If he's familiar with the Bible, we'll try to use hellfire verses to enhance this fear of punishment. Then we might try to instill a reward thought to the subconscious by suggesting developing a consensual love relationship instead, and that this good behavior would produce more happiness in this life and lead to obtaining the reward of eternal life in heaven. We can do all this almost instantaneously, and you sense our influence more on an instinctive and intuitive level."

Nick's lower jaw dropped open and his eyes widened, as he shook his head. "I'm beginning to understand the depth of the mind-fuck you guys have been putting over on humanity for thousands of years."

"I'm not sure I approve either," Valerie said. "And watch the foul language, mister, or I'll take your video games away for a week."

"Fine," Nick said. "But then I'll just point out that you have no right to object to the Balazons. Threatening to take away my video game system is no different than what the Balazons do. You're using the same primitive reward and punishment techniques to manipulate my actions."

Suddenly Valerie felt as if Nick's words were a baseball bat and he'd just reached over and smacked her upside the head. He was right! What a terrible mother she must be to manipulate her son and interfere with his freedom of speech. She felt her face flush and her cheeks got hot, and she felt as if something like a hot dagger stabbed her mind. She felt terribly guilty, just terribly so.

Wait a minute. All parents have to set limits and teach right from wrong. She had punished Nick in much more severe ways over the years. This shouldn't bother her so much. She pushed the thought away as ridiculous, and suddenly felt normal, as if a weight had been lifted from her shoulders. "Hey, what just happened to me? You made me feel guilty, didn't you?"

Acin-om nodded. "Yes, I intensified my influence, just to give a demonstration of how we use the implant."

"I felt terrible too," Nick said, "for swearing and back talking. But then it went away."

"Notice how you both rejected the thoughts," Acin-om said. "I quickly pushed your consciousnesses to the limit so you would instinctively push back and reject the thoughts. I wanted to show you how we can only exert influence. You make all your own choices. Your own strong opinions and emotions often negate our efforts. But we still try to do the best we can."

Valerie frowned. She was annoyed. This felt like a type of mental rape, a violation of her most private inner thoughts.

"I'm sorry if you feel violated," Acin-om said. "But I know you understand our good intentions."

Valerie suddenly felt embarrassed, as she realized Acin-om was monitoring her every thought. But this kind of thing had been going on her whole life anyway, and she never knew it. There was no use trying to hide, and no use feeling ashamed about the reality that just was. Nonetheless, she couldn't help feeling exposed and naked, and like she couldn't trust her thinking now, as there was no way to really know which thoughts were exclusively her own anymore. "Are you influencing me even now to accept the things you are saying?"

"Of course, we love the entire human race and will always, in love, continue to do everything we can to help you. We make no apologies for that. The only difference between what we were doing yesterday, and what we are doing today, is that we are now visibly showing ourselves and plainly explaining all the reasons behind our mysterious workings with you humans."

Valerie thought again of her own methods in raising her kids over the years. She loved them dearly and did her best for them always, which entailed some encouragement and rewards for good behavior at times, and many instances of threats of punishment or actual disciplining. At times, her own children had accused her of trying to control them too much. She had felt so hurt that her own children had viewed her actions as manipulation, devoid of any love. But they had eventually matured enough to understand, and she hoped the same would prove true for humanity.

Raising children was not easy at all, and she realized in a deeper way now how the whole human race was evolutionary children to these beings. She totally understood now how love was motivating the Balazons to do anything and everything they could, even seemingly manipulative mind games, to ensure the survival of their "children", the entire human race. She would expect no less commitment from herself or any good parent.

"Then we're just like animals!" Stephanie suddenly said, voice quaking and almost breaking out into a sob. Valerie could tell from the tone of Stephanie's voice that her resistance was fading. "There's no God, no heaven. When we die, we just die. Never to think or feel again!"

Acin-om leaned forward and reached out a long skinny hand to Stephanie. "It's not as bad as you think, dear child. Take my hand and I will telepathically project images into your mind of what might be. I think you will be pleasantly surprised."

Stephanie recoiled with disgust and fell out of her mother's arms. "Stay away from me! Don't touch me! Don't even come near me!"

Stephanie picked herself up as Acin-om moved in closer, ignoring her commands. With the fierce determination of a child refusing to give up her belief in Santa Claus or the Easter bunny once she had learned the truth, she ran past Acin-om and bolted for the front door of the house.

She was halfway down the main hall when Valerie stood up to chase her. "Stephanie! Get back here this minute!" Valerie almost added, "And apologize to Acin-om," but stopped herself. That would be expecting too much, too soon. If she could just get Stephanie to listen, it would be enough.

Stephanie was blindly hurtling for the door. It seemed as if she was choking on the thick air of shattered dreams and to breathe a whiff of the outdoors might revive her. Her single-minded obsession drove her forward without thinking, brain apparently incapable of handling its own struggles and coordinating movement at the same time, for she tripped at the top of the stairs.

"Oh God!" Valerie said with alarm, and then realized the irony. It almost sounded as if she were praying to a being she no longer believed even existed. She witnessed her daughter fall headfirst down the long flight of stairs, several feet away from being able to pull her to safety. Valerie lost sight of her for several seconds, but thumping noises filled her mind with horrible images. She reached the top of the stairs in time to see Stephanie crack her head on the hard unforgiving linoleum floor. She was powerless to do anything except stand there.

"Oh my God!" she said again as she raised her hands to her cheeks and felt them hot against the palms of her hands.

Valerie ran down the stairs. Stephanie was out cold, and her head had a huge bloody gash on the side. She didn't try to move her, but felt for an evasive pulse which, once found, was frighteningly low. Valerie looked up at Nick at the top of the stairs. Acin-om was beside him.

"Call an ambulance," she said.

Nick, wide-eyed and unable to move for several seconds, eventually nodded his head in agreement and started for the kitchen phone. Acin-om held out her skinny arm and blocked Nick's progress. As Nick looked up with eyes that asked for an explanation, Acin-om gently shook her head.

"There is no need," she said calmly.

"What do you mean?" Nick asked.

Acin-om didn't reply, instead went downstairs and knelt at Stephanie's side. Valerie didn't say anything, but watched in amazement. Acin-om rested her hands on Stephanie's head, closed her huge alien eyes, and tilted her narrow bald head up to the ceiling. Soon Stephanie's gash disappeared from her head and reappeared on the same spot on Acin-om. The Balazon winced for a few seconds as if in pain, and the gash disappeared from her own narrow head as well.

“Stephanie will be all right in a few hours,” she said. “She needs to rest now.”

Valerie checked her daughter’s pulse again. This time it was strong and healthy. She thanked Acin-om profusely as she picked up Stephanie in her loving arms, took her upstairs to her bedroom, and tucked her under the quilt. Valerie spent a few minutes holding Stephanie’s hand and stroking her hair, thinking how grateful she was to Acin-om for the miracle healing but worrying about how she could help Stephanie upon awakening.

When Valerie finally came back downstairs, Acin-om and Nick were sitting on the couch. The alien said, “I was just telling your son about the very thing I had planned on telepathically communicating to Stephanie before she ran off. I was explaining that no humans born since sentient status have ever really died. They physically die of course, but we preserve their essences, storing them inside other humans.” Acin-om looked at Valerie hopefully, as if unsure of how Valerie might react.

“Reincarnation,” she said slowly, fascinated at the mere idea, and sat across in the love seat.

“Not quite,” Acin-om said. “At the moment of death, an individual’s basic essence—their spirit, or soul if you will—is released into the atmosphere, where it’s drawn to the strongest natural radiation source, the sun. If allowed to reach there, it would quickly burn up, except we have this entire planet encased in an invisible containment shield. A team of Balazons is solely dedicated to collecting these souls and depositing them in host bodies.

“You see, though we are very powerful, there are certain things we cannot do: we cannot create higher forms of self-conscious life.

That is something the universal force of nature must do over a slow process of millions of years, but we can preserve life's higher essence once it has sprung forth. Perhaps now you can understand a little better how Xsalma's misplaced love for humanity drove him to do what he did. He knew a few deaths now would make no difference in the end, for everyone is really alive."

Nick said, "That's also why some have had near death experiences."

Acin-om nodded. "To humans, death resembles being pulled through a tunnel towards a bright light. In the past, we sometimes deposited people back into the same physical body they had come from so they could come 'back from the dead' and reinforce the belief in an afterlife to others. But for those allowed to completely expire, we immediately deposit their human essence into another person. Anyone will do. We have found similar species' essences are so compatible that one human could potentially hold trillions of individuals."

"Then why don't I remember those past lives," Valerie asked, bewildered.

"You don't fully understand," Acin-om said patiently, as if she were a teacher explaining a difficult concept to a student. "Every human is a distinct and separate individual, but he or she can also serve as a storage tank, so to speak, for many more individuals. The dead are dormant, lifeless, and unconscious inside their human hosts. You won't even be aware they're there."

"Unless you hypnotize yourself," Nick added.

"True. Sometimes, in a deeply relaxed or meditative state, one can reach inside their mind and vicariously live the experiences of the other individuals inside them, but mostly they lie dormant until the exultation stage. As humans evolve to become like us, the many individuals within also evolve, eventually emerging to becom many separate exultation entities. If even *one* human can be alive at the moment the transformation takes place, that human will contain more than enough storage space to birth every human born since sentient status. Think of it. One single human being, an egg if you will, bursting forth to release untold trillions of life forms.

"Once you die, this transformation will seem to take place immediately. You won't be aware of the passing of time, even billions of years, while you are dead. So from your perspective, you will indeed 'go to heaven' immediately after you physically die. Your next conscious awareness will be as if you have just awakened from a restful sleep to a new and wonderful life. For instance, the baser side of your human nature— the so-called evil side of hate, lust, selfishness, desire for power and the like—will no longer influence you, but you will be full of love, joy, peace and contentment. And you will desire, like us, to help other races in the universe attain the same ultimate potential you will have achieved."

"That's so wonderful," Valerie said. "So everybody goes to 'heaven' in the end, regardless of anything 'good' or 'evil' they have done."

"Well, yes and no," Acin-om said. "There is still a danger. We've seen it happen on other planets before, even after a fairly successful unveiling. This revelation does not positively motivate everyone, but rather some become emboldened to start actively resisting their conscience-bubbles because they no longer fear death. They choose to live lives of selfish, passionate, hedonism, which can eventually destroy the implant. Over time, this attitude slowly spreads to others, who do likewise. And the more we try to reassert influence and control over people, the more resentment and rebellion against us grows. Eventually, we are totally rejected and have no choice but to abandon the planet. Left to your own devices, self-extinction usually soon follows. Of course, if this happens, then nobody is going to 'heaven'. Everything is a delicate balancing act, and we cannot do it without your support. We need your help in order to help you."

Acin-om took a deep breath and motioned with her hands, as if she were gearing up to tackle another difficult subject. She started a sentence, stopped as if searching for the words to communicate, and then started again. "You asked me earlier why anyone would want us to leave. In addition to the dangers I've already outlined, what happened with Stephanie is a graphic answer to that question. Many humans find it difficult to give up their belief systems in favor of new understanding and will bitterly oppose us, even to their deaths, all in the name of religion. Religions we, ourselves, had inspired as a temporary preserving influence until full knowledge could be openly shared."

Valerie nodded. "I believe it." When she thought of the horrible wars and atrocities done through the centuries in the name of religion, she knew the Balazon spoke the truth. Fanaticism would always be alive and well on planet earth. All she could do was choose to react positively and hope enough others would do the same. She wondered how her husband would react when he found out.

Jeff!

She suddenly looked at her watch and realized it was almost six.

She leapt from the love seat and raced for the kitchen phone. "I think I'd better call the police," she said. "Jeff should have been home by now."

Acin-om immediately jumped up and followed behind. By the time Valerie had grabbed the handset, Acin-om gently reached over, took it from her hand, and hung it up.

"I already know where he is," Acin-om said. "After Xsalma's people attacked him last, I sent him to Darryl's place for help. Jeff is fine and will be home shortly."

Chapter 6

The police lined the streets on all sides, also paddy wagons, and what looked like the army. And all of them carried long futuristic looking shoulder rifles, which looked like ray guns from a bad science fiction movie. Jeff stopped his car and asked a police officer why they were out in force.

"We're a precaution. In case things get out of hand."

"Does this have something to do with the Balazons?"

The cop nodded his head. "Don't worry, sir. We've been prepared for the worst. Best thing for you is to get home and stay home. Things might be getting ugly soon." Jeff didn't pry further. The officer's look demanded he move on.

Ignoring the pain in his shoulder, Jeff drove the last few blocks as quickly as possible. When he got home, he cautiously opened the door to his house and peered inside. Valerie was talking to someone. He entered the living room and saw one of *them*.

Jeff pointed his finger and started to say, "I want you out," but stopped mid-sentence. He stared at the creature, dumbfounded for a short time. There could be no mistake.

"Hi, Monica," he said casually, as if he had expected to see her.

"Monica is not my true name. I am Acin-om."

After a short pause he said, "I've already heard Khur-ak's explanations. I've thought about it a lot and come to the conclusion it's all a bunch of crap. I don't know what game you things are playing, but I know danger when I see it. Go away and leave us alone."

"It's too late for that, Jeff," Acin-om said. "We must make the best of the situation. You may not wish to accept us, but others will."

"What do you things really want? What's your hidden agenda? If all this stuff about conscience-bubbles is true, take mine out and let's see if I revert into a caveman. I dare you. You can't because it's not true."

"The effect of doing such a thing before you are ready would be disastrous. Besides, once we have implanted it, only the individual can remove it."

"I don't believe you. I don't think you have the power to do the things you say. Do some miracles. Rise up my dead grandmother."

"We can't reanimate a dead person once their essence has been deposited into a host body."

"Oh, convenient excuse."

"Give me another test," Acin-om said.

"Why not make wine out of water." Jeff ran to the kitchen and came back with a glass half full. He handed it to Acin-om and it turned red.

"Drink it," she said.

Jeff did; it was indeed wine. He threw the glass across the room, staining the wall on impact. "I don't care about your parlor tricks! I don't trust you."

"I have the power to heal as well," Acin-om said and pointed at Jeff's injured shoulder, the mere reminder initiating a stab sensation that seemed to travel along his collar bone to the base of his neck.

It was then that Valerie noticed it too. "What happened?" she asked.

"Nothing. It's a long story." He turned to the Balazon. "Look, while I admit it might be nice to..." He stopped, curious that Acin-om suddenly decided to close her exaggerated eyes in mid-sentence. The alien seemed to be concentrating, as she lifted her long arm and pointed slender fingers in Jeff's direction. Then he noticed the pain was gone.

He tore off the shoulder dressing. Nothing. It was as though he'd never been shot.

"It is my gift to you," Acin-om said and opened her eyes. "I can not take it back."

Jeff sighed. "It doesn't change a thing." It was his heart that needed the miracle, but it wasn't one he thought the Balazons could provide. He went to the kitchen and stared out the window, trying to determine what it would take for him to let go.

When Valerie got up to follow him, Acin-om said, "It will take a while, but he'll come around."

She went over and hugged her husband from behind. "Please try and stay open-minded," she said. "Remember the cult? After that experience, you gave up on all mystical things. I thought you would like the concrete reality of what the Balazons represent. No more ambiguity to deceive you. They're being very direct and open."

There was no response.

Jeff didn't want to admit a part of him did believe, and after the horrible experience he'd had with the cult, he had totally given up on religion. It had been very difficult for Jeff to come to the realization that he was being lied to and manipulated by the religious group, and he couldn't shake the same sinister feelings he was receiving now about the Balazons. The aliens were lying and manipulating mankind. Jeff might not be able to prove it, but he could *feel* it, almost as clearly as he could feel the rough scar tissue that had healed over his own flame scarred forearm. He rubbed the area, raised and callous, something he liked to do when he needed a reminder to think for himself instead of following anyone else, human, alien, God…whoever.

Khur-ak was the cult leader and the rest of the aliens were his blind obedient followers, spinning their deceptive lies for some evil manipulative reason. The aliens would show their true colors eventually. The cult leader had also been slow to reveal his true evil nature but eventually it happened. He'd been down this road before, a road of light that seemed so deceptively right, but led to disaster. The only difference now was that the fancy Bible talk was coming from aliens that actually had some power to back up their claims with miracles.

But even if Jeff could dismiss the cultic overlay he was imagining on the Balazons, after the terrifying things the aliens had done to him, he didn't know if he could open up to them. They seemed so powerful after all. He could only shudder to imagine what else they might do to him if he let his mental guard down for a moment.

Jeff went back into the living room and sat down. Valerie followed him. "I was attacked today by a longtime customer of my store. Did Xsalma's followers take over his body?" he asked. "Wouldn't it have been more efficient to simply create a body, such as the one you made for yourself, and try to terrorize or kill me with that?"

Acin-om closed her eyes for several seconds, concentrated, and changed shape to become Monica. "To do this requires more mental energy than simply taking over a human host; they needed all they could to muster a proper attack. Besides, there is more terror in being inexplicably attacked by those you know."

Jeff's facial grimace conceded to Acin-om's statement. He remembered how horribly shaken he had been. "I don't claim to know everything, but I do know you creatures aren't as altruistic as you claim. Surely you don't need to resort to lying, deception, terrorism, and murder to help us poor earthlings out of our primitive condition. That makes you no better than us. If that's your idea of help, I'd rather not have any."

"You are presently incapable of comprehending our motives. Someday, if you become like us, you will understand."

"I understand better than you realize. Valerie, have you ever seen the movie 'V'?" Jeff stared at Acin-om. "It stands for *V*isitors. In it, aliens land on earth claiming to be friends, but in the end it turns out they need humans for food."

"Oh, Jeff," Valerie said. "Do you know how ridiculous that sounds?"

"No more ridiculous than what she's told me so far." He continued to stare at the Balazon, searching for some type of reaction, acknowledgment perhaps.

Acin-om started to say something, but then stopped. Jeff continued to vent his feelings.

"How do I know this isn't so?" he asked.

"I suppose you don't. You'll have to trust us."

"No way. I'm going to call my friend Brian. I'm sure he'll want to interview me for his TV show. I'll tell the viewers about your assaults on me. We humans aren't as stupid as you think, Acin-om. When people like me start telling their stories, you'll see how determined and unified we can be at opposing evil beings like you."

Valerie sighed. "That's exactly what Xsalma and his followers were trying to do. Sow fear and mistrust so Khur-ak wouldn't unveil. Don't let some misguided aliens manipulate you like that, Jeff. Listen to Acin-om. I think you will find everything the Balazons have done up until now very logical and well thought out. They had no choice but to do the things they did."

"No way", Jeff said. "I'll never trust them."

"If enough people think like you, humans will automatically

be condemned to extinction," Acin-om said. "You need our help to survive."

"We don't need anything from you. How do we know you're not lying to us again for some twisted reason? I may not be a genius but I trust my instincts."

"We are here to help humans, Jeff. The choice you and everybody on this planet must make is whether or not to accept that."

"I can't." Jeff turned to his wife, a sour look on his face. "What did they do to you to make you so agreeable? Did they take over your mind and body too?"

"Oh, Jeff," she said. "We must listen to them, or all dreams of immortality will be lost."

"I don't care," Jeff said. "Being mortal, maybe that's a good thing. At least I'd have a chance of dying a natural death instead of whatever these things have in store for me. Living forever would become boring."

"Be honest with yourself," Acin-om said. "Your own feelings reveal death is unwelcome. Search your heart and you will see the conscience-bubble is holding out the possibility of eternal life to you."

"I've got good reason not to trust your kind."

"You've got a point, Jeff. I'm terribly sorry about what happened. But if most of the people on earth think as you do, there will be little we can do for humanity."

If only Valerie could have experienced the full horror he'd gone through, she might understand. "I think I've heard enough," Jeff said. "I don't want to be here right now." He got up to leave.

"Where are you going?" Valerie asked.

"Out for some fresh air. Don't worry I'll be back." He would be back all right, back after contemplating what he should do next and fearing what that might be. He wasn't much of a fighter, but if he felt his life and family was in jeopardy, he would have to do something.

He quickly grabbed his coat and went outside. Neither Valerie nor Acin-om tried stopping or following him.

Chapter 7

Jeff slowly trudged down Kirkwood Avenue, as a windy chill pelted his leather jacket and bounced off. McDonald Park was a block away, and he had a deep desire to sit in its grass and gaze at the water of the miniature lake.

Jeff's street ran roughly parallel to the main street business section, several blocks down. He could see activity, police cars, foot patrol, other people walking— perhaps feeling the same as himself. But *his* street was virtually empty. Occasionally, a car drove by.

Jeff shuffled his feet and kicked various stones as he entered the front gate. Then he picked up a few pebbles and sat near the edge of the small lake. The rippling surface looked beautiful. Jeff tried skipping a few stones, as he had often done as a kid. Somehow, he couldn't get it to work this evening.

If the Balazons were being truthful, he could live his life as normal, doing whatever he wanted, perhaps even live longer due to medical advances, and hopefully die at an old age, having done everything in life he had wanted to do. He would live again millions of years later, regardless of his accepting them, or getting too close. Perhaps, at least, he could remain neutral. Nothing in the Balazons' philosophy demanded otherwise.

On the other hand, he couldn't ignore the feeling they were up to something sinister. It was a gut instinct, something deep down inside him, but he had learned to trust those instincts ever since they'd helped him escape from a mind-controlling cult. He had the same feeling he was being manipulated and lied to as he had in those days.

A shrill scream suddenly pierced the air. It was a woman's voice, sounded as if she were being tortured. He got up and ran in the general direction of the voice, but it stopped. Then it shrieked again, coming from a large tree on the other side of the park.

Jeff's heart was pounding. As he neared the screaming voice, he could make out a man and woman rolling in the grass. He moved in closer, careful to be quiet.

The man had the woman pinned to the ground. He was holding both of her arms above her head with his left hand, and attempting to pull down his pants with the other. Her skirt was above her waist, revealing torn nylons. She was squirming, screaming, and biting her attacker. Every now and again, the man would curse and slap the woman in the face or punch her in the stomach.

Jeff's mouth went dry. He had always wondered what he would do in a situation like this—what kind of hero, if any, he would be. He still didn't know. "Hey," he croaked lamely. "Stop that."

The man stopped moving momentarily, as if unsure he'd heard anything, then continued his assault.

Jeff cleared his throat. "Stop that!"

This time the man whirled his head around. "Go away, man. I'm just having some fun."

Jeff could hardly believe the indifference in the man's eyes. "You'd better stop or..."

"Or what!" The man got up and spun around, with the woman held tightly in his grip. He flashed a long knife in his left hand; it glinted, reflecting the sunlight. "I intend on doing her a favor. After we have some fun, I'm gonna send her off to the exultation stage. You know, man. Where you go after you die. Guess now I'll have ta do both of you that favor. Like the man sez on TV, ain't no hell, just heaven. And we all go there regardless. I bin wantin ta do something like this fer years, but the fear of the Lord and all you know. My daddy'd pounded that into me since I'z a kid. But now it don't matter. Live and let live. Eat drink and be merry, for tomorrow you die and live forever." The man laughed and looked up to the sky. "Ain't life wonderful? I got me lots'a makin up ta do."

The woman suddenly bolted out of his grip. The man didn't even try chasing her. "Darn. Now look watcha done. Oh, well. Plenty more where that come from." He looked at Jeff. "But you, buddy, are gonna get your exultation papers early." He lunged at Jeff, knife pointed straight at his chest.

Jeff grabbed the man's hand and held it away, as they both fell to the ground in a desperate struggle to see who could stab the other. They rolled over twice before Jeff managed to fully point the knife's direction towards the man. On the third roll, the man moaned, stopped moving, and lay on the ground face down. Jeff stood up and moved several yards away, watching for any signs of life.

He picked up a stone about the size of a baseball and slowly inched nearer until he was a few feet away. When he kicked the man over, Jeff saw the knife sticking out of his chest. He checked for a pulse and breathing, but there wasn't any.

Jeff felt no pity for the man, but he *should* contact the police. He took a shortcut through the park, and started to walk towards where he had seen the conglomeration of police vehicles.

When he got to main, he saw a mini-war going on. A group of people, young and old alike, were hurling stones and Molotov cocktails at an overturned police car, behind which several officers were hiding for protection. In front of the overturned car, rows of police were wearing riot gear, but instead of shooting tear gas, they blasted what appeared to be rapid-fire flashes of light, which looked like laser beams. Every time a light bullet hit a rioter, he fell to the ground. Then some other men in gray uniforms would come and load the bodies into a paddy wagon.

The unveiling was quite a shock, but Jeff could hardly believe the docile town of Star City would start rioting. At least for the moment, the Balazons were acting peacefully, and he had a hard time believing most people were like the rapist he'd killed in the park. Then again, he understood the unbeliever's viewpoint.

Even though he called himself an atheist, he felt constrained by an inner sense of right and wrong. If he were convinced his feelings were merely due to a conscience-bubble, there were no objective standards for good and evil, and he could live forever regardless of his present behavior, he might like to experiment with his wild side too.

Jeff flinched with the sound of a nearby explosion and ducked behind the nearest building he could find, a hardware store. He periodically peaked around the corner to view the action, quickly hiding again when it appeared as if someone might spot him. He started to think he should try to get home safely and call the police from there, but his house was straight through the fighting. Then there was the tempting possibility he could go in the opposite direction, to the police station. It was a greater distance, but at least it was clear.

Jeff opted for what he thought was the safest route. He'd almost made it to the station when he was confronted by a gang of middle-aged men and women brandishing handguns, rifles, knives, and any other kind of weapon they could carry. Jeff guessed the crowd of malcontents numbered at least two dozen.

"Whose side are you on?" a big man who looked like their leader asked. "Those marauding aliens or us humans?"

Jeff sensed that he shouldn't respond indecisively or claim neutrality. "Of course I'm on the humans' side. Who do you think I am?"

"Just checking." The man eyed Jeff suspiciously. "It's hard to be sure these days, with our own government selling us down the tubes and all." He reached into his side pocket, pulled out a gun, and offered it to Jeff. "You won't mind fighting with us then?" It was less of a question, more of a command.

"I'm afraid I can't. I'm going home to get my own Colt forty-five; I don't feel right taking a gun somebody else could use, especially when I have my own at home waiting."

The leader cocked his left eyebrow and looked at Jeff a little less suspiciously than before. "Well, when you get it, meet us on main for the showdown. We're not going down without a fight."

Jeff noticed movement within the crowd. A forty something aged woman slithered through the crowd, a snake winding its way to the front looking for prey. Her hair was frizzy and she took position beside her leader like a loyal guard dog. Her back arched up slightly like a cobra ready to strike. "He's one of *them*," she hissed. "Demon!" Her head lunged forward again and again, as she repeated the venomous word, sinking fear into Jeff with each bite, as he imagined she might leap on him at any moment. "Demon, demon!"

The leader raised his arm and blocked the woman's plunges. "Now, now, Bertha" he said. "Calm down. I know a human when I see one. You can tell from the eyes. I trust him. This one is on our side." The woman hissed again but backed up slightly. "Go home and get your gun, Sir. Meet us on main when you have it."

Jeff nodded curtly and walked away as quickly as he could.

After that little run-in Jeff changed his mind about going to the police station and headed home as discreetly as he could, using back-alleys to cover himself, even grabbed a long metal pipe from a garbage can and carried it with him for protection.

Things continued to deteriorate. It seemed as if everyone in Star City were leaving their homes and protesting the Balazons' presence. He heard various shouts of anger against alien interference, trickery, government sellouts, and even a few more demon slurs. Many others were shouting for no reason at all—destroying property and looting for fun, since morals were but a concept of the mind.

Jeff almost made it home when a band of malcontents rushed into his alley; police cars soon closed off both ends. Almost immediately, a barrage of light rained down on their heads, and bodies began to drop. Jeff tried to duck behind some garbage cans but a bolt of light struck him. Every inch of his body started to tingle. Then he lost consciousness.

Chapter 8

Jeff slammed the front door and raced upstairs to find Valerie exiting the main bathroom, holding one pink towel around her limp wet hair, another wrapped around her body. Jeff almost mowed her over in his haste to get into the shower.

"What's your hurry?" she asked.

Jeff stopped and stared at his wife. The upper left corner of his lip rose in a snarl. "I've been away all night and that's all you can say? There were riots going on. I could have been killed! I'm sure you wouldn't have minded, though. Then you could marry your sweetheart Acin-om."

Valerie's hands dropped from her head, taking the towel with them. "What?" She rolled her eyes, threw her arms in the air, and headed for the bedroom. "You're being ridiculous. I knew exactly what happened to you. The police stunned you last night and took you into custody. You were being held in a make-shift jail cell in Star City High School for rioting."

"I wasn't rioting! How did you know anyway?"

"Acin-om told me."

"Of course. I should have known. And here I thought you'd be worried because they wouldn't let me call."

Valerie allowed the towel covering her body to drop to the floor and ignored his comment, while selecting a comfortable pair of jeans and sweatshirt from her closet. "Acin-om is a really nice person. I wish you'd realize that. She's even helping out your boss at your work."

"She doesn't know anything about pharmacy. Allan wouldn't allow it."

"I'm afraid he already has. It's not just you. They're helping people all over—at work, home, play—"

"I'm calling the police. She can't do that." Jeff raced for the phone and started dialing.

"Don't even bother," she told him. "The government has already passed emergency legislation that allows the Balazons to do whatever benevolent miracles they wish. You see, this is the time they prove their sincerity. Besides, the police have better things to do, such as patrolling the streets for more fanatical rioters." She emphasized her last two words, but Jeff restrained his anger.

"They've also set up a special twenty-four hour information channel dedicated to the Balazons and the things they're doing. If you want to read about them, books and magazines are expected to flood the market in about one week, mostly written by scientists and top government officials. They wish to educate us, Jeff, about themselves and so many more things we can't even begin to imagine."

Jeff didn't respond. Lost in thought, he trudged into the shower, adjusted the water temperature, and pulled the handle to redirect it through the nozzle. He found the water warm and inviting, and wished he could stay there for quite some time. Soon, however, the water became cool, despite repeated attempts at turning it up.

Jeff got out of the shower, dressed, and went downstairs. Valerie had already set the table for breakfast. Even before he had reached the last step, he smelled the delectable aroma of bacon and eggs. His mouth started to salivate.

"Good morning," Valerie said cheerfully.

Jeff frowned and sat down. "What is Acin-om doing at work?"

"Are you still worrying about that? Acin-om isn't out to steal your job. Go to work if you want or stay home. I don't think it matters today. Eventually, though, you'll have to go because you have to be retrained."

"But who gets paid for the hours she's worked?"

"I'm sure Mr. Armstrong will pay you. If not, Acin-om can miraculously supply all our needs. Acin-om says eventually—thousands of years from now, in the new world—people won't use money. Won't even need to work for a living. We'll be able to spend our time on pleasant, fulfilling, and exciting tasks instead of the hum-drum jobs we do now."

"I don't plan on being around in thousands of years."

"So you're saying you want to get all you can right now?"

"That's not what I meant," Jeff said, voice rising.

"Oh, forget about it. Let's not argue." After a moment's pause, she said, "Your friend Darryl called this morning. He's very excited about the Balazons and wanted to talk to you."

"Yeah, I believe it. I could see he was going to fall for all this crap the other day."

"You'll come around eventually too. You're just confused right now."

Jeff's lips puckered up as if he had swallowed alum or sour orange juice. "If anyone is confused, it's you."

Valerie shrugged as she stuffed a bite-full of egg into her mouth, and didn't say much for the next ten minutes. Valerie never had been one to argue, usually went out of her way to avoid it. When they had finished, she started to clear the table.

Jeff grabbed his keys and coat and opened the front door, determined to carry on with life as usual. He wasn't going to avoid work simply because Acin-om was there. Besides, if he did go, he might be able to find out something to confirm his gut feeling.

"Please don't let the kids talk to Acin-om while I'm gone," he said. "I want to minimize our contact with them as much as possible, until I know more about them. OK?"

Valerie didn't answer, just kept doing the dishes. Jeff figured that that was about as good a response as he could expect and left it alone.

On the drive to work, he listened to the radio.

"An independent poll shows forty-two percent of Americans are still distrustful of the Balazons. Another forty-seven percent believe them and eleven percent are undecided. When asked how it affected their moral perceptions, the forty-seven percent category almost unanimously agreed conventional morals are now obsolete and expressed a desire to remove their conscience-bubbles.

"American Balazon spokesperson Mordak said it might be possible to remove the implant at some time in the future, but refused to comment on how long that might be, stating it depended on the human response to their presence and other factors beyond their control. Mordak said their primary focus is to help humans become accustomed to their existence and the future would, hopefully, take care of itself.

"In other parts of the world, the Balazons have received a more favorable response. In Africa, approximately eighty percent have accepted the aliens and their commitment for aid. By the end of the day, it is estimated the Balazons will have fed and clothed thirty percent of the poor and prevented the spread of most communicable diseases. Apparently the Balazons could do more, but are cautious about initiating changes too quickly, claiming people need time to adjust. When asked what their ultimate goal was for the continent, African Balazon spokesperson, Esta, commented they hope to fully end racial discrimination and provide full and equal access to improved education.

"In a special announcement this morning, Khur-ak indicated a group of Balazons are presently combining their mental energies to affect the world ecological system, hoping to restore it to the tropical paradise it was before the dark stage. Over time they will repair the ozone layer, regenerate desert lands, and affect the climate to become more moderate."

Jeff clicked off the radio. It was starting to irritate him.

When he arrived at work and parked in his usual spot, his car started to glow brightly.

"What the heck," Jeff said as he leapt out, fearful of what might happen should he stay. When he took a few steps back, he got his answer. "What are you doing?"

"I am Talazon," the Balazon said. "I am designated for this area of space. To help people whenever possible. I have repaired your car."

"Oh," Jeff said. "But there was nothing wrong with it."

"There were several small dents in the exterior, a minor oil leak, and your right front wheel CV joint needed repair. Is there anything else I can do for you?"

"Yeah," Jeff said with a resolve to test Talazon's limits. Give me a million dollars."

"I am sorry but I am not authorized to grant that request."

Jeff snorted and walked away, berating himself for liking the special treatment. He heard a man drop a grocery bag and curse; Talazon jumped to his aid.

The entrance to Armstrong's pharmacy was lined up with people, so Jeff entered through the back. Betty noticed Jeff and said, "Wow, it's incredible. When I saw them on TV last night, I never dreamed they could do so much. It started with just a small group watching, but soon crowds came. And before you knew it, we couldn't beat them away with a stick."

"What do you mean?"

"Go into the dispensary and see for yourself." Betty pointed at the swinging door.

"I think I will, thank you."

There were scores of people crowded around the dispensary, some even had prescriptions. The owner, Allan Armstrong, was in the corner, sipping coffee, smiling, and watching everything happening with obvious unbridled joy. Acin-om was spending most of her time with the people, answering questions about herself and patient counseling, while another Balazon seemed to be mentally directing the dispensing operations.

When someone would hand Acin-om a prescription, she would set it on the counter. The other Balazon would just glance at it and move the script aside. Then the computer would type automatically, print off labels, and the stock bottle would float off the shelf as if a ghost were directing it; the bottle would unscrew its lid, pour the exact amount of medication into a prescription vial, and the label would attach itself. Acin-om would then motion with her long skinny fingers and the vial would float into her glowing hands. The alien pharmacist didn't seem to frighten the customers either, who were mostly curious or amazed.

"There you are Mrs. Reichston," Acin-om said and handed the old lady her medication. "Take one tablet per day and it should completely clear up all symptoms of your arthritis. There are absolutely no side effects."

This was the kind of incompetence Jeff was afraid of. Patient response to medication varied. There was no way she could make such a claim. He pushed his way through some people and into the dispensary.

"Good morning, Jeff," Acin-om said, but the other didn't reply.

Jeff immediately brushed by the other Balazon too and grabbed the stock bottle that had been used. The label read Zanthatar. He had never heard of it. The bottle didn't yield any clues about its identity either, as there was no other writing such as therapeutic classification, generic name, manufacturer, or dosing directions: nothing except the name Zanthatar in big black letters on a white bottle. He turned to Mr. Armstrong.

"What's going on here?" he asked.

"She's been creating new drugs for everybody."

"What? Untested drugs? She can't do that."

Mr. Armstrong crinkled his nose up slightly, and waved his hand nonchalantly. "Don't worry about it, Jeff. I trust the Balazons. Besides, this morning's legislation approves it."

"But it doesn't seem right. I mean what... what...."

Mr. Armstrong smiled knowingly. "Don't worry, Jeff. I know what you're thinking and there is no need for concern. The Balazons are here to help, not destroy our economy and way of life overnight. You will notice we are charging a reasonable fee for every prescription, certainly no more than the price of medicines already on the market. She assures me she could simply heal everyone and I believe her. But that's not the way the Balazons do business. Our society requires time to adjust. The Balazons don't intend to do away with every pharmacist, doctor, lawyer, judge, or police officer immediately. It will happen eventually but that's many years into the future. In the meantime, I think your livelihood is safe. Accept the artificially engineered environment they create and go with the flow."

"I don't want to go with the flow. I'd rather get there myself, thank you very much."

Mr. Armstrong's expression became hard. "As long as you work in my store, you'll do things my way. I like what we're doing here. I feel good about it. You can adjust or get out." Allan Armstrong left.

Jeff stood in the center of the dispensary, bombarded on all sides by the activity. Bottles flew around his head like angry bees, and computer keys rattled off, sounding like machine gun fire, while new stock bottles were constantly materializing out of nowhere.

"I'm going for a coffee break," he mumbled and stormed out, feet clicking hard on the tile floor. He swung the staff room door open hard enough to make a loud thud as it rebounded off the wall.

Nobody was in the small room.

Jeff poured himself a cup of freshly brewed coffee and sat down, noticing a discarded newspaper on the table.

The first page read "Aliens-Friends or Foes?" The article described how one person had been abducted and taken on board a space vessel and tortured. Another person had objects in her house fly around at random, sometimes hitting her. In another family, a five year old had cursed her parents with the foulest of words before attacking them with a steak knife.

Further down the page Jeff read that Mordak had an explanation for each incident. The story went into great depth about Xsalma and his reasons for doing what he did, but Jeff skimmed it quickly as he'd heard it all already.

Jeff took a sip of coffee and flipped through the paper. One article was titled "Xsalma—Sorry for Millions of deaths." It explained how Xsalma now regretted his decision to oppose Khurak, and believed he should have waited for the wisdom of the Council to decide the matter. The article ended on a positive note, promising those millions would live again if humanity could somehow see fit to forgive the Balazons, accept their aid, and survive until the exultation stage.

Jeff read another article by several prominent scientists, who detailed and summarized vast amounts of technological data on the aliens. Basic to their research, the scientists studied several Balazon volunteers to learn about the source of their power, a plentiful energy reservoir called Forsacon. The Balazons had the ability to mentally harness this raw power source that surrounded all organic and inorganic substances in the universe, enabling them to do seemingly miraculous things. The reason humans had never discovered Forsacon before was because its vibratory signature phase shifts it into the seventh dimension, making it undetectable by mankind's primitive science. The scientists went on to conclude that this energy was more powerful than nuclear, and easily manipulated by highly evolved minds, but only highly intricate and complex machines—currently beyond human technology—would ever be able to harness it.

The editorial section talked about the continued need for moral constraint. The writer pointed out humans should still try to act as if there was a God who assigns people to heaven or hell. Humanity was still in a precarious position and shouldn't take their new found freedom too far.

Jeff sighed and took another sip of coffee. The world he'd always known was dissolving around him, being replaced by the new information flooding the earth every second the Balazons remained visible. He felt a nagging fear sear his brain like a hot iron, as if a sixth sense was warning him of danger.

"I won't trust them, no matter what others think or do," Jeff whispered.

Don't let fear rule you, his inner voice said. *Open up to new possibilities. They are who they say they are. What other explanation could there be?*

No, it was impossible!

Men used to think it was impossible to run the mile in under four minutes, fly, harness nuclear energy, break the sound barrier, or go to the moon. Change your way of thinking and admit the possibility and you will see.

No! Jeff frantically flipped the newspaper, eyes and hands working in perfect unison. He was searching for something, not sure what, but he'd know when he found it.

"There!" Jeff said out loud as he pointed to the headline, giving more force to his words. "There is your proof. For every expert who says one thing, I can find another who will say the exact opposite."

The headline read "Michigan Scientist explains the real truth about the Balazons." Jeff quickly devoured the article. The scientist's name was Tim Forger, and he'd worked in a top security chemical weapons division of the Armed Forces before retirement. He theorized the whole Balazon controversy could be due to a leak of powerful hallucinatory chemicals they'd been working on for use in combat. One part per several trillion could induce massive hallucinations to the population of an average sized state.

If a small amount of the gas had escaped, light winds could have conceivably spread it across the entire North American continent. In reality, people were most likely sitting or standing in one spot with their eyes half-closed, looking like drugged out hippies from the sixties. The rest of the world was probably wondering why Canada, the United States, and Mexico had stopped working and were babbling gibberish about Balazons.

It was no more a far out suggestion than omnipotent beings pretending to be God.

The sound of the staff-room door opening snapped Jeff to attention. It was Kim and Gabriella, cashier and merchandiser respectively. They both poured some coffee and sat down.

"So what do you think about the universe today, Jeff," Kim asked cheerfully as she took a sip of the hot liquid.

"I'm really not sure yet," he replied. "How about you?"

"Oh, I think it's wonderful. I've been watching Acin-om and

her friend all day and I'm amazed at what they can do. Imagine the benefits of learning from them."

Jeff crinkled his eyebrows up in a thoughtful pose. "You accept them then?"

"Oh, yes, definitely."

"How can you? You know what they did. I was one who survived their attacks. Believe me, they are capable of much cruelty."

Kim's look hardened a little. "I've been attacked too, Jeff. My physical life wasn't in danger, but my beliefs and everything I held dear to me was assaulted. You see, I have been a Christian since I was twelve, and had believed the Bible to be the inspired Word of God—up until last night. The Balazons have helped to re-focus my understanding of reality. Quite frankly, I feel much freer now, as if a burden has been lifted from my shoulders. Religion can be quite restrictive. I don't harbor any grudge against them for being slightly dishonest. They love us so much, after all."

"Slightly dishonest?" Jeff shot back. "Love? I don't consider blatant deception for six thousand years slightly dishonest. Any creatures who truly loved us wouldn't have done that."

Kim lightly pounded her fists on the tabletop. "I have feelings too, and believe me, they're as real to me as yours are to you. But I know emotions can be deceptive. My Balazon representative explained it to me last night. When I first became a Christian, I felt very 'spiritual'—but this was really just psychological rewards offered by the conscience-bubble because I heeded its moral message to my heart.

"Why, I even prayed for my big brother who was in a wheelchair, paralyzed since a car accident when he was ten. He was healed instantly and jumped up! Boy, the whole house was so excited we told everyone about it. I prayed for many others in those days too, strangers even, and a lot of them were healed. Now I find out the Balazons had performed these 'miracles' as a confirmation to others of the validity of my message. I brought many people to Christ in those days, or should I say Khur-ak. I did my part to be a positive influence in the world. Like the Scriptures say, be the salt of the earth to keep it from being destroyed in the dark stage."

Jeff snorted. "Show me where it says that. I'm not an expert in theology, but I don't think it does."

"That's what it means. You shouldn't automatically disregard everything they say because you had one bad experience."

Jeff looked at Gabriella. "What do you think?"

"I'm not getting in the middle of this argument. I haven't been terrorized or threatened in any way."

"You don't have to have been to be affected."

Then Gabriella seemed to relent. "Well, I'm still undecided. I do think extra-terrestrial life is possible, and I can't deny their powers, but as to their motives..."

She tilted her head to the ceiling and said slowly, "W-e-l-l it might be like a friend told me. Perhaps they're inter-galactic scientists doing one big psychology experiment. They take a belief we have about God, and create all the necessary alibis to work themselves into that role to see how far we'll believe them. Then maybe they'll tell us the truth to see how we'll react. However, I don't think they're out to harm us; if they were, they could have done it before now. They certainly have the power to do so."

Jeff turned to Kim again. "Well at least they haven't taken away *your* job."

Kim shrugged her shoulders. "They're not here to steal anyone's job, just to help. Once today, I had a lineup of five customers. Before I could call for another till, a Balazon popped out of nowhere, waved her hands over the top of the keypad, and the buttons started beeping. Soon, the sales total had rung up and the customer's items floated over to me. All I had to do was hold the bag and in they went. Wow! Nobody seemed to mind either. I think seeing them in a store grants them credibility they wouldn't find elsewhere. She disappeared for the rest of the day, but it was nice to know she cared and was there to help me when I needed it." Her tone became somewhat chiding. "They're here to help, Jeff. They're sacrificing their time and energy to lift us up, not bring us down."

"I had a similar experience," Gabriella said. "I was upstairs trying to find some facial tissue but couldn't. I was getting pretty frustrated when one popped out of nowhere and told me to look under a pile of boxes in the corner. It actually gave me a weird feeling to realize these things are watching us all the time, waiting to materialize and do some good deeds. Why, I bet there's several in this room right now. Ask them to show themselves and they probably will."

Jeff shook his head. "Let's not, OK?"

She was right, though. It was eerie to think the Balazons had watched not only his own life, and all humans' lives since the beginning of time—every private act, crime, or indecency has been open to the Balazons. No one was exempt. The Balazons were everywhere, like the air, invisible, but sometimes exhibiting a definite effect when it decided to blow. The reason more didn't show themselves, he supposed, was humans were still a little uneasy. In time, that would change too.

Jeff got up to leave. "I suppose I should go do some work."

He felt calmer now, as he gently opened the door and walked past the vitamin display. Everything seemed so orderly, as if nothing unusual was happening.

The pharmacy was still quite busy, but Acin-om was resting in the corner with her eyes closed. "Hello," she said without opening her eyes, as Jeff approached. "Don't mind me. I'm renewing my mental energy. The amount required to restructure random atmospheric matter into specific molecular designs is enormous." She opened her eyes. "But I'm glad you're back now so I can bring you up to date."

Jeff's grimace showed he was sure. "I wouldn't even be listening to you if Allan wasn't forcing me to."

"I know. But I'm willing to carry your disdain now in the hope you will someday carry my joy."

"That's not going to happen."

"Perhaps, but that's not what we're here to discuss." Acin-om briefly introduced her companion, Parfon; Jeff grunted a non-polite response. Then she turned to face the cupboards and opened one at center chest level. The shelves revealed a whole array of new drugs. "The system is very simple. There is one drug for every major therapeutic classification. By the end of the day, I will create about two thousand new drugs to cover the less common disorders."

Jeff's eyes trailed across the shelves. The products were lined up alphabetically from Albathem in the top left corner to Xtantor on the bottom right—all boring white bottles with their names in big black letters. Dromolin floated off the middle shelf and glided over to the other Balazon dispenser.

Acin-om said, "At this very moment, Balazons are equitably distributing to drug companies all necessary information to make these drugs themselves. We are simply creating them as a short term solution."

"We need difficulties and trials to overcome ourselves," Jeff said. "You can't hand everything to us on a silver platter. Humans aren't built to work that way."

Acin-om calmly raised her hand in a gesture that said relax. "You're still thinking in the old pattern. You will understand one day."

Jeff's eyebrows rose in astonishment and suspicion. "What do you mean?"

"I'm not at liberty to say. There is much you must learn and embrace beforehand. But believe me, it will be beyond your wildest dreams." Jeff's upper lip curled in disgust as he prepared to let loose a verbal assault, but Acin-om abruptly left to help Parfon.

Jeff took a prescription for Cardizem from a lady and started to fill it. But he couldn't decide which of the new heart drugs he should use, as they weren't labeled properly. All they had were their stupid names in big black letters.

"Having trouble?" Acin-om suddenly asked, peering over his shoulder.

Jeff thought she almost sounded arrogant. "I'm not having more difficulty than any normal human would have. You haven't labeled these bottles properly."

"Oh," Acin-om said with a smile. She waved her hand and all the bottles instantly became labeled with therapeutic classification. She also created a list of the new drug names cross-referenced against their human counterparts. "This should help you too."

Jeff snorted as he grabbed the bottle marked Antihypertensive. The word above this classification read Potatal. "Who makes up these stupid names anyway?"

Acin-om seemed unmoved by the comment as she said, "The group of Balazons in charge of medical advancement."

"You Balazons think you're so great," Jeff said as he counted out the Potatal. "Your wonderful plans are probably as stupid as these drug names."

Acin-om ignored Jeff's snide comment and calmly kept working. The vial Jeff had filled suddenly leapt from his hand. A label attached itself, and it floated over to Parfon.

As Parfon counseled the person, an elderly man came to the

counter with a new prescription, and Jeff went to take it. The script was for Voltaren, a drug for arthritis. "It'll be about ten minutes."

The elderly man nodded. "I've been hearing lots about how you're handing out alien medication. I want you to know right now I don't want none. I'm not going to let you use me as a guinea pig. I know Voltaren has worked before, and I don't want to try anything else." The man leaned forward and motioned to Jeff with his finger for emphasis. "You understand me?"

Jeff nodded. He didn't have any qualms about sticking to the old methods. He was looking forward to telling Acin-om what to do with her version of Voltaren. If she protested, too bad. Patient's request after all. Even Allan wouldn't refute that one.

Acin-om came over to Jeff's side. "I overheard your request," she said smoothly. "I assure you our drugs are completely safe and effective."

"No way," the man responded. "I don't trust your alien potions any more than I trust you."

Jeff smiled. This was his kind of customer.

"But you will get total relief from any inflammation and—"

"I said no and that's final!"

Acin-om closed her eyes, as though she were concentrating on something. "I can sense you are upset. You are currently experiencing a great deal of pain."

"Way to go Einstein," the man said. "How did you figure that one out?"

Acin-om quickly opened her eyes and reached out with her long skinny hand. The man recoiled, but was not fast enough. Acin-om had touched him before he could step back.

"What do you think you're doing?" he asked.

"I decided to make an exception."

"An exception? What do you mean?" Then, after a few seconds, comprehension shone on the man's face. "Hey, my pain is gone! It was aching to beat the band when I came in, but now it's gone."

"Yes," Acin-om assured him. "For the rest of your life, arthritis will never again haunt you."

Tears started to appear in the corner of the man's eyes. "I've suffered for years. Used to take almost an hour to get out of bed in the morning because I was so stiff. I think the pain made me a little miserable. I was wrong about you. How can I thank you?"

"By not telling anybody what I did," Acin-om said.

The man looked puzzled, but didn't argue. "No problem. Your secret is safe with me." He turned and walked away.

Jeff understood. Acin-om probably didn't want people to know, or there would be even bigger crowds around the pharmacy. Nobody would want to buy drugs if they could get a complete healing.

The rest of the day seemed to pass rather quickly. Jeff mastered the new "system" rather easily. Other than in name, they were all very similar: one drug for each disease state—one tablet taken per day, no side effects. He was never able to get a rise out of Acin-om either, despite repeated insults; she remained very clinical and detached for the rest of the day.

At five o'clock, Jeff took off immediately, while Acin-om stayed behind to show the night pharmacist a few things. He wanted to get home before Acin-om went to his house and Valerie let her in to start infecting the kids again. If Jeff got there before her, he would carry more weight in preventing it.

Chapter 9

Jeff woke up past eight and headed for the bathroom.

"Where are you going?" Valerie asked. She was in bed, facing the opposite way.

"It's my day off. I'm going to the city to meet with my support group. Remember? I told you last night."

"Oh, that again."

"Yeah, that again." Jeff sneered visibly. It was a good thing Valerie was facing the other way and couldn't see his facial expression. Since the Balazons' unveiling, they did plenty of fighting and he was already late.

The members of the Xsalma Survivors Group met once a month. Many had gone through similar experiences as Jeff and considered themselves lucky to be alive. Others had been fairly mild, such as hearing strange voices and seeing ghostly images. But Jeff went for another reason besides moral support. He enjoyed meeting and talking with others who didn't trust or like Balazons. Even his daughter had been eventually brainwashed. A few days ago, Jeff had watched the newest Saturday morning cartoon, Balazon Rescue, with Stephanie in the three dimensional virtual reality TV room, or VRT for short.

Jeff still got a mild pain in his stomach sometimes when he thought about the technological advances the Balazons had initiated in *only* the past three years or so. He didn't have a problem with the technology itself, more so the fact *they* had simply given it to humans. Well, that wasn't totally true. The Balazons had set up research facilities in which they showed scientists and engineers how advancements could be perfected and expanded to be used in everyday life. But to Jeff, it sounded more like a sixth grade science experiment than actual discovery.

The cartoon show Jeff had watched with Stephanie dramatized the Balazons' invisible influence throughout history. The time was the Second World War, and the aliens were trying to decide how to stop Hitler from destroying the world. The German leader was a rare individual who'd managed to totally remove his conscience-bubble on his own. From behind the scenes, Khur-ak decided to try to bring the military might of America into the war by subliminally suggesting to the Japanese ruler to attack Pearl Harbor. It was supposed to be an educational program for kids, but Jeff still didn't like it. He didn't believe his children should be watching as much of the VRT as they did, but it was nearly impossible to drag them away. They spent most of their free time there.

Jeff entered the washroom and the light automatically came on. He thought how good it would feel to transport back in time a few years, even for a minute or two, and enjoy the chore of hitting the switch himself. He closed the door and went over to the shower.

"Usual temperature of 100 degrees, Jeff?" the built in home computer, named Bert, asked as it sensed Jeff near the shower.

"Let's try a little higher today, one hundred and five degrees Fahrenheit." Jeff thought of the very first time the computer had asked him that. Around room temperature had sounded good. "Seventy-five degrees," he'd said, but yelped. It was too cold. He increased his original estimate by multiples of five until settling on one hundred, never again forgetting what temperature suited him.

The water came on.

Jeff had resisted getting all the new gadgets installed at first, but eventually relented. Valerie and the kids begged for them, and everybody else was doing it, and they were reasonably priced, so he figured, what the heck. Besides, he knew deep down the advances were good. His problem was with the creators. All the flurry of activity, new surprises by the Balazons, new discoveries, and endless turmoil of his changing world would never make him forget. Others enjoyed it and went with the flow, but Jeff refused.

After his shower, Jeff went downstairs to get some breakfast before heading for the city. He went to the food dispenser and verbally requested Golden Grahams cereal.

"That item is presently out of stock," Bert said. "Would you like to try another brand?"

"No," Jeff said and paused, "I want Golden Grahams. Bring up the grocery store on the other world and I'll get some."

"I know what you are trying to say, Jeff, but I don't like responding to slang. I prefer a more formal atmosphere. Please restate your request." Jeff liked the new hands free computing. One hardly had to touch a keyboard or mouse these days, with the new voice recognition capabilities and all, but some of the artificial intelligences had too much attitude for his taste. He'd much rather dictate to his word processor, a "dumb" computer, and have it dutifully translate his words into text than argue with the "smart" computers.

"Is that really necessary, Bert? If we can't get along, remember I still have one year to exchange your AI brain for another."

"I don't respond well to threats, Jeff," Bert said in a soothing voice but sounded very threatening nonetheless, reminding him that a machine could be a cold thing. He couldn't shake the feeling that his computer might turn on him someday if it ever gained the ability, despite manufacturer's claims to the contrary and no confirmed cases of such a thing to date. "I'm sure you would miss me. Aren't I efficient in every other way?"

Jeff sighed, silently agreeing. The previous household AI he'd tried, Shelley, frequently forgot his preferences, especially shower temperature, which really annoyed him. The machines were becoming more like humans than he was totally comfortable with. He realized he was going to lose this fight and complied. "Connect with Eddy's Groceries and transfer the image to the VRT room…please."

Jeff heard an electronic beep. "Program initiated. You may enter when ready."

Jeff went into the living room and closed the collapsible partition so the projection devices would have the enclosed area they needed to operate. The objects in the room disappeared, as their molecular patterns were analyzed by the VRT scanners, dematerialized, and stored in computer memory. New molecular patterns sprung forth to form Jeff's favorite grocery store around him.

He walked down the cereal isle, marveling at the illusion the VRT could project.Even though he understood his living room floor was actually rotating beneath him like a treadmill and he was really only walking in one spot in his living room, the white tiled floor of the simulated grocery store seemed as solid and stationary as the real thing. It seemed so real that he was walking down a long grocery isle, "reality" shifting around him to give the illusion of movement. He found the box of Golden Grahams, picked it up, and took it to the checkout.

The computer generated image of a woman rang up his purchase and asked, "Hand or forehead?"

Jeff held out his right hand. The lady scanned it with a world database reading device. The display on the register showed electronic funds transferring to the food store. The cost was a paltry one dollar. "Please have it transported by u-band immediately. I want to be able to eat it right away."

The lady smiled. “Certainly, sir. Have a nice day.”

Food was cheap now, since shortages were a thing of the past. Food could be created easily now instead of having to grow it. All the food company needed was the molecular design, the permit to create it, and the technological know-how. The governments strictly controlled the technology and what food each company was allowed to make, since the industry’s workers were still in transition to other jobs and the world needed time to absorb them. Plans were in the works, though, for all households to one day be allowed to have their own food dispensers, and then the food industry was slated to disappear altogether. For now, people still had to use grocery stores.

Jeff waited for the lady to complete the transport before he said, “Bert, end program.”

“P-l-e-a-s-e.”

“Please,” Jeff added, weakly giving in to Bert’s insistence on formality and politeness.

The surroundings became Jeff’s living room again. He went into the kitchen and ate his cereal. Jeff had to admit the VRT did have some useful purposes. He could also use it to send himself on exotic vacations, moon trips, and space shuttle flights, at significantly lower cost than the real thing, but the price gap closed daily.

The Balazons were introducing replication technology into all raw manufacturing sectors, such as steel and lumber. Hardly any resources had to be mined from the earth these days, just seemingly created out of thin air. Companies still had to assemble products themselves, but Jeff could imagine the day not far off when he would simply feed specifications into a computer and create his own private mini space shuttle at probably the same cost today of a fake VRT experience of the same thing.

Jeff finished breakfast quickly and headed for the door. He saw a Balazon candy bar wrapper on the floor and cursed as he picked it up, went back into the kitchen, and threw it into the garbage disposal. The wrapper dematerialized and went into the magical realm of waste storage. He could retrieve it up until the time he pushed the button that transported it into deep space.

By now, people were so comfortable with the Balazons they were on every street corner, in every place of business, and most homes. There was nowhere left to run, nowhere to escape the most popular creatures on earth. Companies marketed Balazon dolls, posters, board games, and potato chips; others made comic books for children and Balazon Weekly magazine for adults. They appeared frequently on talk shows, book of the week specials, and did private appearances.

Jeff shook his head with disgust. He looked at the round, white clock hanging on the wall. Eight-thirty. He'd better get going. It took an hour to get to the City of Newellen and another fifteen to the old McLeran Baptist church, where today's meeting was to be held. It didn't start until half past ten, but he was supposed to meet Brad privately beforehand about some new secret information. He'd been trying to find solid incriminatory evidence against the aliens for a long time, but the Balazons covered their tracks too well. This was the best lead he'd ever had.

Jeff headed for the door, endeavoring to keep his head up, lest he be tempted to waste time if any more Balazon paraphernalia lay around. Once outside, he noticed the next door neighbor entering his Toyota Corolla. His smile communicated, "Good morning, what a wonderful day, aren't the Balazons wonderful?" He had commented so to Jeff too many times before. Jeff smiled back, not wanting to appear rude, but didn't say anything.

He got behind the wheel of his Prelude and took off, thinking he would never get used to its quickness and quietness since the conversion of gasoline engines to more efficient and environmentally cleaner electric motors. Energy stations selling power packs had replaced gas stations. There were also rumors circulating about u-band travel for humans. That was going too far! There was no way Jeff was going to be dematerialized and shot through space to some other destination. He had to draw the line somewhere.

Jeff connected onto highway thirty-three. He grimaced at the huge billboard outside Star City. The smiling face of Khur-ak advertised the Balazons' slogan—one world, one people. The Balazons had managed to politically unify the world under ten general regions, zone one comprising the United States, Canada, and Mexico, and also known as the North American zone. Each country still had their own elected leaders, who were subject to the elected zone leader, who in turn answered directly to Khur-ak. It was a more limited form of self-governing democracy that Americans slowly adjusted to over time. Jeff saw it more as a veneer of respectability to cover the aliens' controlling ways, even though Khur-ak claimed full awareness of the fine line he needed to walk to prevent a post-unveiling rebellion such as had occurred on other worlds, often promoting the aliens' second favorite slogan—we need your help to help you.

Jeff was not much of a political man, so could only remember the other zones that really interested him most, such as zone five, the European Union, now renamed the United States of Europe. Jeff had always had a fascination with European history, and it awed him that the continent was able to come together, albeit with alien interference, to form a unified core that now surpassed the United States in productivity and GDP. The biggest unifying factor had been enabling a common language in the "Reverse Babel Project", a voluntary project that most Europeans eagerly embraced.

The name was in reference to the Biblical Tower of Babel story, a time in ancient history when man had been unified under a common language, and the Bible records how "God" had scattered the people by creating many different languages. Khur-ak explained that the Balazons had confused man's languages in order to prevent humans working together too much and progressing faster technologically than mankind was mature enough to handle. But now all willing people could have this effect reversed by allowing the Balazons to once again modify the language center of one's brain to instantly understand Balazonese, the new common world language and text.

It was still an optional procedure, in respect of some people's queasiness about letting aliens modify their brains, but Jeff would have refused to submit anyway. Everyone still understood English in the North American zone and most other parts of the world Jeff might ever visit, so he didn't think he needed it. Besides, if he had to travel to a foreign country, he could always rely on the technological equivalent that did the same thing, the new Universal Translator Kit, comprised of hearing aid to convert languages he heard into English, microphone to convert his speech to any other language, and special eyeglasses that recognized foreign text and projected the English equivalent onto the back of one's retina.

Jeff also knew of zone three, comprised of North Africa and the Middle East, as it was a continuing source of inspiration to him that a once volatile war region was now working together quite cooperatively. Once the Balazons helped to end terrorism and depose radical dictators worldwide, including most of the Arab states, the Muslim populations proved very reasonable people. Their deeply held religious convictions proved a strength, as once they could see and talk to their "God", they passionately embraced Khur-ak's leadership as if he were the Allah they had always worshipped. Israel just seemed relieved to finally have peace, but was surprised how the world, including Arabs, honored their place in history as the nation that the Balazons directly built to secretly bring knowledge of themselves to the world.

Jeff was glad to finally see the end to anti-Semitism, but he never forgot who inspired religious bloodshed in the first place by creating the concept of "God". Most people got angry when he pointed this out to them, defending the aliens' bad behavior by claiming they had no other choice. This reminded him too much of his cult days. In the name of salvation, he'd accepted all kinds of excuses to rationalize the leader's verbal, emotional, and physical abuse of himself. Never again. The world seemed happy to blindly follow the cult of Balazon, but Jeff refused.

Despite much visible external success, such as the worldwide economic database and world political union, Khur-ak still had a lot of work to do. Invisible boundaries—mostly nationalistic and territorial—still hindered the alien leader's progress towards a new world order. Many nations, including the U.S. and Russia, were still negotiating terms under which to surrender sovereignty of their nuclear arsenals and military machine to Khur-ak's world-state. Jeff was glad the elected leaders were being cautious in favor of protecting American interests, although some insisted it set a bad example.

Sporadic wars still broke out between nations, and Khur-ak refused to forcefully stop them, claiming he didn't want to appear dictatorial and try to rule with an iron-hand, lest the world unite against the Balazons, as had happened on other worlds before. The aliens seemed so nonchalant about people dying, and justified this attitude with the promise that the essences of the dead would continue and be reborn in the exultation stage, but to Jeff this sounded like more cultic rationalizations to justify a form of abuse by passivity. However, the aliens did encourage the more stable nations to go restore order themselves, which often occurred.

Jeff was jolted from his highway hypnosis when a police car flew overhead, only about 20 feet off the ground. He nervously looked at his speedometer, cruise control locked at sixty miles per hour. Since the creation of invisible bullet-proof body shields, quark radar guns, and new road-side sensors capable of distinguishing between alcohol, marijuana, cocaine, or plain Tylenol, it seemed the police had little to do but roam the sky looking for people to hassle, especially since the advent of perfect lie detectors meant officers had to spend zero time in court trying to prosecute crime. With the device, a judge usually could quickly and easily determine innocence or guilt, which greatly reduced crime, since nobody could obfuscate the truth in court.

Jeff refused to buy one of the new flying cars, as they were quite a bit more expensive than a regular vehicle, and the special license one needed to operate them required re-certification every three years. A cheaper alternative was to retro-fit normal vehicles with an anti-gravity conversion kit, but the resultant machine consumed more energy than one built properly from the manufacturer, so Jeff figured he'd end up paying about the same in end anyway. The whole thing seemed like too much hassle, so he decided to stick to the standard mode of travel he was used to.

As the patrol car grew smaller, he calmed down and turned on the radio. It was already tuned to station GRN, or Global Radio News, the radio equivalent of GNT, Global News Telecast, the two broadcast mediums solely dedicated to bringing the world new information about Balazon activities, Khur-ak's motivational speeches, and technological and world political changes. Jeff felt compelled to keep himself updated, as reality around him seemed to be constantly changing and getting faster with each day. He forced himself to spend some time everyday listening or watching these channels. A news bulletin announced that Friday, five days away,

Khur-ak would give another world-wide broadcast, apparently unique in that it would signal the beginning of something wonderful beyond comprehension. Jeff was sure his family would be thrilled, but he felt a gnawing pain in his abdomen as his stomach started to churn. Something wasn't right.

He put it out of his mind as he navigated the outskirts of Newellen. They wouldn't be meeting at Sue's place anymore, all future meetings to be held at the Baptist church. Brad had given him the address, but this was the first time Jeff had tried to find it.

Churches hadn't held any worshippers in a long time. Eventually, after considering the evidence, Muslims, Jews, Hindus, Christians, and most other faiths abandoned their beliefs and simply cooperated together as humans. Khur-ak may still have his difficulties uniting a stubborn race, but at least one of the biggest excuses for war and hatred was gone: religion.

Lately though, some fanatical religious groups were trying to start riots or gain followers by insisting the Balazons were the devil and his demons deceiving the world. Since the unveiling, some religious holdouts had always proclaimed the demonic origin of the Balazons, but the groups seemed to be growing in number and influence lately. Random evangelistic campaigns were popping up everywhere, but if the proselytizing didn't produce enough converts, the fanatics would shoot everybody and take off, claiming all who didn't believe in God must die. Almost daily, the media reported ugly news of their barbaric attacks, and warned people to flee from any such preaching venture and immediately report their whereabouts to the police. The fanatics were constantly changing locations.

Other opposition groups were more secular, such as the Earth Freedom Party, or EFP for short. The EFP was an underground terrorist organization that committed random acts of violence in hopes of coercing the Balazons to leave, as they simply hated alien interference in human affairs and did not trust their leadership. Jeff could relate to the frustrations of this group, as he was also convinced the aliens were up to no good, but Jeff wasn't prepared to step into cult territory again by believing in supernatural things like demons. He was much more rational these days.

Jeff eventually found the building and walked up the front steps, feeling a sort of reverential awe despite himself. God may not be real, but the building still affected him. Once inside, he went up the steps left of the sanctuary, now used for theater productions, and turned to the first door on his right.

He found Brad Stockwell in a chair by the window. Brad became startled and jumped. "Oh, it's only you." He gave Jeff a solemn look. "I think you'd better sit down."

Jeff pulled a gray plastic chair over to Brad. "Go on. What did you find out?"

Brad shrugged. "Not much. Not much hard evidence anyway. But if my intuition could convict them, the Balazons would be in jail by now."

Jeff yawned inside. He'd heard the paranoia before. He wanted something real this time, but understood why Brad hardly ventured out anymore, except to go to survivors' meetings. Compared to what he'd had gone through, Xsalma had merely said, "Boo," to Jeff.

Xsalma's followers had physically appeared to Brad and said, "If aliens unveil themselves and say there is no God, don't believe it. We are God's messengers sent to prove to you there is a hell." The aliens then ripped Brad's essence out of his body and dragged him into the ground. He remembered feeling a cool sensation as they passed through solid earth, which slowly became warmer. Suddenly, he saw the brilliant yellow-orange of the earth's molten core and thousands of souls bobbing about in it, screaming in agony, chained inside the tumultuous fire so they couldn't escape.

They chained Brad as well, but he remembered only feeling slightly warm. It didn't seem too bad.

"Now feel the full fury of the flames of hell," the Balazons said, and searing pain exploded his body. He screamed in agony and begged to be let loose, but the Balazons disappeared. Brad said he could sense he was still somehow connected to his physical body but felt its life slipping away, his pain diminishing proportionately to his nearness to death. He was fading into nothingness and wanted it to happen quickly.

The next thing he remembered was being in his apartment and a middle aged man was slapping him in the face. The man apologized for not helping sooner but said he couldn't; he didn't offer any further explanations but simply walked through Brad's closed front door and disappeared.

Ever since then, Brad lived in stark fear about everything concerning the Balazons.

"Give me specifics," Jeff said. "What did you find out?"

"I talked to a friend of mine in Washington who was directly involved in coordinating Khur-ak's unveiling to the public. He had firmly believed in them."

"Yes, go on," Jeff said, feeling impatient. Brad had worked for the CIA before his Xsalma incident traumatized him so much he retired early and moved to Newellen. At first, Jeff thought the man must be somebody important because he always claimed the aliens were stalking him. Later, when Jeff realized Brad wasn't quite all there mentally, he was cautious what he believed of Mr. Stockwell's myriad of stories.

However, given Brad's credible sources and connections, Jeff would gladly embrace any solid evidence Brad could produce to prove the aliens' evil ulterior motives, not just paranoid delusions but actual evidence this time. Without something solid, the world would stubbornly choose to remain blind, just as the followers in the cult had done. Jeff remembered how after he had escaped the mind control of his cult, he had gone back and tried to convince the other followers of the leader's evil nature, but they refused to see. Simple logic, reason, and common sense had no effect, as Jeff had tried to convince people that the psychological and physical abuse the leader slowly but inevitably unleashed on all of his followers was wrong.

The leader always seemed to have a way to spin the scriptures and one's mind to "prove" that everything he did was actually a loving thing, at least to his followers. He had a charismatic personality, and a magnetic aura about him of hypnotizing and supernatural quality. Khur-ak was no different. The alien leader spun the Bible, evolutionary dogma, and love talk pretty good too, and had undeniable power to back him up. But no matter how much the Balazons would spin everything they had done in history as a loving thing, and no matter how many good things the aliens did now, Jeff judged the Balazons untrustworthy, and would never forgive their history of lying, terrorism, and murder. It was just too cultic for him, but he knew he needed hard evidence to have any hope of convincing others.

If he could have gone back to the cult followers with evidence that the leader was running a hidden child sex ring or some similar thing, maybe people would have been shocked awake, but the leader had been much more subtle than that. He eventually hid his evil right out in the open and rationalized and justified it with masterful spins of scripture and the concept of love, not much different than what the Balazons were doing. If only Brad had evidence of secret wrongdoings by the aliens, Jeff planned to take it to his friend, Brian Ferster, and then let Brian use his investigative VRT program to expose the truth about the Balazons to the world. It had to be an exposé on some hidden evil though, since the world had already excused the blatant wrongdoings of the aliens to date. Brian had been brainwashed too by the Balazons but was always chasing ratings. Jeff was sure he'd air any real evidence, for fame and fortune if for no other reason.

"My friend had something so secret to tell me that if he was caught talking about it, they might kill him. Many who found out about it and opposed them have already disappeared."

"Yes. Yes. What is it?" Jeff leaned forward in his chair.

"He couldn't reveal much over the phone. He said it had to do with a special VRT broadcast, deception at the highest levels, and a conspiracy to eliminate all who found out the truth. He also said to be at this address at eight o'clock tonight to learn more."

Brad handed Jeff a slip of paper with an address on it.

"He was supposed to fly down and meet me, but his plane crashed," Brad said.

Oh great, Jeff thought. Another lead dried up. "How did it happen?"

"The official story is the EFP was responsible," Brad said. "But I think they killed everybody just to keep him from talking to me."

"Who killed him? The government?"

"No, the Balazons. Don't you get it, Jeff? Nobody really knows how dangerous they are, but I do. They follow me wherever I go. Even as I left my house this morning..."

Another typical paranoid tirade. Jeff drifted off.

Chapter 10

Jeff parked his car in an angle parking slot just inside the gate of Star City's McDonald Park. The lot was only about half full, and he could see people gathering near the miniature lake in the center of the park.

"Are you sure this is the right address?" Jeff asked as he turned his head towards Brad on the passenger side.

"Positive," Brad said. "I even checked a map before we left Newellen."

Brad had been reluctant to come with him, fearful as he was of just about everything connected to Balazons, but Jeff finally managed to persuade him when he refused to go on his own. Brad's paranoia about the aliens killing his contact scared Jeff just enough that he wanted company if he was going to do this. They had no idea of what to expect.

Jeff got out of the car and breathed in a deep breath of the cool night air. The sun was going down and the air was chilly and damp. He could hear some murmuring in the crowd ahead, but couldn't quite make out what people were saying.

"I guess let's follow the crowd," Brad said and pointed towards the gathering crowd by the lake. "My contact didn't give any more details so we'll just have to play this by ear and see what happens."

Jeff led the way, following a well worn path through the short grass. They approached the crowd with caution, and waited patiently, lingering near the back.

A group of people near the front of the crowd had set up a small raised platform with a podium and microphone. They turned on an overhead floodlight to brighten the area and then one man approached the microphone and started to speak.

"We are here tonight to tell you the truth about the Balazons," the man at the microphone said. "Most of you are here tonight because one of our agents has directed you here or you heard about our meeting from a friend. Our numbers are growing everyday, and the truth is spreading. God's Spirit of revelation is being poured out in these last days and the Lord wants to save you tonight!"

Jeff felt adrenaline start to surge through his body and he started to panic, as he realized this must be one of the murderous fanatical religious groups that the news had been warning the public about. He could only imagine what timid paranoid Brad must be feeling.

"We are not going to harm you," the speaker continued, as if he had read Jeff's mind. "The media is the devil's tool to spread lies about us. They are the murderers not us! We only want to tell you about God's son Jesus Christ and about how he died on the cross for your sins, but Khur-ak doesn't want you to know this truth. You see, Khur-ak is actually the devil in disguise and the Balazons are his demons!"

The man's voice was rising and he started to jump and wave his arms in the air for emphasis. "They are deceiving the world in the Biblically prophesied last days deception! You must not follow them anymore or trust anything they say. Rebel! Kill them, or they will deceive you to hell! We have supernatural weapons that can help you kill the demons! Come follow us, or when you die, you will burn forever in hell! Confess you are a sinner, believe on the Lord Jesus now, and receive forgiveness before it is too late!"

Jeff turned to Brad. It looked as if he had tears welling up in his eyes, but Jeff couldn't be sure in the dim night. "Let's get the hell out of here, Brad. I've heard about these crazies."

A murmur was rising throughout the crowd, a feeling of nervousness becoming palpable.

Brad started sobbing. "But it's true," he said softly. I spent time in hell. I know it's true. I've been denying it all these years, running from the truth. I need to come to Jesus."

"What?! Are you losing your mind? You survived an attack from Xsalma, who was trying to prevent the unveiling. None of your perceptions were real. It was just an illusion."

Brad continued to weep. "No. I can't deny it anymore. I need to come to Jesus." Brad's chin sunk to chest level and he covered his face with his hands, continuing to cry.

"Look, I don't have time to be polite here. You've always been a little bit of an unstable wacko, understandable seeing what you have been through. But these cult types are dangerous. Haven't you been watching the news lately? We've got to get the hell out of here."

"No. I can sense the Lord really speaking to me in my heart. That's why God told my contact about this meeting. God wants to save me. I need to come to Jesus…I need to come to Jesus."

Jeff shook his head in disbelief. He was used to Brad's erratic behavior, but he picked the wrong time to lose it. Jeff wasn't about to endanger his life one second longer. The news warnings had given very specific recommendations for anyone who came across a preaching venture. Leave and report their whereabouts to the police immediately, or you could get killed.

Jeff grabbed Brad's coat collar and started to drag the man back to the car but he resisted. He kept mumbling about how he had to come to the Lord. Other people started leaving too, starting a trend that couldn't be contained.

"Infidels!" the speaker screamed into the microphone. "We offer you truth and salvation and all you can do is run? Then die like the demonic Balazon puppets you are!" The speaker reached into a black bag and pulled out a machine gun.

"Shit," Jeff said, and he felt more adrenaline surge his system. Brad seemed oblivious. Jeff slapped him hard, which seemed to snap him to attention. "They've got a gun. Move your ass now!" Brad nodded curtly, seemingly instantly clear in his senses, and turned and ran for the car, Jeff only inches behind him.

Rattling gunfire split the quiet night and people started screaming and running. The speaker yelled obscenities and continued firing at the crowd, but Jeff and Brad had been far enough on the periphery of the crowd that they weren't as clear a target as some of the other people. They made it back to the car without taking any bullets.

Adrenaline coordinated Jeff's movements with swift ease, as he flung open the car doors, slipped the keys in the ignition and hit the gas. Brad was already on his cell phone, reporting the fanatics to the police.

Jeff felt safer after about ten minute's drive from the park.

"The police said that was the second attack in Star City this week," Brad said. "I'm sorry I lost it back there."

Jeff didn't respond. He was still pissed at the man's stupidity. He turned on the radio for a distraction, and tuned to a soft country station. He kept the volume low, just something calm and soothing in the background.

"I can't explain it, but something happened to me back there. I just felt this instant conviction and belief in the Lord. I know there's a God now. The Balazons are deceiving us."

"Oh, don't give me that supernatural nonsense."

"I think you're suppressing the truth too because of your fear of falling into another cult."

Jeff instantly flared hot. "You idiot! I guess I should just go back and join that group then, huh? How stupid can you be?"

"I'm not saying join them. Obviously, they were nuts but that doesn't mean there wasn't some truth in what they said."

"You're nuts. I should take you to the hospital for a psychiatric evaluation. I've no doubt the Balazons inspired all our religious traditions. I can't deny the reality around me like you seem to be doing. I just also know deep down in my gut that they are evil too and will show their true colors sooner or later."

"Then you should understand how I feel. I too just know, deep down in my gut, the truth now. That's the power of belief, Jeff. You might not be able to prove it, but you just know that you know." Brad paused. "Wow!"

"What?"

"I just felt the Lord speak to me very strongly. He asked me to consider why the media has only recently become so focused on warning about these preaching ventures where the speakers accuse the Balazons of being demons. I mean, the Balazons claim to have inspired all our religions and beliefs about God. If that's true, what about the devil? The concept of evil spirit beings exists in every religion too. Surely they must have inspired a belief in Satan too then? Why haven't they explained their rationale for doing this before now? It's like they've been clouding our minds from asking that obvious question."

"I don't know, but one thing I've learned in life is one should search for truth boldly, head on, asking honest questions, and facing legitimate doubts. Ok, Mr. Bigshot believer. How about this? Let's just go home and ask the Balazons that very question."

"I don't mind. I'm curious too."

Jeff was surprised at Brad's reaction. He thought for sure he could rattle him with that suggestion. "Aren't you afraid? You avoid Balazons like the plague."

Brad smiled. "You know, I was raised Catholic but was never really afraid of the concept of hell until the Balazons terrorized me with it. But that's all gone now. I can't explain it. I have peace in my heart and no fear anymore."

"We'll see about that." Jeff drove the rest of the way in silence, marveling at Brad's miraculous change of demeanor, but doubting its staying power. He knew the man too well. He had only been about five more blocks from his house, and within a few minutes, they were parking the car and approaching Jeff's front door. Brad still seemed as calm as ever.

Jeff opened the door and led Brad inside. The collapsible partition to the living room was closed indicating people were inside being entertained by the VRT. Jeff ripped it open, causing the transmission to shut down automatically.

"Aw, dad," Nick wined. "What are you doing? That was a good program."

His wife and two children were huddled together on the sofa, no Balazons in sight, but he knew he could bring them out with a word. They were just beyond human perceptual reality, somehow tuned to a person's thoughts or words, and ready to appear at a moment's notice. Khur-ak had specifically assigned a personal Balazon to each person on the face of the planet, ready to assist, answer questions, or just chat. All one had to do was ask: Garlez was for Valerie, Marcach was for Stephanie, and Stro-kar was for Nick. Acin-om was for Jeff, but he hadn't called on her in a long time. No matter.

"I don't care. We've got business to attend to. Acin-om, show yourself!"

Almost immediately, a bright light flashed and a mild warmth filled the room. "It has been a long time, Jeff," Acin-om said. "How may I assist you?"

"I have a few questions."

"Yes, I know you do. I'm aware of your encounter at the park."

"You were there?"

"Hmmm…not exactly. It's rather difficult to explain. Let's just say that we have a constant awareness of what our human assignments are thinking and doing."

"We could have been killed. Aren't you supposed to be protecting me or something?"

"Not at the expense of other higher priorities, such as walking the fine line of exerting influence but not interference in human affairs."

Jeff requested Bert to bring up the conference room simulation, closed the collapsible partition, and waited for the room to change. Then he had Valerie and the kids call up their Balazon representatives, and was only mildly surprised when Brad spontaneously did the same thing, still seeming totally at ease in a room with now five Balazons visible. Jeff motioned for the aliens to sit on one side of the simulated rectangular oak table and humans on the other.

"What's this all about, Jeff?" Valerie asked, looking him straight in the eyes and with a scowl.

Jeff got right to it. "We were attacked tonight by some cult fanatics who raised an interesting suggestion. The Bible says God has spiritual enemies, the devil and his fallen angels. I want to know how we can know for sure you Balazons aren't demons trying to deceive us for some evil purpose."

"Oh, come on, Jeff," Valerie said. "It's been years since the world has had to contend with mysterious supernatural nonsense.

You of all people should be more level headed. Do I have to worry about this cult taking over your mind?"

Jeff ignored Valerie's sarcastic insult and kept his eyes on Acin-om, trying to read her reaction, but she only smiled and nodded her head. The other Balazons were smiling the same condescending grin. Nick and Stephanie started protesting too but Jeff raised his hands in a stop gesture and told them to be quiet.

Acin-om said, "For a period of time after an unveiling, we need to suppress a species' minds from full understanding of how the conscience-bubble influences individuals with the more negative aspects of spirituality. It might embolden rebellion and possibly increase the risk of self-annihilation. So we suppressed people's minds from seriously considering we might demons. We'd still prefer not to talk about it."

"Well too late," Jeff said. "I want to know right now what you're hiding."

Acin-om sighed. "Very well. We can only suppress this idea for awhile anyway. It was inevitable that we would have to address this question sooner or later on a worldwide scale. There's actually a very straightforward explanation. The reality is that an actual devil doesn't exist any more than does one all-powerful God that created everything, nor do literal angels and demons exist. All such things are simply concepts we use on your minds, as I'll try to explain further in a way you'll understand.

"Almost every religion has this concept of a great cosmic struggle between spiritual forces of light and darkness, where the light side is stronger and wins in the end. These implant-inspired beliefs are just a microcosm of your inner struggle, as the conscience-bubble tries to subtly inspire hope that that person, as well as mankind collectively, will one day overcome their dark nature and evolve to become like us, god-like beings, entities of pure energy, light and love, the highest form you can attain. So really each individual is both the 'light' and the 'darkness' in this struggle, although every person starts out life as predominantly 'darkness'.

"Thousands of years ago, the only way your primitive awakening consciousness could understand these evolutionary realities was by us enumerating them to your subconscious in the form of simple stories about a battle between God and an evil arch enemy, and we use these concepts to accelerate your consciousness. By way of a biological analogy, you could say our involvement with humans is the equivalent of intentionally inducing genetic mutations into physical organisms to more quickly adapt them to the environment and accelerate growth into higher forms."

"More evolutionary mumbo-jumbo, just like when they first unveiled" Brad said. "I don't believe it anymore."

"Let's hear what they have to say before getting critical," Jeff said. "And why do you want to keep this a secret?"

"Because we still use the conscience-bubble and we need it to work as maximally as possible in order to help you. Our experiences on other worlds has shown that too much understanding of how the implant subtly uses fear, especially right after an unveiling, can embolden people to actively start resisting it, increasing the likelihood of rebellion, rejecting our help, and eventual self-extinction.

"You see, at your current stage of development, you have a conflicted nature between your lower animal-like qualities, the dark forces, and the higher god-like essence you are evolving towards, the light forces. Through the implant, we simply use these ideas to inspire people to cooperate with the natural upwards pull of evolution so they can better win the battle over their brutish, self-centered animalistic nature that currently seeks, through natural selection and survival of the fittest, to dominate or destroy others, horde all resources, live as long as possible, and spread their DNA to the next generation. You need our help to resist this dark side of your human nature, or you won't survive the millions of years necessary to reach our state of existence, your 'heavenly reward' for living a life of obedience to the ideals of love.

"We reinforced these concepts when Khur-ak walked the earth as Jesus, by taking over people's bodies by so-called 'demon possession' and letting Jesus 'cast us out' to convince people of his power and authority over these 'evil forces'. We wanted people to follow his teachings. But really mankind is both the light and the darkness in this imagined cosmic struggle for supremacy between God and the devil. We're trying to help your race reach exultation, where there is no longer any conflict. Then you easily and naturally always operate from the standpoint of pure love. Until then, the implant is programmed to use fear of sharing the fate of the dark forces to motivate you."

"I don't think like the religious folk at all, Acin-om," Nick said. "So you're gonna have to explain that one a bit more about using fear to motivate us."

"It's a very subtle effect that the implant exerts on the subconscious. It still directs you too, Nick, in various ways but you're just not aware of it. Basically, almost all religions pick up on the implant-inspired idea that the fallen forces of darkness, the fallen angels in the case of Christianity, are doomed to hell forever and God will never forgive their rebellion against Him even if the rebels desired it. So if God is that hard and unforgiving to some of His creatures, it follows that humans could also sin to a point that God will never forgive them. However, by not precisely defining at what point this could happen, it creates some subtle fear to control your behavior. Although every human baby starts out life basically like a 'demon', a bundle of selfishness, we try to bring each person to a point of balance in their lives. The idea is we want to hold people in the middle between hope and fear, believing all your choices are slowly making you either an 'angel' or a 'demon', ultimately sending you either to heaven or hell, and motivating you to keep striving for the ideal of love, lest you cross some vague point of no return and become forever damned to a fabled hell with the imaginary devil and his angels."

"I never *could* believe in a God that would torture His creation in a literal hellfire forever," Nick said. "It's disgusting. How does your implant so effectively convince people of that kind of drivel?"

"Again, it's a subtle thing, affecting even you, that works deep on the subconscious, whereby we use your own base human nature against you to convince you hell is true. The concept of God we created is one who is Almighty and can do anything, and yet He allows all the suffering and injustice that you inflict upon each other on a daily basis, such as crime and wars, as well as the daily suffering of diseases, natural disasters etc… So, it follows that this God could conceivably also allow the suffering of a literal eternal hellfire in the afterlife. So we used the 'hell' of your daily existence, to reinforce the concept of greater suffering beyond this life for those who are disobedient to the promptings of the conscience-bubble and Biblical directives. Add to that, on some deep level, most people could imagine causing great suffering to someone if they believed they were sufficiently justified to do so, so you naturally project this capability onto God and convince yourself that He is capable of doing such a thing.

"We want you to move beyond these simple beliefs that we used to imprint evolutionary realities into your subconscious minds to moderate your actions. We'd hoped not to have to reveal all of this too soon because once a person has a better understanding of how we use subtle fear to manipulate your minds with these concepts, it will lessen the effectiveness of the conscience-bubble. We have found that subconscious fear is a very effective behavioral modification tool for beings as primitive as you, even after a successful unveiling."

"This makes sense to me," Nick said. "You're using our own imagination and ability to think in abstract concepts to influence us. If you think about it, it is pretty hypocritical that God says in the Bible that we're supposed to love our enemies and forgive our enemies, but God doesn't have to love and forgive His enemies, the devil and the demons. Now I get it. God does love demons, which is who mankind is! I am an incarnation of a 'devil', already burning in the symbolic hellfire of our daily suffering existence, and God will forgive me and release me from 'hell' if I truly repent! Hellfire is a good thing then, if it refines my character and makes me perfect in love! I just have to overcome evil on the human plane of existence by accepting Jesus and living a life of love by faith and… yada, yada, yada…" Nick laughed and rolled his eyes. "I suppose I shouldn't get too sarcastic. Many intelligent people have struggled with these kinds of things over the centuries."

"This is kind of insulting," Valerie said. "I don't like to be compared to a demon."

"It's only an allegorical concept we use on your mind," Acin-om said. "You also have potential to become light beings, if you let us help you. Your own Bible says these very things in many subtle ways."

"That's interesting," Stephanie said. "I used to be something of a Bible thumper. Show me where these things are in the Bible." Stephanie requested that the computer create a holographic version of what used to be her favorite Bible, the King James Version, and handed it to Acin-om. Jeff remembered many a fight in the past where Stephanie had used it as a weapon against Nick.

Acin-om opened the book and flipped some pages before settling on one section and handed it back to Stephanie. "Notice Khur-ak says in John 6:70, 'Have I not chosen you twelve, and one of you is a devil?' By comparing a human to a devil he is insinuating that humans are the so-called 'fallen angels', metaphorically speaking of course."

"That scripture is talking about Judas," Brad said. "It just means he was an evil man. Jesus wouldn't call any of his true followers a devil."

"Not true. Please turn to Mark 8:33". Acin-om waited until Stephanie found the passage before continuing. "Here Khur-ak rebukes Peter, one of his closest disciples, saying, 'Get thee behind me Satan: for thou savourest not the things that be of God, but the things that be of men.' So by calling Peter the arch-demon Satan, he's insinuating that people of all different stripes, true followers or not, are actually the 'devils'."

Jeff wondered how Acin-om could so easily quote verses from memory, and hypothesized that the alien's massive brain power must have the entire Bible memorized, perhaps even all the different versions.

Brad's face soured. "That just means Peter was acting like a type of Satan in that he was tempting Jesus to divert from his mission to die for the sins of the world. Peter didn't do it on purpose though, and it shouldn't be taken literally."

Jeff marveled that Brad was so boldly challenging the aliens. He figured the man would have lost it by now for sure.

"That's one level of meaning, but you must understand that Khur-ak had full memory and knowledge by this time. He knew exactly what he was saying, and he was also trying to hint at the full truth so that we could use his words down through the centuries."

"What do you mean by use his words?" Nick asked.

"The Bible was an authority for many people down through the centuries, and we utilized it as much as possible, especially Khur-ak's words. Another example is in Matthew 25:41 where Khur-ak says, 'Depart from me, ye cursed, into everlasting fire, prepared for the devil and his angels'. Again, by describing people being thrown into hell, and then specifically saying hell was created for the devil and his angels, the subtle subconscious suggestion is that humans are the so-called 'fallen angels'."

"Interesting," Nick said. "It's sort of logical that if God prepared hell specifically for the devil and his angels, then He would only throw beings in there that actually fit that description. So describing humans going there too means that's who we are. But I've never heard of such a possibility ever even being suggested by *any* Christian denomination, not even some of the weird cults and sects. Why has nobody made this connection before?"

Brad made a lame rebuttal that the only demons in the room were the Balazons, but it didn't sound very convincing to Jeff. Jeff might not like the Balazons, but Acin-om's explanations sounded more realistic to him at this point than Brad's insistence there was a God. However, his continuing steady demeanor impressed Jeff. He figured surely the man would have lost nerve by now.

"That's because we suppressed your conscious minds from comprehending the full meaning and purpose behind the fictitious archetypical images, so that people could only read and understand the Bible at a certain conscious surface level. That way the implant was more effective at causing people to take the verses with symbols of hellfire, and imagery about angels and demons quite literally. Then we use those same verses to speak secret meaning to the subconscious, sort of like subliminal messages. But it's not all negative. There are equally many positive Bible verses we can use to subliminally suggest to people that they can become holy angels and children of light, such as Ephesians 5:8, John 12:36, and 1 Thessalonians 5:5. I could go through the Bible in great detail, if you're interested, and explain the many subtle levels of meaning we were trying to communicate to the writers."

"I'll pass," Nick said. "Thanks anyway."

"We're not always negative, but unfortunately, given your current state of development, we've found most people's minds respond better to threats of eternal punishment in hell and comparisons to becoming fallen angels, than positive messages about rewards in heaven and comparisons to becoming something like holy angels and children of light. We still use these concepts and images on your subconscious to moderate your actions, but now that you have a deeper understanding of how the implant uses the negative aspects of Biblical imagery, there is a greater risk of people feeling emboldened to resist the implant at a subconscious level, which is mostly where it does its work. Now that you understand all this, your conscious minds will eventually work this revelation deep into your subconscious, which may prove damaging to your psyche. At the very least, for the greater good of the survival of your species, please keep this information to yourself and don't let it become common knowledge."

Brad shook his head. "See how clever they are. They turn it all around and make us into the demons. Amazing! All I can say is you spin a good yarn, Acin-om, but evolution is just a demon inspired abstract philosophy you're using to deceive the world that there is no God and no judgment for sin after death in hell! I don't believe it anymore."

Brad suddenly shuddered and gasped. "Here is your proof you are a liar, Acin-om. The Holy Spirit of God has just spoken to me deep in my spirit. The true God has supernaturally popped scriptures into my mind to show me how your demonic deception was prophesied long ago. 2 Corinthians 11:14 says that Satan, that's you 'Balazons', not us humans, is transformed into an angel of light. Oh, today's secular-scientific mind might dub you aliens of light, but the meaning is the same and clear. You are deceiving mankind! And all the lies you are spouting are summarized nicely in 1 Timothy 4:1 where it says that 'in the latter times some shall depart from the faith, giving heed to seducing spirits and doctrines of devils.' You are the devils, not us, trying to seduce us with your lies! Galatians 1:8 warns that 'though we, or an angel from heaven, preach any other gospel unto you than that which we have preached unto you, let him be accursed!' You are those false fallen angels from heaven, the true devils of your master, Satan, preaching another gospel, and I pronounce cursing on you, as the Bible says to do. In the name of Jesus I curse your lies!"

Acin-om simply smiled and calmly said, "All those verses you are quoting are from our agent, the apostle Paul. Like Jesus, we eventually appeared to Paul and explained everything to him and also did 'supernatural' things to affirm his ministry. We could tell that Paul was an exceptional person who would willingly work with us if we let him in on all of our secrets, so we did, in order to make him a more effective witness to the risen Khur-ak, otherwise known as Christ to his followers. Paul absorbed scientific evolutionary realities as best as his first century mind could digest, though we often had to explain it to him with Old Testament quotes like Psalm 82:6, 'I have said, Ye are gods; and all of you are children of the most High'. Then he could accept that the scriptures testified to the fact that humans are evolutionary children of this concept of 'God', and gods themselves, evolving into gods, as it were, given enough time. Once convinced, he then willingly labored the rest of his life to spread the new message we wanted mankind to embrace. The man was a fanatic, but of the good kind once properly directed. We regularly appeared to Paul and taught him deeper and deeper truth as he was able to take it in. I knew him well and consider him a friend. I look forward to fellowshipping with him again millions of years from now, assuming mankind survives long enough to evolve to the exultation stage."

"No way," said Brad. "Then why did Paul warn us of an end-time demonic deception from seducing spirits, fallen angels, from heaven?"

"Haven't you been listening? I've already explained that concepts like angels and demons are but fictitious archetypical images that we use to moderate your actions and enhance evolution of your consciousness to exultation. Like religion in general, concepts about evil supernatural entities were meant to be but a temporary preserving influence, and are no more real than the ancient gods Zeus and Thor. Paul understood this and was simply continuing in Khur-ak's tradition of speaking about these entities as if they were real. Mankind, in general, was not ready for the full truth back then, minus a few exceptional men like Paul. Paul had to try and threaten and intimidate the early believers with fear inducing talk to try and preserve what we were trying to do. As with Jesus, we tried to psychologically enhance Paul's fear statements, but general apostasy and spiritual anarchy eventually ensued anyway, as our future forecasts told us was likely. Mankind is exceptionally stubborn and rebellious. But we continued to work with mankind down through the medieval centuries until finally, only now, are we able to tell the world the full truth, not just rare individuals like Paul."

Brad frowned and his mouth curled up in a snarl. "I'll never believe you! You make up great sounding lies, but the spirit of God tells me Jesus is the true God and you are demons! There is a hell and you're going there, and so will any humans who fall for your lies!"

"Calm down," Jeff said. "This is getting out of hand. We're just trying to get to the truth. No need to panic."

"I'm not panicking," Brad said. "I don't know what to say to convince you all. I know the truth now, even if I can't think fast enough to outmaneuver demonic explanations. The Bible testifies of the devil's power to deceive. He is very good at what he does, twisting logic, scripture, reason, evolution, science, anything and everything to deceive you into following him to hell." Brad rose from his chair. "I won't stay here any longer and listen to this." He went over to the collapsible partition and opened it, immediately ending the holographic simulation and left without another word.

Jeff spent a few more minutes soliciting opinions from his family about what they had just heard, but none seemed to show any concern, accepting all the aliens' explanations. Jeff wasn't that accepting, yet not willing to take the opposite leap of faith into religion like Brad had done. He still couldn't bring himself to blindly trust the aliens anymore than he would another cult leader, as Jeff had learned to trust only his own intuition after that experience, and something still didn't *feel* quite right.

"Mankind's collective consciousness is waking up," Acin-om said. "More and more people are asking these kinds of questions, considering these possibilities, a common thing that happens several years after an unveiling. We can't suppress this awakening forever; only delay it for a few years. But we're pleased with the progress mankind is making. We believe most people are now ready to assimilate this new revelation without undue damage to their conscience-bubbles and are mature enough to reject any notion that we are demons. Nonetheless, as I said earlier, if you desire to help others, please try to keep these details to yourself. We disseminate this information on a need to know basis, and for those who insist, we would prefer to tell them ourselves."

Jeff nodded his head, seeing no harm in the restriction for the time being. He went to bed early that night, and lay awake for several hours, unable to fall asleep, meditating on everything that had transpired that day. Eventually, he totally wrote the demon theory off as nonsense, but still refused to embrace the aliens, trusting that instinct inside him that told him something was still wrong. But he figured at this point he might have to wait patiently to see if and when the aliens might reveal an evil persona, just like his cult leader had eventually done. He was sure he'd just lost his best ally in trying to discover any rational ulterior motives of the Balazons, as Brad seemed stuck on his theory that the aliens were demons.

As he took comfort in accepting that he would just have to play things by ear, he was able to find peace and fall asleep.

Chapter 11

"Come on, dad," Nick said excitedly. "It's almost time for it to start."

"Oh thrills," Jeff said. He had been sitting at the kitchen table reading a book. He found lately he liked reading fantasy, for it took him off the earth and into another universe where Balazons didn't exist. For a few short minutes, he could escape the unwelcome reality of his own time and space.

For the past several days, the Balazons refused to leave his house. They moved in as if part of the family: Acin-om, Garlez, Marcach, and Stro-kar, one for each member of his household. Acin-om was trying to be Jeff's personal Balazon, but he hardly ever talked to her. Despite Jeff's repeated efforts at getting her to leave him alone, she would not, as she was supposedly under strict orders from Khur-ak to try to win his trust before the special broadcast. Jeff was convinced, however, she was trying to drive him insane.

By the time Jeff got to the VRT room, his wife and kids were already huddled on the couch. They looked as if they were ready for an exciting movie, popcorn and coke the only things missing. Stephanie fidgeted with excitement and urged him to hurry up and activate the VRT.

Jeff closed the partition to the VRT and sat in the reclining chair across from the couch, while Acin-om joined the three Balazons standing in one corner like silent sentinels watching over their prisoners.

"Computer, please turn on the VRT room," Nick said. "Channel GNT. Volume level twenty."

"My name is not 'Computer'."

"Sorry," Nick huffed. "Bert turn to GNT then."

Nothing happened for several seconds. "I'm waiting," Bert said. "You know what you must do."

Nick sighed. "Bert, p-l-e-a-s-e turn on the VRT room, channel GNT, volume level twenty."

Instantly, they were in a bright studio. Khur-ak sat behind a wide brown desk, appearing in his native state, a shining alien of light, having long since shed the human disguise he had worn years ago at the initial unveiling. Behind him, pictures showing the positive advancements the Balazons had initiated since the unveiling flashed across a screen.

"Good evening, ladies and gentlemen," Khur-ak said. It is good to be addressing you again. I feel we have come so far in the last several years. You have responded to our presence better than expected. What a joy! Once again you humans surprise us.

"I will get right to the point. We desire to do something wonderful for you, but it requires your direct involvement, or it will be ineffective. You, the people, must embrace what we are about to tell you with all your hearts, minds, and wills."

Khur-ak stared at them lovingly. "Even before we appeared, you had progressed beyond your infancy and were reaching out with your spaceships, telescopes, science and technology. You yearn for the freedom only knowledge can bring. I knew Xsalma was wrong." Khur-ak nodded his head with satisfaction. "And I was right. I have found that once an evolving race becomes as technologically advanced as you are, the exultation stage is near—with a little help, of course. It's going to be so wonderful; you're going to burst forth from your physical ties and fly out to the stars like a caterpillar bursting out of its cocoon and soaring through the skies."

Khur-ak stopped talking and closed his eyes for several seconds before opening them. "I can sense many of you are eager to hear more. You are still limited in many ways, but this need not continue. However, you must voluntarily leave your old life behind. We can help you become a new creation, but we cannot do it without your support. My dear children, if you accept our assistance, together we can bring you to a place of unbridled joy."

Khur-ak closed his eyes again, pausing to absorb the emotions of his audience. "The exultation stage will not happen for you for many millions of years yet. However," he said with emphasis and opened his eyes, "we can speed up the process. Within your own lifetime, you can experience the thrill of exultation if you will do as my representatives tell you.

"I will leave you now, for my fellow Balazons will explain the rest."

The VRT projection of the studio suddenly shifted to a news room, and a man and woman began discussing Khur-ak's speech and its probable impact. Jeff was too stunned for words, and he imagined his family must feel so too.

Nick was the first to speak. "Wow, cool!" The newspersons' images kept talking, blissfully unaware of anything except their own computer world. "I want to be like you, Stro-kar. Tell me what I need to do."

"You must admit you need our help and fully accept us into your heart and mind by a conscious act of your will," Stro-kar said as he broke rank with his fellow Balazons and knelt beside Nick. "Let my essence merge with yours and we will become one being. Then I can remake you from the inside, renewing your mind and body with changes that would naturally occur if you lived for millions of years.

You will feel an immediate difference when I come in, but we will need to work with you over time to cause full integration. Eventually, you will become like us, exultation entities, with mental powers beyond your ability to fully appreciate right now."

"Wow," Nick said. His eyes were glazed over with the possibilities.

The rest of the Balazons, including Acin-om, knelt by their human assignments. "I hope you can be open-minded about this," Acin-om said to Jeff.

"No," Jeff replied. "Don't even come near me. I don't like looking at your face, let alone allowing you to affect my mind. Go possess somebody else."

"What we are proposing here goes far beyond merely taking over a body temporarily, as we have done in the past," Acin-om said. "We need your help for this to work, as it is a cooperative process that, over time, will eventually elevate your consciousness and essence to our plane. Why don't we just merge for a short time and I can show you how it works? If you become uncomfortable, I can always leave."

"I'm already uncomfortable! Get lost!" Jeff looked at his family and panic started to overtake him. "Don't do it, kids! Valerie! Valerie!" But they ignored him. They had gotten used to his protests and knew there was little he could do.

Stephanie seemed a little reluctant. Jeff stood up to help her, but Acin-om used her mind powers to push him into his seat.

"You are not permitted to interfere," she said. "Everyone must make their own choice."

Jeff was in a hazy dream. He moved in slow motion, and when he spoke, the words were drawn out. He could see Acin-om smiling.

"What are you doing to me?" he said. He was a helpless prisoner watching his family drink slow-killing poison. Already, Stro-kar was dissolving into Nick as if Stro-kar was water and Nick was a sponge. The alien was merging with his son as easily as if Nick was simply putting on a new set of clothes.

Jeff struggled with all his might, but barely managed to stand up. He tried moving but became paralyzed and floated through the air at Acin-om's direction: she took him outside.

Jeff could move again, but Acin-om wouldn't allow him back inside. Another walk in the park was what he needed. The setting sun and cool evening air would help him feel less tense.

Acin-om followed close behind.

They were halfway to the park when a young woman came up to Jeff. "Good day, mighty warrior," she said.

Jeff stopped walking. He looked at the young lady, then Acin-om, then back to the young lady. There could be no mistake. "It's you! Monica!"

Monica nodded and said, "Acin-om has been lying to you. She is not me."

"Who are you talking to?" Acin-om asked.

Jeff's eyes became slits of anger. "You made yourself look like her. I can't believe I didn't suspect anything. That's what's been bugging me all these years."

"Come," Monica said as she took Jeff's arm firmly and motioned in the direction she had come from. "This way please."

As they started to walk away, Acin-om angrily demanded Jeff come back. But she was whirling around and screaming at the empty air. Apparently she could no longer see him. He tried asking Monica questions but she wouldn't answer.

They turned right and left down various streets and walked for blocks, until Jeff found himself in an unfinished section of town. The only car in sight was a white van with a mini-satellite dish on its roof, parked beside a tall, antenna-like structure.

"You must go inside," Jeff's escort commanded and pointed to the van. Jeff looked at it curiously. He was about to ask his kidnapper why, when he noticed the woman was no longer holding his arm. He whirled around, but there was nobody there.

Jeff shrugged his shoulders, walked up to the back of the van, and tapped on the door. There was no answer. He tried the handle and heard it click. As he slowly opened it a crack and peeked inside, he heard men talking. Then he saw them.

"Do you have the satellite uplink secured yet?" one of the men asked.

"No," the other replied. "They must have already changed the prefix code. Our informant died in vain to give us this information."

The other man's face became downcast. "Try it again." Then they both noticed Jeff. It almost seemed as though they were both afraid of him. They held their breaths and didn't say anything.

Jeff was the first one to speak. "I'm sorry. I think I'm lost. I was out for a walk when a lady dragged me here and said I had to go inside. I'll be on my way."

The two men exhaled, obvious relief on their faces. "No problem," the brown-haired one said. "My name's Len. This here is Ellis."

Jeff hesitated. "My name's Jeff Saunderson."

"Don't be frightened," Len said. "We know why you're here. Come on in." Len turned to his comrade and said, "Call headquarters and tell them we've got another one."

As Ellis turned to grab the CB, Jeff entered the van cautiously and closed the door. He noticed complicated looking electronic equipment lined both sides of the interior. One small monitor had an image on it like a radar view screen.

"Don't worry," Len said. "He's called you to be here. We'll send a car to take you to our hideout."

Ellis finished with the CB and said, "They're sending a car right away. It'll be here in about ten minutes."

"Would someone please tell me what's going on here. You guys sound like spies or something."

The two men looked at each other and smiled as if understanding some private joke. "In a way we are," Len said. "We're enemies in a foreign land fighting for freedom and truth."

"That's nonsense," Jeff said. "We're citizens of America, the land of the free. Or are you guys Russians?"

Ellis laughed. "No, we were born in this country, but we're not free."

Jeff nodded. "You mean the Balazons."

"Yes," Len said. "Have you felt free since the unveiling?"

"No," Jeff conceded. "So you're a part of an underground organization fighting the Balazons?"

"Yes," Ellis said and added, "but it's much more than that. It would take too long to explain and there's no time. We have urgent work to do before the authorities can get a fix on us."

"What are you doing?" Jeff asked.

Ellis seemed a little reluctant to answer. "Should we trust him?" he asked his friend. "Mavis hasn't had a chance to certify him as one of us."

Len rolled his eyes. "You're being overly cautious. If he wasn't one of us, how did he find the van? Anyway, it's not like they don't know we've been trying to do this uplink for some time now."

Ellis shrugged.

Len said, "We've been trying to connect with the Balazon channel to interrupt their broadcasts. We've got a message on this tape we'd like the viewers to see." Len pointed to a VRT disk on top of the main instrument panel.

"What's it about?" Jeff asked.

"They'll explain everything at headquarters."

The two men politely excused themselves from further conversation and continued their work. Jeff silently watched Len push buttons on a computer keyboard and keep getting the message "Access Denied." Ellis fiddled with the computer on the other side. After a few minutes, they heard a knock on the van's back door—two knocks, a pause, one knock, a pause, and then two knocks.

"That's for you, Jeff," Len said. "Go with them and do exactly as they tell you. Don't worry about anything. They won't harm you."

Jeff didn't know why, but he trusted them. After blindfolding him, the men put him in the back seat of their car, and drove on without saying much. In reality, it was a short trip, probably ten minutes since that was how long it had taken them to pick him up, but it seemed longer.

When they stopped the car, the two men escorted Jeff through rough terrain. He felt soft mud and dirt beneath his feet. Soon he heard a large, creaking door open and they walked through a building smelling of manure. He heard shuffling noises as if animals were moving about. After a short distance, he heard another door being opened.

"Go down there," one of the men said. "When you get to the bottom knock twice, once, then twice again." They hurried him down a few steps and closed a door behind him.

"Is anybody there?" Jeff asked. There was no reply, so he took off his blindfold. He was at the top of a flight of concrete stairs leading down to another door, cement walls on either side. Soft white lights dimly lit the corridor. Behind him, he saw the cellar-type door he'd come through. Out of curiosity, he tried to open it, but it was locked. On the right hand side there was a small numeric keypad, probably used to enter a pass code.

He walked down and knocked as he'd been told.

The door made an unlocking noise and opened. Come in, Mr. Saunderson," a lady said. "I'm Mavis, the greeter." She held out her hand to shake so Jeff offered his. She grasped his hand, held it tightly, and closed her eyes. "Oh, the Lord has got great things in store for you. He sometimes gives me visions of the future. Yours is glorious."

"What are you talking about?" Jeff asked, as he pulled away his hand.

Before Mavis had a chance to reply, a big bearded man came up to her. "Well?" he asked her.

"He's one of us, all right," Mavis told him.

"Then come with me." The big man motioned for Jeff to follow him.

Jeff followed his new escort through a tunnel that opened to an area as big as an aircraft hangar. Cars, trucks, and white vans were lined up along one wall and hundreds of people were scurrying about doing various tasks. Elaborate electronic equipment was randomly stationed throughout the room.

The big man led Jeff up another flight of stairs to an office with a window overlooking the activity below. Jeff entered the room, and a tall man in a suit and tie greeted him.

"Welcome, Jeff, my name's Lawrence Shumacker" the man said as he held out his hand. Jeff was reluctant to shake after what had happened the last time, but he did anyway. "You can leave now," Lawrence said to the big man before turning his attention back to Jeff. Lawrence sat down behind his desk, and motioned Jeff to sit across from him.

"So, what brings you to our humble abode?" Lawrence asked.

"An invisible woman," Jeff said bluntly as he started to relate his story. Lawrence listened patiently to Jeff for the next few minutes, occasionally nodding his head.

When Jeff finished, Lawrence took a deep breath and said, "Doesn't surprise me. A dozen others have joined our ranks today, all with similar stories."

"Who are these invisible kidnappers? Who are you?"

Lawrence cocked his head to one side and seemed to be searching for the right words to say. "I don't know how much you know, but I'm going to tell you plainly. After all, you wouldn't be here if you weren't one of us." Lawrence paused for a moment before continuing. "We believe the mysterious strangers are angels sent by God to lead His people to places of relative safety. Very soon now, Khur-ak is going to start destroying this planet, as well as all people who have been deceived into following him."

"I see," Jeff said as seriously as he could, humoring the man. He knew what these fanatical religious groups were capable of. "So I take it you don't believe the Balazons are who they say they are."

Lawrence shook his head slowly. "No. Khur-ak is the devil in disguise. Everything he says is a lie. The Balazons are his demons, likewise deceiving the world with their humanistic religion of evolution to virtual god-status. And many are buying it because they want to believe they can have eternal life without repenting of their sins. The Bible says the deception in the last days would be so great God's own people would fall away if it were possible. Well Jeff, now is that time."

"You're starting to sound like my psychotic friend, Brad. He went off into religion too. I just can't stick my head in the sand. There's something to the scientific concept of biological evolution. Didn't the first computers cost millions and fill warehouses?"

Lawrence nodded.

Jeff pressed. "Now they've 'evolved' to become small and cheap and they're available everywhere. My cell phone has more computing power now than the first computers."

Lawrence nodded again. "I can see you are an intelligent man, and it might not be easy to break the hold Satan has on your mind. I'm not saying what scientists have discovered about evolution is totally false, but the concept has many logical flaws. Yes, computers have 'evolved' in a sense, but human intelligence was bettering their own invention and guiding this evolution, just as God has been guiding biological evolution for millennia."

"Good comeback. I guess that was a stupid analogy. That should have been obvious."

"No, it's an excellent example, as it shows how easily we humans can tend to forget that intelligence must be behind all forms of evolution. Let me give you another example that will cut right to the chase. When you were, say 7 or 8 years old, could you have even understood the concept of biological evolution?"

Jeff shook his head and said, "Probably not. I was too young."

"Exactly. Your mind, your consciousness, had not grown enough, matured enough, 'evolved' if you will, to be able to fully comprehend the concept. But now you can process a deeper abstract way of thinking. As an adult, you have many mental faculties your younger self just didn't have."

"That's just because I grew up. That naturally happens to everybody."

"Ah, but that's what evolution is all about, growing, getting better, more complex, more capable, more adaptable to real life, becoming something greater than what existed at earlier stages. To use your analogy earlier about computer evolution, you can now easily admit that humans must have guided this process, right?"

Jeff nodded sheepishly.

"But were you there in the computer design house to witness it personally?"

Jeff shook his head.

"You only saw the completed products, the new models that came out and were better and better and more powerful. Even your own consciousness development from childhood to adulthood is an evolution of sorts, but you don't see the invisible God guiding that process any more than you saw people guiding the design of computers. But you can perceive God's completed product, a fully developed adult mind, capable of complex abstract thinking and reasoning. The final stage in consciousness evolution for any human is when God brings a person to a choice: to accept Jesus as Lord and Savior or not. We only get one life to make that choice, as Hebrews 9:27 says it is appointed unto man once to die and then be judged and go to heaven or hell. We will all live forever somewhere, Jeff. Heaven or hell. It's your choice. Make it a good one. I believe the Lord brought you here to make a good one though, and we're going to help you with that."

"Nice way to try and smooth out the scare tactics. I'm not going to respond to something out of fear. I'm still not convinced. How do I know for sure the aliens aren't right, and that evolution just happens by natural forces that no being, not even the Balazons, can fully explain? Maybe we *are* evolving into 'gods' somehow."

"You're very bright, Jeff. There will always be some mystery, of course, but that's where faith comes in. Yes, we are gods of a sort, as even Psalm 82:6 says all humans are gods and children of the Most High. But we can never evolve to become fully like Father God. That's Satan's trick. He throws a little bit of truth in with some lies to confuse and deceive people. God the Father as the ultimate authority is not just a concept like the Balazons want you to believe, nor does God rule His creation by some sort of democratic consensus. Rather the Lord speaks His will and all of His sentient creation willingly and lovingly and wholeheartedly obeys Him out of passionate love for who He is... at least the angels on God's side do, and you could say we believers are in process. Obviously, I don't mean to say Satan and his followers happily obey God, but they do obey Him nonetheless.

"Father God is a personal being that is Almighty and even Satan answers to Him, as the book of Job clearly shows. Satan tormented and destroyed Job as much as he could, but the scripture records that God put the limit of life on Satan. The devil was not allowed to kill Job, and no amount of power Satan might have brought to bear to try and kill Job would have been successful. Satan didn't even try it. He would have failed anyway, and he knew it, and would have suffered more than Job for even trying. Satan has certain power and authority but he's nothing like the real God, and though some sort of evolution is happening, and human beings will one day be something like God, there's only One Almighty Creator and all the universe is soon going to learn that."

Jeff shrugged. "The bottom line is the Balazons have an explanation for just about everything and are very convincing," Jeff said. "And what about their powers? How do you explain that?"

"God is allowing the devil to use his evil power to deceive those who are not His. Even in the Old Testament when Moses was contending with Pharaoh, the Pharaoh's magicians were able to duplicate *some* of the supernatural miracles Moses did, but they could not duplicate them all. Likewise, the Lord has told me He will soon send His people out in such power that the signs and wonders they will do will dwarf everything the Balazons have done to date. They will go forth to warn the world about the coming Judgment and the only way of escape—forgiveness of sins through repentance and the blood of Jesus Christ."

"Very interesting."

Lawrence noticed Jeff fidgeting. "Is there something wrong, Jeff?"

"No, nothing. I think you've made a mistake here, though. I'm not a Christian."

Jeff immediately wondered if that had been a wise thing to admit. They might kill him. But if he pretended he was, they would want him to stay and take part in their preaching bloodbaths—something he just couldn't do.

Lawrence looked puzzled as he crossed his arms and frowned. "That's very strange. Mavis has certified you as one of us. She's *never* wrong. God has given her the gift of discerning true believers from false ones. Perhaps you're a Christian but don't know it. Sometimes the Lord sends people to us who haven't had the conversion experience yet. Others were genuine saints at one time, but have let themselves be taken captive by the enemy, falling into sin and unbelief. If you're one of the latter groups, Jeff, the mercy of the Lord is still available. I have people here with the ability to cast out demons and free you from bondage."

Lawrence picked up the phone and hit an intercom button. "Mara report to my office please."

Jeff craned his neck around to look at the hangar behind him.

"Pretty impressive, huh, Jeff?"

Jeff looked back at Lawrence. "Yes, I find it hard to believe you could build all this in a few months." That might not have been a wise thing to say, Jeff realized. If Lawrence knew Jeff had been watching negative news coverage about them lately, it might set him off.

"A few months?" Lawrence looked at him incredulously. "Oh, no, Jeff. Before my dad died, he had been working on this complex for years. You see, the Lord had seen fit to bless my dad by talking to him in an audible voice. About seven years ago, the Lord told him to start building this complex. He gave my dad very explicit instructions on how to do it and where to get the money."

Jeff was getting uncomfortable, and he was sure it showed.

"I know you're probably thinking he was schizophrenic; so did I at the time. I wasn't even a Christian, but my father was a strong believer so he obeyed the voice. My dad went right up to the wealthy businessmen the voice told him to and said, 'The Lord told me to tell you I've come for the money.' He was amazed when they immediately wrote out checks for hundreds of thousands of dollars. I guess the Lord had already prepared them. At any rate, when he was done collecting the money, he had more than enough to complete the job exactly the way God told him to. He did everything God said, right down to the brand name of hammer He told my dad to buy."

"Sort of like Noah building the ark," Jeff mused.

"Not exactly. At least Noah knew he was building an ark because of an impending flood. God never did say what this was for. My dad always told me he'd disappear one day in the rapture, but I didn't believe him. I thought religion was for kooks. Well I'll tell you, when millions disappeared off the face of the earth and several thousand reappeared in this complex along with myself and my dad, I got right with God pretty quick! My dad and I had been having lunch at our favorite restaurant and then suddenly we were just here! Now God has seen fit to bless me with the same gift my father had and leads these people through me. Although some weren't ready to come here and be prepared for what is to come, God made sure places of relative safety would be available for those who would become Christians throughout the great tribulation."

"Wow," Jeff said, half-believing Lawrence because of the sincerity with which he spoke. And there could be no denying the superstructure surrounding him. But what was this rapture thing he was talking about? He asked Lawrence to explain it further and also asked him how his dad had died.

"It was quite a shock when we first all found ourselves here. My dad started obediently explaining to the people what God was telling him to say. Apparently, the most commonly held Christian view was that the rapture was a term given to describe the Lord's taking His saints to heaven before the great tribulation, a time of great deception and distress in the world. My dad admitted that he had believed this too, but the Lord was now telling my dad that he had been influenced by a mistaken notion that God would allow His end-time saints to escape trouble. That was not God's plan. This confusion about the rapture issue was similar to the confusion the Jews had around the Messiah's appearance in history, as the Jews did not understand that the Messiah would come first as a physical being, and His second coming would be as a spiritual being. Likewise, there was to be a physical rapture first followed by a spiritual rapture later.

"The first physical rapture was to these relative places of safety, complexes that had been constructed all over the world, and the people were to be prepared for going out and preaching the gospel about three years later. Many would die in the future battle to preach the gospel as a witness and a warning to the whole world, and then the end would come, when Jesus would return to earth, and a spiritual rapture would take place when all true Christians, both dead and alive, would be changed in a twinkling of an eye and become spirit beings, just like the Lord Himself. Well, some couldn't accept they had been wrong in their interpretation of the Bible. They thought it was all a demonic deception or a government conspiracy or something and some rushed my dad and killed him. Then God started talking to me and told me to complete the message. I was scared they would kill me too but the Lord told me not to fear, and somehow I trusted that voice, and spoke God's words."

Jeff leaned forward in his chair, curious to hear more. "Then what happened?"

"I explained how the Lord told me to say that what He was doing was consistent with God's revealed character in the Bible. For example, during the worldwide flood judgment of Noah's day, God saved His people in the ark, both a supernatural and a natural saving in that Noah heard from God, but Noah also took action in the natural to build the ark. Another example is God sending angels to remove Lot and his family from Sodom and Gomorrah before raining down fiery judgment on the city for its sins, supernatural in that angels assisted but natural in that Lot and his family still had to physically run from the city. Similarly, God supernaturally directed the building of the worldwide network of complexes and miraculously transported His people to protect them from the alien deception, but these hidden places of safety are also a natural means of protection and were still constructed naturally by human hands. Ever since that first day, we've been praying, fasting, and studying God's Word, the Bible, in preparation for reaching the world for Christ."

Jeff shrugged. "Obviously you said the right things. They didn't kill you too."

"No, the Holy Spirit shamed the crowd into acquiescence when I relayed the Lord's words. I said their escapist attitude was wrong, and they should consider it an honor to be chosen to suffer and die for Christ. Jesus had suffered and died for God's glory, and almost all the early apostles had been martyred, along with countless millions down through the centuries. I asked why they thought they were all so special that they deserved to be exempt from persecution and suffering?

"After a moment for silence and reflection, I proved I was hearing from God by prophesying that at that very moment fallen angels disguised as aliens were revealing themselves on TV and deceiving the world. We turned on the complex's large projection screen TV and watched Khur-ak's unveiling firsthand. I couldn't have known that otherwise, as the so-called alien presence hadn't been revealed yet. I plainly said Satan was pretending to be the alien leader, Khur-ak, and was about to pull off his masterful deception. With all of the true Christians taken away, it was fairly easy for the devil to mentally suppress people's minds from seriously considering the possibility that the aliens were demons in disguise. They didn't want to believe the truth anyway. In the deepest parts of their souls, those left behind desired to believe evolutionary lies, wanted to believe they could evolve into gods themselves without having to obey the one true God, Jesus Christ. So the Lord allowed the devil to deceive people with the lies that they wanted to believe."

Jeff frowned and shook his head. He was finding this all very difficult to believe.

"For those God brings here, this is always difficult to accept at first. But the reality is that it wasn't Xsalma who caused the disappearance of millions. Rather it was God. Those millions disappeared because they were true believers, walking by faith in the Spirit and ready to come here and be prepared for what must come. Even my dad's murderers totally repented and changed their attitudes, proving their true allegiance and worthiness. Of course, I forgave them, even though it took me some time to work it out, as I was a new believer thrown into a leadership position and had a lot of adjustments to make in my way of thinking. God showed me how we all make mistakes in life, even serious ones. Salvation is about grace and forgiveness for the past and learning to do better for the future. We are all prepared now to endure the horrors of the persecution to come, but it will also be a time of great glory for God. He will pour out his Spirit without measure, and His people will do great things." Lawrence paused. "You're thinking about Monica, aren't you?"

"How did you know?"

"God just told me the devil has been deceiving you about her. Acin-om is a demon pretending to be Monica, and the real Monica was actually an angelic protector God sent to protect you from behind the scenes until you had a chance to accept the truth and be saved. The devil has been trying to kill you for a long time now. Satan realized you were one who would be left behind and might become a Christian after the physical rapture. You could possibly frustrate his plans."

"That sounds pretty incredible to me. Are you saying this whole Xsalma thing is a cover-up to hide Satan's attempts at murdering potential believers and distracting the world's attention from the physical rapture?"

"Precisely. It also gives them a good excuse to do all kinds of deceptive miracles to make up for what happened. Many are impressed. But don't believe it. It's all a lie."

Jeff paused. "This doesn't make sense. When Xsalma's people attacked me, they looked like Balazons. Aliens. Not demons. Well, I've never actually seen a demon, but I imagine they look different than Balazons. And the people in my support group have similar stories. If the devil wanted to kill us, why not do it quickly and efficiently? Why all the games? And why disguise themselves as aliens?"

Lawrence nodded his head in understanding. "Because Satan knew his attempts might be thwarted by God's angelic protectors. In such an eventuality, the devil wanted to have an alibi in case the survivors tried revealing his true identity to the world. It worked. And the devil even has the power to transform himself into an angel of light, so don't be surprised if he disguises himself as an alien when it suits his purposes."

Jeff shook his head. "I still don't understand. Monica came into my life about three and a half years ago. Why would God let me be deceived for all this time, no more messages from the real Monica?"

"The Lord's timing isn't something I try to figure out. The Bible records how God let the Israelites suffer persecution at the hands of their enemies, the Midianites, for seven long years. Then He suddenly appeared to a man named Gideon, and used him to free the nation. Why wait seven years? I don't know. And God could have freed His people Himself, right? Why use Gideon?" Lawrence shrugged his shoulders. "All I know is God's got a reason behind everything He does, and His timing is perfect, even if we can't understand it all. And He does need us to do our part. That's how this spiritual war is fought. He's been working behind the scenes all this time to prepare your heart to accept Him. You were to continue on in unbelief until your appointed time. Now is the hour of your destiny, Jeff. You know the truth, and must make a choice, like Gideon did, to follow the Lord or not. Which will it be?"

A lady opened the office door. "You wanted me for something?"

"Yes, come in, Mara." Lawrence motioned for her to sit down beside Jeff. "I want you to tell me what you think of this man."

Mara sat down, closed her eyes, and began whispering a prayer. Jeff could only make out odd phrases such as "Lord hear me," and "reveal to me, Lord." After several seconds, she started to twist and turn. Her body seemed to be writhing in agony as it contorted and convulsed uncontrollably. Lawrence remained calm.

"Is she OK?" Jeff asked.

"She's fine. It won't be long now."

Mara stopped moving and began to speak. "Pain, anger, turmoil. Disappointment, disillusionment. He wept for hours. His tears will fill the bottle of God's remembrance for eternity. He would have made it, but gave up the fight. He's locked in so many chains now he can't even see the light. He turned his back on God and returned to his old lifestyle. Even so, the Lord has chosen him to be his possession forever. He will come back."

Jeff's mouth started to get dry. Suddenly, he didn't care what they might do to him. "What is this junk she's saying? Tell her to stop. Tell her to stop, or I'm leaving."

Lawrence shook her gently and she immediately opened her eyes, seeming as fresh as the moment she had entered. "Tell me more," he said.

Mara turned towards her leader. "He was a baby Christian, and nobody helped him. The devil stunted his spiritual growth at infancy and eventually succeeded in overcoming him."

"Go on," Lawrence said.

"He became a Christian about a decade ago, but had a very bad experience with a cult. He became so disillusioned he simply decided not to believe anymore in a Being he couldn't see or hear. So sad." She looked at Jeff. "The devil succeeded in totally extinguishing the tiny flame within his heart. He fell away from the God who loved him."

Tears came to Jeff's eyes.

Mara looked at him with compassion. "The enemy is a deceiver, Jeff. Only you can allow the devil to extinguish the fire of God's Holy Spirit. But the Lord is an eternal flame and doesn't need oxygen. Even in a vacuum, He can be ignited again. And He can grow to engulf any prison that holds Him, consume all things in His way, but you must allow this to happen."

Something started to stir in the depths of Jeff's being. He wanted to believe it could be true, but was almost beyond feeling. He had been so for many years and had grown used to it. It was comfortable.

He'd long ago pushed away all thoughts of God and ridiculed believers, including sometimes his own wife—back in the days when she believed that is.

"God works all things for good," Mara continued. "He has been using this difficult experience to help insulate you from the Balazon deception by fueling your fear of being deceived again. It has kept you suspicious and questioning until you could come to us and be exposed to the truth. I know a person who can pray for you, Jeff. We can help set you free."

"No! I'm not a Christian. Never have been. Religion is for weak-willed fools. I'm not going to let you control my mind. I won't let it happen again."

Mara said, "I know you're afraid, but there is a difference between cults and us. We don't want to mold you into our likeness, just listen to *Him*. Then you will fit into the body of Christ perfectly, and you won't feel guilty for not being exactly like everyone else or for not obeying a million nonsensical rules." She reached out her hand.

Jeff wasn't sure if she was trying to comfort him or pray for him. Either way, he wanted no part of it. "I don't need you or God, and I don't want to have anything to do with your organization. I don't know how you're able to know these things, but then again, I don't understand the Balazons' powers either. Perhaps you're both from the devil. But I do know I want to leave now. Either let me go or kill me."

"The media is Satan's puppet, Jeff," Lawrence said. "If you want to go, you're free to do so. Reports of us killing people are lies fabricated to discredit us."

"Not true," Jeff said. "I was attacked by religious fanatics myself."

"Yes," Lawrence said. "The devil has some false preaching groups that kill people as a counterfeit to our own efforts. Their purpose is to scare people by creating bad press. They want to prevent people from listening to the true gospel message from our own groups. But Satan is driving these people. We have nothing to do with them. We believers have been waiting for years for the Lord's command to go forth and start evangelizing the world and these false groups are just Satan's way of trying to stop us. As a sign of good faith and sincerity, I will let you go home without a blindfold."

Lawrence called the big man with the beard to his office. When he arrived, Lawrence said, "Take this man back into town and drop him off wherever he wishes. And don't blindfold him."

"Yes, sir," the man replied without hesitation.

"You see, Jeff," Lawrence said, "we will not force you to do anything you're uncomfortable with. However, Satan's cohorts will be watching you. If you show signs of believing, you might become a target again. The demons have the ability to constantly monitor your thoughts and whereabouts."

"I know. My personal Balazon, Acin-om, told me she was aware of my every move but couldn't interfere too much in my life. Something about needing to follow the higher priority of walking the fine line of exerting influence but not interference in human affairs."

"That's another lie, Jeff. You can't see it, but there is a mighty battle going on in the spirit realm. Truth is, God simply doesn't allow the demons to do certain things. The Lord is still restraining the evil and deception to some degree, but this will not last for much longer. I urge you to consider all I have said and come back to God before it is too late. And remember, our complex abounds with God's supernatural protection. The demons can't follow you here, and you can be totally free of their influence if you come over to the Lord's side. You are welcome to join us anytime."

Jeff nodded stiffly and left with the big man. After they had gone, Mara said, “Are you sure that was a wise thing to do? He’ll know our hideout location now.”

“It was the right thing to do,” Lawrence said. “The Lord told me to do it. He also told me he’d be back.”

Mara didn’t say anything more.

Chapter 12

Jeff asked to be let off several blocks from his house, so he could walk in the comfortably cool night and gaze at the twinkling stars, an activity that often helped him clear his thoughts and zero in on exactly what was bothering him. The moon was out in full, casting a comforting glow in the night sky, almost confirming to him the magnificence of creation and the possibility of a Creator behind it all. The air smelled clear and crisp, and silence enveloped him, as not a car or person was in his vicinity.

It disturbed him how Mara knew so much about him. He didn't understand her powers anymore than the Balazons but she was right. He *had* been an immature believer and let a bad experience deter him from growing spiritually, eventually losing what he had in the beginning. He'd turned his back on Jesus, the One who loved him enough to die for him. He wondered if God could still love him after that, wondered if He would accept Jeff back if he came begging on his knees. No! Jeff refused to let his mind become tortured again. God would have to reveal Himself to Jeff personally. He wasn't about to blindly follow humans anymore, even ones doing supernatural things.

Seeing his house nearer in sight now, Jeff picked up his pace. He still didn't trust the Balazons, but that didn't mean he had to embrace another weird cult. If they wanted any converts, they would have to get them somewhere else.

Jeff fumbled with his keys in the dark before opening the door. Stillness and darkness greeted him inside the house. He flipped on a hall light and went into the living room to find Stephanie mindlessly staring at the wall. She was swaying her head forward and back as if spaced out on drugs. After what they had done to his little girl, if he saw a Balazon right now, powers or no powers, he would likely rip its head off. Jeff turned up the lamp beside her, but Stephanie continued to stare at the wall, no signs of alertness.

"Snap out of it, girl," he said.

Stephanie slowly came back to reality. "Oh, dad. Hi."

"Where's the Balazons? Where's Valerie and Nick? What happened to you?"

Stephanie talked like a stoned hippie from the sixties. "Relax, man. The humans are asleep and the Balazons have made a retreat." She laughed slightly. "Hey, that almost rhymes. But they'll be back tomorrow for another treatment. Look what I can do." She waved at an object across the room. "The picture on the wall. Watch it."

"Nothing's happening," Jeff said.

"Can't you see it flying around the room? I've already got some of the Balazons' telekinetic powers."

"Stephanie! Snap out of it. The picture isn't doing anything."

"Yes it is!" she insisted as she put her head between her legs and started moaning and mumbling. Suddenly, Jeff thought about God with disgust. This was further proof that God didn't exist. If He was real, He should prevent innocent children from being brainwashed, or at least show Himself to Jeff by releasing his daughter.

If you knew Me, we could do it together, a voice suddenly seemed to say. Jeff didn't hear anything audible, but the words were as real to him as the conversation he'd had with his daughter.

"Who's that?" Jeff said out loud, but there was no reply. "I don't know what you mean. Tell me more."

Jeff wondered if he might be going insane.

However, Jeff was willing to do whatever it took to free his daughter. He remembered the words he'd heard once at a miracle healing crusade. The preacher used the name of Jesus to supposedly cast out demons and heal people. Maybe he could do the same to cure Stephanie. He didn't know if it would work, but he decided to try.

However, Jeff's mental denial was still operating. He didn't think he could invoke the name of Jesus if he didn't believe. He tried to force himself to say the words, but it was no use. It seemed ridiculous anyway.

Jeff thought of taking her to the hospital, but didn't think they could do much. Perhaps he should take her to a hypnotist, regress her back mentally to before any of this happened. Then, despite himself, he thought of a title he had heard once for Jesus Christ: the Great Physician. No! He wouldn't think about such things.

Jeff suddenly had a vision.

He saw a mirror in front of him. His reflection was that of an ugly, grotesque, monster, dripping slimy ooze. The next second, he was himself again, and clean—wearing robes of purest white, shining like the sun. Jeff understood. God had shown him what his real difficulty in praying for Stephanie was: sin. Jeff couldn't say it, not after having lived for years in rebellion. He didn't feel worthy. He had walked away from God and lived his life for himself, ignoring any convicting nudges from the Lord's Spirit.

But he also knew God was telling him that he could be clean again if he truly repented of his sins and renewed his relationship with Jesus. Jeff started to feel clammy, as he realized he must muster the courage. He had to get his heart right with God. His daughter's life and perhaps both of their eternal destinies were at stake.

Jeff struggled for several minutes before he managed to ask God to forgive his sins and accept him into His family of believers. Immediately, a warm tingling sensation pulsated throughout his body. He felt rapturous joy and the sensation of a huge weight lifting off his head. He felt content to revel in the feeling but decided not to waste any time.

"Wake up child, in the name of Jesus Christ." He felt kind of silly saying the words, and there was no sign of response from Stephanie, but he put his hand on her head and continued. "Demons of darkness, I come against you in the name of the Lord Jesus. I command you to release my daughter from your power! Leave her body now and don't come back."

Stephanie's head suddenly shot up. Her eyes shot daggers. When she talked, her voice was low and gruff. "You fool. We will not leave. We have permission to be here."

Jeff took a deep breath and moved back a bit. "Who gave you permission? Who are you?"

"The girl herself invited us in. We are a part of her now." Stephanie smiled and nodded, obviously satisfied. "Go away. She has made her choice."

"She's young. She couldn't make such a decision properly. You must leave her."

Stephanie laughed a shrill laugh and the deep voice spoke again. "Go away unbeliever. We've won! He will not accept one who has strayed so far for so long. You are nothing."

Guilt started to creep over Jeff, and a feeling of despair assaulted his mind, but in that moment, Jeff cried out for help and received an answer. "You're a liar!" he said with conviction. Jesus Christ has won! In the name of Jesus, I command you to come out of her, and I ask now Lord Jesus that you fill Stephanie with your Holy Spirit and save her soul!"

Stephanie's eyes welled up and one small tear fell from her right eye. She nodded her head slowly, the best she seemed able to do to acknowledge her acceptance and agreement with Jeff's words. But that was the only step of faith the Lord needed.

The shrill scream returned as Stephanie ran around the room clutching her head. She fell to the floor in seeming pain and continued to scream. "We will not leave," she said in defiance, but within the next second, she was calm. "Dad? I'm free!"

Jeff hugged his little girl and thanked God. "It's OK. It's over now. Everything's going to be fine."

He grabbed his daughter's hand with new found strength and faith, and headed upstairs.

"What are you doing, dad?" Stephanie asked.

"I'm going to free your mom and brother, as I did you. If you've been affected, I'm sure they have too." He stormed into Nick's bedroom first and then Valerie's, flipping on the lights and commanding the demons to come out of them.

Valerie got very upset and started yelling, not shrill screaming such as he'd heard from Stephanie, but her own voice. She continued to yell and throw things until he had backed past the door's frame.

"That's it," she said. "I've had enough of your ranting and raving and small-mindedness. I want you out of this house. I'll be filing for divorce tomorrow." She slammed the door in his face.

He was stunned as to why it didn't work. With Stephanie, his faith hadn't even been very strong. He didn't understand but there was someone who might. He grabbed suitcases for himself and Stephanie, packed a few things, and headed out the front door without looking back.

"Where are we going, dad?" Stephanie asked.

"To the hideout."

* * *

"The Lord works in mysterious ways, Jeff," Lawrence said from behind his desk. "I don't know why you couldn't cast out the demons from Valerie and Nick. And the Lord hasn't given me any special word on the matter either. Perhaps you jumped to conclusions and they weren't possessed yet?"

"Maybe," Jeff said. "Valerie must have at least been influenced by them at that point, the way she just cruelly told me she wanted a divorce and all. Valerie is the most loving, kind, tender, forgiving person I've ever met. I've never met anybody I've felt as connected to as her. That wasn't her talking."

"Just keep trusting in Him," Lawrence said. "You do believe now, don't you?"

"Yes. The real clincher came when I renewed my relationship with the Lord. The moment I asked for forgiveness, I could feel my mind being released. It was as if a claw tightly fastened to my brain for over a decade suddenly left. I could think clearly. Instantly, God gave me the faith to believe in Him again. I can feel His presence now. I can't see Him with my physical eyes, but He's as real to me as you sitting across this desk from me. His Spirit is at one with mine. I know I'm a child of God. And when the demon spoke to me, it reaffirmed what I then knew to be true."

"I feel it too, dad," Stephanie said. "I realize now I never really had Jesus in my heart by the power of His Holy Spirit. I knew lots about Jesus, and much doctrine and Bible verses, but I never really knew the real person, who is alive and now in my heart. He is in me and I am in him. Jesus said the same thing about His Father. So many things Jesus said in the Bible make sense now. All the fights I had with Nick about religion were more about being right and one-upmanship than really seeking love and truth. I love God and desire to obey Him now. I never felt that before."

"That's because God has renewed your heart," Lawrence said. "It's not about religion, but rather a supernatural love relationship with a very real Jesus. It's natural to want to please those you are close to and love. We knew your transformation would happen. We've all been praying for you here. With these many spiritual warriors behind you, you were as good as free. Not only that, but God told me you'd be back tonight."

"Please pray for Valerie and Nick too," Jeff said. "I won't abandon them totally. I have to go back periodically and try to reach them."

"We will. We will."

"So what happens next? Where do I go from here?"

"We'd like you to join with us. Both you and your daughter can stay here in the complex. There's plenty of room."

Jeff turned to look at his daughter, who was smiling. "I think we'd like that." He looked back at Lawrence. "How can I help with your cause? What can I do?"

Lawrence scratched his head. "Have you discovered your gifts and calling yet?"

Jeff shook his head.

"Well, God will reveal it to you sooner or later. Until then, I'd like you to stay with us and attend the daytime Bible classes. There's nothing more important you can do now than grow in the Word of God. If you like, you can talk to any of the gift counselors. They're usually quite good at discerning others' abilities and offering sound advice on all sorts of things."

"Sounds like a good idea to me," Jeff said as Lawrence called for an escort on the intercom. A long blond-haired woman came to the door. She was wearing a pink jump suit which hugged her petite figure closely. Lawrence introduced her as Sandy and asked her to show Jeff to a two-person room on the far south side of the complex.

They exited the small office.

"So, how long have you been here?" Jeff asked as they headed down the stairs.

Sandy tossed her hair to one side and smiled. "The Lord led me here shortly after the rapture, during a time when I was searching for answers."

"What's your gift?" Stephanie asked.

Jeff scolded his daughter gently.

"Oh, that's OK," Sandy said. "I don't mind telling. I know ahead of time when the police are arriving. You know, when we're out spreading the gospel?"

A look of mild surprise flashed over Jeff's face. "I see. So you help the group get away before the authorities can arrest you on false charges or kill you."

"Exactly," Sandy said. "I can visualize them in my mind. While they're still many blocks away, I warn everyone to flee. But sometimes people don't believe me."

"And get killed," Jeff said.

"Yes. The police shoot everybody and blame it on us. Most of the new Christians we take with us, but the others don't always believe me or react fast enough. They scoff, calling us religious fanatics and everything, until it's too late. At least in the beginning they did. Nowadays, it can be difficult to keep a crowd listening because people are afraid. They've all been brainwashed by the media."

"Yeah, I can imagine," Jeff agreed. "I was scared when I first came here for that very reason."

They reached the bottom of another set of stairs. Sandy led them up and pointed at the third door down the hall. "Well, that's your room," she said. "There's no lock. You won't need one."

Jeff stood at his door and stared at Sandy, trying to think of something to say.

"Say thanks, dad," Stephanie said.

"Oh, right," Jeff said. "Thanks for everything. See you tomorrow?"

Sandy laughed slightly. “Sure,” she said as she walked back down the stairs.

“She’s pretty isn’t she, dad.”

“Yep,” was all Jeff said and opened the door.

The next day, Jeff and Stephanie spent their time in Bible classes, which were held in various rooms near the front tunnel entrance; they started at nine in the morning and went until five in the evening, with a one hour lunch break. It was a rather grueling pace physically, rather reminded Jeff of university, but he didn’t mind as he was soaking up Bible knowledge like a sponge. His spirit was very willing, even if his body occasionally got tired. Every hour they would switch rooms and be taught by a new instructor who would talk about his or her own gifts and experiences. It was more of an open seminar than a class.

One of the instructors, who could cast out demons, explained to Jeff in greater depth what had happened earlier. Jeff learned about the power and authority Christians yield in the name of Jesus, and the instructor explained how God has given believers authority over all the powers of darkness.

“Then why couldn’t I cast out the demons from my wife and son,” Jeff asked.

“I don’t know,” the instructor replied frankly. “It could be they weren’t fully possessed yet. Sometimes you need greater faith. Sometimes I think God leaves them there to teach a person a lesson. At times, with non-believers, He may leave them permanently and demonstrate His power by defeating their purposes through us. But in your specific case, I don’t know. You should talk to Conner in your two o’clock class. He has a gift for understanding the divine perspective on everyday events.”

Jeff took his instructor’s advice, but Conner was not much help either.

"Sorry, Jeff," Conner said. "All I'm getting is the Lord wants your family under their influence. As for how long or why, I can't tell."

Jeff didn't understand it all, but it was enough for him to realize that it was God's will for the time being, so he left it alone.

Later, sitting with his daughter in the complex's cafeteria, Jeff gulped down the last bite of his roast beef and potatoes and looked at his watch, about a quarter past six. Sandy had stopped by his prophecy class and told him that she would meet him for supper. She'd said to start without her if she were late.

Jeff spotted Sandy enter the room and go to the sandwich bin. She grabbed something which had lettuce sticking out of it, poured herself a cup of coffee, and sat beside them.

"If that's all you eat for supper, no wonder you're so slim," Jeff said.

"I'm not sure if that's a compliment or not," Sandy joked.

"It is." Jeff looked at his empty plate. He had unashamedly taken advantage of the free food. The dinner smorgasbord of carrots, corn, gravy, roast, fresh buns, and mashed potatoes had overflowed Jeff's plate, not to mention the cherry pie for desert. "So what's the big news you were going to tell me?"

Sandy swallowed a bite of what Jeff could see now as a turkey and lettuce sandwich before answering. "I've talked with Lawrence and he said the Lord wants you to come with us tonight when we hit the park."

"I don't understand what she means," Stephanie said.

Jeff looked at his daughter. "I think she means one of their preaching ventures."

"Exactly," Sandy said. "Stephanie can stay here; it'll be safer. But we need you to come along."

"Did Lawrence say why? I mean, I don't know if I'm ready for this yet."

"The Lord wouldn't call you if you weren't ready."

Jeff slowly nodded his head in agreement. "OK, I'll come."

Sandy daintily ate her sandwich for the next few minutes. She talked about her experiences on the battlefield and how dangerous it could be. They had lost one of their preachers only several days ago when they had spent too long pleading with the lost crowd. The police arrived before they could get away, and shot him in the chest, killing him instantly. She said it was hard losing a preacher. In the complexes spread throughout the world, those with the gift of effectively communicating the gospel message were highly cherished and guarded.

"How many more complexes are there?" Jeff asked. "How do you survive? How do you communicate with one another?" Jeff explained he didn't know very much about their operations. He'd never heard anything about God or believers on the VRT or radio. Nothing positive anyway. Now that he'd become a Christian, he wanted to know more.

"There are thousands of complexes hidden throughout the world," Sandy said. "Each one is mainly responsible for evangelizing its own general area, although in our own case, we've occasionally gone as far south as Mexico, and as far north as Canada. We simply go where God directs, and He provides for and protects us in mighty ways. Take this food for instance. We only have enough food in each complex to feed everybody for one day, but each morning new food miraculously replenishes the previous day's depleted supply. God's taking care of us as He did the early Israelites, when millions were fed each day with manna from heaven. We would be dead by now without Him.

"As far as communicating, we do have some radio equipment, but the authorities might track our hideouts if we used those, so they're mostly reserved for mobile work. Mainly, Lawrence communicates with other leaders the same way he communicates with God. He then updates us on our world progress. Don't ask me how that works. I don't know, and I don't think it's important."

Jeff shook his head in awe. By faith, he knew what she said was true, but he found it difficult to picture people in Africa doing the same things they were doing. Maybe he was too used to VRT news coverage, and needed to see images in order to feel as though it were true.

Jeff folded his hands together. "How can Satan keep knowledge of your existence such a tight secret, and hunt you down privately without resistance. Aren't there any good people left?"

"Sure, they get added to our numbers every day." Sandy smiled. "And the devil can't keep our existence a secret. We're starting to make a big impact. Soon the whole world will know the truth."

Jeff didn't say anything, but nodded his head in fascination.

"Wouldn't it be great if tonight we discovered your gift is preaching?" Sandy asked, changing the subject. Jeff realized Sandy had probably heard these types of questions many times before. She was probably more interested in what God was doing now.

Jeff shook his head. "I don't think so. I'm not very articulate."

"So far, the best ones have always been those who say they're no good. I guess we'll have to wait and see."

Jeff nodded in agreement as he thought about that night.

* * *

"There's hardly anybody here," Jeff said as he helped Sandy set up the last two speakers in the center of Star City Park. "Are you sure this is going to work?"

"It'll work," Sandy said. "The Lord always makes sure people are here at the proper time."

Len and Ellis set up more electronic equipment behind the portable platform. Everyone continued to fiddle and finetune, while Jeff sat in the back of the van. After several more minutes, all four of them gathered around the platform.

"Are we ready?" Jeff asked.

"We're ready," Sandy said. She stood on the platform and closed her eyes. "I see throngs approaching the front of the park's entrance. Most felt led to go for a walk, and have found themselves here. They're confused. They don't know why, but they keep coming. It won't be long now." Sure enough, Jeff saw scores of people starting to make their way to the platform.

"It's your turn now, Len," Sandy said as she got down.

Len took his place and started preaching before the people reached the van; some turned around, fearful of fanatics.

"Don't be afraid," Len shouted. "We won't harm you. Come gather around. The Holy Spirit has drawn you here for a reason. You have a longing in your heart to know God, and you can do so tonight."

That seemed to settle their fears, most mustering the faith to continue walking, only a few going the opposite direction. A crowd of all types quickly grew around the van and platform, from the young and healthy to the old and weary. Jeff saw one older lady wearing dark glasses. She must be blind, for an elderly man led her by the hand. Jeff saw Mrs. Cobb, a lady who used to frequent Armstrong's Pharmacy, and whom Jeff knew to be on welfare, as well as Mr. Gelinas, one of Star City's richest businessmen.

"The Balazons are liars!" Len shouted into his microphone. "Khur-ak is not the leader of a group of super-beings who have created a belief in God. No one has created God, for He is from everlasting to everlasting." Len went on to say Khur-ak was Satan, the devil, disguised as a beautiful angel of light, deceiving the world, trying to drag as many as will follow him down to hell, but the Spirit of Jesus had drawn them to the park to break the power of the enemy and release them from captivity.

Jeff could see Len was merely warming up. His voice started to rise and he waved his hands around for emphasis. After several minutes of very blunt warnings about the Balazons, Len pointed at an elderly man who was bent over in a wheelchair. The man's hands were deformed as if he had severe arthritis.

Len shouted, "In the name of Jesus, stand up and walk!" The man's limbs straightened out and he immediately stood up, shouting for joy.

While the man rejoiced, Len said, "Lester Cranleigh, come forward!" A young man came out of the crowd. He walked with crutches because he had no leg below the right knee. "Throw those away. Walk!" The man let out an astonished yelp, and dropped his crutches, as a new leg grew out of the stump which had existed previously. "Since the unveiling, the devil has done many miracles to deceive you, but when have you seen humans do mighty things in the name of the Son of God? Search your hearts and know the Spirit of God is with us!"

Len walked over to the blind lady Jeff had noticed earlier, who now stood near the front, and threw her dark glasses off. "You can see!" he declared. "Jesus has given you sight!" The woman screamed with delight, while Len went back to the podium.

"I can see!" she yelled. "I can see!"

"God can do greater things than this," Len said. "But He has done these miracles so you might believe in the living Jesus, who reigns in heaven above. The real Jesus was God manifest in the flesh. He died two thousand years ago on a cross to pay the penalty for your sins. If you repent and receive Him now as your personal Lord and Savior, you will become a child of God and receive a place of honor when He comes to take you home.

"We are living in the last days when the devil's deception is permeating the entire earth. You no longer need to be a part of it. You can come to Jesus and be set free. If you've already started merging your minds with the Balazons', it is even more imperative you come now. The longer you wait, the harder it will be to respond to Him, for the demons will slowly take over your minds. He is standing at the door of your hearts, drawing you, asking you if He can come in. He wants to forgive you. For your own sakes, give Him a chance. Open the door."

The intoxicatingly beautiful presence of God filled the air. Jeff tingled and he knew the listeners felt it too because many came forward when Len asked if they wanted to be saved from Satan's grasp and receive Jesus as their Lord and Savior. Then the newly born Christians began worshipping God, singing praises and lifting their hands upward.

Jeff sat back and smiled. He had never seen anything like this before. A new sense of intensity came over him, a feeling of power he'd never experienced before, an unparalleled closeness with the Lord. God seemed to tell him, "When the time comes stamp your foot on the ground."

"What?" Jeff said. "What do you mean?" But he couldn't sense any response.

Sandy was sitting at the opposite side of the van. Jeff went over and asked her what she thought.

She was smiling and rejoicing, but turned to look at Jeff. She had to talk loudly to be heard. "I don't know what it means, but I'd suggest you do it when the time comes."

"But when's that!" Jeff said.

"You'll know when the time is right!"

For all he knew, the authorities were near. He might not have time to think about it, let alone do anything. "When will the police be here?"

Sandy closed her eyes and prayed. "I don't sense anything. They might not even find out about this one."

Len continued to preach for the next fifteen minutes, trying to reach the minority that still hadn't committed their lives to the Lord despite all they had seen. Jeff estimated that out of the approximately three hundred there, about two hundred and fifty were saved. This wasn't good enough for Len. He wanted them all.

With a background of rejoicing and dancing, Len set his microphone on the podium and walked amongst the crowd, continuing to do miracles for the hurting, and telling them marvelous things about God's Kingdom. He appeared calm and relaxed as he leisurely moved about, allowing God to express His love through him. Len performed powerful miracles, and with the electrifying presence of God's Spirit, few doubted His existence. The atmosphere was so absorbing that, at first, nobody saw several armored trucks enter the park.

Jeff was the first to say anything. "Sandy. Look!" He pointed at the trucks.

Sandy was speechless. "Why didn't He warn me? God always tells me when they're coming. Why would He betray us this time?"

Jeff wasn't listening. He had already jumped on the platform, and grabbed the microphone. He was about to scream a warning when he heard the Lord say, "Now!"

"What?" Jeff said into the microphone and got some confused looks from both Len and the audience. Everyone became quiet as they sensed something was wrong, but didn't know what. Then it slowly dawned on people as they noticed the armored police trucks. Someone started to scream and Jeff knew full-scale panic was mere seconds away.

"Wait!" Jeff said. "Don't fear." For the first time, he understood what the Lord was telling him, and for some unknown reason, they listened. "In the days of old, when the pharaoh's mighty army was about to crush the Israelites, Moses stretched out his hand and divided the Red Sea. The Lord delivered them from their enemies that day. So too, I say do not be afraid, for the Lord will deliver us." Jeff set the microphone on the podium, as men in uniforms made their way out of the armored trucks and lined up behind the crowd. They nonchalantly pointed their machine guns in the crowd's direction and began walking forward.

Jeff lifted his right leg, and with a wide smile, stomped down hard. There were a few tense seconds in which nothing seemed to happen. Then the ground began to rumble. The rumbling became louder and the ground started shaking. Soon, the whole world—except the van, platform, and crowd of three hundred—began to convulse violently.

The officers covered their heads in fear, for soon large hailstones began to fall on their heads, but Jeff's group and the crowd were safe, as if by an invisible bubble. Jeff grabbed the microphone again. "Sandy, Len, start packing." He gestured at the crowd. "All who want to can come with us." At that point, everyone who had been unsure about Christianity overcame their doubts very quickly and obeyed Jeff's instructions.

The turmoil energized people to quickly pack the van. Jeff got into the passenger side, while Ellis got behind the wheel. Len and Sandy piled the back with as many people as possible, while the rest ran behind the van as it slowly crawled along. And wherever they drove, the quaking and hail stopped temporarily, starting again once they'd moved on.

Unimpeded by the authorities, they slowly drove to the complex. As soon as they arrived, Jeff and his friends introduced the newcomers to the gift counselors.

Jeff went to his room. He had been constantly active since this morning's early classes and thought he deserved the evening off. However, no sooner had he opened his door than Lawrence announced over the intercom Jeff's group was to report to the main office.

He arrived to hear Len mildly protesting to the lady behind the counter they should get some sleep, but Len took the itinerary from her and said, "The Lord's will be done."

"How bad is it?" Jeff asked. Working for God would undoubtedly have its good and bad times, but he wouldn't miss the personal joy and satisfaction he'd received from his experience today for anything. He was prepared to go right back into the field if needed.

Len glanced up from the paper he was staring at. "Not as bad as I thought. We're through for the night, but we've got big jobs ahead of us. Probably won't be back in Star City for awhile."

Chapter 13

Star City, several years later

"God's judgments are meant to move you towards repentance," the preacher said while standing behind his podium on Baker street, a light set up behind him so the crowd could see him better. He had just healed a blind lady. A few of his companions stood to one side, hiding in the blackness of the night. The moon couldn't give much illumination either because two weeks ago it had turned blood red and stayed that way. The signs you have seen lately are not natural phenomenon. They were prophesied in Revelation long ago." There were no stars visible in the night sky, except for the odd one which streaked across the heavens every few minutes and burned up.

A few hundred yards away, a long finger of fire flashed from heaven and scorched the ground, filling the air with the smell of acrid smoke. A large hailstone as big as a boulder fell from the sky and pulverized a parked car, shock waves from the explosion causing those in the vicinity to cover their ears. "These signs, along with the plagues and scorching heat of the day, are to make you realize His judgment of sin is very real. Don't wait until past death to feel the full fury of it. Come to Him now while you still can." Everyone who was listening to the message, approximately three hundred, responded.

The speaker finished leading everyone in a sinners' prayer, as Shaun led his gang silently through the crowd, sneering at the weaklings who were listening. He motioned for Nick, Chris, and

Mark to circle around behind while he and the others took up positions in front of the podium.

"Who is your master, preacher-man," Shaun said.

The man paused. "Jesus Christ."

Shaun pulled out a gun and pointed it at the woman beside him. "Is this your wife?"

The man nodded.

Shaun grinned an evil grin. "Tell me your master is Satan."

The man paused briefly before shaking his head in deliberate fashion.

Shaun blew the lady's head off and pointed the gun at the man. "Say it!"

The man shook his head again and calmly said, "No."

"I hold the power of life and death over you."

"You have no power over me except what is given you from above. God has already told me my physical life is to end today, but I know I will live again. You can have that assurance too if you come to the foot of the cross."

"Screw you," Shaun said, as he put his gun in his holster. He pulled out a long sword from a sheath on his left. The man didn't try to get away, but Mark held his arms anyway, and Shaun slowly pushed the long blade through his belly. The man gasped short breaths, as Shaun methodically twisted and turned the sword. After a few seconds, he fell to the ground. Then Shaun said, "Kill everyone who came with him! And everybody who listened to him too!"

His men mercilessly carried out their orders. Nobody even tried escaping. Nick hesitated for a moment, a part of him resisting, but the stronger dark power of Stro-kar pushed him to kill. After he was done, he found he had enjoyed it.

"Collect the Christians' bodies," Shaun said. "They'll fetch a handsome price with the demon authorities."

However, before they could do so, a Cadillac zoomed around the corner. Several men hung out the windows and started shooting. Shaun ordered his men inside an abandoned hardware store for cover.

It was their rivals, the Falcons, trying to steal their prize.

They returned fire and succeeded in killing the driver. The Cadillac lost control, and overturned. The surviving Falcons jumped out of the Cadillac and took cover behind some trucks across the street.

Shaun and his men ran forward and took refuge behind the Cadillac, where Nick saw a Falcon pinned underneath the passenger side and pointed his gun at the man's head.

"No! Don't kill me! I can tell you where to get grenades, man."

"All right," Nick said and put away his gun. "I won't shoot you if you tell me."

"We have some in the trunk in a bullet-proof container."

Nick's left eyebrow rose in mild surprise. "Good boy. Thank you very much." Nick pulled out a switchblade.

"No! Wait!"

Nick smiled as he slit the man's throat. "I kept my promise. I didn't shoot you." He relished in the sensation of slicing flesh and drawing blood, look of fear and pain adding to the excitement.

Shaun peeked over and rattled off several Uzi rounds, but couldn't aim very accurately in the darkness. Shaun's second in command, Mike, hurled a Molotov cocktail. The explosion lighted up the surroundings to show it had fallen short by about three yards. The Falcons returned fire, and Mike ducked behind the relative protection of the car-shield with the six other gang members.

Life was very different now that Khur-ak was in full control. Some people had been afraid at first but slowly most fully integrated with the aliens. Somewhere along the way, though, things went bad—very bad.

"The grenades in the trunk would take care of them pretty quick," Nick said.

Khur-ak had eventually openly declared his true identity to be Satan. By then, many didn't care, for they had totally enmeshed with the fallen spirits, becoming creatures that loved to behave like animals—brutal, selfish, and unfeeling. The demons were in complete control and plunged the world into utter depravity, simply because they loved it. When their hosts died, they would join another. Many demons could live inside one person. The fallen angels had transformed themselves into aliens of light, and had managed to totally deceive the world.

Since Satan claimed defeating God required rebellion against all good, Satan's new world government was very iniquitous. Murder and other forms of violence were widespread and nobody cared or tried to stop it. In fact, torturing and killing Christians brought a handsome price with the demon authorities. Basically, anything one wanted to do was allowed. Over time, the demons had managed to destroy people's consciences and do away with moral restrictions.

"Really?" Ronny said. "I didn't think the Falcons had such hardware."

"I guess they have a new contact," Shaun said. "I think I've got a plan." Nick knew Shaun would love to torture the Falcons, but he was also practical. It would be easier to blow them away. Even though Nick was infested with Stro-kar, he would never understand Shaun's viciousness.

Nick began to feel uneasy as Shaun stared at him. Their leader was the wickedest person he'd ever known, unpredictable and brutal. Even without demon possession, he must have been born that way. It seemed so natural to him. But Nick still struggled with Stro-kar.

Shaun pointed at Kevin, who was beside him and crouched low. Kevin hadn't let off a single shot yet. "You're the most expendable. You've been a coward since day one." Shaun quickly reached into his belt, pulled out his revolver, and shot Kevin in the head. He slumped to the ground, mouth frozen open in silent protest. "One clean shot. The less holes in him the better."

"Watcha got in mind, man?" Ronny asked.

"Nick's going to use him as a shield. Tear me a strip from your shirt."

Ronny immediately complied. Their leader tied Kevin's limp legs to Nick's. "There," Shaun said, "that should keep him from flopping around." He grabbed the back of Kevin's jacket and pulled him up straight.

Nick was stunned at what had happened and hesitated.

"Well, grab it," Shaun said and Nick slowly obeyed.

"Everybody cover him!" Shaun said. "He's going to get the grenades!" Nick didn't want to, but disobeying orders meant instant death, so he had to try.

All gang members acknowledged with a curt nod. As Nick jumped into the open, they opened fire on the Falcons. Nick shot open the trunk and quickly grabbed the only metal container he could see. Kevin's body recoiled as it took a few bullets. Within seconds, he was behind the shelter again.

Shaun opened the metal box, at least a dozen grenades inside. "They would have used these on us. I'm going to give them some of their own medicine." Shaun pulled the pin on one small handheld bomb and hurled it without looking. A loud explosion rocked the Cadillac. "Did I get them?"

Ronny peeked around the corner. "No."

Shaun pulled another pin. "Cover me!" Everyone started

shooting simultaneously. This time Shaun carefully judged the distance before throwing.

Another explosion rocked the street as the bomb clearly hit its target. One person staggered about, clutching his head and screaming; he was on fire. Shaun took aim with his gun.

Nick could hardly believe his eyes. Here Shaun had an opportunity to watch a man slowly burn, and it looked as if he were going to shoot him. It seemed out of character.

Shaun let off rapid-fire rounds, overshooting the man by several yards, and then adjusting appropriately to riddle his legs with holes. The man collapsed and screamed as he burned. Shaun laughed. This was more like their leader, Nick thought.

The gang went ahead to investigate the carnage, but Nick lagged behind to talk privately with Ronny. Even now, Stro-kar urged Nick on, pushed his inner self to let go, but Nick resisted. Usually, though, he was unsuccessful. The battle was too difficult and he was too weak.

Nick remembered how it had seemed so right at first to merge with Stro-kar, how free he had begun to feel, as he let what he believed to be a benevolent alien transform his mind. Over time, ideas of good and evil, right and wrong, began to meld as one in his mind, and nothing was to be condemned, all was allowed, everything was relative. The demons transformed the world slowly at first, by reinforcing and pushing the world's growing acceptance of immoral sexual lifestyles, such as homosexuality. They started with giving the world medical solutions that removed all negative consequences of any sexual behavior, perfect birth control, perfect antibiotics and perfect antivirals that cured AIDS, gonorrhea, syphilis, and any other sexually transmitted disease that existed or might ever come into existence. Then they started encouraging sexual "freedom". Under this cloak of freedom, most people's consciences did not detect the subtle damage the demons were doing to people's minds, as the "aliens" pushed for more and more sexual license.

Following on the heels of worldwide legalization of homosexual behavior and same-sex marriage, the governments of the world had quickly codified many types of perverted sexual behaviors as lawful, including polygamy, incest, and pedophilia, since it seemed so logical to their demon infested minds that total sexual freedom should be the norm and judging any type of sexual behavior was wrong. Any people with dissenting opinions to this new standard had been viciously muzzled by beefed-up hate speech laws, which demanded immediate and indefinite incarceration upon proof of any written or verbal condemnation of any type of sex act.

The world had fully bought into the lie that mere expression of disapproval of certain sexual practices constituted hateful speech that must be suppressed, since all sexual behavior groups had become classified as persecuted minorities with special legal protections. The Bible had soon become banned as hate speech, since it soundly condemned many types of sinful sexual behaviors but had long since been proven false in the eyes of the world, since most believed there was no God. Mere possession of a Bible could land one in jail for ten years, an edict that had inspired mass burnings of a book that had come to be mostly considered an irrelevant collection of stories about ancient man's interactions with alien-gods and full of outdated beliefs and hateful writings, not a serious guide to sexual morality. But in reality, the hate speech laws were simply demon inspired legal justifications to destroy any conscience left in society.

Despite some mild religious protests, to help aid in the evolution from old religious faith to enlightenment, claiming belief in Jesus as the only way of salvation was also outlawed as hate speech. In the eyes of the world, it seemed so narrow-minded and hateful for religious holdouts to stubbornly cling to exclusive claim that Christ was the only way to eternal life, especially in light of all the knowledge and advancements the "aliens" had brought mankind. The proof was in what the Balazons could do. Eternal life would be wrought by internal transformation to exultation. Khur-ak had promised it. It would be done.

Soon sexual laws seemed passé to the evolved and enlightened beings that humans were becoming and people began pushing the envelope further. Emboldened by the new legal protections, people began engaging in sexual activity in open public places, or at work, then soon with dead bodies, animals…any sexual behavior was allowed and encouraged, anything with anyone, anywhere, anytime, the more outrageous the better. With the aliens' help, mankind was "evolving" beyond the need for sexual moral restraint.

"I wish they were gone," Nick said to Ronny. He spoke quietly, so the others wouldn't hear. Nick felt he could only be open with Ronny, who likewise sometimes struggled with his inner evil companion. He started to reminisce about life before the Balazons' unveiling.

Those were the good old days, Nick started to think, but the demon Stro-kar forced that part of his personality back. Nick let out a small scream of agony.

"What's wrong?" Ronny asked, but instinctively understood. "Wrong thoughts are punishable. How many do you have now?"

"Still just Stro-kar, but that's enough. You know, Ronny, I wish I had never heard of the Balazons." Nick continued to speak in low tones. "They suckered us like patsies. Now we know the truth but still we can't do anything about it." He wined slightly. "He causes so much pain inside me. My mind feels like a hot iron sometimes. I can't resist his dark power."

"I know what you mean, man," Ronny said, equally softly. "I've got two of them. Sometimes I wish—" Suddenly, he let out an anguished yelp, facial grimace vividly showing his internal punishment for rebellious thoughts. “I wish nothing.” He spoke louder so the others would hear his affirmations of allegiance. “I am at one with my masters. I will do as they tell me. We love to roam free and live to please our every whim and desire.”

Then a sorrowful expression came over Ronny’s face and he quietly said to Nick, “They want me to rape another woman. I don’t know if I can do it.” There was a slight pause before Ronny screamed and fell to his knees.

The gang members looked back, unconcerned. At one time or another, each had resisted and experienced punishment, so they were tolerant of Ronny’s weakness to a degree. Even Shaun had admitted to mild rebellion during the early part of his conversion. Eventually, however, they fully surrendered to the darkness within. They also knew Nick wasn’t totally given over, but tolerated him too. Both had been loyal gang members, and Shaun said that in time, they would become full partakers of Satan’s spirit.

After awhile, Ronny stood up and said, “Let’s go get us some women.”

Nick nodded. He felt a sudden urge to inflict pain on a child. He remembered how violence had seemed the next logical phase in advancing sexual freedom, as Stro-kar soon bent his mind to think rape was just another form of free sexual expression, which had to be upheld at all costs. The governments of the world agreed and passed the Sodom and Gomorrah act, which legalized rape and basically transformed the world into the licentious Biblical cities after which the act was sarcastically named. Then it wasn’t long until the world abandoned laws altogether, except the law of the jungle, survival of the fittest. Ironically, soon after this phase of alien enlightenment, many like Nick and Ronny had awakened to the reality of what they had become, and some semblance of conscience had returned to them.

It hadn't been too long after this renewed awareness of conscience that Nick had encountered an outdoor preacher. The man had been preaching from the book of 1 Corinthians chapter six, which talked about sexual sins. The preacher had warned that verse nine explicitly said people who practice sexual sins will not inherit the Kingdom of God, but will eventually end up in hell. The man went on to conclude verse eighteen nicely summarized what had happened to the world since integration.

Verse eighteen talked about how all other sins were outside of one's body, but sexual sin was an intimate personal violation that one did to his or her own body in a very unique way. The preacher said that when the world had embraced all sexual behaviors as normal, the worldwide degradation that followed was just a natural consequence of the inner destruction of the souls of people who blur moral lines to such a degree as to accept all sexual behaviors and lifestyles. Without even fully realizing what they were doing, open acceptance of all things sexual violated an intimate spiritual boundary that soon enabled the "aliens" within to confuse people into fully accepting their evil philosophy of moral relativism to the extreme, basically turning people into animals, driven by brutish instinct, passions, and the natural code of survival of the fittest. The preacher had claimed Jesus was the only hope of escape from this downward spiral and the only hope of salvation.

Nick had been driven into a rage at the preacher's words and only briefly considered calling the police and pressing charges for the hate crimes of judging sexual behaviors and claiming Jesus as the only way of salvation. Instead, Nick chose to violently beat the man to death with his bare hands. It had been his first kill, and he had enjoyed it, which terribly confused him. He thought the alien merging was supposed to make him a better and a more enlightened and evolved person, but Stro-kar hadn't done anything to prevent him from killing. He started to question everything in the aliens' philosophy and what was happening to him. But it was too late. Stro-kar's hold had grown too strong, and Nick had realized with despair that he had accepted an ethic of sexual anarchy with homosexuality as its lead issue, volunteering for a slide into a moral cesspool under the guise of "safety", "tolerance", and "freedom".

Khur-ak then moved to the final phase of control, as he openly revealed his true identity to be Satan, the devil, and admitted that the Balazons were his demons. Satan explained that a renewed conscience was God's Spirit striving once again to convict the world of sin, and demanded that all must fully cooperate with the demons inside them or suffer his wrath. Satan plainly revealed that full surrender to the dark beings within was equivalent to accepting the spiritual mark of the beast, symbolized in the Bible by a mark in the right hand or forehead, which indicated your mind and body had fully surrendered to evil. Once fully given over, people would be damned to spend eternity with Satan and his fallen angels in hell. Satan and his minions taunted and tormented people from within, as they enjoyed slowly damning people to hell, daring anyone to try and resist them. Those that did resist were more sport for the fallen ones, and not even suicide was an option for people, as the demons mercilessly tortured any mind that even thought about trying to take such an easy way out.

Nick was losing the inner battle. Stro-kar's hold grew stronger every day. The point at which evil spirit and human were individual beings was becoming indistinguishable. They thought like one, acted like one, and enjoyed what they did together as one. Nick felt sick when he would torture, kill, or rape someone, but a part of him loved it too. Then the part which felt sick would feel even sicker because he had enjoyed it. But he had to keep some small remnant of himself alive that detested these things. If he didn't, he would end up in hell. It hurt to fight, but even if a little bit, he had to continue the struggle.

How the others were able to live without a care, Nick hoped he would never fully understand. But, at least to some degree, he had to pretend. Otherwise, he'd end up like Kevin, an example of what happens to those who fail to be all that Satan wanted. Nick wasn't sure if Kevin had fully taken the mark or not, and wondered if he was in heaven or hell right now. He shuddered to think about it, and realized how vulnerable they all were to stepping into eternity at any moment without the Lord's mercy. He tried to encourage himself sometimes with the idea that if he just kept surviving a little while longer, things might one day change for the better. He was probably just being delusional, so he pushed the thought away and dutifully picked up the dead Christians and followed his leader.

Shaun delivered the dead bodies to the demon station on main street, a small office building kept open twenty-four hours a day. As the gang entered, Nick smelled the pungent odor of rotting flesh.

A short, fat, slimy demon came around the front desk. Since they dropped the Balazon charade, the demons appeared in their natural state. This one had a wide mouth containing hundreds of razor sharp teeth. "Some more, eh?" he said. Good. The master will be pleased. Throw them into the chute." He pointed at the wall.

Shaun ordered his men to obey. "These ones were doing miracles," he said. "We get extra for that."

Nick knew Shaun hated dealing with these low ranking demons. He'd frequently told the gang he adored Satan but wished certain others could disappear.

The creature smiled and stroked his sharp teeth. "Certainly. That is the arrangement." The demon closed his eyes and seemed to be concentrating, probably telepathically confirming their story with the dark creatures inside them. He opened his eyes and motioned Shaun over to the front desk. "Put your hand under the scanner." Shaun obeyed.

"They told us the blistering sun and diseases are due to God's supernatural judgment of sin," Shaun said.

"Yes. If you want it to stop, we must purge the earth of all good. Then we will win and my master will stop the judgments. Keep bringing me bodies like you do and we won't have anything to worry about." The stout beast hit a few buttons on a keyboard and said, "There, I'm done."

Shaun looked at the tally on the financial scanner. Although Satan's iniquitous world system had abandoned law and order, it retained the concept of money, specifically so people had something to selfishly fight and kill over. "One thousand credits? Is that all? Last week I got double for half as many bodies." Shaun must have angered him when he asked for a greater reward, but he immediately closed his mouth. He knew what happened to those who questioned Satan's minions, even low ranking imps. Besides, the gang had opened the chute to the body bin, and the smell of rotting flesh had fully flooded the room. Shaun held his hand to his mouth, undoubtedly eager to leave. "I'm sorry. It's good enough."

The demon eyed Shaun hatefully. "Don't question me again. If you weren't such a good customer, I would kill you right now. Get out of here before I change my mind."

They immediately complied. Shaun led his gang to Armstrong's Pharmacy, where they bought Virtua, the newest mind-trip drug. You didn't even need a prescription, only credits, or something of value to trade. Nick enjoyed it for another reason as well. While high, he didn't feel as bad about himself.

The perfect medicines Nick's dad had told him the Balazons had made were long since discarded. Nobody cared about the sick and the dying, the aged or the unfortunate. Everyone was out for themselves. Humans took what little technology the demons had given them and made new drugs, crap which fed their fantasies and desires.

After collecting the drugs, they stalked the streets for more prey. Then Shaun abruptly said they were going to sit in a private spot he knew. Nobody questioned him, just followed. The poor were begging for money or food. Most had some type of infectious disease, so if they got too close, Mark shot them. At one point, Chris stepped around some garbage and sewage, sending huge mutated bugs and rats scampering, which Mark used for target practice.

The streets were battle-scarred. Everywhere Nick turned his head he saw overturned and bombed-out cars, craters that explosions had made, dilapidated buildings, dead rotting bodies, and skeletons. The refuse accumulated everyday, as people didn't care to clean it up.

They eventually came to a small, secluded, grassy, area. Their leader was the first to swallow a Virtua tablet, lie down, and look up at the shooting stars. He handed the vial to Mike.

Mike popped a pill and passed it on.

Ronny was the last one to take the drug. "Can you imagine coming out here in the day?" he asked Nick.

Nick said, "I've tried it. You can actually stay out for about two hours with a strong sunscreen. Longer than that and you need one of those silver suites that cost a fortune. I'll only do it if I have to. Mostly I sleep in the basement until night."

"Ironically," Ronny said, "war sort of makes this town more peaceful."

Nick looked up at the sky. "Yeah. Less people out. Everyone holes up at home. But everyone has to leave eventually to buy food or work. Then we have our fun with them." Nick talked for the benefit of the others. Deep down, the greater part of him—so he liked to think, if he could get it to stand firm—hated it.

"Why are we just sitting here?" Ronny asked Nick quietly.

Nick whispered back, "Shaun's probably waiting until the drug takes effect before going to work. It'll be more of a kick."

Stealing was their main source of revenue. Many did it these days because the so-called one world government was really just anarchy; the demons had seen to it. The new world government had no standards for law and order. Satan wanted everyone to do as they pleased, and nothing was prosecuted. If one was strong enough to take what one wanted, the demons applauded your abilities. At other times, to avoid uncertain battles with equal or greater opponents, it made sense to trade something of value or use electronic currency.

As a result, the most popular job these days was private armed guard, to protect against the bold attacks by looters. The guards were too expensive to have around all the time, however. The cool of the night was usually the best time to steal, especially since Shaun's informants gave him the times and places of unprotected stores.

Nick knew of at least three unguarded shops at this very moment. "Whatever his reasons are," Nick said, "I'm not going to ask. You know what happened to the last guy who did that."

Ronny sighed and changed the subject. "You ever wonder about getting a regular job? A fair number still do that."

Nick looked away from the sky towards Ronny. He knew his friend was joking but it still irked him. Ronny knew as well as he the only way out of the gang was death. "We don't live in a normal society anymore so why pretend?" Nick looked beside him and noticed Chris eavesdropping. "And I enjoy it. As long as the guards don't catch us, it's usually quite lucrative."

"I agree." *So I don't see why we're sitting here*, Nick could almost hear Ronny thinking, but Ronny kept his mouth shut.

Nick saw a dark figure about a block down. The street light barely illuminated it. When it glided by, Nick identified it as an enforcer demon. These days, most demons preferred to inhabit human hosts, but a few remained outside the body to encourage evil and enforce the elimination of godly people. Anyone caught aiding and abetting religious people was immediately tortured to death.

If the demon had caught them doing nothing, they might have been in trouble. The enforcers wanted you to be continually engaged in spiritual worship, living out the wicked desires within you. On Saturday, they made you gather at the school gymnasiums to worship and sing praises to the devil. Any large territories that defied them were nuked off the face of the planet; individuals who defied them were slowly tortured to death.

Nick heard a scream and looked down the street. The enforcer had stepped into the light of a street lamp and Nick could fully see his grotesque features. He was about the height of two men and had three bulging oval sections for a body. With the wings on his back, he sort of looked like a huge bee, but he stood on two thick hind legs like a Tyrannosaurus Rex and had a spiked tail. The scream had come from a man who'd been sleeping on the sidewalk. The demon had lashed out with its two razor sharp claws and sliced the man's arms and legs off.

Nick looked away. He couldn't bear to watch. The other gang members laughed and relished in the man's pain and misfortune.

Ronny saw it too and whispered to Nick, "I hate those things. It's bad enough they're inside us, but to do that."

Nick agreed.

"Hey, man," Mike suddenly said to Shaun. "Why don't we knock off a fast food joint? I haven't had a burger in ages." Since Mike was second in command, he was sometimes allowed to make suggestions.

"Don't be stupid," Shaun said. "You know they're under protection from Jarius Armed Guards Ltd. Those guys don't fool around."

"But they aren't ready for this," Mike said as he pointed to Shaun's metal container.

A sly smile crossed Shaun's face. The challenge of doing something bold visibly energized him. "Yeah, Jarius has always been the one with the major hardware. I think it's our turn."

"It will take reinforcements at least five minutes to respond,"Chris said. The gang looked at their leader expectantly.

Shaun stared at them intently before nodding his head. He told everyone his plan, gave them their positions, and one grenade. Mike and Shaun kept the rest, as their job was the most important.

It didn't take long to reach the burger joint Shaun had in mind, adrenaline rush giving them energy to run most of the way. Nick hid behind a bush near the front entrance and the rest took up similar positions around the perimeter.

A young couple carrying machine guns walked up to the entrance, paid the guard the customary bribe, and entered the restaurant. The door was dilapidated and falling off its hinges. The walls were riddled with bullet holes and gaping bomb blasts from earlier encounters. The guard wore bullet proof black body armor that was made of a light plastic. Nick had heard the armor afforded some protection from the plagues too.

The young couple could easily be carrying Dermalgia, an ailment which caused excruciatingly painful sores to appear over one's body, and not even know it. Not even the best scientists knew how it was transmitted, although some suspected drinking the contaminated water brought it on.

Most water supplies had mysteriously become bright red, killing many plants and sea creatures. People didn't want to drink it, but if you were poor, you had little choice. Now Nick knew why these things happened: God's judgment. But he doubted Satan would stop the disasters if he defeated God, as he loved to inflict pain and suffering.

When everybody was ready, Nick started shooting. The guard was momentarily knocked off his feet, but quickly got up and returned fire. Within seconds, many more guards ran out the door and began shooting. Nick gave the signal which ordered a retreat across the street. The guards ran after them, and that's when the grenades hit.

Mike and Shaun revealed their positions on top of the restaurant. They tossed every grenade they had and opened fire. Nick and the rest also tossed their mini-bombs and continued shooting. Caught in the middle, the guards were soon destroyed.

"Yahoo!" Shaun shouted as he came down. "I knew we could do it, and we didn't lose a single man. How's that for my supreme leadership capabilities."

"You're the master," Mike said, and everyone agreed. "But we'd better move fast. Jarius will be sending his goons after us."

Shaun's gang burst through the entrance and ordered the clerks to give them all the food they had. Each gang member soon had an armload and ran out the door, but Shaun ordered Nick to stay behind and kill the witnesses.

"Hurry up, man," Ronny said, standing at the entrance. "We haven't got time to waste."

Nick was sweating and felt pain shooting up his leg, but was unable to act. "I'm having another weak moment. I don't think I can do it."

Ronny nodded his head with understanding. Nick looked away, while Ronny shot the people.

"Please don't tell the others I couldn't do it," Nick said as he turned to see bloody bodies strewn over the floor.

Ronny nodded his head and they left.

"What took you so long?" Shaun asked when they got outside.

"Nick wanted to have some fun," Ronny said. "He tortured one guy for a bit."

Shaun's smile indicated his approval. "Well, we've gotta go. Now!"

Shaun decided they needed to steal a car and retreat to Nick's place. They found an average-sized house, clean on the exterior. Undoubtedly, the owner wasn't excessively rich or he would've had guards posted outside, but he likely had a vehicle in the garage. Hopefully, the owner had money to fill the tank too. Shaun had one grenade left so he used it to blow open the garage door. They quickly ran inside and smashed the window of what Nick could now see was a Plymouth Acclaim.

Ronny was an expert at hot-wiring, and within seconds, was navigating the streets like a race-car in some frantic pace to cross the finish line.

"No fooling around," Shaun ordered as they turned down thirty-seventh street. "Jarius is going to be looking for anything suspicious so go straight to Nick's."

Ronny was pulling into Nick's driveway within minutes. He dropped the gang off and drove away to dispose of the car.

Nick led the way to the front door. "Careful of those wires," he said as he pointed to the ground. "Mom's got the whole perimeter booby trapped. You don't want to find out what those can do to you."

Nick unlocked the front door and heard the attack dogs barking wildly. "Stay!" he said and the Doberman pinschers, recognizing their master's voice, quieted. He opened the door and led inside. The dogs growled when they saw the gang members. "Do you know I could say one word and both of these dogs would leap at your throat?"

Mark swallowed hard and looked at Nick. "I believe you."

"Good. But don't worry. I'm a nice guy."

All the gang members laughed, including Nick, but a part of him seriously wished he could turn the dogs lose to destroy the perverseness around him. He wished they could protect him and help him feel clean again. Nick felt the pain of Stro-kar's warning and knew he had better change his thoughts.

They plopped their loot on the dirty kitchen table. The entire house was filthy, as it hadn't been cleaned in years. Garbage was everywhere, and most of the furniture was already ruined from earlier house parties.

Shaun had the honor of tasting the first burger. "Just not the same," he said as he swallowed. "Ever since they've had to start using the local chickens and cows, the burgers have tasted like crap, but go ahead and dig in."

Chris shoved a handful of fries into his mouth. "The home-grown potatoes aren't the same caliber either. I guess fallout gives them that irradiant taste."

Nick laughed, but briefly thought he would like them to die of radiation sickness. Stro-kar punched him from within and he changed his thoughts."That was a long time ago, and many miles away. The winds have carried away the radiation by now." He opened the refrigerator and grabbed a beer. Anybody else want one? My mom has her own brewery machine. It's not like the real stuff either, but it'll get you drunk."

As Nick suspected, they all wanted some.

Nick suddenly heard a loud knock. "It's probably Ronny. I'll get it. Help yourselves."

Nick calmed the dogs and let his friend inside. "Have a brew, bud," he said as he tossed a bottle at Ronny.

Ronny opened it and took a drink. "Where's your mom?"

"Oh, she's here somewhere," Nick said and led Ronny into the kitchen. "Probably in bed with a bunch of people."

Chris was going upstairs to use the bathroom, and Nick threw him a chicken burger sandwich. "It's mom's favorite," Nick said. "If she's up there, you might as well give her one before they're all gone."

Chris nodded.

After a few minutes, Chris came back downstairs and said he'd been asked if the gang would like to join them. Nick wanted to throw up. A part of him was repulsed, but Stro-kar jumped at the suggestion. He-it wanted to, thought it would be enjoyable, but he-it also wanted to run. The warning pains started.

The gang was thrilled at the idea, except for Ronny, who privately expressed his reservations to Nick, not wanting to appear weak before the others. When Ronny finally agreed, that settled the matter in Nick's mind. There was no use resisting. It would be enjoyable-horrible, pleasurable-painful, beautiful-disgusting, and normal-perverted—but at any rate, he would have to obey.

Chapter 14

The next morning, Nick and Ronny sat on the Saundersons' living room couch; the rest of the gang had already left. They had their heads between their legs and were moaning. Ronny would periodically try patting Nick on the back and comforting him, as Nick would grab for the pail beside him and throw up a watery brownish-yellow liquid that smelled like a combination of rotting fish and raw eggs. It burned his throat on the way up and left a taste like bile in his mouth.

"I don't know if I can take it anymore," Nick said. He could only remember flashes of the night before, but what he did remember made him want to throw up even more. At the same time, he would salivate and tingle all over, remembering the pleasure he'd experienced.

He vomited again.

After the invitation, the gang had gone upstairs, done a few lines of cocaine, and injected themselves with some new wonder drug called Erotica, which one couple had brought with him. It was supposed to heighten all of one's senses. Nick supposed it had done that, but it sure made you sick the next day.

He hazily watched as Ronny threw up this time.

The drug also had the unfortunate—or rather fortunate, Nick thought—side effect of partial memory loss. Oh God! Nick knew he needed God's help, but didn't know what to do. If he had to live one more day like this, he didn't know if he could keep his sanity. He just wanted to be free of Stro-kar.

Nick felt another stomach heave, but it settled down before he could throw up. He imagined his mother must be going through the same thing, but to a much lesser degree, because with repeated use Erotica caused less sickness and memory loss. Every night, and several times a day, Valerie had men and women coming and going. It paid the bills, but barely, since the rest was used to buy more Erotica. She was very popular since she had a good immune system which kept her fairly clean.

Most prostitutes had the new diseases which made AIDS look like the common cold; diseases that caused you to constantly scream in agony as your flesh slowly dried up and peeled away like a dry leaf in the wind. The latest one caused every nerve fiber in one's body to swell to three times normal size, causing every synapse in one's brain to constantly register pain at the slightest impulse, even a light breeze. Nick wondered why they didn't just kill themselves. He supposed it might be the survival instinct preventing it. Then again, it was more likely the demons.

Nick had tried committing suicide several times, but Stro-kar never let him finish it. He was able to put a gun to his head, but it was as if his hand would fight against him. He simply couldn't pull the trigger.

"Where's your dad?" Ronny asked.

Nick's eyebrows rose in mild surprise. "He used to come fairly frequently, but I haven't seen him now in months. The last time my mom's demon was driven into a wild frenzy. She spoke in a deep voice, levitated into the air, and said she'd kill him if he came around again. Dad knew she wasn't kidding and hasn't come since. He always talked about forgiveness of sins and deliverance from bondage." Nick snarled with disbelief. "I don't think such things are possible."

"Forgiveness, or deliverance."

"Both. But I've got to admit, he always looked in good shape. God is taking good care of dad. Well fed, clean, healthy, no drugs. A contagious person could cough right in his face and he wouldn't get as much as a sniffle. I never understood what he wanted me to do, though. He always talked about receiving Jesus and junk like that. How do you receive a dead person?"

Ronny shrugged.

"If he comes around again," Nick said, "I'll do anything to get free." He suddenly screamed in pain, doubled over, and started crying.

Ronny moved away as if Nick had caught some new disease he didn't want to risk contracting. "I wish we both could have known sooner," he said. "They're eating up our souls, replacing us with themselves."

"Don't leave me, Ronny. Help me." Nick screamed and doubled over again.

"You've got to help yourself," Ronny said. "Give in. Wrong thoughts are punishable."

"No!" Nick fell to the floor and started weeping and gnashing his teeth. He sobbed and ran his hands up and down his body, quickly, as if trying to scrape off a myriad of ants. After a brief struggle, Nick lay on the floor and breathed heavily, sweat flowing off his face as if it were a wet sponge being squeezed tightly.

"Is it over?" Ronny asked.

"Yeah. It's no use. Stro-kar called for reinforcements. There's three more inside me now." He felt violated, raped, and left to die. It was as if he had invited a friend into his house, but the friend turned into a monster, locked Nick in the cellar, and wreaked havoc. Then he invited his buddies in to party. Nick had let Stro-kar into his heart and mind as a friend, and that friend had turned out to be evil.

Valerie came downstairs and sneaked into the kitchen to make breakfast. She usually made noise, knocking pots and pans and jingling utensils, but today was opening and closing drawers as quietly as she could.

Nick was recovering from Erotica, and felt he could walk without heaving. He got up from the couch and slowly trudged into the kitchen, realizing he would have to face his mom eventually. Perhaps she would try and pretend nothing happened.

As he came around the partition separating living and dining room, he saw his mother gingerly putting strips of raw bacon into a semi-clean frying pan. Unlike everything else, Valerie tried to keep cooking utensils clean to prevent food poisoning. The oven was dented and chipped, but the front right burner worked. With the cost of electricity so high, she was giving them an expensive treat using the stove to cook anything, especially bacon.

Nick stood in the kitchen, staring at his mother, waiting for her to make the first move, but she kept on robotically cooking. He was sure she could see him out of the corner of her eye, but didn't look at him, probably as ashamed as he was of what they had done, ashamed of everything they had become since the Balazons' unveiling.

"Mom...I...I..." Nick stopped stuttering and took a deep breath. Before trying again, he tried to articulate in his mind what to say.

Valerie flashed a look at him and turned back. "You boys sit at the table. I'm going to make you a good breakfast. I'm going to take care of you and..." She collapsed on the counter and started sobbing. "Oh, Nick. I'm so sorry. I hate what I...we've become. In the beginning, I thought I had control and did things on my own. But they tricked me. It's not even me anymore. I couldn't stop if I tried."

Nick went over to his mom and touched her shoulder. "I know. It's OK, mom. Everything's going to be OK."

Ronny came into the kitchen and sat at the table. “Have you ever thought forgiveness and deliverance *might* be possible?”

“Don’t even think such things,” Nick said. “You know what they’ll do to you if you try to resist.”

“I’m not fighting them. God is. I never told you, but last night I did something I haven’t done in a long time. I prayed. I said, ‘God, if You really love me, please set me free.’”

Nick looked at Ronny with a solemn gaze. “What happened?” He grimaced with pain. “Even now, they don’t like me asking, but go on.”

“I haven’t been able to break free totally, but I’m more in control than I’ve ever been. I have this deep feeling I must talk to someone who knows God. I don’t understand why, but I feel such a person can help me.”

Nick left his mother’s side and sat across from Ronny. “Aren’t you in pain? Don’t you feel the incessant pull within you? How can you resist?”

“I don’t know. It’s not easy. I’m being bombarded right now, but I think He’s helping me. I think that prayer did something.”

Nick let those words sink deep. Even his mother was intrigued and sat down to listen. He felt the first pains of warning, remembered he now had four, and began to fear. Desires began to bubble up to the surface of his being, sexual thoughts, hatred, and an overwhelming urge to kill. He was being warned that if he continued listening, he would be forced to do such despicable acts as had been unrivaled to date. “I’m sorry, man. Maybe I’m not as strong as you, but I can’t resist. I know if I try my mind will be pushed to the brink.”

“You don’t have to be strong,” Ronny said. “God will be your strength for you. I think if you pray a simple prayer like I did, He can help us.”

Nick closed his eyes as if to try, and immediately let out a scream of terror. “I can’t. I won’t.”

“I agree,” Valerie said. “Let God make an example of you. If you can be truly set free, then maybe we’ll believe you. If you’re still in one piece when it’s over, we’ll give it a try.”

Ronny looked at Nick with an expression Nick hadn’t seen before, pity almost. What a fool. He was in the same position as the rest of them. Ronny had admitted that himself.

“You’re right,” Ronny said. “Even now I feel the pull. They’re telling me to go somewhere. I’m not sure, but I think it’s out of town. Do you feel it?”

Nick nodded slowly. “Since I got up. A strong feeling that late tonight I should walk down McDonnell trail. It grows, beckons me. I must obey.”

“Yeah,” Valerie said, “me too. At the end of the trail, we should turn left. Why do they want us to go there?”

“I don’t know,” Ronny said. “But we agree we have to do it. Right? You said it yourself, Nick. It’s no use resisting. They’ll make us pay if we try.”

“Yeah,” Nick agreed. “Let’s see what they want us to do.”

Nick remembered old man Stypinski’s farm was in that general direction. Mr. Stypinski was an elderly man who loved cats, must have at least two dozen wandering the yard, and another twelve favorites that never left the house. Wouldn’t it be cruel if the demons wanted them to go there just to kill some cats? Cruel, but not out of character. Still, a perverse thrill rippled through his body at the thought. They would go tonight. They had no choice.

Chapter 15

It was night, and they were on their way to a farmhouse when Lawrence abruptly called them over the radio and gave them new instructions. They drove east on highway nine for exactly seventeen miles, abandoned their van at the side of the road, and walked east through the nearby forest. After about one hour, they approached a huge circular clearing in the woods, where thousands were waiting to hear the gospel.

After hearing the good news, all were saved and delivered from demons. Jeff didn't know how the people got there, and it didn't matter. The main thing was new believers were added to God's Kingdom. But he didn't know how they were going to bring them all back to the complex.

Len closed his eyes and concentrated before opening them and staring at his companions. He looked behind to the thousands crowded into the circular clearing in the woods, fresh smell of pine filling the air. Everyone was quiet, only chirping crickets in the background breaking the silence, as they all expectantly waited for Len to lead them in what to do next.

"Well?" Jeff asked.

"Lawrence told me as long as we get them to the van everything will be OK," Len said.

Jeff would never understand how Len was able to telepathically communicate with Lawrence, but he didn't understand Lawrence's ability to hear God either. It didn't matter to Jeff whether communication came directly from God, through Lawrence, or from

Len via Lawrence, as long as they received direct guidance. Granted, though, it took a lot of faith to obey some human being who claimed to be hearing from God. Jeff was extremely cautious because of his earlier cultic experiences, but God had given him an ability to discern which directives truly came from the Holy Spirit.

"What happens when we get to the van?" Sandy asked.

"I don't know," Len said. "But I know there'll be a way when we get there."

"We don't have to understand everything," Ellis added. "Just obey."

Everybody nodded their heads in agreement.

Len organized the huge crowd into horizontal lines of ten and had them march through the woods in the direction of the van. Len and Ellis led the way up front, while Jeff and Sandy followed behind to make sure nobody got lost. The people were excited and happy, talking together and singing praises as they marched, but Jeff could still hear the night sounds. The air was cool and breezy, causing rustling leaves and swaying trees to throw an eerie chill into Jeff's spirit. Or was it something else? The red moon's mild illumination was enhanced by the flashlights most had brought with them to the clearing.

After about fifteen minutes, the air become decidedly cooler, cold almost. The moon and flash-lights seemed to dim, as the night became darker. Something was wrong. The crowd sensed it too, for they slowly stopped talking and singing. They were new Christians and possibly didn't recognize the source of the disturbance, but Jeff did. It was evil. They were being stalked by something not human.

Ellis ran to the back. "Do you feel it?" he asked Jeff.

"Yes."

"I sense it is Methsaela," Sandy said.

Jeff's eyes widened. "Oh, great." They had tangled with Methsaela before. They knew what they had to do.

Jeff, Sandy, and Ellis knelt in the dirt and began praying fervently, while the new Christians silently marched onward.

"We need Len," Sandy said.

Jeff shook his head. "He can't afford to stop. It'll be upon us soon."

Ellis nodded his head in agreement.

They all joined hands. Jeff and Ellis poured out their hearts to God, praying for His power and protection, while Sandy quietly sang songs about faith and courage and praised the Lord for His love and care.

As the sounds of marching became fainter, Jeff could hear low snarling and growling over the rustling leaves, and what sounded like horses galloping. The sound became louder and louder. They were approaching, but from where Jeff couldn't tell, seemed to come from all different directions.

"There's more than one," Ellis said, and Jeff opened his eyes to see Sandy nodding her head. Jeff could sense it too, a whole legion of demons.

"Why?" Jeff asked. "What does it mean? They've never marshaled such force against one small preaching venture before."

"God has bestowed one of the new believers with a power they desperately want stopped," Ellis said. "But I don't know what it is."

Suddenly, Sandy fell back and started moaning. "Torment...power...the flames of hell they can evade no longer."

"Is she OK?" Ellis asked.

"She's fine," Jeff said. "She's receiving a message, but I don't know what it means."

Sandy stopped moving and lay in a coma-like state, occasionally twitching.

Jeff could feel evil approaching. The hoof beats grew louder. Then the sounds abruptly stopped. "They're here."

Ellis swallowed hard.

The sounds of rustling leaves became louder as the wind picked up force. Suddenly, it blew Jeff backwards until his spine smacked against the solid trunk of a towering tree. Immediately, long branches encircled his limbs and torso like a spider web, pinning him tightly.

"Jeff!" Ellis screamed, but he soon had problems of his own. The ground beneath Ellis's feet started pulling him in like quicksand. Ellis clutched at the loose dirt in front of him, but to no avail.

Jeff felt his chest shrink, as the branches squeezed tighter with every exhaling breath, like a python snake crushing its prey. *Into Your hands I commit my spirit,* he thought.

But Sandy suddenly shot up and shouted, "Release my friends or I will invoke his power by proxy!"

The branches gave one last defiant squeeze before they loosened. Ellis crawled out of his hole; the forces of darkness had pulled him chest level into the ground.

Jeff ran over to his friends' sides. "What happened?" he asked Sandy. "How did you do that?"

Sandy said, "God has given a person named Dan Schuster the gift of damnation, sending demons to hell before their time. This terrifies them. They want him dead."

"If you could invoke this person's power, why didn't you do it?"

"I wasn't sure if it would work. I was bluffing."

"Then try it now," Ellis said.

"I can't. They've gone ahead. You have to be in their presence."

"We have to warn them," Jeff said. Ellis and Sandy agreed. They started running, flashlights blazing a trail ahead, ducking tree limbs and leaping over rocks and other obstacles.

Jeff scratched his arms and chest on branches repeatedly but ignored the pain. He figured they were halfway to their destination when a tall dark figure suddenly blocked their path. Jeff was ahead of Ellis and Sandy, so he stopped and held out his hands to restrain them. Directly ahead was a black bear, standing on its hind legs, snarling. The eyes glinted red, and the snarl it made was unnatural.

Jeff could sense an evil presence again. "It's possessed," he said.

Sandy went around Jeff's outstretched arms and cautiously moved forward.

"Careful," Ellis said.

"I will invoke his power," Sandy threatened.

The bear snarled and moved ahead slightly.

"He's calling her bluff," Ellis whispered.

The bear came down on all fours and reared back, as if readying for a charge.

Sandy said, "In the name of Jesus I invoke the power of Dan Schuster to damn you to hell!"

The bear reared on its hind legs, frantically scratching its head with its forearms. It let out a wolfish howl and came down on all fours again.

Sandy backed up. "It didn't work."

She was right. Jeff could still feel the evil presence, see the red glowing eyes, and hear the inhuman snarl.

The bear started charging, scattering them in different directions.

Adrenaline pushed Jeff's body beyond its limits as he ran, hearing sounds of the lumbering bear just behind him. His heart raced as he bounded through branches, over rocks, shrubs, and fallen trees. The air whistled past his ears. He was about to leap up a tree when he was knocked down. He rolled over and saw the jaws of death. "Help, Lord!" he screamed.

The bear became stiff. Was it playing with him? *Where's your faith, Jeff*, he thought.

He didn't waste time trying to figure it out, but quickly scrambled from under the bear, and leapt up the tree he had targeted. Perched high above, he quietly watched the bear move again. It looked around as if puzzled. After a short time, the evil gleam left the animal's eyes, and it nonchalantly walked away, unconcerned with its whereabouts, content to go on with life as usual.

When Jeff was fully convinced it was safe, he climbed down and cautiously scouted out his immediate area. He called to Sandy and Ellis, but didn't hear any response.

He'd lost his direction in the chase, so he prayed for guidance before starting. When he felt sure, he set out in a brisk walk. Eventually, he broke into a run, hoping to reach Len and the others before it was too late, slowing down only to catch his breath. All the trees seemed the same and he wondered if he was running in circles, but the inner compass of God's Spirit kept leading him forward.

When he finally found the group, they were huddled in a tight ball. The wind was blowing dirt and debris into their eyes, blinding them. People were screaming as trees fell and crushed unsuspecting victims, or branches strangled the life out of them.

Jeff ran into the middle of the war zone. He found Len near the center, on his knees, praying, one eye open in case he had to leap out of the way of a falling tree.

Jeff had to yell over the sound of the wind and screams. "Len! Where's Dan Schuster?"

"Who?" Len yelled back.

"Dan Schuster!"

"I don't know who that is."

"Help me find him. We must find him."

Jeff and Len ran through the crowd, shouting out Dan's name, as they leapt over dead bodies, and fallen trees. Jeff stopped to help as many injured as he could and asked them if they knew Dan. Eventually one person pointed and said, "Over there!"

Jeff saw a small boy being crushed by some branches. An older woman, presumably his mother, was trying to pry them off. A tree fell and Jeff jumped, narrowly evading it by a few inches.

"Len!" Jeff yelled over the wind's roar. "Come with me."

Len nodded and followed. They tried prying the branches off the boy's windpipe, while the mother concentrated on the ones crushing his chest.

Even with Jeff and Len struggling hard to break tree's hold, the best they could do was to loosen them a bit. The boy coughed and gasped for air.

"Damn them to hell, Dan!" Jeff said.

"What?" the boy said.

"Command the demons to go to hell."

The boy's left eyebrow rose in puzzlement. "Demons go to hell," he said. Nothing happened.

"Say it again in Jesus' name," Jeff said.

Dan repeated his command in the name of the Lord.

The sound of blowing wind transformed into the sound of inhuman wailing. The branches loosened and the wind died down. Balls of white light appeared and moved through the crowd. As the lights flew into the distant horizon, the wailing became fainter and fainter. It was over.

Jeff surveyed the carnage. Trees and dead bodies were lying all around and the injured were moaning.

Sandy and Ellis came running out of the woods. They spotted Jeff immediately and approached him.

Sandy nodded at Jeff. "I can imagine what happened. Is he OK?"

"Yeah," Jeff said. "Dan saved the day, but I'd estimate we lost about a quarter of the new ones. Others are hurt. We'd better get them back to the complex."

Len sighed and set out to organize everybody. As he walked among the crowd, he said, "OK, we have to keep pressing on. I want horizontal rows again of ten..."

Len's voice became fainter.

"We tried finding you but didn't have any luck," Sandy said.

Jeff nodded. "Do you think we'll run into anymore surprises on the way home?"

Ellis and Sandy didn't say anything, but they knew as well as Jeff that where demons were, possessed humans were usually not far off. He tried to put the thought out of his mind.

Dead people had to be buried under lose dirt, shrubs and rocks. Jeff wanted to bring them to the complex for a better burial, but acquiesced when Len explained they didn't have the time or manpower; some family members were upset too, but likewise understood the difficulties of the situation. After Len organized everybody, they marched on again for about twenty minutes, with the physically fit helping to carry the injured.

They had almost made it out of the woods when Len suddenly stopped and sniffed the air, sensing danger. He yelled, "Get down!"

Ellis, Jeff, and Sandy immediately obeyed, for they trusted Len's instincts, but the others hesitated.

Seconds later machine gun fire rattled off high in the treetops. Possessed humans, seeming as wild-eyed and unkempt as vicious beasts, were aiming their guns at anything moving. The first several rows of people were cut down before the rest took cover behind trees, boulders, or anything else which afforded some protection.

From behind a sloping incline, Jeff watched Len crawl over and talk to Dan. The boy shouted something and shook his head. Then Len crawled over to Jeff, narrowly escaping several stray bullets.

"Can you start a quake, Jeff?" Len asked.

"It would be better if Dan could damn them."

"Tried that. Didn't work. Must only work on free roaming spirits, not those sheltered inside humans."

"Well, I have to be standing when I stomp on the ground."

"You're our only hope."

"He's right," Sandy said. She joined hands with Len and they both started praying aloud for Jeff's safety.

When Jeff felt led by the Spirit, he stood up and prayed for his special power to flow. After he stomped on the ground, he got down quickly.

The rumbling started, quaking, then huge hailstones fell from the sky.

"Move out," Len shouted as he led the way. "Leave the dead. There's no time."

The group scrambled through the remaining woods. They were close to the highway so it didn't take long. By the time they exited, the earthquake had stopped, and Len had organized everybody again. Jeff and Sandy were some of the last ones because they had stayed behind to help carry a man with a broken leg.

They came out to see a mass of organized people, but nobody moving.

Jeff and Sandy went to the front to see what the hold up was, and saw a circle of armed guards around their van. The guards were a fair distance away and hadn't spotted the group yet because it was still dark, but it was easy to see the guards because they had set up lanterns around the van's perimeter.

Jeff turned to Len. “Are you sure we have to get to the van,” he whispered.

Len nodded. “Perhaps another quake would distract them.

Jeff shook his head. “Too dangerous. We’ll be too close.”

“What do we do then?”

Sandy said, “Let’s all join hands in prayer. I mean everybody. Including the new Christians.”

Jeff was the first to grab Sandy’s hand, the beginning of a long chain of interconnecting hearts. Soon, Jeff felt energy flowing through him towards Len, who had a strong impression in his spirit and said, “I think God is saying we should walk right up to it. But that’s ridiculous.”

“Is it?” Jeff asked. “Sounds like something He would tell us to do. Do we have the faith, though?”

“I’m going to check with Lawrence first.” Len paused and closed his eyes. After a few minutes, he opened them again. “OK. Let’s do it.”

Everybody moved forward cautiously. Closer. Closer. No reaction from the guards. They stepped into the light of the roadside lanterns and continued forward. Still no reaction. Len quietly opened the driver’s door, while Jeff got in the passenger side, and Ellis and Sandy loaded as many into the back as possible. When it was full, Ellis went to the driver’s window and tapped.

Len rolled it down. “Yes.”

“Now what?”

Len closed his eyes. “Have everybody touch the van.” He opened his eyes and said, “or touch somebody who is touching the van.”

Ellis nodded and disappeared. After a short time, the back door slammed shut and Ellis said they were ready.

“Whatever You’re going to do, Lord,” Len said, “we’re waiting.”

Jeff looked out the window. Several people stood beside his door, but most had instinctively crowded around the back, probably expecting the van to go forward. The guards still stood and stared into the woods, but the van started to rise. Jeff rolled down his window and peered out. Everybody in the group was rising into the air as well. The guards became smaller as they continued to rise, still no recognition the van was gone.

They glided through the dark sky, several hundred feet in the air, skimming the trees along highway nine. At one point, a fireball fell from heaven, nearly hitting the van. Jeff looked out his window and saw the fire devour a group of people who had been encircling another group below. Jeff guessed Scott Sheppard from complex seventy-three must be amongst the group in the center. Scott was a protector, like Jeff, able to supernaturally defend against attack.

Jeff began going over the day in his mind. They had started early that morning because Lawrence sent them to a small town about three hundred miles south of Star City. Once there, they preached and saw virtually the entire town come to Christ. The biggest miracle that impressed the townspeople was God had given Jeff's group and the town special immunity that day against the scorching heat of the sun.

It would have been too dangerous for the new Christians to follow them to Lawrence's complex though. Instead, Len mentally communicated with Lawrence, who said they should wait until dark, at which time a group of Christians from a complex in New Mexico would arrive and miraculously fly everybody back there. Jeff arrived home by late afternoon, rested for a bit, and then went to the clearing in the woods from which he was returning.

Jeff looked out the window again and saw they were approaching Star City. They flew over the town and touched down outside the complex. Lawrence immediately came to greet them, and Jeff rolled down his window.

"Welcome back," Lawrence said. "But don't get too comfortable. Do you remember the farmhouse I'd sent you to before there was a change of plans?"

"Yeah, I remember," Jeff said wearily.

Lawrence smiled.

Chapter 16

They had to miss the Satan daily devotional hour, the time when everyone on earth tuned their VRT to channel 666 and worshiped Satan's image while he talked to them. The demons would do something to make their hosts go into a trance. When they awoke an hour later, they wouldn't remember anything, but somehow that hour reinforced their evil hold. If you missed one episode, the demons punished you severely.

"I still think we should've brought the dogs," Nick said as they walked along McDonnell Trail, which led out of town.

Ronny shook his head. "Our automatic guns will be enough protection." Ronny didn't know why Nick had thought they were supposed to let the dogs kill old man Stypinski's cats. He hadn't said anything to Valerie or Nick, but was fairly confident that wasn't their mission.

As they walked, the street lights became fewer and fewer, until they were surrounded by deep blackness, only their flashlights an aid to lead the way. Only occasionally would a car drive by and light up their surroundings, as most could barely afford food and clothes let alone cars. The air smelled sulfurous, like the smell left lingering in the air after an enforcer demon walked by. A light rain drizzled and Ronny tasted the drops with his tongue, feeling a slight sting as he did. It tasted acidic and he spit it out.

When Ronny had cried out in desperation the other night, he'd received a very distinct message. He didn't hear anything audible, but knew nevertheless to go to this location and God would have somebody there to help them. Ronny hadn't told Valerie and Nick this, as he was sure they wouldn't have come.

Ronny had been mildly surprised, but very happy, when Nick and Valerie said they were having the same urge, but remained unaware of its origin. If they were really going to have an encounter with God, Ronny would prefer company. He'd never done anything like this before and was frightened.

Ronny wondered if the demons were aware of what was ahead. None of them felt an overpowering urge to stop. On the contrary, they kept walking, compelled but not knowing why, at least not Valerie and Nick.

After a long distance, Nick stopped walking. "I'm getting a funny feeling. Maybe we should go back."

Ronny could sense their destination up ahead. They had passed right by Stypinski's place, but there was another farmhouse about two minutes walk away. "We're almost there, Nick. Don't stop now."

"He's right," Valerie said. "I feel we must do this."

Nick finally relented. They continued on and found themselves amongst a crowd of thousands. There was a white van parked near the house, and in the middle of the yard, there was a raised platform with four speakers in front. Also on the platform was a podium with a microphone.

"There's something strange going on here," Nick said. "I don't think I like it. Let's get out of here."

"Just wait a minute," Ronny said. "We'll find out soon. Be patient."

Nick asked several people beside him what was going on, and received three "I don't knows" before someone mentioned they suspected a speaker was going to talk about God. The mere suggestion got him visibly nervous.

"I'm leaving," Nick said and was about to turn back when several people got on the platform. He froze, shock tattooed on his face.

Ronny looked at the podium and realized what had shaken his friend: Nick's dad was on the platform.

* * *

Nick was paralyzed. The Stro-kar part of him wanted to run, but he also wanted to stay. The yard light illuminated the platform, a few in front, but very little else. "You were not brought here tonight by accident," the speaker said. "God has drawn you here to hear His message."

Nick started to feel very uncomfortable. He nervously looked around and noticed his mom seemed a little rattled herself. She was fidgeting and licking her lips. Only Ronny seemed eager to hear more; he was half-smiling, leaning slightly forward, and bobbing around to see better.

Nick's heart started to beat faster and his face felt flushed. He wondered if he should try to get away while he still could. The demons would probably kill him if he tried converting to God's side.

An inner tug told him to run. If he didn't, something weird might happen. Unexpectedly, however, Nick didn't feel any pains of warning, only inner thoughts deluging his mind; even now, he was lusting for the beautiful lady standing beside his dad. But the thoughts were more controllable. He wondered if Ronny could have been right, and perhaps God was helping him somehow. He hadn't even asked for any.

"We didn't advertise," the speaker continued, "yet you all came here tonight. Thousands of you. That was no coincidence. You didn't hear about us through the VRT or radio or even by word of mouth, but you did hear from God."

The preacher moved about the platform for emphasis. “Satan and his demons are not going to win this war and you don’t need to fear them.”

Nobody in the crowd said anything. There was a deathly hush.

Nick swallowed hard, as the speaker continued to talk. Something deep in the pit of his stomach responded, and shame fell upon him like a ton of bricks. He felt as if he had heightened senses, or perhaps a new sixth sense.

Nick didn’t know why, but he suddenly felt as if he were being watched by millions of eyes, which could see deep into his soul. He bobbed his head above the crowd, eyes darting wildly, head moving right and left. Nobody was staring at him, but he felt exposed.

The man on the podium pointed his finger at one section of the crowd and fanned it out over the rest. “But even though you’ve turned your back on God, and have asked demons to come into your heart instead of Jesus Christ, He can, and will, forgive you and restore you if you come to Him.”

Nick wanted desperately to believe it could be so. He had lived for so long now, it seemed, weakly giving in to sensuous desires. But he was afraid. If he tried but failed, they would punish him severely, perhaps make him torture himself to death.

Nick looked at his mom. She was clenching her jaws and pounding her fist into her hands. She looked as if she wanted to use her machine gun to kill everyone in the crowd, but especially those on the platform. However, she was constrained by forces Nick didn’t understand, nor could see. It was as if she were being held by an invisible force field, unable to act until allowed, until the message was finished.

Ronny was smiling an idiotic grin, wider than a happy clown. He swayed his head back and forth as if in some beautiful dreamland, constrained from shouting praises to God in so far as he didn't want to interfere with the message. Nick wondered if, perhaps, Ronny had already experienced the mysterious freedom the speaker was talking about.

"The Scriptures are very clear." The people on the podium gazed solemnly at the audience. "It says all have sinned and fall short of the glory of God. But I know I will go to heaven when I die. I will not go to hell and be punished eternally for my sins. Why?"

Again, there was a slight pause as the speaker let the audience soak up his words. Then he told them how God loved them so much He gave His only begotten Son to die for them, and by believing in Him they could have eternal life; God's grace was sufficient to blot out all of their sins. The man even told them about his own past, when he too had been deceived and possessed. He encouraged them to come forward and receive the same deliverance he had experienced long ago.

Nick felt as if a huge weight was being lifted off his back, and a metal clamp which had tightly gripped his head was being loosened. The words of encouragement and hope were so soothing. A tingle went through his body as he felt, for the first time in a long time, there might be real hope for him. Then the fear hit.

Nick looked at the many shadowy faces created by the yard light above the platform. Some were twisted and seething. These same people were wringing their guns in their hands, waiting for the moment to act. Nick still had his survival instinct. Despite what the speaker said about living forever after death, Nick wasn't sure he wanted to experience it yet. The angry people were going to open fire the first chance they got. When exactly that was, he didn't know, but he knew it would happen. Perhaps God was temporarily restraining them, but Nick didn't trust He would continue to do so.

His mother was clenching her gun now too. She must have totally given herself over to the dark powers. If he wanted to stay alive, he would have to do the same. Nick didn't feel proud of himself, but he was a survivor. At least he'd make it home alive, back to the gang, even though a part of him didn't want to go back.

He remembered he still had a Bible stored somewhere in his basement. If he could just get home, Nick could dust it off and read its contents. Surely, if these Christians were speaking the truth, he could experience deliverance at home as easily as here. And he wouldn't have to risk being killed. In fact, if he sneaked out now, it would be all the better.

As he contemplated the possibilities, his fear destroyed the tiny ray of hope he'd experienced. Nick felt the weight fall back on his shoulders and the metal clamp, once again, gripped his head, squeezing tighter than ever before. He realized he couldn't sneak away, for Stro-kar had other plans. Nick let out a muffled groan, as the evil impulses of Stro-kar deluged his mind. He knew what he had to do. Nick was to open fire as soon as God released him from constraints.

Constraints?

Nick looked at his sweaty hands, wringing his gun in anticipation. He found he couldn't move either—he was held tight. He felt as if his mind was inside another body. This wasn't him, not the real him, the new mind which had started to surface.

After a while, the part of him that had responded to the message was relegated to the back recesses of his mind. Nick was his old self again, no longer a stranger in a foreign body. He was Stro-kar-Nick, waiting for his opportunity, relishing in thinking of the bloodshed he would soon cause. His only regret was he was commanded to simply kill them. It would be better if he could slowly torture them to death.

"Time is running out," the preacher said, as if he knew what Nick was thinking. "If God has been drawing on your heart, come to the front of this platform."

Thousands flocked to the platform, some screaming and fighting themselves, but moving nevertheless. Ronny was one of the happy ones. Without hesitation, he ran to the front, like a child ecstatic to meet his long lost father.

For several minutes, Nick listened to the gentle encouragement to come forward and make a commitment to Christ. When he strained his neck to the right and left, he saw several hundred like himself, frozen and clutching guns.

Finally, the preacher commanded the demons to leave the people's bodies in the name of Jesus, and led them in a prayer. "Dear Lord, I know I'm a sinner and need your forgiveness," he began and they repeated after him.

Nick watched the blond-haired lady whisper in his father's ear. His dad nodded and seemed to take that as a cue to mouth something which looked like a prayer and stomp on the ground.

Suddenly Nick was free. Now! Stro-kar was telling him to act now! He pulled back the bolt on his gun and aimed at the crowd, but it was difficult as the ground started to shake.

Somebody beside him let off a few rounds and bodies started to drop. Nick congratulated himself that he wasn't part of the new converts. The trusting religious fools had been betrayed by their God. Bullets tore their backs open before they fell to the ground. Oddly enough, Nick noticed everyone who died had a smile on their face.

The tremors become violent convulsions, knocking Nick to the ground. His mother and several others fell on top of him, but he was glad because they served as a canopy of protection from the large hailstones which started plummeting from heaven.

One man clutched a twisted and bleeding nose, as he writhed on the ground. He was being systematically beaten to death, but the group leaders and their new followers were calmly loading the van. When they were done, they drove away with a huge crowd running alongside. Nick noticed the earthquake and hail lessened the farther away they got.

Chapter 17

"Oh, Valerie, Nick," Jeff lamented as he sat at the foot of his bed. "If I'd only known you were there, I would have done something more to save you."

"There's nothing more you could have done," Sandy said. She was sitting beside Jeff.

Ronny sat at a desk in the corner, periodically flipping pages of the Bible he was reading. He turned to look at Jeff. "She's right, Mr. Saunderson. Nick and your wife made their choice. There's nothing you can do now."

"Call me Jeff," he said as he went over to the curtains and opened them. Down below, he could see the complex's main floor. Thousands of new Christians were excitedly milling about, talking to one another and shaking hands. Lawrence was down there too, organizing everybody into groups and assigning them to gifted leaders.

"What happens now, Jeff?" Ronny asked.

Jeff was still daydreaming as he looked down below. "Humm? Oh, I don't know. It's different every time. Lawrence just does what God tells him to. Some will stay and help us here. Others will be sent to other complexes. In all cases, individuals will find out what gifts and talents they have and be equipped to carry out their particular role. Everyone also receives a certain amount of Bible training, depending on their particular calling. Preachers get a lot more, and cooks and janitors get a lot less. But we're all important. Nobody is allowed to lord their gifts over anybody else. We all need one another."

"Where do you get the food to feed everybody?" Ronny asked. "Many are starving on the outside."

Jeff smiled. "God provides the food and the cooks prepare it. You've never tasted food until you've eaten here. But anyway, you should be down there too."

"Sorry," Ronny said and pointed at the Bible he had been reading. "Can I take it?"

"No," Jeff said. "It's got a lot of my own study notes in it. Besides, we've got thousands of Bibles. If you were down on the floor like you should be, you'd get your very own tonight."

"Wow," Ronny said. "Where do you get them?"

"God told Lawrence's dad exactly how many he would need on hand to be able to hand one out personally to every person who would ever come through this place."

Ronny shook his head in amazement.

Jeff took on a semi-smiling, semi-serious look. He didn't want to be rude, but he wanted to talk to Sandy alone. "I appreciate your telling me about my family, but it's time for you to get going." He pointed down below.

Ronny smiled and trudged out of the room. When he was gone, Jeff sat beside Sandy again. "I want to go and get them," he said.

"We're not scheduled to preach again in Star City for two weeks. Lawrence said we're supposed to go to a town in Wyoming. Then we're to go to the rural areas north and..."

"I don't care, Sandy!"

"What?"

"Don't you understand. This is my family, my wife and son. I still love them, and it pains my heart to know they were so close and yet so far. God was obviously drawing on their hearts or they wouldn't have been there. If I could only get to them I'm sure I could.... That's if they're even alive." Jeff lay back on the bed and stared up at the ceiling. Tears started to well up in the corners of his eyes. He missed them so much. He wiped the tears from his face.

It had been so long. Many times, Jeff had felt like giving up on them, but continued to pray. Lawrence had reluctantly let Jeff make periodic visits, which were always depressing, constant rejection and the last time a threat of death. That had been the last straw. He knew Valerie wasn't kidding, and Lawrence said Jeff couldn't go anymore. Now to see his small ember of hope almost burst forth into flames was more than he could manage. He had to go to them one last time.

Sandy looked at Jeff, tears of her own forming in her eyes. "I'd like to help if I could, but..." She looked away. Jeff understood. For a long time now, he knew she had once loved him.

Sandy had made her feelings very plain after escaping the mob at the Sheriff's office, the place where the local professional protection mogul, Jarius, had set up shop. They had seen at least a dozen of Jarius' men come to Jesus, before Jarius got angry and tried to kill them. Jeff used his God-given power to get away, but Sandy had taken a bullet in the arm. Back at the complex, the doctor removed the bullet and bandaged her arm, but the brief brush with death seemed to fill Sandy with the courage to speak her mind.

She talked quickly, a flood of words pouring out almost faster than Jeff could listen, of how she'd fallen in love and wanted to marry him, of how she thought of him first thing upon waking, all day, and right before falling asleep.

Jeff, on the other hand, didn't feel the same. While he cared deeply for Sandy as a friend, he still loved his wife. As long as Valerie was alive, he would keep waiting and hoping. "But she has repeatedly committed adultery," Sandy had said. "You can get a divorce." That was true, but he still didn't want to. He was lonely for intimate female companionship, but he didn't love Sandy in that way.

Jeff was definitely physically attracted to Sandy, though, perhaps a little too much. He even asked Lawrence to transfer him to a different group, but to his surprise Lawrence said no. Apparently, God had other plans for them. It didn't seem smart to Jeff, but he didn't question God's judgment. Now, much later, he could see the good in it. Eventually, any of Sandy's romantic feelings disappeared and he developed a very deep, abiding friendship with her. He could be very honest with her about his love for Valerie and how much he missed her. Sandy accepted Jeff the way he was and never even got jealous or envious. But now, the prospect of Jeff reuniting with his wife seemed to frighten her.

"We'll always be friends," he told her as he sat up and put his arms around her. "You don't have to worry about losing me." When she looked him in the eyes, Jeff knew he'd guessed correctly.

"Are you sure? We won't be able to spend as much time together."

"Yes we will. To me, you've become a part of my family. Like a sister. And I know Valerie, at least the real Valerie, not the thing she's become. She won't mind us being together. Trust me."

"OK. If you say so."

"I actually think this is just the kind of situation that calls for Stephanie's unique abilities."

"But don't you think we should ask Lawrence first?"

"Yes, let's do that." They exited the room and made their way to Lawrence's office. The door was open, as Lawrence liked to demonstrate an open atmosphere with his people as much as possible. He smiled as Jeff and Sandy approached and asked them to come in and sit down.

"It's nice to see you two," Lawrence said. "The Lord has already told me about your situation."

"So can we go get them and bring them back here for Stephanie to work on?" Jeff asked.

Stephanie had developed into quite the little spiritual warrior over the years. God had given her the ability to enter into a person's mind and battle demons personally, a skill needed in those rare cases where demons could not be cast out of a person in the field. Some demons were so strongly entrenched in a person's mind that God would sometimes have the preaching groups bring people back to the complex, where Stephanie would enter the person's mind and expel the demon or demons.

She used to travel with the preaching groups personally, but was now confined to a wheelchair since one particularly difficult encounter with Daimagon, Satan's second in command and only marginally lower in strength than Satan himself. Over the years, Stephanie's skills had grown so fast and so strong that she had become a bit overconfident. Daimagon was finally expelled from one man after days of mental battle, but as the demon was leaving the body, Stephanie dropped her guard for just a moment, thinking the battle was over. Daimagon struck one last defiant blow when she wasn't expecting it and then fled the man's mind. Stephanie may have had the ultimate victory, but she was left paralyzed from the neck down in her physical body after this fight. No matter. She gladly continued to battle with any demon possessed people that could be brought to her. Her body might be frail now, but when she entered one's mind, her spirit was indomitable.

"I'm afraid the Lord's answer is no, Jeff."

"But why? This is a perfect case for her. She's never failed yet and—"

"The answer is no, Jeff," Lawrence said a little more forcefully. "Valerie and Nick didn't respond when they heard the message. They had their chance to repent. Their fate is in the Lord's hands now. All He will say to me is *patience*."

"Does that mean they will get another chance later?"

"I don't know. But the best thing we can do for them is obey God and pray for them. We all must learn to wait on the Lord's timing."

"That's difficult for me to do when it comes to my family."

Lawrence smiled. "God's doing a work in all of us, Jeff. Learn faith and patience. All who are meant to be in God's family will be eventually."

Jeff gritted his teeth and nodded slowly. He and Sandy left Lawrence's office and started to make their way back to Jeff's room, but Jeff passed his room and continued down the hallway.

"Where are we going?" Sandy asked.

"I think we should talk to Stephanie," Jeff said.

"What would be the point. You're not thinking of doing something stupid are you?"

"I just need to talk to her." Sandy shook her head and sighed but followed him to Stephanie's room. Jeff knocked on the door and heard Stephanie say, "Come in, dad."

He opened the door and entered the room, marveling at her senses as he closed the door and sat down across from her. "I'll never be able to surprise you, will I?"

"Not within about a 100 foot perimeter," Stephanie said. "But my senses don't reach much beyond that."

Jeff could feel his daughter's presence now too.

He had a special connection with his daughter in this way, but only within about 10 feet for himself. Even though Stephanie was not in his mind fighting demons, he could sense her spirit filling the room as though it were a thick smog that only he could see. Others usually didn't feel a thing but only saw what appeared to be a physically frail young woman in a wheelchair, arms and legs atrophied from immobility.

Jeff told her the whole situation and asked her what she thought.

"I don't care what Lawrence says. We're talking about mom and Nick! I say go get'em, dad. Bring them to me and they're as good as free."

"This is what I was afraid of," Sandy said. "You two running off like lone rangers or something. We need to trust the Lord here."

Jeff sighed. "I just know I have to do this."

"You might be endangering us all."

Jeff silently got up and walked to the window, staring at the activity below. "I don't see how that's possible. I'm going tomorrow morning. By myself if I have to. I'll be the only one in danger. I'd like you to come but I understand if you don't want to."

Sandy got up, walked over to the window, and stood beside Jeff. "Count me in," she said.

* * *

"I don't know, Jeff," Sandy whispered. "I'm really starting to wonder about this. Kidnapping is not God's ideal way of evangelizing."

Jeff squirmed inside what used to be his and Valerie's closet. It was filled with boxes full of junk, a baseball bat, drugs, and moldy clothes. He supposed the cost of cleaning must be high, judging from the smell.

He touched the pair of handcuffs tucked inside his belt. Sandy had her own pair. The plan was for Jeff to grab Valerie and handcuff her before she could react. Sandy would find Nick and do the same.

"Don't think of it as kidnapping," Jeff said. "Think of it as de-programming. I know Stephanie can help them back at the complex. Once they're free of the demons' influence, I'm sure I can lead them to Christ."

"How can you be sure? They can come back if the person lets them."

"God's Spirit drew them to the meeting. That's how. They wouldn't have been there otherwise. If Jesus fills them with Himself, they won't go back to Satan."

"I hope you're right. They stayed behind to shoot at us, so they're still under the influence of the fallen spirit world in a mighty way. And I still don't feel totally comfortable doing this when Lawrence specifically said we shouldn't."

Jeff pushed back any doubt. He wasn't entirely certain, but was driven beyond rational thought. Apparently, God needed a little help where his family was concerned. No. Rather, Jeff decided, this must have been God's plan all along. He was here, and would stay until they came home.

Perhaps they were dead. No! He refused to entertain such thoughts. Besides, they had gone back to last night's farmhouse, and hadn't seen Valerie or Nick among the dead bodies.

Jeff and Sandy stayed in the closet all afternoon, determined to wait it out. Eventually, Sandy opened the door only a crack to get some air; it squeaked badly, and Jeff didn't want to be heard closing it again if Valerie and Nick were to come home.

It wasn't until later in the evening that Jeff heard the front door unlocking. He closed the closet door as quietly as he could.

"Did you hear something?" Valerie said from down the hall.

"No," Nick said. The dogs started growling and barking, apparently sensing his and Sandy's presence. Jeff had forgotten about the two Doberman pinschers which usually guarded the house.

Sandy whispered her concern, but all Jeff could do was shrug his shoulders. Whatever happened, there was no turning back now. As they had often done in the past, they would have to continue as planned and trust God to work out overlooked details.

Nick ordered the dogs to be quiet, and Valerie must have shrugged it off too because she didn't say anything more, but came into the bedroom. Jeff peeked through a crack in the door, and saw Valerie carrying armloads of clothing and other personal items. Jeff recognized a dress as being similar to one the neighbor's wife used to wear. They had probably been raiding the neighborhood with that gang of thugs Nick hung around with lately.

Jeff hesitated, wondering what would happen in the next few minutes. Then he took a deep breath and whispered to Sandy he was going to make his move. He quickly opened the closet door, and grabbed Valerie. Both fell on the bed.

Sandy grabbed the bat in the closet, and ran down the hall to get Nick.

Valerie screamed and struggled, but Jeff was stronger and forced the cuffs on her.

"You idiot," Valerie spat. "You're not going to get away with this. Nick! Kill these fools!"

Sandy came diving back into the room headfirst, as bullets shattered the door frame, one of the dogs chasing behind. She turned in time to see the dog leaping for her throat. But she still held the bat in her right hand and swung it hard, connecting with the dog's head, making a loud cracking noise as if scoring a home run. The dog fell to the ground and didn't move again.

Sandy said she was a little shaken up, but not hurt.

Jeff reached for Valerie's gun, which had fallen on the bed. He poked around the corner and let off a few rounds into the air as a warning.

"I'm sorry," Nick yelled. "It's you, isn't it, dad? I just remembered your little blonde friend from the other night."

"Yeah. It's me. I want to help you."

"I've missed you. Come out into the open where I can see you better."

Sandy gave Jeff a look which said, "Yeah right."

Jeff wasn't fooled either. If his wife was any indication, he could tell this wasn't going to be easy. He poked his head around the corner and brought it back just in time to prevent his brains from being splattered, as bullets riddled the door frame again.

"Kill them, Nick!" Valerie shouted. "Walk right in here and kill them. They haven't the guts to shoot you."

"Gag her mouth," Jeff said.

Sandy found a sock and shoved it in Valerie's mouth. Jeff heard what sounded like running footsteps down the hall. Within seconds, the other dog entered the room and leapt for his throat. He shot it in midair and it fell to his feet. Valerie screamed through her gag, obviously upset her pets had been killed.

"You wouldn't hurt me, would you, dad?" Nick yelled from down the hall. "I'm coming up. We can talk. Like old times."

Jeff started to panic. He could hear his son walking up the stairs, footsteps sounding methodical, as if he were stalking a wounded animal. Soon, Nick would be in the room, and Jeff was sure he wasn't going to talk about old times.

He couldn't shoot his own son.

Jeff mouthed a quick prayer to God, but sensed no answer.

He got up, prayed again quickly, and stomped on the floor as hard as he could. God would shake the house and throw Nick off balance.

Nothing happened.

"I'm almost there," Nick said. "My gun's at the foot of the stairs. Don't shoot."

Yeah right, Jeff thought to himself. He looked at Sandy and mouthed the words, "What do I do?" With panic written on her face, she shrugged her shoulders. They were out of options.

"Forgive me, Lord," Jeff said as he blindly aimed his gun around the corner, but he pointed more to the floor than full body height. Jeff pulled the trigger and heard Nick moan and fall with a loud thud.

He poked his head around the corner. His son was clutching bleeding knees and grunting with pain, gun lying beside him.

Jeff ran down the hall, and Nick grabbed for his gun again, but Jeff kicked it away. "You're coming with me, son," he said as he slapped on the cuffs.

Chapter 18

Lawrence walked right up to Jeff and Sandy, frowning. Either God was giving him a special message, or he was angry. Lawrence looked away and peered into the window in the center of the door. "You shouldn't have done it, Jeff," he said. "You should've trusted me. It wasn't the Lord's will for you to have gone at this time."

Jeff was silent. He felt like a young child being scolded for misbehaving. He worried slightly at what Lawrence might do as punishment, such as kick him out of the complex, but pushed the thought away quickly. Lawrence wasn't that kind of person. Besides, Jeff had learned long ago God could take the worst situations and turn them into something good, and Jeff knew God was at work here somewhere. Otherwise, He wouldn't have healed Nick.

When Jeff had first carried Nick in, he took him straight to the doctor. Nick's knees were mangled, and his blood practically soaked every fiber of Jeff's shirt. But when the doctor prayed over him, he was instantly healed and started fighting again. So, Jeff dragged him to this holding cell.

From where he was standing, Jeff could only partially see through the window Lawrence was still looking through; inside, Valerie and Nick were locked in straight jackets, cursing and swearing at those looking in, throwing themselves against the walls in frustration. Luckily, the walls and floor were padded.

"But the Lord tells me He knew all along you would," Lawrence said and looked at Jeff. "You are impetuous, aren't you. Well, I'll call for Stephanie and see what she can do. In the meantime, I'm going to my study for private meditation. I'll ask the Lord what He wants us to do next." Lawrence walked away and Jeff could tell he was indeed angry, something in the way he stomped down the hall.

Jeff decided to take another peek inside. The room about 20 feet by 20 feet and almost soundproof. His wife and son were mouthing curses, but he could hardly hear them. Nick was frothing at the mouth as he flung himself against the wall repeatedly. Valerie was wailing and squirming on the floor as if she were being overrun by ants.

When Jeff was done, Sandy took a look.

"I hope Stephanie can do something," Sandy said. "She's never failed before, but then we've always stayed within the Lord's boundaries before. I wonder if your losing your gift today is a sign."

Jeff hung his head in a somber gesture. "Yeah, except for today, I've always been able to call down an earthquake. Nothing happened when I stomped my foot."

Sandy looked back at Jeff. "Are you saying you think the Lord might not free them?"

"I don't know anymore." Sure, he knew God could free them, but whether or not He would was another matter. Jeff began to have some doubts, realizing how reckless he had been. He should've known better than to rush God. If God wanted them saved, He would have done it in His own time. Perhaps this would be his punishment, watching his family being tormented by demons, locked in a tiny padded cell for the rest of their natural lives, knowing an eternal hell awaited them upon physical death and being helpless to save them.

After several long minutes, Stephanie came whirring by in her electric wheelchair. "I'm all prayed up, dad, and ready to kick some demon ass." She smiled and Jeff felt her special presence grow as she neared. Such power and love started to pelt his mind, a stronger feeling than he had ever sensed from her before. Understandable, he thought. She was fighting for family this time. She used her mouth to push some buttons on the navigation bar that was fastened to the wheelchair and positioned in front of her face, and the wheelchair slowly came to a stop in front of him.

At this distance, Jeff almost fell to his knees from such an awesome and overpowering feeling of love, both from his daughter and mixed with a strong sense of the Holy Spirit's love and power. He started to weep. However wrong Jeff and Sandy may have been, Jeff realized God's gifts were never withheld from His people, which increased his confidence that Stephanie would be successful in the battle about to begin.

"I'd like you to stand by my side for this one, dad. I think it'll give me strength and comfort to know you are there."

Jeff nodded and wiped his eyes. He entered the room with her. Sandy stayed outside. For several hours, Stephanie simply stayed in the center of the room, praying and speaking the Word of God over Valerie and Nick. For the most part, they cowered in one corner and periodically cursed Stephanie, but they never attacked her. Eventually, she closed her eyes and Jeff could sense her entering a mind, but he wasn't sure which one.

Jeff had never stood by Stephanie before during an exorcism, and felt unsure what he should do next, so just grabbed her hand and held it tightly. He was amazed to find that the special connection he had with his daughter suddenly increased dramatically. Usually he could only sense her presence and some emotion, but now he could see a vague picture in his mind of what she was doing, a strange sensation he had never experienced before, seeing something in his spirit but not seeing it with his physical eyes.

He could sort of envision Stephanie approaching a large black castle, and felt the sensation of red, then an image of the castle walls dripping blood popping in and out of his mind. Fire…a mote, castle surrounded by a mote of fire, yes that was clearer now. The castle seemed alive and opened its drawbridge partially, as if the bridge were a mouth. The castle seemed to recognize Stephanie and asked for help, and Jeff just somehow knew the castle represented Valerie's mind.

"I'm here mom," Stephanie said. "Don't worry. These ones are no match for the power of God."

A jolt of electricity shocked Jeff's hand as Stephanie said this, and he felt his daughter's faith surge and a feeling of raw power traveled up his arm. A blurred image raced towards the castle, a boulder, or something like a rock. Jeff focused his mind and concentrated and sensed the rock was Stephanie, focused harder and for a few seconds could see an image of a six foot tall woman with shoulder length red hair now standing at the drawbridge. The woman was broad shouldered and muscular, and Jeff could only recognize the woman as Stephanie by the flowing red hair, just like her mother's.

"Drop that drawbridge and face me, demon," Stephanie said firmly. "Or I'm coming in."

A bright yellow flash blinded Jeff's mind, and he saw something like fire or molten metal spitting out of the castle windows and enveloping Stephanie. When the flash cleared he could picture a rock within a clear bubble, protected from the fiery assault from the castle above. The bubble popped and the rock opened its mouth to speak.

"Is that the best you can do, demon?" Stephanie said. "I've been doing this a long time now. Your gonna have to have something better in your bag of tricks or this is gonna be real quick."

Way to go girl, Jeff thought and felt another jolt of power electrify his body.

A chorus of voices, at least several dozen, shouted defiant words, and he saw a blurred image of people rushing atop the castle.

"So you're more than one. At least that'll give me more of a workout."

He felt sorrow, anguish, and pain in his spirit… coming from the castle…Jeff started to weep again, as he felt Valerie's pain. The drawbridge opened wide and a loud voice pleaded for Stephanie to enter. Then the castle screamed in pain.

"Leave her alone, you sons of bitches," Stephanie said.

A feeling of anger, turmoil…the images shifted quickly. Jeff saw a blur rush across the now open drawbridge and enter the castle. Soon, flashes of white light and blood began to spill over the castle walls. Black and red figures where thrown high up into the sky, simply to come crashing down into the castle again, and then be thrown up again into the sky. Jeff couldn't make out the black figures clearly but several red figures hovered in the sky momentarily, and Jeff could make out creatures that looked like a cross between a dinosaur and a dragon, with faces something like the head of a Tyrannosaurus Rex and massive wings like a Pterodactyl.

Stephanie grunted and her head vibrated noticeably, rocking her wheelchair. She started to breathe heavily and beads of sweat started to form on her forehead.

Jeff could see blurred images of black and red continuing to flail over the sides of the castle, enter the castle again, and be thrown out again. Then the red and black figures changed tactics and started spewing bluish fire at the castle walls.

A strong sensation of anguish and pain overwhelmed Jeff's spirit…physical pain, confusion, emotional turmoil. His spirit felt like it was on fire and he just couldn't hold on anymore. He let go of Stephanie's hand and even had to step back a few feet to lessen the sensations he was getting off of his daughter. In the corner of the room, Valerie suddenly began to scream and wrestle in her straightjacket.

"I'm sorry," Jeff said. "I just can't do this anymore."

Stephanie was sweating profusely now, and grinding her teeth. "N-o…n-e-e-d to…apologize," Stephanie grunted out in short bursts, obviously unable to hold a normal conversation and still maintain focus on the mental battle.

Jeff shook his head in awe and admiration for what Stephanie was able to do. He figured she must endure everything he had just experienced but even more intensely. Despite some insulation provided by years of training and experience, it was obviously a struggle beyond his ability to fully comprehend.

"G-o…d-a-d. Noth—ing…can d-o…a-n-y-way."

As he exited the room, Valerie started to scream again and tears began to well up in Jeff's eyes. He pushed back his own feelings of anguish and closed the door behind him, muffling his wife's voice as he did so, confining her screams to the small padded room but carrying her pain with him in his own way. He tried to encourage himself with the idea that it would be more productive to simply go back to his room and pray, and he did so.

For the next several days, Jeff would go and visit his wife and son. Stephanie ceaselessly battled and battled. She vowed she would keep fighting until her mom was either freed or God told her to stop; everyone in the complex was also praying for Jeff's family. This went on for a week, and Jeff refused to go on missions for the entire time. He moped around the complex, visiting his family and praying. Sandy stayed behind for a few days to comfort him, but eventually went back on the road.

Stephanie had supernatural physical strength when locked in these types of demonic battles. Jeff had seen her go at least a week without food and water, but for some reason, this time after only three days had past, the doctor had to hook Stephanie up with intravenous feeding tubes, as her body began to emaciate and shrivel.

Lawrence would periodically call Jeff into his office and try to encourage him to go on missions. He would talk about how much weaker Jeff's team was without him, how they needed an earth-shaker, how dangerous it was without him, but Jeff doubted if his gift would work. Lawrence was always sympathetic and tried to convince Jeff that God had forgiven him, but Jeff continued to be depressed. All he did was eat a little, sleep a lot, visit his family, and pray. Slowly, even his prayer life started to slide. He became so discouraged his joy started ebbing away and he hardly read his Bible anymore.

At the end of the week, Lawrence called Jeff into his office again. "Please, have a seat," he said as Jeff opened the door. Jeff sat in a chair opposite Lawrence's desk.

"Any word yet from the Lord about Valerie?" Jeff asked. Almost daily, Jeff asked Lawrence this question and was usually told that this battle was not fully ordained by the Lord at this time and so it would be a more difficult struggle. Whether or not they ever would be freed, Lawrence could never say, which added to his anxiety. Today, he sensed in his spirit that Lawrence had more insight from the Lord.

Lawrence sighed. "I'm sorry to say that the word God gives me is *death* for one of your children."

Fear overwhelmed Jeff's mind and he felt as though someone had just stabbed him in the heart. "What does that mean? Just physical death, or spiritual death too? For one or both of them?"

"Stephanie is sealed by the Holy Spirit and can't experience spiritual death in the lake of fire. The blood of Christ covers her. Other than that, the Lord hasn't given me any more details about what that means. Just prepare your heart for that outcome, whatever it means. He also tells me life for both Stephanie and Nick had you waited."

Jeff started to sob and begged Lawrence to intercede on his behalf but Lawrence refused. "This is the way it has to be, Jeff. The Lord is hard on His people sometimes. He has high standards and expects obedience. That's just the bare minimum He expects of everyone. You are spiritually mature enough to have known better. He expected better of you."

"Then punish me instead!"

Lawrence just shook his head. "There's something else I must tell you."

Jeff nodded meekly.

"For many years now, I've run this operation as best as I could. The Lord has been with me mightily, giving me wisdom to lead wisely, and the privilege of hearing His voice audibly."

Again, Jeff nodded.

"Everyone here has been marvelous, a blessing to me and each other. The Lord has given us wonderful diversity, and yet there has been very little division. Each has been given a remarkable portion of grace, able to really love one another and work together. They have been willing to obey God and trust me as His servant. And I've never abused that trust. Everyone has seen my hard work and knows I'm sincere."

Jeff nodded once more, starting to feel uncomfortable.

"This never ceases to amaze me. Sure, we've had minor disagreements about how things should be done, but in the end, it has always worked out. Everyone communicates openly and honestly and is willing to submit to those in authority over them. This is how God wants His children to behave, but again I'll say it—I'm amazed. When I read the Old Testament, I see how Moses had difficulties leading the Israelites. They grumbled and rebelled against his authority. God even opened the ground on one occasion and swallowed up some rebels. In the New Testament, I read Paul's letters exhorting believers to submit to one another in love and to obey those in authority over them. Not only that, but Paul had to continually resist and rebuke improper behavior in the churches.

Even Jesus had to contend with His own disciples' evil desires for power and prestige when they were arguing over who would be the greatest. I seem to have been mightily blessed as a leader. Everyone here has their priorities straight: God first, others, then themselves."

Jeff didn't feel like nodding anymore. He thought Lawrence was leading up to something, and felt convicted of his own wrong behavior. Lawrence would probably now rebuke Jeff again for his refusal to go on missions. He might lecture for a few minutes, and command Jeff to shape up. And he should; Jeff knew that. But Lawrence was also kind and sympathetic. He would do his best to encourage Jeff. "I think the power of His Spirit helps a lot," Jeff said.

"No doubt. In other times there hasn't been such an abundance of gifted individuals working in unity."

"I know what you're going to say, Lawrence, and I agree. I've been the black sheep around here lately, but you don't have to worry about me anymore. I'm going to dust off the cobwebs and get back into the action again. There's work to be done." Jeff had been leading up to this decision for the past several days, but this little talk had persuaded him not to wait any longer.

Lawrence smiled. "That's very commendable. Actually, I knew you'd say that, but it's not why I asked you in here."

"Oh?"

"I wanted you to know it's not all your fault. This is also the way the Lord wants it to be. All complexes will meet the same fate. From this disaster our people will be weaned from the security of home-base. They've all been adequately trained. Now God will be with each of them in a mighty way. Each small group of believers will experience all the gifts. You will even hear His voice, Jeff. Like I do now. The people will no longer depend on me for direction, or the complex for safety, but they will depend totally on God. They will be forced into every conceivable corner of the world, and the gospel of Jesus Christ will go with them. This is what the Scriptures meant when they said the gospel would be preached as a witness unto all the world and then the end would come. He's coming back very soon now, Jeff, very soon."

Jeff frowned. "What are you talking about? What disaster?"

"They're coming for us, Jeff. It's like in the Old Testament. You know, when one Israelite would disobey God, the whole Israeli army would be punished and lose in battle. But it was only a temporary defeat. Soon, God would glorify Himself by turning the situation around and giving His people the victory again."

"I still don't understand."

"You disobeyed God when you went to get your family. You didn't even realize it, but several members of Nick's gang were in the area and heard the commotion. They followed you here. Jarius has wanted to find our hideout for some time. Now he knows. Since then, they've been planning to raid us, even enlisted extra men in their army and amassed more weapons and explosives."

Jeff's jaw fell open and he stared at Lawrence. "Wha...when will this happen. I mean I'm sorry. I couldn't have known." He knew the Lord had already forgiven him, but still started to feel guilty, realizing what all was going to happen because of his mistake.

"It's all a part of His plan, Jeff. You're going to go out and fulfill your destiny in ways you've never dreamed of. And I've also got good news. God has decided to free Valerie within the hour."

Jeff imagined his face must show a distorted picture of emotions. He was relieved and happy for Valerie, yet sad and afraid for his children. Then guilt started to creep over him once more, as he considered the pending assault on the complex, but he pushed it away, deciding not to dwell on the past. It wouldn't do any good. He couldn't go back and do it differently. He instead focused on the positive side: *God would give His people the victory again*. "What about Sandy? I can't leave without her, and you never told me when this will happen. Where will we go? Who will we go with?"

"Calm down, Jeff. I've already recalled the missions. Sandy's team is returning from Texas and will drive straight through the night until they get here. She should make it just in time."

"And when will Jarius' men be here?"

"Tomorrow at 2:12PM exactly."

"That doesn't give Stephanie much time to work on Nick. It's taken a week to get Valerie free. How can we save Nick in…" Jeff looked at his wristwatch and noted it was almost six o'clock in the evening. "…only about twenty hours?"

"I don't know, Jeff" Lawrence said flatly. "I told you to prepare for death for one of your children. I'm sorry…I'm sorry."

Jeff exited Lawrence's office and ran to his room to pray fervently for Nick's salvation.After fifteen minutes of begging the Lord, he felt absolutely nothing positive in his spirit about Nick's fate, so he tried to distract his mind. He looked around the room and thought about the many things he would have to take tomorrow: clothes, towels, personal hygiene things, and books. He took several suitcases out of the closet and placed them on the bed. Then he thought about transportation. There weren't enough vehicles in the complex for everyone. And then he worried about where they would stay. It wasn't safe outside. He started to doubt God's loving care, as he mourned again for his son, and started to think the whole evacuation idea was crazy. Jeff looked at his watch, about forty minutes before his wife would be freed.

Lawrence's voice suddenly boomed over the speaker system. He explained to everybody about the impending assault, and split them into groups, stressing they shouldn't bother packing because God would supply all their needs. Finally, Lawrence closed with a good luck and the admonition to go wherever God told them to, as soon as they felt led.

Well, that took care of that idea, Jeff thought as he tossed the suitcases off the bed and onto the floor. Jeff need only wait. He put some hymns on the cassette player, turned the volume low, and lay on the bed, praying in his mind for Nick. Within minutes, he fell asleep.

* * *

Jeff was awakened by a knock on his door. "Wake up, Jeff! It's Valerie. She's ok."

Jeff shook off his sleepiness and looked at the clock on the wall. He'd been asleep for nearly three quarters of an hour. Valerie was right on schedule.

Jeff jumped up and opened the door. He saw a young boy standing in the doorway, a face unfamiliar to him.

"Stephanie sent me to give you the good news. Several minutes ago, the demons were forced to leave your wife."

Jeff smiled. "Thank you."

He ran down the stairs to find throngs of people already milling about in preparation for the onslaught tomorrow. He zigzagged through the maze of bodies and ran down the corridor near the main entrance. Before he even reached the end of the hallway, Jeff saw Stephanie exiting the holding cell with Valerie, both appearing exhausted and about five years older.

Valerie looked up. "Jeff!"

The joy of the moment seemed to knock the five years off and she ran to meet him, Stephanie whirring close behind in her wheelchair. Somewhere in the middle, they all met and embraced.

Valerie squeezed Jeff tightly. "I love you, honey. I'm so sorry for everything. I didn't know what I was getting myself into. The things I did..." She began to sob.

"Forget it," Jeff said. "It's all in the past now. It's forgiven and forgotten. I'm just glad I got you back. Did Jesus fill you with Himself?"

"Yes. I feel wonderful. It's been so long since I've had a pure thought."

They all had a refreshing cry before Valerie and Jeff started back up the hall. "I'll take Valerie to my room," Jeff said to Stephanie. "If you feel able, please get to work on Nick right away. We don't have much time. I'll come back to the holding cell as soon as I can and explain more."

Stephanie nodded and immediately turned around and headed right back to the padded holding room.

Jeff gave Valerie a quick verbal tour of the complex, but didn't bother showing her around. It would be fruitless; time was short and it would soon be destroyed anyway. Then they navigated through the mass of people, up the stairs, and into his room.

"It's not very big," Valerie said.

"Doesn't need to be," Jeff replied. "We're hardly ever here anyway. Most of us are on the front lines, fighting the spiritual battle."

Jeff and Valerie sat together on the edge of the bed.

Valerie almost started to cry again. "I know what it feels like to be on the other side."

"Don't cry, honey,"Jeff said. "As far as I'm concerned, that was the old you. You have been given a new life through Christ. Live it joyfully."

"I still feel a bit guilty. I mean, I know you're right. It wasn't totally me, but it was. You'd have to experience it to fully understand. I was losing my identity, their thoughts and desires becoming mine. When the demons would act, it was me doing it and vice versa. Such a horrible predicament."

"But there was a part of you that didn't want to, right?" Jeff asked.

Valerie nodded.

"That was God influencing your life. He never fully gave up on you. That's why you're here today. And it's the same for many more out there. That's why we keep pressing on to reach the world. Lawrence said God would give us the power to finish this war when we leave this place."

"I'll be happy if I can help. I'll never forget what it felt like to be a prisoner in my own body. For the entire week Stephanie was battling, my mind felt like it was being seared by intense heat. The demons fought with everything they had to stay, but on the last day, I felt more peaceful. I sensed it was nearing the end and the pain would stop soon, one way or the other. I really didn't care if I died. I just wanted it to be over."

"I'm glad you didn't die. I wanted to be able to tell you I love you, Valerie. I always have. Even when I handcuffed you and you yelled at Nick to shoot me, I wanted to say it, but I knew you couldn't receive it then."

"I can receive it now," Valerie said and gave Jeff a big hug.

Jeff explained about the mass exodus tomorrow before Jarius' men would arrive and about his deep abiding friendship with Sandy. "We have to wait for Sandy. I'm not leaving without her. She's been such a good friend to me."

"I understand. When will she be here?"

"We're not sure. Sometime tomorrow before Jarius."

"You two must have had some amazing experiences."

"Definitely. God has sent us all over Star City, the surrounding areas, the whole continent in fact. When we each do what God has called us to do, we're able to reach the world in supernatural power. Now Lawrence told us *all* the supernatural gifts will be fully expressed through each small group. I still find this hard to believe, but I don't doubt God will do it. My gift used to be causing earthquakes and hail storms to cover our escapes. When God pours out His Spirit's power on us, we'll be able to preach powerfully, cast out demons, heal the sick, talk to God..."

"Will I be able to do all that too?"

Jeff shook his head. "Lawrence said all the gifts will be expressed through each *group*, so I think everyone will still have different gifts which work together."

Valerie frowned, disbelieving. "But I haven't had your training. How can that be?"

"God can do anything. He can miraculously imprint every Bible verse into your memory if He wants to, and He can give you full revelation and understanding in a moment. Don't doubt it for a second."

"Wow," was all Valerie could say. "So where are we going?"

"I don't know. The Lord will tell us when the time is right. We should trust until then."

They continued to talk about the past, the future, and about their fears, desires, and hopes. All the time Jeff kept eyeing the clock on the wall. He wanted to give Stephanie at least an hour for the warm-up praying she usually did before tackling an exorcism, but now he felt it was time to go warn her about Lawrence's prophecy. He was also procrastinating telling Valerie the full truth, but it had to be done sooner or later, so he got to it.

"I have some bad news about one of our kids," Jeff said, as he explained the Lord's pronouncement that one of their kids would die.

Valerie gasped and her cheeks turned beet red. She doubled over on the bed, clutching her stomach, and started to sob.

"Don't lose hope. I've seen Stephanie do amazing things. God is in her gifting in a powerful way. I'm holding on to the hope that all Lawrence meant is physical death, which is nothing. It's spiritual death that I'm most worried about, being cast into the lake of fire to burn forever. I have to go talk to Stephanie. She needs to be warned about the death prophecy and that she only has about nineteen hours left to free Nick. Please, just stay here and pray while I go talk to her."

Valerie nodded and wiped her eyes, as Jeff got up to leave.

He left the room and gently closed the door behind him, muffling Valerie's sobs as he did so, reminiscent of how he had muffled Valerie's screams in the holding cell the day before, and feeling the same dreadful concern, but this time about Nick's fate. He walked as briskly as he could to the holding cell, hoping against all hope that Stephanie would be able to bring Nick back from the brink.

Chapter 19

Stephanie's natural inclination had been to pray for at least two hours before entering Nick's mind, but the Lord had other plans. She had only prayed for about five minutes when she strongly felt urgency from the Holy Spirit that she should go *now*.

So she did.

Nick was on his knees huddled in one corner of the small padded room, one lone hanging lamp dimly illuminating his corner of the room. Stephanie kept the room dark, a concession she made out of love for Nick, as his natural inclination was to prefer the darkness. But now it was time to come into the light.

God's presence leaked off her like a strong perfume, and Nick reacted like a man allergic to the smell, struggling against his straightjacket, determined to get free and flee the room lest the aroma of God's presence cause anaphylactic shock and endanger his life. But he was held tight.

She could smell the pungent odor of sweat in the air from her mom's earlier battle and knew the floor would soon be dripping with the sweat of both she and Nick, perspiration the closest thing to a bloodletting that either would face. This was a battle for the mind.

The lamp beamed a ray of hope over Nick, a silent physical witness to Jesus, the light of the world that lights every person who comes into the world. Nick's face and shoulders were slumped to the right, keeping his face out of the light, as if it were acid that might burn his face.

"Turn your face into the light!" Stephanie said.

Nick cursed and started to reposition his head as commanded, but then cursed again and slumped his face into the darkness.

Stephanie moved her wheelchair in closer. "In the name of Jesus, I command you demon to look into the light!"

Nick let out an inhuman wail and immediately shot straight up, pupils contracting to pinpricks in the glare. "Little sister gonna save me?" he taunted. He cursed again and spat in Stephanie's direction, now only several feet away, and landed a direct shot in the middle of her face. She felt the spit run down into her mouth. "You can't even wipe that off your face, you crippled fool! How you gonna save me?"

Stephanie focused her mind, and in the spirit, she saw a tube of light extend from her forehead and fasten above Nick's eyebrows. He squirmed. The end of the tunnel was blockaded in darkness.

"Sorry, Nick. I have to do this to help you."

She forcefully projected her consciousness down the tube and rammed the dark entrance to his mind, breaking through it like it was tissue paper. She heard Nick scream before she lost awareness of the outside world.

* * *

Stephanie found herself enveloped in total darkness. Her heart started to pound and she started to breathe rapidly, as she realized that she had no conscious psychic link to her physical body in the natural world. This had never happened before. She had always maintained awareness and connection in every exorcism she had ever done before, could even talk with people on the outside. Now she felt so totally alone. And cold. Something wasn't right. She wanted to break the connection and flee Nick's mind, but love for her brother kept her still as a statue.

She silently prayed for the Lord's direction and felt His strong presence, as He told not to fear and that she was free to leave anytime. But the Spirit also warned her to proceed with extreme caution if she chose to stay, because her experience would be different than any she had ever had before.

That sealed her decision. As long as she still felt the Lord's strength and direction, she would stay for Nick's sake and see this through to the end. She decided to exercise her authority in Christ to conform Nick's mind to her command.

"Light fill this space!" she said, and light flickered around her slowly, like a reluctant fluorescent light at startup, before it suddenly blazed forth. She felt uncomfortable with the time it took for her command to affect her surroundings, wondering if the hesitancy was a premonition to expect more of her powers to be muted.

Stephanie found herself in a fun-house of mirrors that immediately made her think of a childhood memory, a time at the country fair. She and Nick had entered a fun-house of mirrors but Nick had disappeared from her sight. When she had rounded the corner, Nick had yelled, "Boo!", and scared her silly. This looked like the exact same fun-house.

They had both had a good laugh then. But this was no laughing matter.

"Little sister come out to play?" a voice said, as if over a loudspeaker, deeper than Nick's normal voice but still recognizable as his own. "Remember what happened that day? Come around the corner and let big brother give you a scare."

Not this time, she thought, as she stared at her reflection in the mirrors. She wore a white warrior's uniform, cutoff at the shoulders but with a deep V neck, a one piece suit that crisscrossed at her stomach, leaving her belly button exposed, and finishing in flowing miniskirt about midway to her knees. Her flame red hair reached to her shoulders and flowed freely down the sides and back. Her shoulders were broad and thick muscles rippled around her entire skeletal structure.

"Shield and sword appear," she said and slowly her requested weapons materialized, solid metal but lightweight shield appearing in her left arm, and long broad sword appearing in her right hand. Again she felt uncomfortable with the delay. Perhaps if she concentrated more.

She focused her mind harder this time and said, "Muscles increase!" Instantly her reflection seemed to puff up, especially her biceps and leg muscles seeming to double in size. That was better, she thought, realizing muscles were irrelevant anyway, for everything she saw was a mentally projected illusion. The battle was for the mind, and that's where her strength was.

She commanded the fun-house mirror illusion to disappear but it would not. She focused harder and commanded again for the fun-house to disappear in the name of Jesus but nothing happened. This did not bode well at all.

"Little sister having trouble?" Nick said. "You don't give orders here in my world! Leave while you still can."

"That's not going to happen, Nick. I'm going to free you whether you like it or not. I love you with the love of the Son of God."

"You mean the one and only Son of God?" Nick said. "Jesus is not so unique, you know. I'm already one of the *sons of God*. What do I need Him for?"

"No you're not. Sons of God is a phrase used in the Bible to refer to angels, spirit beings, not humans. You're a human being. You're my brother. I love you and I've come to take you home."

"Little sister thinks she's so smart, but she doesn't even know her theology. Stro-kar has taught me many things since we've become so intimately acquainted. Did you know the phrase *sons of*

God appears in numerous places in both the old and new testaments and is used to refer to both angels and humans?"

Stephanie felt a chill go down her spine, as she tightened her grip on her shield and sword and took up a fighting stance. She didn't understand what Nick was trying to say, but something began to stir deep down inside her, a primal fear she had never felt before.

She pushed the thought away and slowly moved towards the corner, knowing Nick was around the bend but not knowing what to expect, pushing back any apprehension by powering up her mind with the idea that she was a lion stalking her prey. Her faith surged a bit and she started to glow. But she already knew this encounter was going to be different, her powers not being totally up to par, not knowing why but trusting the Lord's leading anyway. Perhaps she was just exhausted from the recent battle to free her mother.

She knew Nick was probably monitoring her thoughts, so she broadcast an image of herself moving slowly and methodically down the long corridor of mirrors and locked this image in her surface mind, while hiding her true intent. Then she ran down the corridor and quickly rounded the corner, hoping to take Nick by surprise.

She saw a blur of red and white before she felt a strong furry arm blast her face. She was hurled several feet away and landed on her back.

A creature stood before her with the head, beak and wings of an eagle, the body of a lion, and the tail of a scorpion. It stood at least eight feet tall on its hind legs and had red fur covering its entire body, except for hands and feet which were covered in white fur, and its fingers and toes ended in sharp talons.

The creature lumbered a few feet towards Stephanie and spoke with Nick's voice. "You think you're so smart. You think you're saved? You're no better than me. If I'm going to hell, then I'm taking you with me."

They were on a round slice of land, about a twenty foot perimeter on all sides. The patch of dirt was floating on an ocean of molten lava, which gurgled and made popping noises. A smell of something like sulfur and rotten eggs wafted through the air. The fun-house she had perceived just a moment before was nowhere in sight and the sky was a light pink, peppered with only an occasional white cloud.

Stephanie rose from the ground, sword and shield still tightly gripped in her hands, fighting the urge to run again, primal fear pulsating up her spine and assaulting her mind. She had never felt this way in any battle before, some sort of power in Nick's words that weakened her.

She steeled her will and got ready to charge. This part she was familiar with, fighting the demons into submission in whatever form they took. She couldn't kill them, but then neither could they kill her. It was more a battle of wills that manifested in this thought realm as a physical fight.

"You're going to be sorely disappointed," she said to Nick, but more addressing the demon. "You're leaving my brother's mind one way or another."

The Lord's Holy Spirit had always been with her in mighty power. She had never failed before and she wasn't about to start today, not with Nick's eternal life in the balance. Her plan was always to inflict enough pain that the demons were forced to eventually accept defeat and vacate the victim's mind. Stamina was the key, as the longer she battled, the more God's power flowed through her body and the stronger she became. How and why it worked that way, she didn't totally understand. It was a paradox, sort of like fasting, in that the longer one deprived oneself of food and should be getting weaker, the more spiritual power they would attain. The longer she fought, the more spiritual power flowed through her. Victory was simply a matter of time.

Nick cackled, and his eyes flared red. "I know you're afraid like you've never been before. You have to learn how to use the fear to your advantage, let the hate and rage well up and focus it towards God, convert it into raw power, strong enough to destroy even God Himself. Stro-kar showed me how. Come, let me teach you."

"That's the demon talking," Stephanie said. "You're deluded. There's no way you can destroy God. You don't have the power."

"Really? Let me show it to you. There is no forgiveness for the *sons of God*, the angels who rebelled! You're an evil angel and you're going to burn in hell forever!"

Stephanie fell to her knees and started to gasp. "No…I'm a human, a child of God, forgiven by the blood of Christ."

"All humans existed as angels before they ever came to earth! You still sin everyday just like everybody else. That makes you no better than even the devils. You're an imperfect fallen angel, and all imperfection must burn in hell forever!"

Stephanie grunted but started to rise to her feet. "I'm not perfect, but God doesn't expect perfection, just a repentant and contrite heart, and to do your best not to sin."

"No! He expects sinless perfection. Matthew 5:48 'Be ye therefore perfect, even as your Father in heaven is perfect.' You fail everyday loser. You're an evil spirit being and you're going straight to hell!"

She felt as though Nick's words were a hammer that just cracked her on top of her head, and she fell to her knees again. His words and thoughts were being pushed into her mind against her will, something she had never experienced in battle before. She realized he was even using her revered translation against her, the King James version, much like she had similarly used it against him as kids when they had had fights about religion. But she had never had power to affect him like this.

"You're a liar," she said weakly. "Humans and angels are an entirely different order of creation."

"No, stupid, truth is you are simply an evil spirit being living a human experience! You betray Him everyday by sinning, you Judas. Devils have no forgiveness. Burn in hell!"

Stephanie's mind fogged and she started to loose touch with her surroundings. "There is no forgiveness for devils," she said hypnotically and started to sob. "I have no forgiveness?"

Nick said, "Job 1:6 'Now there was a day when the *sons of God* came to present themselves before the Lord, and Satan came also among them,' and Job 2:1 'Again there was a day when the *sons of God* came to present themselves before the Lord, and Satan came also among them to present himself before the Lord.'"

It was true, she thought. God's word was clearly referring to angels in the book of Job. The New Testament used this phrase often in reference to humans. Humans and angels *must* be one and the same. Her sins were so many, each day, so true…she was far from perfect. Then she must be a fallen angel, destined for hell. She began to perspire heavily, as a confused mixture of emotions assaulted her mind, fear…guilt… remorse…condemnation…

Stephanie's conscience started to burn, her mind on fire. Panic stricken, she instinctively thought to call on the Lord for aid but she was suddenly terrified of Jesus, a feeling she had never felt before. She needed His help but couldn't ask for it.

Instead, she decided that her memory must be failing her. The phrase in the New Testament must be *sons of Man*, referring to humans. She was human and humans could always repent and seek forgiveness. She didn't have to be perfectly obedient like angels, one little slip up sending her to hell forever. Encouraged, she began to stand up.

"Wrong again!" Nick said. "New Testament quote John 1:12 'But as many as received him, to them gave he power to become *sons of God!*'" Stephanie fell her knees again, gasping, dimly aware that Nick was using her thoughts against her, but powerless to defend herself against his quotations that seared her mind like a hot iron.

"Romans 8:14 'For as many as are led by the Spirit of God, they are the *sons of God*,'" Nick said. "The Spirit has left you little sister. You are NOT being led by the Spirit of God because you are a devil, doomed to eternal hellfire."

She clutched her stomach, feeling an ulcer-like pain.

"Romans 8:19 'For the earnest expectation of the creature waiteth for the manifestation of the *sons of God*.'"

Her esophagus burned and a taste like bile formed in her mouth.

"Philippians 2:15 'That ye may be blameless and harmless, the *sons of God*, without rebuke…'"

She threw up a brownish-yellow liquid.

"John 3:1 'Behold, what manner of love the Father hath bestowed upon us, that we should be called the *sons of God*.'"

Suddenly, the Holy Spirit pushed through the fog in her mind and encouraged her by simply reminding her that not all angels were destined for hell and that she needed to trust Him completely.

"John 3:2 'Beloved, now are we the *sons of God…*'"

She felt only mild warmth in her cheeks this time and stood up stiffly. Then the Holy Spirit began popping scripture verses into her mind. "Even if what you say is true, I'm not a devil anymore. At the core, I'm a changed spirit, Christ has renewed me! 2 Corinthians 6:18 promises that God will be a Father to his people, and His people will be as sons and daughters. I'm a forgiven daughter of

God! Psalm 23:4: 'Yea, though I walk through the valley of the shadow of death, I will FEAR NO EVIL!'"

Her faith surged, as her strength returned and she started to shine. "Fear is of the devil. I won't let you put it on me anymore. Timothy 1:7 'For God hath not given us the spirit of fear, but of power, and of love, and of a sound mind.' So stick that in your pipe and smoke it, demon!"

She ran forward and swiped across Nick's chest with her sword before his huge clawed hand slashed her face. She was flung to the ground, blood flowing from huge gashes on her face. The creature roared and stepped back, blood oozing out of the open cut.

"Stupid bitch," Nick said, as the cut closed like a zipper on a pair of pants and disappeared.

Blood from Stephanie's face stained the ground red, but she thought the wound away and new flesh closed in on her wound as quickly as Nick's chest had just healed itself. She rose from the ground just in time to put her full weight behind her shield and barricade herself against Nick's charge. He hit the shield full force and was thrown to the ground.

Nick got up, roared, and extended his razor sharp talons, like a cat opening its claws to slice some prey. He snarled and lunged forward, slashing the air with knives for hands, pummeling Stephanie's metal shield and making screeching noises that sounded like fingernails on a chalkboard. He knocked her back with each blow, and she tried to push back but he was too strong, a powerhouse reminiscent of the time she fought Satan's second in command, Daimagon, but she realized Nick's strength dwarfed even that evil being.

Stephanie held the shield high and blindly slashed back with her sword. She saw an opening and plunged the blade deep into the lion's chest, right where its heart should have been, pulled the blade out quickly and got splattered all over her body with gushing blood. While the thing was still stunned, she slashed horizontally across its eyes, cutting them both deeply and blinding it temporarily.

The creature wailed and roared and stepped back, flailing its arms in a defensive gesture. Within seconds, the creature's wounds had cleared and it charged again, stopping just a few feet in front of her and swiftly turning to one side. Stephanie only caught a glimpse of its scorpion tail before it swept her legs out from under her.

She landed on her back and the thing pounced, engulfing her in a blur of red and white fur, knocking her head about like a punching bag while it slashed at her face. She could feel warm blood spilling over her cheeks and gasped short breaths, kicking at Nick but unable to throw him off.

She could see nothing but blackness, and her eyes stung as if sulfuric acid had been thrown in them. As she covered her face with her arms and focused her mental energy on healing her eyes, Nick grabbed her by the hair and dragged her along the ground, gurgling sounds from the molten lava getting louder, a feeling of warmth getting stronger. Her vision cleared in time to see a huge fury white claw grab her by the throat and plunge her head over the side of the circular plot of land and deep into the molten lava.

Stephanie's faced burned and she opened her mouth to scream, only to swallow a mouthful of hot lava. Nick pulled her out of the hot viscous fluid and held her high above the ground by the neck, laughing. His grip slowly tightened like a vice and she could only inhale in short gasps. She had dropped her shield but still held her sword tightly, and used it now to plunge the doubled sided blade deep in his chest, sawing it back and forth rapidly until he dropped her.

Stephanie shouted a warrior's cry and flung all her strength into a forward charge, knocking them both clear across the patch of land and into the molten lava on the other side. The sensation of being blasted with a thousand flame throwers racked her body, but she dropped her weapon and held the creature tightly, as it flapped its massive wings and tried to propel itself from the lava.

"I'm not letting go until you leave his body," Stephanie said.

Its wings beat the air rapidly, wind pelting her body and cooling the fire somewhat, but she was determined to hold tight. Soon, they both started to rise straight up, slowly at first, then faster and faster. Nick viciously kicked with his hind legs, razor sharp talons slashing her arms repeatedly until they were severed at the elbow.

She dropped through the air, hurtling towards the molten lava below, as Nick laughed and started to fly away. She willed her arms to rematerialize and for wings of her own to spout from her back, mind focused by enough of an adrenaline rush to push aside the dampening effect of Nick's world and her thoughts immediately came to fruition. She flapped her massive wings and took off after Nick.

She pursued him across the sky, closing the distance with each mile, the bright yellow-orange molten ocean below seemingly endless, but as she closed the gap to within about one mile, she could see land rapidly approaching on the horizon. By the time she was only a few feet behind him, they were directly over the landmass and approaching a huge castle. Stephanie gave one last push of her massive wings and tackled Nick to the ground.

They tumbled and rolled on the hard unforgiving dirt, littered with small sharp pebbles that ripped at her skin with each turn. Nick stopped their forward rolls by steadying himself with his scorpion tail, then quickly plunged its spiked end into Stephanie's abdomen, instantly sending its fiery venom throughout her every blood vessel and racking her body with pain.

"Let's see how brave you are in my castle," Nick said. "I have lots of friends."

While she steadied herself and willed the venom to clear from her body, Nick flew over the castle wall. She created a new shield and sword, took a deep breath, and flew over the wall after him. She landed in the middle of the outer court and found herself surrounded by dozens of Nick creatures.

"Little sister gonna have some real trouble now," the creatures said together in perfect harmony. "You gonna burn in hell forever."

At Nicks' words, she felt the blood rush from her face and she almost fainted, but the Lord spoke strongly to her spirit that she was His forevermore and she stood firm.

"That's Stro-kar talking," Stephanie said. "I'm not afraid of anything you try to throw at me. The Lord is with me and we will prevail! Take your best shot, demon!" She tightened her grip on her sword and shield.

The Nicks laughed and said together, "Stupid girl doesn't even know yet that Stro-kar is already gone."

Stephanie reflexively reached out with her mind to search Nick's heart, an instinct within her wanting to confirm Nick's statement was a lie…but she sensed no presence other than her and Nick. She had sensed such a malevolent evil when she had first entered Nick's mind that she had just assumed all along it was the demon, but it was true that only she and Nick were here. Confusion overwhelmed her, as she realized they shouldn't even be fighting then, just repent and invite the Holy Spirit in and they could all go home.

Then the Lord revealed to her the real reason she was having so much trouble handling Nick, and ordered her to flee Nick's mind immediately.

"Oh, no, Nick…no, no, no…"

"Stupid little sister finally understands."

"No, Lord. Let me stay. I volunteer to do whatever it takes."

The Holy Spirit commanded her more forcefully this time to leave. She pushed back her emotions and obeyed.

* * *

Stephanie rolled her wheelchair out of the room. She wailed loudly and found that her friends, Tim and Rhonda, were already waiting outside for her. They tried to ask her what was wrong and console her, but she couldn't catch her breath.

She saw her father, Jeff, walking towards her. Then he started to run. She continued to wail and as he neared, all she could say was, "Oh, dad, it's horrible," and sobbed some more.

"What!?" Jeff said and stopped directly in front of her. "What is it? What's the matter? What happened?"

"I'm sorry, dad. I'm so sorry. There's nothing I can do for Nick."

"What are you talking about? You've never failed before. Did someone tell you about Jarius' assault tomorrow? Don't worry. If we have to, we can take you both with us and continue to work on Nick far away from the complex."

"No, you don't understand! Nick totally gave his mind over and fully integrated with evil! He's committed the unpardonable sin, blasphemed the Holy Spirit! He's branded with the mark of the beast now, doomed to hell forever. Nothing can be done to change his destiny."

Jeff's face went white. Then he fainted and collapsed in front of Stephanie's wheelchair.

Chapter 20

Jeff opened his eyes and immediately felt a splitting ache racing up the back of his skull. He was in his room lying on his bed. His wife lay beside him, apparently sleeping, but the doctor was hanging over her head and peering into her eyes with a light.

"You cracked your head when you fainted," Stephanie said. She was at the foot of his bed.

"You have a bump but it isn't anything serious," the doctor said. "We can get you a Tylenol if you like."

"I think I'll be alright," Jeff said. "What's wrong with Valerie?"

The doctor pocketed his light. "It seems she is in a coma. I'm not sure why. All we can do wait."

"She didn't react well to the news about one of our children dying," Jeff said. "Maybe that had something to do with it."

Stephanie said, "Then if she wakes up, I'd hate to see how she'll react to what I told you about Nick."

"If you'll excuse me," the doctor said, "I have some other people to attend to." He left the room.

"Are you positive there is nothing you can do for Nick?"

"Sorry, dad. I don't think so. But I asked Lawrence if I could have a private meeting with him as soon as you woke up. Maybe he can give me further direction. Why don't you stay here and look after mom and I'll go talk to Lawrence?"

Jeff agreed, and Stephanie left the room, heading towards Lawrence's office. Along the way, she thought about Nick's unusual theology and how he was able to use it to torment her mind. His position had felt so believable at the time. He made her feel like she was a demon doomed to hell. Although they only fought over the *sons of God* phrase, she could sense many other scriptures he was just waiting to use against her, and she could also sense his entire theological system. He had a way of looking at the scriptures that she had never considered before, and it all made sense to her at the moment. She couldn't refute him. If the Lord hadn't helped her, she didn't know what would have happened. She was eager to see what Lawrence had to say about it all.

She approached Lawrence's office and saw him sitting behind his desk, door open as usual. He smiled and invited her in, then rose to close the door behind them. "I don't want us to be disturbed. The Lord tells me you have many questions. Often, He gives me answers before people even ask, but for some reason, He's given me nothing more on you. I'm very curious what this is all about."

There were two chairs in front of Lawrence's desk, and he moved one aside to make room for Stephanie's wheelchair. She whirred to a stop in front of Lawrence's desk, and he sat down across from her, asking her to fire away.

"I left Nick's mind after I strongly heard God tell me Nick had blasphemed the Holy Spirit. Is it possible God can yet save him or is he truly lost forever?"

"Is it possible for a camel to pass through the eye of a needle?" Lawrence asked.

Stephanie shook her head.

"And yet after Jesus said it was easier for this to happen than for a rich man to enter the Kingdom of God, he also said with God all things are possible."

"So there's hope? Even though I clearly heard God say Nick had committed this terrible sin?"

Lawrence smiled. "There's always hope with God. All sin is

terrible. As humans, we tend to categorize some sins as worse than others, but to God it's all the same. The Lord's standard of perfect obedience to Him always, motivated only by a pure heart of love towards Him, rather than thoughts of rewards or fear of hell, leaves us all condemned without the forgiveness and mercy Christ's death bought us on the cross. All fall short of God's ideal for us. James 2:10 says if you've committed one sin, it's the same as if you have committed all sins. I have to believe that includes blasphemy of the Spirit, which we've all done to some degree or another, but it seems Nick has gone over to such an extreme that God has given up on him. While there's always room for hope, in the final analysis, your brother's salvation is just between him and God. They have to work it out together, but if Nick's not willing to repent of his sins and accept Jesus as savior and Lord, then God has no choice but to eventually judge him after death and throw him in hell. Most everyone likes the savior part, mercy and forgiveness, but Lord is another matter. Lord implies obedience, which Nick has become unwilling to do."

"But I don't think Nick is even capable. He's not even demon possessed anymore, but he acts exactly as if he were. Stro-kar has corrupted his mind to such a degree that he seems to think he existed as a fallen angel before coming to earth and since all fallen angels are doomed to hell, he's given up hope."

"Ah, then that explains it. Whether or not one goes to heaven depends only on one's relationship with Christ. If Nick believes he is an actual incarnation of a devil, then he will never come to Christ for forgiveness of sins because on that point he is right, the devil and all his fallen rebel angels are going to hell. There is no hope for them."

Stephanie sighed. "I hope that's not the case. I know the idea of preexistence seems to go against what Christianity has historically taught, but I was intimately connected to his mind. I understand why he thinks so. There is certain logic to it all. If there is any hope that I can do anything for him, I need to get your input on it all."

"Well tell me more, and we'll see what we can come up with together."

Stephanie nodded and started. "The beginning of the gospel of John is clear that Christ existed as a spirit being, God Himself, before coming to earth. Correct?"

"Yes."

"Then if God can become human, why is it so impossible to believe that all people might have lived as spirits before becoming human?"

"Well, Christ was a special exception. All other people come into existence at the moment of conception. He is God and has always existed. All other beings were created by Him. Let's not forget, that Jesus was born of a virgin too and the rest of us aren't. We can't compare ourselves too much to Jesus."

"Yes, the prophecy in Isaiah says a virgin shall conceive a child as a *sign*. But perhaps it was just that, a supernatural miracle done simply as a sign. How do we know that God didn't just supernaturally take genetic material from both Mary and Joseph and combine it to make a fetus, and then place the pure essence of the spirit being of Jesus inside the fetus and plant it in Mary's womb? Having a spirit that was untainted by sin, Jesus was able to perfectly struggle against His flesh and never sin even once. The rest of us, God just lets the natural conception process take place, but He still places the essence of spirit beings into fetuses as His special act of incarnating His spirit children, specifically fallen angels, into flesh existence. Of course, our spirits start life corrupted and we sin from birth. That's why you never have to teach kids to do bad things like lie, cheat, steal, or disobey their parents. The struggle comes in trying to teach children to be good. We naturally do wrong from birth. We are born with a sin nature and now we know exactly where it comes from. Now it makes more sense why Jeremiah 17:9 says the human heart is deceitful above all things, and desperately wicked."

"Pure speculation. We'll never know for sure the answer to these kinds of things until we get to heaven."

"Maybe, but this is what Nick believes. I got this directly from his mind, and he believes he received this as special revelation from Stro-kar, a mystery that has been kept from humanity until the very last days."

"He's foolish to believe anything demons say. They are pure liars."

"Granted. On the other hand, if we're to have any hope of helping him, I think we have to understand how he thinks and why. Only then can we shine the light of truth on his errors and help lead him to Jesus."

Lawrence sighed. "Ok, continue."

"The only two types of spirit beings we know exist are those on God's side, Holy angels, and those on the devil's, fallen angels. If you had to choose, which type of spirit being do humans most closely resemble in character?"

"I suppose fallen angels, seeing as how all people sin. But while nobody's perfect, most people aren't as wicked as demons unless possessed, so I just can't agree that's who we were in the past."

"That's because God works with people on the human plane of existence by His Spirit to restrain their evil and purify their characters. Even so, history is replete with examples of many people who acted as cruel and as wicked as any devil, even without apparent possession. However, God is in the business of transforming enemies into friends. He doesn't work with fallen angels on the spirit plane, only once they enter human existence, where as part of their punishment and learning process, they must struggle to find Him, repent, and overcome sin.

"That's why demons in the spirit realm hate humans so much. They know the stakes and what is going on, and they hate that some people are making good on their one life's chance at reconciliation with God the Father. They hate that God has made the way so difficult, many are called but few chosen, narrow is the way to life etc…that kind of thing. Most demons have messed up their human life, many more have yet to get a chance to live a human life, but know they will probably fail. The demons are angry that God will not simply accept them as they are, but that He demands that they learn obedience through suffering on the human plane of existence, and demonstrate it throughout a lifetime of learning to walk in faith, trust, love and obedience, the thing they hate most and couldn't do on the spirit plane. But then even Hebrews 5:8 says Jesus had to learn obedience through suffering. Why should demons be exempt from learning obedience in the same way?"

"I don't agree. God says he will forgive humans but not demons. That's just the way it is."

"I'm just telling you what I got from Nick. He's convinced all humans existed as fallen angels before the world was created. As angels, we had no doubt of God's existence, power, and what He desired of us. But it still wasn't enough and we rebelled with Satan in the angelic rebellion anyway. This is why God is so mysterious and hides Himself and makes things so difficult, because seeing God and knowing exactly His will obviously didn't make a difference and disobedience still occurred anyway. So now we must suffer on earth and struggle to figure these things out and overcome, while God hides Himself, but works with us subtly by His Spirit. Yet God makes a way back home for those who are sincere. This is also why He lets demons attack our minds and thoughts, deceive us, and even possess us because we must learn to overcome the lies of our fellow evil spirit brethren, lies about God's character and ways that we obviously believed or we wouldn't have followed Lucifer, who became Satan the devil. We all chose to become 'devils' before we ever came to earth."

"I have no memory of such things, so it's hard to comment. Again, speculation."

"Just because you have no memory of this, does not mean it's not true. Do you have a memory of, say, being two or three years old?"

"Of course not."

"Exactly, you have no memories of that time but you know you were alive and experiencing life. In a similar way, you were alive and experiencing life as a fallen spirit being before ever coming to earth, even though you have no conscious memory of it, anymore than you have conscious memories of being very young. But the realities of that existence are buried deep in your soul, the same as our childhood experiences form our characters at a young age."

"The unveiling showed us the deceptive power of spin. You can make up nice sounding arguments to 'prove' just about anything. Show me in the scriptures that this is so and I'll believe it."

"Ok, how about the Tower of Babel story where God instantly confused the unified language of men at that time to prevent them from building the tower? Point being, if God can instantly alter people's brains so they start talking in different languages, then for sure He has the ability to suppress the memories of our preexistence as spirit beings. Or how about the example in the book of Daniel of how Nebuchadnezzar lost his mind for seven years? Or Peter being led out of prison by an angel and the guards didn't even see it, or the visions people received in the Bible? All examples of alteration of mental perception."

"I'd like specific scriptures that say humans are angels."

"Ok, when I was battling Nick he repeatedly hit me with this phrase *sons of God*, which occurs in the Old Testament and refers to angels. Right?"

Lawrence nodded.

"Well, the same phrase occurs numerous times in the New Testament and refers to humans. Proof we are one and the same."

"Not necessarily. It could be that *sons of God* can refer to both humans and angels. To tell which, you would need to consider the context of the passages, and perhaps even special revelation from the Holy Spirit."

"Maybe. Or perhaps it's another clue God is giving us that humans and angels are the same. How about Luke 20:36 where it talks about resurrected humans being equal to the angels, not greater or lesser, but equal, showing we are one and the same type of being."

Lawrence grabbed an NIV Bible to look up the reference, and Stephanie asked that he use the King James, which was her favorite and most accurate in her opinion. Lawrence looked up the reference in the King James, and read it. "Good memory. How did you remember that passage so precisely?"

"I have many passages burned into my memory that Nick was waiting to use on me. He was relentless in attacking me with this concept until the Lord stepped in."

Lawrence nodded. "Ok it does talk about being equal, but that could just be referring to the fact that humans are destined to be resurrected and transformed into spirit children of God, a similar essence of spirit, so equal in a sense, but humans are a higher form of life than angels, and destined to be greater."

"Ok, now I'll say the same thing to you. Prove that to me from the scriptures."

Lawrence turned some pages in his Bible and said, "1 Corinthians 6:3 says we will judge angels. So if we're destined to rule over angels, that means we will one day be greater than them, full sons and daughters of God, a higher type spirit being than angels."

"Not necessarily. You are our leader and you 'rule' over all the people in this complex, but that doesn't make you a higher level being. You are just a human being like the rest of us. Position doesn't necessarily denote superiority."

"Good point, Stephanie. Ok, how about in Genesis where it says that humans were made in God's image, proving we are His master creation, destined for greatness, to be like our Father in heaven. Angels were never made in God's image."

"Angels are recorded in the Bible to have arms, legs, etc…if that's what you mean by image. But to be made in God's image has more to do with having sentient consciousness, to be able to think, rationalize, make moral choices etc... The angels can do these things too. Revelation 22:9 indicates John about to bow down to an angel and worship him, but the angel refused and said John should only worship God, saying he was a fellow servant of God, just like John. Humans and angels are both servants of God, just as they are both called *sons of God*, indicating sameness."

"I can see you believe what Nick impressed in your mind but—"

"I'm not saying I believe it all, but I can't dismiss everything I got from Nick either. How about this one? Jesus says we're supposed to love our enemies and forgive our enemies, right?"

Lawrence nodded.

"Well, don't you think God loves his enemies too, the devil and his fallen angels? Though enemies, Satan and his demons are also God's children, evil though they may be. It's not logical for God to expect something from humans that He is unwilling to do Himself.

The Lord must love and forgive His enemies too. Don't you think God would make a way for even the devil to be saved if Satan really wanted it?"

Lawrence raised his eyebrows. "Ah...well maybe He does love His enemies, maybe even forgives them on some level, but that doesn't mean they can be restored. The Bible is clear that the devil and his angels are going to hell. Christ died for humans, not angels."

"Not all demons go to hell. Some fully avail themselves of the probationary chance God gives them to live a human experience, repent, and change their ways. That would be you and me and all the rest of the believers in the world. And yes, Christ technically died for humans only, but now we understand that really He died for His fellow spirit brethren, the demons, and even the devil."

"That's crazy. The Bible is clear. The devil is going to the lake of fire."

"Yes, but that's because of his choice. To show fairness, God even gave Satan a human life and worked with him as much as any person, but, of course, the devil rejected Christ. Maybe Satan lived the life of Hitler or something. I didn't get a lot of specific details from Nick's mind, other than the general concept and many scriptures to back it up."

"If your brother is so messed up that he believes this stuff, I don't hold out much hope anything can be done for him. We don't understand all the details of the spirit war, but when we get to heaven, it will all make sense and we will agree God has always been perfectly loving, just, and fair."

"I don't doubt God's character, but I'm trying to understand how Nick thinks, trying to find some way to turn his theology to our advantage. For instance, Nick is convinced he's totally messed up his chances, and his fate is sealed. He also doesn't think the Holy angels need to come to earth and work out their salvation because they never rebelled, as this life is only for the devils. Maybe there is some way I could convince him Holy angels come to earth too, and that he is one of those? The idea might encourage him enough that he can just put his faith and trust in the Lord and accept God's love, grace, and mercy."

"It's a long shot, but I'll support your decision if you want to go back in and try again."

"I think I need to find some way to restore a sense of balance in him. In one sense, his ideas sort of balance both God's love and wrath for His enemies, a wonderful possibility to consider God loves His enemies enough to give them a chance to change their ways on the human plane of existence and avoid judgment. But a terrible truth that even the devils won't be able to complain on judgment day that God hasn't been fair. We all get one human life to get it right, as Hebrews 9:27 says it is appointed unto men once to die, but after this the judgment, where we either go to heaven and get reinstated, or go to hell as the fallen angels we are. Nick figures he's already had his judgment day and failed miserably, his entire human existence just an intermediary probationary state, a one time chance to change his destiny that he's messed up."

"I'm still not buying this spin. What about ruling and reigning with Christ in the millennium? Mere angels don't rule with Christ forever. The true children of God rule with Christ."

"It's not forever. Yes, we assist Christ during the millennium, a time when the final batch of devils incarnate and get their chance, proving even under ideal conditions most won't change, as Revelation records another rebellion occurs at the end of the 1000 years. But not even Christ rules forever. This position is just a temporary responsibility, as we lusted after God's power and position in the preexistence, so the Lord is going to give us a taste of how difficult it is to lovingly rule over hardhearted individuals.

Even 1 Corinthians 15:28 says after all things have been subdued under Christ, then Jesus Himself will step down and become subject to the Father, so that God may be all in all. Jesus will just be our elder brother then, and we will answer directly to the Father. Jesus won't need to rule anymore, and neither will we, as all those who are willing will have become perfectly obedient immortal spirit children of God our Father. A wonderful future, but then there will still be hell for those rebel angels who refuse to change, which are many. Bible says broad is the road to destruction, many are on it, and many are called but few chosen. At the end of the millennium, everyone's fate is finalized, either heaven or hell forever, all evil spirits having been given their one life to get it right. At least now we fully understand why those destined for hell get exactly what they deserve. I mean they saw God and everything and it made no difference, rebelling anyway!"

"I can see why a demon influenced mind might buy into what you are saying, but it's just not scriptural."

"Look at it this way. You say the vast majority of humans don't know Jesus and are going to hell to burn forever. They are eternal spirit beings and cannot die."

"Yes."

"But you said earlier that people come into existence at the moment of conception. How can that be if we are eternal spirit beings, who by definition are outside of time, being eternal, and therefore must have existed before becoming human?"

Lawrence paused and frowned. "Well, there are certain mysteries. I don't pretend to know everything."

"You also say the devil and all demons are doomed to burn forever in hell. They are likewise eternal spirit beings and cannot die."

"Yes."

"So what's the difference then? Even if you don't believe what

I'm saying is true, humans and demons might as well be the same, as the end result of rebellion is the same."

"The difference is God is willing to forgive repentant humans that change their ways, not fallen angels."

"You've proved my point. The human plane of existence is where change must occur. But in many respects, that's the only distinction between humans and fallen angels. In a way, what Nick believes isn't much different than our traditional understanding of things, just a little deeper understanding of the back-story. I've always wondered how it could be fair that an unrepentant person could be sentenced to hell forever for only seventy or eighty years of sinning. But we really are eternal beings that can't die, and prove our willingness or unwillingness to change in this life. Everybody in heaven, and even everybody in hell, will know that God has done everything He could to redeem His creation, even sending His Son to die for our sins. Everyone, redeemed and unredeemed, will then acknowledge that God has no other choice but to execute final judgment, as even millions of more lifetimes would make no difference, everyone having proven their heart and sealed their fate one way or another." Stephanie paused. "Maybe Nick did influence me too much. I'm willing to consider more of your viewpoint. There are many more scriptures I could cite for discussion. Nick had a lot of them."

Lawrence shook his head. "We could go back and forth on this all day. The devil is good at spinning lies and I think he's just really messed up your brother. Satan probably wanted to deceive Nick with these lies so that your brother would despair enough to stay committed to a rebellious and hateful attitude towards God. Without direct revelation from God on this matter, I will never agree."

"Why not ask Him then?"

Lawrence nodded his head, closed his eyes and bowed his head for a few minutes. When he opened them, he said, “I asked the Lord for the truth about this issue. I’m not sure I like the answer I got.”

“What did He say?”

“He said, ‘It is not for you to know the times of the seasons, which the Father has put in His own power.’”

“What does that mean?”

“I understand what He is saying. I’ve learned how to interpret His way of talking by using reference, analogy, metaphors etc... This is the same response He gave in the book of Acts, after His resurrection, when the disciples were asking when He would restore the Kingdom of Israel. Basically, He’s telling us it’s none of our business and He’s not going to answer the question.”

“Does that mean I’m right?”

“Not necessarily. I’ve learned not to jump to conclusions when He says stuff like this, rather just take a wait and see attitude. Obviously, there is much we don’t fully understand about the spirit war, what happened before humans came along, and all God’s mysterious dealings with His creation. And He’s just not going to tell us right now. Faith wouldn’t be real if we understood everything.”

“In Nick’s case, I got the deep sense that he thinks God is vindicating His justice to His loyal angels, as not even Nick argues now that he deserves hell. He has come to fully understand and agree with God that he deserves his fate, and he doesn’t think he can avoid it.”

“Yes, predestination. People have debated that for centuries, but the mystery is we have a choice too. I don’t believe things are set in stone, not for humans anyway.”

“Nick doesn’t believe this. He thinks he’s crossed the line and God will never forgive him. He’s full of hatred, rebellion, unforgiveness, and bitterness, towards God. He's jealous and angry that God loves others but not him."

"God loves all His creation but there is such a thing as crossing the line. Maybe he *has* done that. He seems to have developed exactly the attitude one acquires when they've committed blasphemy of the Spirit. This sin is more of an extreme hardness of heart and total rebellion and hatred towards God, and total unwillingness or ability to love and obey Him. Jesus warned the Pharisees of His day that they were in danger of going to hell because of this attitude, since they accused Him of casting out demons by the power of the devil, obviously not true and they knew better, but they were so full of pride they'd rather burn in hell forever than submit to the truth."

"What takes a person to that point?"

"I guess in many ways the issue is the same for humans and demons. Between free will beings, somebody has to have the final say on things otherwise there would be anarchy. God insists on being the one to ultimately define what is right and wrong, and He expects obedience as a minimum standard. But this has to come from the heart because one loves God. He is the Creator after all and He says love for Him is demonstrated through obedience to His commands, a reflection of who He is. If one wants a relationship with Christ, one has to care how He feels about things. Same goes for a relationship with anybody. If I treated you like crap, we wouldn't be able to have any kind of relationship now would we?"

Stephanie shook her head.

"If God is hurt by your desire to lie, steal, hate, cheat, murder, commit sexual sins like adultery and homosexuality etc…then you shouldn't do those things, assuming you want a love relationship with your Creator that is. God loves all of us, even when we are deeply trapped in sin, be it sexual sin or any other type. It's all the same to God, but He insists we repent and commit to changing our ways if we want to be forgiven. Since we are incapable of loving God fully like we should, He tries to regenerate our heart by His Holy Spirit and show us how to love, but we still have a choice to make. The bottom line is, Nick has totally rejected this convicting work of the Holy Spirit and adopted the fallen angels' definition of freedom, do whatever you want and submit to others only as made to do so by force. Satan rules his demons by pure power, as I believe he could single-handedly defeat them all if he had to.

"Jesus' way is voluntary submission and obedience because you care about God's feelings and desire to love the Lord back in gratitude for dying for your sins, in the case of humans, or simply for giving you life, in the case of angels. Any other motivation just isn't good enough. Nick has lost the ability to understand this, as he thinks like a demon and can't understand love. He thinks the reality of hell makes God no different than Satan, the threat of eternal fire making God just like Satan in a way, as Nick thinks God uses fear to try and force obedience, just like Satan. He's lost sight of the love, mercy, forgiveness, and restoration Christ offers too, and if he can't come to believe in that and submit to God in love, that is why he has no hope.

"We really are saved only by God's gift of grace, through Christ, but if you don't respond in love to this truth, you give power to Satan to corrupt your mind. However, when you accept Christ's regenerative work on your heart, acting out of love for your Creator eventually becomes natural, as the Holy Spirit helps us to love and obey God with a new heart, in a natural and instinctive way, beyond just legal surface-level interpretations of scripture. Even while demon possessed, God worked with Nick on some level but it seems he's totally gone over and may have no hope."

"Yeah, he just can't believe God loves him, or that Jesus would accept his repentance and efforts to try and obey Him," Stephanie said. "He can't receive the forgiveness and love in the right way, to the point that it actually motivates him to love God back and try to obey Him out of love and gratitude. I guess in the final analysis, that's how a person rejects Christ and chooses instead to send themselves to hell. God has already proven His love through Christ's death on the cross, and each person must individually choose to accept or reject that love, our choice shown out by our thoughts, words, actions, and lifestyle."

Just then, Stephanie heard Lawrence's office door quickly open and make a loud thud as it rebounded off the opposite wall. How rude, she thought. The least the person could have done was knock. This was a private meeting after all. She began to turn her wheelchair.

"Stephanie!" she heard her dad say and turned around to see him holding Valerie by the shoulders, her face an ashen grey but awake and alert. "God has given your mom a gift that might help Nick! But it's going to require you to become a stronger warrior than you ever thought possible."

Chapter 21

"I'm inside, mom," Stephanie said. "Are you there?"

Stephanie had just forcefully projected herself into Nick's mind again, and as before, now lost contact with the outside world. She knew her mom and dad were with her physical body in the small padded room, but she felt so alone again, just as before.

She found herself in a beautiful garden at dusk, but could still make out flowers of many shapes, sizes, and colors, in the setting sun. A confused but pleasant mixture of fruity aromas filled her nostrils. A large round stone was in the center of the garden, and she felt an instinct to go to it now, kneel before it, and pray.

I'm here, Stephanie, she felt her mom say in her spirit. She didn't hear any audible voice, but it was pretty clear, reminiscent of times when she would very clearly hear God speak to her in her heart on the outside world.

After Stephanie's mom and dad had burst into Lawrence's office, her mom had explained how she hadn't really been in a coma, rather a trance, in which she had gone to heaven and received instructions from God on how they could possibly help Nick. The Lord had given Valerie the gift of influencing and guiding a person's thoughts without their awareness and showed her how to use it.

"How can this help Nick?" Stephanie had asked, and her mother had explained that it was the ideal complement to Stephanie's gift. With it, the both of them could go back into Nick's mind, and hopefully reach him with the love of God. Her mother could only subtly manage the environment of Nick's mind though. Nick would still ultimately have greater control over what happened, but Valerie was sure she could exert enough influence to prevent Nick from overpowering Stephanie to the same degree he had last time.

Stephanie remembered how full of hate Nick had been in their last encounter, how she could feel it, and how it made him powerful enough that he could toss her around like a rag doll. He was brazen and totally unafraid of God, but he was somehow able to make her afraid of her Savior. But deep down, she knew he was afraid, since he considered himself a demon.

"If that's true," her dad had said concerning Nick's belief that he had lived before as a fallen angel, "then the 'Balazons' spoke some truth that day many years ago when I came home and challenged them." Stephanie recalled the day the whole family had sat around the conference room simulation in the VRT room and heard the "Balazons" say how humans were actually demons, metaphorically speaking, as Acin-om had put it.

Stephanie remembered how the "aliens" had implied all humans were "devils", citing the scriptures comparing Judas to a devil, and Jesus rebuking Peter by calling him the arch demon, Satan. Even if there were some truth to it all, she had no doubt Peter had finished his journey in life well and was now in heaven. She had to somehow get through to Nick that such an ending could be written for his life as well.

She had to find a way to break through Nick's fear. Even James 2:19 said that demons believe there is one God and tremble at His power, constantly aware of their impending judgment forever in hellfire, but they still don't obey the Lord. Nick had become just as intransigent as demons, but Stro-kar had taught him how to channel that fear into hate and pure evil, which gave him a sort of perverted strength. She had always had success before in other people's minds because the people themselves were resisting too on some level, but

Nick's mind and will were totally committed to resisting Stephanie and so could overpower her with guilt, fear, condemnation, twisting even her own thoughts to believe God didn't love her and that she was going to hell.

"What's happening, mom?" Stephanie said. "Where am I? Where is Nick?"

I can feel him approaching. Be strong. I sense the Lord wants you to kneel by the rock and pray.

She did as her mother asked, comforting to "feel" her mom talking to her in her spirit, but still adjusting to this odd form of communication. She wondered if she could communicate with her mom without words and decided to try it.

As she knelt beside the rock and began to pray, she thought a request to her mom, asking her to create a stream by the rock if she could hear Stephanie's thoughts. Almost immediately, a small stream appeared at the base of the rock and flowed down the garden path.

Stephanie felt comforted to know how close her mom was, and to have confirmation that her mother could indeed affect the surroundings. She hoped the two of them together would be enough to make some sort of difference with Nick, but neither of them had clear direction from the Lord as to what to do or what would transpire, other than to enter Nick's mind in childlike faith and trust the Lord's leading. However, God had told Stephanie to expect the toughest battle she had ever faced to date, warning her that she would have to become a stronger warrior than ever before.

As Stephanie knelt by the rock and began to pray, she started to quake and shudder, as a feeling of terror formed in the pit of her stomach and blasted up her esophagus. She coughed and spat up a brownish-yellow liquid. "Father," she prayed, shivering from fear, sensing Nick's quick approach and not knowing what to expect. "If there is any other way to help Nick, please do so and don't let me have to continue in this place. Nevertheless, I will stay here if it is Your will."

Being in agony, she prayed more earnestly, and drops of sweat mixed with blood fell from her face. A man appeared beside her wearing a white rob, and he had great white wings on his back like an angel. "Be strong, Stephanie," the man said and rested a hand on her shoulder. "Love Nick like the Lord loves him, and you may win his soul." Then the man faded and disappeared.

"Are you doing this, mom?" Stephanie asked. "What's happening to me?"

Trust in the Lord, Stephanie. I'm refocusing Nick's environment as the Lord directs. It's going to get worse before it gets better. Go talk to your sleeping friends.

Stephanie noticed three slumbering women about a stone's throw away and walked over to them. She roused them awake. "Could you not stay awake with me for just a little while?" she found herself saying, almost involuntarily. "Pray, or you might enter into temptation." She shook her head, slightly dazed and confused, feeling like she was an actress playing a familiar role, but not sure of her next line. She was losing herself in the scene, becoming a character, forgetting that it was all a mind projected illusion.

Stephanie heard marching feet and clanging metal near the entrance to the garden. She looked up and saw several dozen Nicks approaching. They all looked exactly the same, and they appeared as Nick normally did on the outside world, rather than the man-beast she had encountered last time. Some of the Nicks were dressed in soldiers' uniforms, wearing helmets, breastplates, and carrying shields and spears. One of the Nicks approached Stephanie and gave her a big hug and then kissed her on the cheek.

"Nick, do you betray the daughter of man with a kiss?" she said hazily, head in a fog.

One of her girlfriends, Petrella, leapt from her sleeping spot and swiped a sword at the Nick who had kissed Stephanie, chopping off his ear. Nick roared and covered his ear with his hand, which started to become a furry white claw, his body slowly changing into that of a lion.

Stephanie's fighting spirit was roused by Petrella's actions, and her mind cleared, fully brushing off the dampening effect of Nick's mind, resolving not to lose focus again. She instinctively reached out with her mind and formed fighters to help her. Legions of angels appeared with swords drawn, ready to fight at her command. Nick shook his head as though confused, then growled and slowly red fur began to appear on his body, and his head started forming into that of an eagle.

Stop what you are doing, Stephanie! This is not the kind of fight that is going to save Nick. I have him sedated. He's vaguely aware of what's happening, more like a dream state. If you wake him up, he'll become that beast thing again and you cannot defeat him in that form. You're going to have to fight God's way if you are to have any hope of reaching Nick.

"I've always fought God's way," Stephanie said. "I've always fought evil head-on with courage and honor, subduing evil in whatever form it manifests in one's mind."

Yes. But there is a higher way to fight. Turn the other cheek, let Nick hurt you.

"What?" Stephanie said, a bewildered look on her face. "That's never been my kind of calling, mom. Sometimes you have to fight. The Lord didn't sit still while the religious leaders of His day falsely accused Him of vile crap. He was a fighter, verbally lambasting His opponents. Revelations 12:7 says Michael and his angels fought against Satan. And the Holy angels fight at God's command! God's a fighter too, mom!" She started speaking more quickly, as her anger fueled her defensive rationalizations. "Sure we should turn the other cheek, but that just speaks to a restrained response to milder forms of evil, not an indication that Christians should never fight ever. Self-defense is justifiable. I'm not going to turn the other cheek if the violation is severe enough, like someone coming at me with a knife intent on killing me and—"

I agree sometimes it's necessary to fight, but you're only facing Nick this time, no demons. While in my trance, the Lord impressed upon me that the highest form of fighting is to suffer in love for those you love. When the time came to lay down His life, the Lord let the people kill Him. God tells me the only hope we have with Nick is for you to be willing to lay down your life for him. It's the only way we can help him.

"What exactly is going to happen to me in here?" Stephanie asked.

Nick's eyes started to glow red, eagle wings began to form on his back, and a scorpion tail began to protrude from his backside.

Trust in the Lord. All I know is you'll suffer greatly, but don't fear, your destiny in heaven is secure. In the end, you may die, and it might not make any difference anyway. Nick may be unreachable, but the Lord tells me the only hope we have is for you to demonstrate the highest form of love and pray that the love and grace of God will shine through you enough to reach him. He's never really known the love of God, but Nick knows you, Stephanie, and if he sees sacrificial love in you, a mere human, it might inspire him to believe in Jesus' love too.

Stephanie paused, considering her mom's words. She had always been a little afraid before any battle, but confident the Lord was with her, and confident in her abilities in a fight. This was totally different and she had no idea what to expect.

You can leave anytime but then Nick will be lost.

"I'm used to suffering in battles. He's my brother and I love him. We'll do this your way. Can you put him to sleep again?"

I think so, if you heal his pain.

Stephanie concentrated and all her protector angels disappeared. She reached over and touched Nick's ear that had been chopped off by Petrella and focused healing thoughts at the wound. The ear grew back. Nick's beast features soon melted and the human Nick stood before her once more.

The soldier Nicks handcuffed Stephanie and she didn't fight back. Then the scene around her changed to become a courtroom. Twelve Nicks, dressed in priestly uniforms, glared down at her from raised platforms that formed a semicircle around her. The high priest Nick, who sat in the center, wore a tall white hat, adorned with jewels and gold. "Do you claim to be a daughter of God?" he asked.

"It is as you say," Stephanie said.

"Blasphemer!" the high priest Nick said. "What need do we have of any further witnesses? We ourselves have heard the lies out of her own mouth."

Talk to him, Stephanie. You represent God to him and he wants to take revenge on you. I can only hold him back so long.

Stephanie shuddered to think what she might have to endure next if she couldn't reach Nick. She had read her Bible many times and didn't relish how this narrative went. "Listen to me, Nick. You don't have to do this. I know you think you're a demon, and God will never forgive you. I know you think God wants to vindicate His justice by sending you to hell, as not even you argue now that you deserve to burn. But believe it or not, that is the best place to be! You have come to fully understand and agree with God that you deserve your fate! That's exactly why you can avoid it! God has a higher form of justice than hell. It's called mercy and forgiveness to those who know they don't deserve it. All you have to do is receive it, and try to honestly respond out of love to love the Lord back. Let's end this scenario and go home. Mom and dad are just waiting on the other side. I don't believe Stro-kar has corrupted your mind so much that you can't see how simple it all is. We don't have to do this anymore."

"Blasphemer!" the high priest Nick said again, louder this time. "Take her to Pilate!"

The scene around her dissolved and reformed into a king's palace. She stood before a Nick wearing a crown and kingly robes sitting on a throne. The chief priest Nicks were around about her. "They say you are a daughter of the King of the Jews," the king said. "Is this so?"

"Yes," Stephanie replied.

"I find no fault with this woman," Pilate-Nick said.

The chief priests became fiercer. "She thinks she's better than us," they said with one voice in unison. "She thinks she deserves to go to heaven but we don't!"

"I didn't say that," Stephanie said. "Nobody deserves to go to heaven, Nick. There are no good people in heaven, just forgiven people. Just receive and respond to the love. You're the one who is refusing to love, serve, and obey God. It's your choice."

"We will not submit to a cruel God!" the Nicks said in one loud voice. "God allowed me to be deceived, in the preexistence by Satan, and on earth by the 'Balazons'. He let me be demon possessed. What kind of a loving Father is that? They tormented my mind, made me do horrible things, and now He blames me for it all! I have to admit I'm a sinner and repent? What about God? Why doesn't He admit to some wrongdoing? Make Him beg me for forgiveness first and then maybe I'll think about it!"

"God sets the standard, not us. God judges us We don't judge

Him. We need God's forgiveness. He does not need ours. Stro-kar has twisted your mind."

The high priest Nick ran up to Stephanie and struck her on the face. "Fuck you, stupid bitch," he said, and his head momentarily started to take on the form of an eagle, but then subsided.

"We all make our own choices, Nick. I was deceived too by the 'Balazons', but it was my own fault. I wanted to believe nonsense about how we all evolved from primordial goop without God because I didn't want to have to answer to the God we all know deep down exists. I was demon possessed too, but I don't blame God for everything. I've suffered from poor choices in my own life, poor choices others have made that have hurt me. I've even suffered for good, as I try to help people like you. If we would all just learn to love and obey God, none of these things would happen. It's the pride and selfishness in all of us that has causes pain and suffering. You can repent and change. You don't have to live like that anymore."

At her words, even the Pilate-Nick seemed to lose sense of his role in the drama and started to scream for her to be scourged and crucified. In the gospel account, Pilate had put up more resistance before turning Jesus over to the Romans for crucifixion.

The scene dissolved around her and reformatted to become an outdoor courtyard. She was chained to a pole and naked, surrounded by Nicks that were laughing and taunting her. She heard a cracking noise behind her and gasped in pain, as a whip slashed her back open, the barbed end wrapping around her front and lodging in the nipple of her right breast before being pulled away, tearing her nipple in the process. The whip cracked again, and again, tearing and ripping her flesh with each strike. She clenched her teeth and endured the agony, fighting the urge to break the bonds and turn and fight. It was all an illusion anyway, she thought in an effort to try and comfort herself.

I'm sorry, Stephanie. I can't stop him from lashing out, only funnel the rage into a scenario that might impact him for good in the end. It's really the God you represent that he is trying to hurt.

"I know, mom," Stephanie said, and relaxed her body, enduring blow after blow. Soon her flesh began to resemble bloody ground beef and she found the pain more tolerable, becoming numb to the brutality.

The Nicks eventually released her from the pole and placed a crown of thorns upon her head. They crushed the crown deeply into her skull, and she screamed in agony, as the sharp thorns bit into her scalp like knives. Then the scene dissolved around her and she found herself carrying a cross up a long hill.

Hang on, Stephanie. The Lord is proud of your endurance and He understands what you are going through. He says your sacrifice can produce a great harvest if you endure.

She carried her cross up the hill. Once at the top, she tried to reason with the Roman soldier Nicks but they were beyond thinking. They placed her on the cross and drilled nails in her hands and feet, laughing in glee, enjoying her suffering. The spikes were fire in her palms and feet, and she bit down so hard against the pain that she broke several teeth in her mouth.

They raised the cross high in the air and there she hung for hours between two thief Nicks on crosses beside her. "Forgive Nick, Father," she said. "For on some level he knows what he is doing."

The Nick soldiers at the foot of the cross mocked her. "Let's see you save yourself, if you think you are such a strong warrior, daughter of God." And a sign was written over the top of her cross that said, "This is a daughter of the King of the Jews."

The thief Nick on her left said, "If you're really a representative of Christ, save yourself and us."

But the other thief Nick rebuked him saying, "Don't you fear

God? We are receiving the rewards for our deeds, but this woman has done nothing wrong."

Stephanie turned to the Nick on her right and said, "Yes, Nick. That's the closest you've come yet to admitting any wrongdoing. I'm doing this because I love you and don't want you to go to hell. I'm trying to demonstrate to you the love of God. Just fully repent, ask God's forgiveness, and change."

"But the Spirit of God has already told me I've revealed myself as a demon in the flesh," the thief Nick on her right side said, and hung his head low. "There's no forgiveness for me."

Stephanie prayed for the Lord's touch on Nick's heart. "Yes, there is, Nick. You just have to choose to believe it. You have to accept God's forgiveness and then forgive yourself. You're hell-bent on destroying yourself. Why?"

"You don't know the things I've done. I feel so guilty. How can God love me?"

Stephanie pushed against her legs to catch a breath, as she felt her lungs crushing and found it difficult to talk. "Your works have nothing to do with salvation, Nick. Stop resisting the Holy Spirit and embrace Him, and He will remove your heart of stone and give you a new heart that desires to love and obey Him. That's it. Forget the past. The whole world was deceived by the Balazons' evolutionary lies. We all wanted to believe we could just naturally and easily evolve into gods without learning obedience to the one true God. We denied our consciences. We all wanted to believe there was no God and therefore no accountability. The demons tricked you, possessed you, used you, but you have to let it go and come to God."

"I was a fallen angel before I came to earth, and I've proven my allegiance again to Satan through the human life I've lived. There can be no forgiveness for me anymore. I've committed high treason by betraying my Creator twice and committing spiritual adultery again with Satan in this life. That's why sexual immorality is so wrong. Sex sin is a physical type picturing the primary sin all humans have: lack of spiritual fidelity to God. I lost that intimacy, connection, and union with God by becoming disobedient and rebellious in the preexistence. And I did it again…I did it again."

The thief Nick hung his head low.

"We don't know that for sure," Stephanie gasped, finding it difficult to speak. "You can't believe everything Stro-kar says."

"No, Stro-kar may have initially revealed it, but I really feel like God confirmed to me that it's true."

She started feeling weak and her legs began to give out, lungs crushing again, and gasped for air. But she found the strength to push up again. "Well, even if that's true, whatever you might have been before you came to earth, as long as you are human and alive, you still have a chance to change your destiny."

The thief Nick hung his head low again.

"You can do it, Nick," Stephanie said. Her legs were burning, but she knew she had to keep pushing and continue the conversation. "This is the part where you're supposed to ask me to remember you when I come into God's kingdom. That's probably all you have to do and we can end this."

"I can't. I'm too much of a sinner. I'm too weak. God can't love me."

Stephanie felt her life ebbing away, and gasped out one last plea to Nick to repent and believe, her speech now broken and very labored. The sun faded and darkness descended around her.

It's almost over, Stephanie. This is the hardest part. The Lord asks you to trust Him. Hang on. Don't come down off that cross.

The darkness of the night invaded her soul, and she began to feel an intense spiritual agony. Body muscles she never knew she had began to contract and convulse violently, as she began to sense

Nick's thoughts in a more powerful and intimate way than she had ever before experienced in any mind. His thoughts were becoming hers and her mind was becoming his. Memories began to flood over her, things Nick had done while demon possessed, vivid details of unimaginable things, rapes, murders, torture, and the pleasure of it all…and the pain. Then she lost any sense of connection with her mom, or even God's spirit.

Stephanie asked in her thoughts if her mom was still there, but received silence in response. She begged for a touch of God's spirit but likewise received nothing. "Mom, God?" she cried out. "Why have you both forsaken me?" She thought of ending it all and exiting Nick's mind, but steeled her will and tried to focus on thoughts of love, determined to stay for her brother's sake.

Despair flooded over her, and she felt as if hot irons were being pressed against her head. She screamed, as her mind seared, and the memory of the point at which Nick gave up fighting Stro-kar invaded her consciousness. When Nick had fully merged with Stro-kar, he broke a barrier whereby Nick believed he became privy to spirit "mysteries". Powerful memories of the demon, Stro-kar, began to merge with her mind too, memories of thousands of years of spiritually torturing and tormenting humans.

She deeply understood now why her words seemed unable to impact Nick, and why Nick was so sure he was doomed, a demon in the flesh. Mere words could never reach him, the depth of his pain and agony something that had to be experienced to be understood. But while Nick was too weak to believe on his own, she had the faith to believe there was no limit to the love and mercy of God, even for His enemies, even if the demonic theology was true. She understood now why she had to merge with Nick in this way, share part of his pain, so that he could share part of her faith, as the merging process went both ways and it was the only way she had any hope of impacting him.

Motivated now only by love, totally unafraid, and willing to endure any pain, she pushed further into Nick's mind, becoming evil incarnate, becoming a devil, feeling the burning of Nick's conscience, a sort of hell of its own. The fire in her mind intensified, but she threw herself fully into the flames, knowing with unshakeable faith that God would not leave her soul in hell forever, even though she was willfully turning herself into a demon, for love conquers all and love never fails.

She fully merged with her brother's thoughts in every way possible, becoming one with his evil nature, becoming one with his sin, becoming sin, losing perception of boundaries where she began and Nick ended. In the process, Nick took on the nature of Stephanie, faith, hope, and love building bridges to heaven that had long since been destroyed. She joyfully went to hell with him, confident that she could also bring him with her to heaven.

"It is finished!" she said, and pushed her legs up one last time to take a gasp of air and say the words that would end her journey. "Father, into your hands I commit my spirit." Then she died.

* * *

Stephanie slumped over in her wheelchair and the doctor's monitoring equipment started beeping. He had Stephanie hooked up with electrodes and wires to monitor her vital signs in case of emergency.

"I've lost contact!"Valerie said, as she dropped her hands that had been tightly pressed against Stephanie's head. The close contact had afforded her some sensation of what Stephanie had been enduring, but the full scope of it was beyond her.

"Move!" the doctor said rudely, and Valerie jumped aside, not at all annoyed at his tone. The doctor began cardio-pulmonary resuscitation.

"You have to bring her back," Valerie said. "I can sense Nick's suicidal despair. He needs his sister now more than ever. If he kills himself in his mind, he'll die here too!"

* * *

Judas-Nick fastened one end of the rope tightly to the bottom of the tree. The tall oak sat at the top of a hill overlooking a valley below. It had one high thick branch that stretched out over the side of the cliff. Perfect place to hang himself, Judas-Nick thought, and shook his head, trying to clear it of a deep feeling of haze. He wondered why the world looked so odd. The grass was a deep pink and the sky was purple.

Lord Stephanie had suffered and died for him, but he had betrayed her. His own sister had been the Messiah, and he had come to know that intimately over the more than three years he had walked with her during her ministry. She had been God in the flesh, and he had been her disciple, witnessing all of her miracles, but in the end he had betrayed her. It was time to end it all, face his Maker, and accept God's judgment, however severe it may be.

He just couldn't live with himself anymore, understanding something of the love of God now in a deeper way, witnessing his sister's sacrificial love for humanity, but knowing it didn't apply to him. They had fought often as kids, full of animosity and hatred at times, but she had been willing to go to any lengths for the sinners of the world. Lord Stephanie had died to bring salvation to the world. But he knew forgiveness didn't apply to him. Even Stephanie had called him the son of perdition. He was damned and he knew it. He deserved to die. And it was time to execute sentence.

Judas-Nick formed the other end of the rope into a noose and flung it over the branch overhanging the valley below, pausing only temporarily to fall to his knees and sob again at what he had done to his sister. He paused, confused, remembering how he had watched her from behind dozens of eyes, but knowing that was impossible, since he was only one person. He shook his head again, trying to shake off a dazed feeling, like he was in a dream world of some sorts. He had a duty to perform.

* * *

The doctor removed the defibrillator pads from Stephanie's chest and the heart monitor beeped to life again, steady and sure. Stephanie opened her eyes slowly.

"You have to go back in!" Valerie said. "When you died, Nick lost connection with your mind and faith. He doesn't know what he's doing. He won't last much longer."

"I wouldn't advise it," the doctor said. "She is weak and needs rest. If she goes back in you might lose them both."

"I don't care," Stephanie said weakly. "I know I'm going to heaven anyway. Nick is the one who still has a choice to make."

She immediately closed her eyes and Valerie pressed her hands against Stephanie's head.

* * *

Judas-Nick fit the noose snugly around his neck and prepared to hurl himself over the side of the cliff. Suddenly, his mood changed, and his faith surged somewhat. Judas-Nick began to realize how illogical it was that Lord Stephanie would want to damn him. She had died for all sinners, including him. Every person had their part in putting Stephanie on that cross. His sin had been so great, though, and he started to despair again.

It was then that he noticed Petrella, one of Lord Stephanie's closest disciples, standing beside the oak tree. "You have to face who you are and what you've done," she said. "Accept the Lord's forgiveness and be a changed person. It doesn't have to end this way."

Nick loosened the noose and removed it from his neck. He came close to her. "What do you know what I've done and how I feel?"

"I felt just as bad as you, in my own way. Lord Stephanie had said I would deny her three times before the cock crowed, and it happened just like she said. I was such a coward. I ran just like all the rest. But I've accepted her forgiveness and I'm ready to die. I know I'll go to heaven."

"She called me the son of perdition. My fate is sealed. Nothing can be done to change it. I might as well just kill myself and go to hell. The longer I live, the more sin and judgment I'll just be heaping on my head."

"No, I forgive you."

It was then that he noticed Petrella wasn't really Petrella, as though scales had been lifted from his eyes. Petrella was actually Lord Stephanie.

"You are risen!" Nick said and fell at her feet. "My Lord and my God."

"No, Nick. I'm just a human being, your sister… and I forgive you. Why do you think Jesus would be any different?"

It was then that more scales fell from his eyes, as memory and total awareness instantly flooded his mind. He remembered everything now, and realized he was really trapped in the hell of his own mind, about to send himself to a literal hell if he had killed himself.

"Steph!" he said as he stood up to face her. "You have all my memories now. I remember us merging."

"Yes, and while here, I can strengthen you a bit with our merged faith. That's why you came down off that tree. But it was all just a demonstration of the truth, Nick, a reflection of Jesus' experience to help you believe. I did it willingly in the hopes it would help you."

"I can't believe what you were willing to endure just to try and reach me, Steph. I can't believe what Jesus actually *did* do for me..."

"That's your whole problem, Nick. Believe it. Stop resisting the Holy Spirit. Surrender and receive Christ before it's too late. You've never really known Christ like I do, but you do know me. And if I forgive you and hold nothing against you, a mere sinful human being, you should be able to understand now how much Christ loves you even more. Whatever you think you know about mysteries of a time before you came to earth, the reality is you are human now, and as a human, you have a choice to make as to whether or not you will love your Creator back, as He has loved you. Obey Him, Nick. That's how you show your love for God. You gave up on Jesus but He hasn't given up on you. The Lord still loves you and He wants you to be with Him in heaven when you die."

Stephanie started to shimmer, and began disappearing from his world. Nick could feel fear and despair pushing into his mind, growing in intensity the more she faded. "I'm dying on the outside and soon my faith will no longer sustain you," she said. "I'm expending all my life energy to be with you now in these last minutes. But you have to make your own choice. My death means nothing. It is Christ's death for your sins that counts. You have to put all your faith and trust in Him to save you. And He will. He'll even give you supernatural desire and ability to love and serve Him, but like the old hymn says, you have to trust and obey, for there's no other way."

Nick fell to his knees and began sobbing uncontrollably. "I will," he mumbled and in his heart, he totally and unconditionally surrendered to the Creator of heaven and earth, Jesus Christ, the Lord God Almighty.

"Lord, forgive me and remember me," was all Nick said, but immediately, joy and ecstasy swept his entire being.

He instantly transformed into a ball of pure light, and merged with Stephanie, who had also become a ball of light. “Let’s go home,” the ball of light said. “Our Father awaits.”

* * *

“That’s it,” the doctor said, after having just tried every thing in his bag of tricks to revive both Stephanie and Nick. “They’re both dead. There’s nothing more I can do.”

Valerie was hugging her husband, Jeff, and crying tears of joy. She wanted both her children back of course, but in the end, it didn’t matter. She was deliriously satisfied with the outcome anyway. “It’s ok, doctor. They’ve both gone home. It doesn’t matter anymore.”

Chapter 22

The ball of light that was Nick-Stephanie hurtled through space, many times faster than the speed of light, but slightly slower than the speed of thought; otherwise they would have been there already, Nick-Stephanie thought. They blasted through the Milky way galaxy, through planets, solar systems, black holes even, on their journey to heaven, then empty space for a short period of time, before encountering more matter from the next galaxy.

What joy they felt together. He and Stephanie were one, yet separate and distinct, combined together and knowing the totality of each other's thoughts and memories in a moment of time, perfect recall of all the good and all the bad things they each had ever done, and every thought they each had ever had about every action. But there was no shame or guilt about anything anymore.

The Lord was in their thoughts too, speaking more and more strongly as they neared heaven, pure instinct driving them home like salmon returning home to spawn.

Nick knew Stephanie's crucifixion firsthand, experiencing it through her eyes, which were his as well. He had experienced it, was experiencing it even now, and would experience it forevermore, as time was irrelevant in the present moment of their spirit existence. But while they had total recall, all pain was gone, only good emotions remained, and a sort of detached emptiness around awareness of any negative experiences they each had ever had.

Stephanie pulled away from him and the one ball of light became two. The light formed into something the likeness of

Stephanie but more gender neutral. Nick formed into a likeness of his former self as well.

He felt emptier and alone now that they were separate, more like being human again, with only his own thoughts for comfort. His awareness of the intricacies of time dulled, and he was unable to share the present moment with as much intensity. But the joy was still there.

"Father is calling me home before you," Stephanie said. "See you when you arrive, slowpoke." She began to accelerate faster than him, and despite his best efforts to catch her, he could not seem to increase his speed. She suddenly took off like a jet, as if afterburners had kicked in, and he lost sight of her.

Galaxies rushed past him until he sensed his destination and thought himself into deceleration. The center of the universe was before him, an immense ball of white energy, something like a sun but millions of times larger and many times brighter. Hebrews 12:29 came to mind: "Our God is a consuming fire." Yet only a mild warmth radiated towards him, and a feeling of being invited. He plunged himself into the energy mass.

Nick's next awareness was of standing outside the gates of a beautiful and immense city, surrounded by a high wall of solid gold. Stephanie approached him from the gates.

"You missed all the excitement," Stephanie said. "Satan and his top Lieutenants were arguing your case before the Lord's court. He was severely pissed that he lost you, and made every argument he could that you had to go to hell with him when the time comes. The devil knows the scriptures backwards and forwards and quoted and twisted God's word like I'd never heard before. I gotta admit. I couldn't see any way around what he was saying, Nick. I thought for sure you'd get here just in time to be escorted to the lake of fire."

"So why am I not going there?"

Stephanie smiled. "Well, then the Lord opened his mouth to speak, and I understand fully now what Romans 8:33 means when it says: 'Who shall lay any thing to the charge of God's elect? It is God that justifieth'. God turned it all around, using the same scriptures, and interpreted your whole life's experience totally differently. Then I believed you had always been a saint since birth. And you were, and you are! This is why none of God's creation can ever again divorce God's input on His own words, Nick. They can be manipulated for both good and evil. Many people are going to hell because deception has them so trapped they can't see this and refuse to follow only the Holy Spirit's leading on interpreting His Word."

Nick was bewildered. "How are such things possible?"

Stephanie smiled again."You had to be there to understand. Satan knew he was defeated before he even entered the courtroom, but he had to spout his vile crap anyway. I was told these kinds of encounters are commonplace in heaven. God uses it as a chance to teach all of His creation the true difference between good and evil, but Satan just uses it as a chance to vent his frustrations, as he loses every time."

Suddenly, the city gates crashed open with a loud clang. A great towering red dragon led twelve hideous reptile creatures of various sizes and shapes through the front gate, escorted by a large angel with twelve equally large angelic cohorts.

"This isn't finished, piss-ass," Satan said and glared at Nick as he walked by. "I wouldn't accept the assignment if I were you. I won't go easy on you this time."

"Yeah, yeah, move along asshole," the leader of the angels said and gave Satan a shove.

"That was the archangel Michael," Stephanie said. "Captain of the Lord's army."

"What did the devil mean by that?" Nick asked.

Stephanie chuckled. "He's just pissed at the Lord's challenge. The Lord agreed to send you to hell only if you refused your special assignment."

"Doesn't sound like I have much of a choice."

"Sure you do. Want to know what it is?"

Nick nodded.

"You have to go back to earth and do for others what I did for you. You are the first person in human history to have totally crossed the line and yet been brought back from the brink. There are other people that have crossed that line and need your help. You really did commit an unforgivable sin, Nick. But you ultimately didn't because the Lord says you didn't. End of story. God's opinion on any issue is the final truth in all matters. It was all the Lord's plan to reveal a new level of grace and mercy to all of His creation. He has a plan and purpose behind everything that happens."

"Are you saying the mystery I thought I knew about having lived before coming to earth as a fallen angel is true? I mean, I'm not so sure anymore. I don't have any memory of that, and now that I'm spirit, I would think I should if it were true."

"Well I can't comment on that because it would affect your ability to complete the task the Lord has set before you. That's why I had to get here before you. The Lord didn't want you to witness all of this firsthand or you wouldn't be able to do what you have to do."

"But I still do have a choice?"

"Yes."

"Obey God or go to hell?"

"Right, but that's really the one and only choice God gives all of His sentient creation. The angelic rebellion and human history have proven that any deviation from this perfect standard eventually results in total failure. After all, if any person's opinion on any moral issue can be placed above God's, then others insist on that right too, an attitude which spreads, eventuating in anarchy. Absolute obedience in childlike trust and faith is the only way that leads to life. But we're focusing on the wrong thing here. The question you should be asking yourself right now is, what is the condition of your heart? What do you desire to do right now?"

Nick beamed. "I want to fall before the feet of the Lord of glory and worship Him!"

Stephanie smiled. "Good answer. But I'm told that would also affect your ability to complete your assignment, as once you are in His presence, you won't be able to leave. You've been forgiven much, Nick, and you just wouldn't be able to tear yourself away. What is the second biggest desire of your heart right now?"

"I desire to be used of the Lord to make a difference for good! I'm willing to go back and do anything necessary, suffer anything, whatever glorifies the Lord!"

"Exactly my point. Nobody forces anybody to do anything here. We all do what we want, and we all want to love and serve God here. If you had any other attitude, you'd be headed to the other place. Well, I'm happy to say then that I am authorized to send you back at the speed of thought. I bid you good journey." Stephanie leaned over and kissed Nick on the cheek.

Nick instantly found himself back at earth, floating above his dead body, which was on a cremation slab, door open to the crematory, fires blazing.

"I wish we had time to find a good burial spot in Star City cemetery," Lawrence was saying. "I'd like to have respected your wishes, Jeff, but there just isn't time. The Lord tells me Sandy will be here in minutes, and Jarius' men will be close behind her."

"I still don't understand why you prophesied that only one of my children would die but now both are gone," Jeff said. Valerie was standing beside him, holding her husband's hand and sobbing lightly.

"The Lord is sovereign over everything, Jeff" Lawrence said. "Just trust Him. At least you know you'll see both Nick and Stephanie in heaven one day."

"Alright," Jeff said. "Push him in."

Nick decided he'd better move fast and willed himself into his body. Then he sat his flesh body up and said, "Don't you think you'd better ask me first?"

Valerie screamed and Jeff stepped back a few feet.

"Don't be afraid," Nick said. "I've been sent back for a special assignment."

"You've been dead for hours!" Jeff said, and both his parents stepped forward and gave him a big hug.

Lawrence smiled and said, "Well, I'm glad you're back. We should be on our way then. I have to take up my position in the center of the complex before Jarius gets here. I'd suggest you three come wait by my side until Sandy arrives."

They all left the crematory and followed Lawrence to a central spot on the main floor of the complex. The place was deserted, with the exception of the odd straggler here and there. Jeff asked Lawrence to tell him again the exact time of Jarius' assault.

"2:12," Lawrence said, and Nick glanced at his watch, seeing it was already 2:08.

"Why isn't Sandy here yet?" Jeff asked. "We can't afford to wait much longer."

Lawrence suddenly stretched out his hands in what appeared to be a gesture which said "Stop." Then he closed his eyes and communicated a message from God. "I see her team. They are three blocks away, speeding here as fast as they can, as Jarius has spotted them and is in hot pursuit."

"She knows I'm waiting for her, doesn't she?" Jeff asked.

"She knows. The team plans to drop her off and escape through the back roads. Jarius will let them go because he is more concerned with destroying the complex." Lawrence opened his eyes. "I'm waiting for them."

"Why exactly are you just standing here, Lawrence?" Nick asked.

"I'm resting my hands against the pillars," Lawrence said.

"What?" Nick said.

"God has revealed to me that my end is to be like Samson. I am to stand here, arms outstretched, touching symbolic pillars. When the time is right, I will push out my arms, bringing down this entire structure around our enemies' heads."

"But you'll be killed!" Valerie said.

"No. Then I will truly live. I will leave this earth to go be with the Lord forever. Do not grieve for me, my friends. My time is ended. This is the way He wants my death to glorify Him. I'm sure Nick understands my feelings, having already been to the other side and back."

Nick nodded, but his father seemed at a loss for words.

They all knew Lawrence well enough to realize there was no way their leader could be talked out of the plan. If Lawrence was convinced God wanted him to die this way, then he would gladly do it. He'd been such a good friend and leader to all of them.

Jeff smiled and nodded. "We'll miss you."

"I know. But we'll all meet again."

Jeff sighed and asked again, "How much longer until Sandy gets here?"

"One minute."

"That's going to be cutting it close."

"Yes."

Jeff turned to Nick and Valerie. The complex was totally empty now. Any last stranglers had fled quickly. "There's a back door in that direction," Jeff said and pointed at a hallway underneath his room and off to the right a bit. "Maybe you two should leave now."

Valerie hesitated.

"We're staying with you, dad," Nick said.

Jeff smiled. "I want you to know how proud I am of the man you've become, Nick."

Nick stood beside Lawrence and his parents, the longest one minute he could remember, until the front entrance smashed open and an attractive blonde woman came running across the wide complex space.

"It's time," Lawrence said and started to move his hands. "I'll give you as much time as I can, but you'd better move fast." The structure started to rumble. Sandy tripped and fell several yards away and Nick's dad went to help her. Before Jeff could reach her however, the door smashed open again and an unending stream of men came running through.

Lawrence moved his hands slightly and the place rumbled again, but Jarius' men kept streaming in. Nick heard gun shots. By this time, his dad and Sandy were running towards him. Then Sandy suddenly fell to the floor, blood gushing out of her legs.

Jeff grabbed her, flung her over his shoulder, and kept moving, more guns rattling in the background. Nick led the way to the escape hallway, his mom and dad close behind. When his parents had cleared the door, Nick turned to take one last glance and saw bloody holes appear in Lawrence's back before he stretched out his arms completely. As Lawrence fell to the floor, the roof started to cave in, and Nick realized his own hallway would be next. He ran forward and didn't look back again.

Chapter 23

Jeff carried Sandy into the open air as dust settled behind them, inhaling the powdery debris that tasted like chalk and coughing it up with effort. The ground was vibrating slightly, and a low rumbling noise filled the air, but soon stopped.

"I was starting to wonder if we were going to make it," Valerie said.

Jeff took a deep breath to clear his lungs. He hadn't been outside for a week, and the fresh air felt good. God must have discontinued the scorching heat judgment, as it was comfortably warm, sunny, and there wasn't a cloud in the sky. "We're OK. Except for Sandy." Jeff gently placed her on the ground.

Sandy grimaced as she looked at the torn flesh of her calves.

"What are we going to do, Jeff?" Valerie asked. "I don't know where to find a doctor."

Jeff didn't know either. As a pharmacist, he'd had some medical training, but had never taken care of bullet wounds before. Suddenly, he thought he heard a voice. "What? Did you hear that?" Everybody stared at Jeff as if he was a bit daft. "Did you hear a voice?"

"What voice?" Nick asked.

Jeff cleared his throat and stood up. "Sandy, the Lord just told me to tell you to heal yourself in His name."

Sandy seemed to forget the pain momentarily, as she looked up at Jeff. She had seen God do many miracles over the years, but Jeff could understand why she was a bit shocked. "You're kidding."

"No. Do it. You'll see."

Sandy paused for a few seconds, then shrugged her shoulders. "In the name of Jesus, I speak healing to my leg. Wounds be gone!" At first, nothing seemed to happen. Then new flesh started to cover the bullet holes, bumpy at first, but soon smoothed out to become like new. Sandy raised her left eyebrow. "I've never been able to do that before."

Jeff said, "The Lord just told me from now on you will have this gift of healing."

"What can I do?" Nick asked.

Jeff said, "You will find out when the time comes. For now we should do as he asks."

"What's that?" Valerie asked.

"He wants us to go north to Edmonton, Canada to preach."

"Why Canada?"Nick asked.

"I haven't the foggiest idea, and I don't care. It's not important to know why, but it is important to obey." Jeff turned to look at his son. "Nick. This is your chance. Take us to Canada."

Nick frowned with confusion. "How? We don't have a car."

"Not that way. Call for your angelic transport to take us there. That's one of your gifts."

Nick requested their transportation in the name of the Lord, and as he finished speaking, all five of them rose from the ground as if they were standing in an invisible helicopter. They flew through the air, seemingly faster than the speed of sound, yet Jeff couldn't feel any G forces or wind. Within minutes they gingerly landed in the middle of Jasper Avenue, Edmonton's downtown district.

The Royal Bank building had a big hole in the front, an entrance through which undoubtedly thieves had gained access to electronic credit transfer machines. The streets were calm but had signs of battle, such as gaping holes or smaller bullet-type holes in various buildings, dead bodies lying around, and all cars were either stripped, turned upside down, or black charred hunks of metal. To the west, the Paramount theater was boarded up with metal plating; a neon sign above showed a naked woman and said X-rated movies only. They probably had done a booming business at one time, but now it looked deserted.

"It's deserted," Valerie said.

Jeff peered up and down the street. "No. They're in the buildings, hiding like frightened mice. I suggest we simply sit in the center of the street and eat a big meal. The hungry people will eventually come out of hiding."

"I'm sure you realize we have no food," Valerie said. "What did you have in mind?"

Jeff was glad to see Valerie had the faith to believe God would do something. "You will supply the food."

Valerie nodded her head in understanding. "Lord, in Your name I ask for physical sustenance. Please give us turkey, potatoes, vegetables, gravy, and bread."

The food appeared along with a table and five chairs.

They sat down and began eating, casually, as if the streets were their usual dining surroundings. Before long, the delectable aromas dragged a man out of hiding, mouth hanging open and visibly salivating. The man walked to within five yards of Jeff before he raised his right hand, revealing a semi-automatic pistol. He pulled the trigger repeatedly, but the gun might as well have been loaded with blanks, for it didn't do one iota of harm to its intended targets.

"My friend, "Jeff said, "you do not need to kill us, for we will gladly share our food with you. We have an abundance of bread. And while we eat, we can share with you the living bread from heaven, Jesus Christ."

The man looked at his gun with confusion and anger. He was frothing at the mouth and grunting. He paused for several seconds before rushing at Jeff, hands grabbing for Jeff's throat and gnashing his teeth.

"Back!" Jeff commanded, and the man was flung several yards in the opposite direction, landing on his back, moaning and sobbing.

Jeff went over and touched him on the shoulder. His right leg was twisted backwards, seemingly broken in two places. "The power of Satan will no longer bind you. Stand up and talk." The man convulsed slightly, vomited, and stood up, leg instantly straightening, and speaking intelligently.

"How did you do that?" he asked. "I haven't been able to speak for years."

"I didn't do anything. The Lord Jesus Christ delivered you as a sign of His power. He now desires to fill you with Himself if you will invite Him into your life."

"Most definitely!" the man said. Right then, Jeff explained the way of salvation; the man kneeled on the ground and sobbed when he understood what Jesus had done for him on the cross. He immediately gave his life to the Lord and sat down to eat with them.

Soon, thousands came crawling out of the buildings, perhaps encouraged by the first man's positive results, perhaps desiring to kill them. Jeff wasn't sure which. They moved slowly, like wolves circling in for the kill. Most were in a similar state as the first man, unable to speak and acting like ignorant cavemen, a manifestation of evil that seemed to predominate in this city. When they got closer, Jeff could definitely see their intentions were not friendly. They carried knives, clubs, guns, stones—anything which might inflict bodily damage.

God told Jeff the people's minds were so controlled that before Jeff could witness to them He would have to free them. So, Jeff and his family walked up and down the streets, commanding in authoritative voices, "In the name of Jesus, demons be gone!"

The people would wail, collapse to the ground, and get up, shaking their heads in confusion.

"How did you do that?" one of the men asked.

"We didn't do anything," Jeff said. "It was the power of God!" They continued until a crowd of bewildered men, women, and children stood around, not knowing what to expect.

Next, Valerie requested food. Instantly, the entire street was flooded with chairs, one long table, upon which was every conceivable type of food, more than enough for everyone. The people ate to their satisfaction while Jeff levitated into the air and hovered over them. His voice was louder than a bullhorn as he boldly proclaimed, "The way of salvation is through Christ!" He could be heard all the way up and down the street.

When he had finished, Jeff only had to ask once for those to gather around him who wanted to repent of their sins and receive the gift of eternal life the Lord had bought for them by His blood. Multitudes came forward so fast it looked like an attack. Only a few hardhearted individuals refused, going away to presumably become possessed again.

"It's time to go to Northtown mall," Jeff said.

Nick raised an eyebrow in surprise but said, "You're the boss." He called for their supernatural transportation.

As they started to rise from the ground a man called out, "Please don't leave us. What are we to do now?"

Jeff motioned for Nick to stop temporarily. "Stay close to the Lord and spread this new life He has given you. Use your gifts and talents to His glory. Tell everyone you meet about God, and direct them to wait at any of the malls in the city. We will appear at each one repeatedly to tell the story of the Savior and give them a chance to receive eternal life."

Jeff nodded to Nick and they continued on their way. When they arrived at Northtown, at Sandy's request, they hovered above the sign which advertised the mall's name. Sandy said she'd received a word from God.

Jeff silently rejoiced that God was talking to the others as well.

Sandy waved her hands and sang joyfully to God. Soon, many lights appeared in the sky, dancing to the melody of the beautiful sounds which could be heard.

People flocked to the center of the display, the spot where they were hovering. Jeff preached God's Word and boldly proclaimed the way of salvation. "All who want to receive life, come forth!" he said as he pointed and beams of light leapt from his finger tips to heal the sick. Meanwhile, Valerie prayed and every type of delectable food floated from heaven.

Virtually everyone came forward when Jeff invited them to commit their lives to the Lord. Afterwards, instinctively, the new believers joyfully sang a song of thanksgiving. But some in the crowd started shooting at the new Christians. Jeff quickly asked God what to do and received an answer.

"Halt and be dead!" he shouted, and instantly everyone who'd tried to do harm collapsed. Even in the face of death, the new Christians hadn't stopped their singing, and now they continued in manifestly deeper reverence.

From Northtown, they next headed to Southgate Mall.

The fame of Jesus' name was spreading throughout the city like a whirlwind. They glided through the air slowly this time because many who'd become Christians at Jasper and Northtown followed them, magnetically adding thousands to the already huge ensemble. Motor transportation was tough to find, but they came on bikes or ran if necessary.

As the young believers followed, they shouted, "Come and see what God will do for you!" One man commanded a demon to come out of a young boy, and it obeyed. This encouraged others to exercise their gifts, starting a whole avalanche of miracles. Jeff was glad people realized they could do such things. All it took was faith. But in Jeff's opinion, to the lost, their enthusiasm was a bigger drawing factor than the miracles. Nobody had seen happy faces in years. Every demon oppressed person, with God's help, was able to come, despite obvious inner inclinations to the contrary evidenced by the strained resistance on their faces.

The crowd grew like a snowball enlarging as it rolled down a snowy mountain top. By the time they reached Southgate, thousands filled the mall's parking lots, adjacent streets, and residential areas. The crowd reached several blocks to the south, past Harry Ainlay High School, and north as far as Lendrum Shopping Center.

Jeff floated above the massive expanse of faces and preached the gospel. Jeff couldn't be sure, but it seemed as though everyone responded to the invitation to receive Jesus.

When they were done, Nick flew his family to West Edmonton Mall, crowd growing rapidly during the slow flight down Whitemud freeway. The mall was huge, fortunate since Jeff needed a large space to accommodate everybody.

People jammed into every available space in the upper and lower parking lots of the monolithic mall. Many more flooded the streets. In all his experiences, Jeff had never seen such positive responses; he felt elated, drunk by the Spirit of God, as he preached, intermittently commanding demons to leave bodies, while his family floated about feeding the hungry and healing the sick. As a further sign, Jeff shook the earth and caused lightning to flash across the sky.

A small band of enraged individuals, fully possessed and unreachable, raised their guns and shot at Jeff, but the bullets became as blanks. They turned their guns on the crowd, but again, no injury came to their intended victims. Then they threw hand grenades, but in midair, the mini-bombs simply disappeared. Jeff was only mildly annoyed, and ordered the would-be assassins to go away. They obeyed. Without any further resistance, Jeff asked if anyone wanted to know God, and the sounds of many voices shouted an affirmative.

After he had introduced the crowd to the Lord, he said, "We must go now! Please do not follow us. You are too many. Instead, have people wait at the malls, or go into the streets and do for others as we have done for you. You can wield the same power we do."

Jeff indicated he was ready, and Nick called for angelic transportation. "Where to, dad?" Nick asked.

"Millwoods Town Center." This time, they moved through the air quickly, as they didn't have to wait for a crowd. As they approached the east side of the city, a large mass of people created a visible landmark of their destination. As previously, response to the invitation to repent and receive Jesus got an overwhelmingly positive response. People flocked to the door of the Kingdom in droves.

When another band of fully integrated humans started shooting the new believers, Jeff was about to call down fire from heaven. But the Lord said, *No!*

"What?" Jeff said, bewildered. He listened with sadness as he heard the Lord say that He wanted to glorify His name by having the new believers die for Him willingly. As they fell by the thousands, they didn't panic or try to flee, and their lips carried a beautiful song of hope for a better world. They had wide smiles in those last moments, totally sure of where they were going.

It was difficult for Jeff to watch Satan unjustly kill God's people, even though he understood their eternal destinies were secure. But in a way, he was jealous. They got to go to their eternal homes in heaven.

When his family asked him questions he said, "I don't understand why God allows what He does sometimes. But I know we should obey nevertheless."

After they had visited every site, they started over again, beginning with Northtown Mall. Even though Jeff got tired at times, the needs of the lost were too great to ignore. He pushed himself, living on a minimum of sleep, family following his example, until they had evangelized the entire city.

Next, God sent them to Leduc, a smaller city south of Edmonton. They flew over Calgary Trail which turned into highway two and led out to their destination. Jeff only saw one car during the entire five minute flight. Once there, they hovered in front of the Safeway food store, while Sandy did another light display. By now, Jeff was getting used to the awesome power his group was exhibiting.

"Gather around!" he yelled as thousands came to hear. His voice was supernaturally amplified, as if a loudspeaker was positioned at every street corner.

"The time to repent is now!" Fire flew from Jeff's fingertips and the earth shook. A few near the front fainted. "The Lord Jesus will be coming back soon. You must be ready for Him or this is all you'll receive!" This time every member of Jeff's family stretched out their hands and a canopy of fire spread out over the town like a large umbrella before disappearing.

"Do not be led by Satan anymore. It is time to turn to Him before it is too late." Jeff made the day become night and then the night become day again. He commanded cars to float through the air like toys he was playing with.

Several men ran up to Jeff. They were drooling and their eyes were black blobs. One snarled and leapt into the air, trying to grab Jeff's foot, which was several feet above him.

"This is an example of Satan's best to defeat God," Jeff said as he pointed below. "It is as if he grasps impotently at the foot of the Almighty." That comment enraged the men and they climbed onto each others' backs to make a human ladder to reach him.

"God can remove the demons from your life as easily as I remove these buffoons!" Jeff swept his hand through the air and a miniature tornado appeared, grabbed the group of malcontents, and carried them away.

The crowd started to recede, a mixture of fear and faith in their possessed eyes. A part of them loved what he was saying, agreed with it, and desired to respond. Yet, another part held back. He knew Nick and Valerie fully understood the pain and turmoil his listeners were going through, and motioned them forward to speak. There were tears in Nick's eyes and Valerie was openly sobbing. Although they had seen much spiritual enslavement, they hadn't gotten used to it.

"I know what you're going through," Valerie said as she started to relate her own story. When she was finished, Nick explained how he'd listened to a message like the one they were hearing but refused to respond. He begged them not to do the same.

Jeff spoke of God's love and the plan of redemption, while Sandy and his family walked out over the crowd, healing the sick and miraculously feeding the hungry. Unlike Edmonton, God told Jeff to call the people to faith first before He would free them.

"Come forth," Jeff said. "You have enough control of your mental faculties to make a decision. Yes or No. God wants to free you and fill you with Himself."

Almost half the crowd came forward, better than he'd expected, since God had told him to expect less outside the city. Jeff didn't worry about why that would be. His job was only to obey and leave the results to Him.

"What?" he suddenly said to himself quietly. "No. Not again. Please Lord." But there could be no mistaking the command. It was the hardest thing he'd had to accept in Edmonton, letting new converts' deaths glorify Him. Jeff understood, but barely, how a trusting, non-bitter, joyful Christian death glorified God before all the angels in heaven, but he still had a tough time with it. It was especially difficult to realize he had the power to do something about it, but mustn't.

Jeff thought of Peter in the garden of Gethsemane, cutting off a person's ear when they had come to arrest Jesus. The Lord had said He could call the angels to rescue Him if He wanted, but wouldn't because He had to do His Father's will, which was for Him to die. He also thought of the Scriptures which say consider it pure joy when you're persecuted or killed for God's sake because your reward will be great in heaven. Jeff clenched his jaw and got on with it.

Jeff invited his listeners to come to God. He looked behind at those who refused, standing stiffly with guns in hand, restrained until the proper time. As soon as he had finished the lead prayer, the new Christians manifested supernatural experiences. Some fell to the ground and started speaking in tongues. Others started prophesying, singing, praising, dancing—all were smiling. Then it happened. Jeff had to dig his nails into the palms of his hands to keep from lashing out.

Satan's followers started shooting the new converts. Jeff did nothing. Sandy and the others ran to his side.

"You've got to do something, Jeff," Valerie protested. "You can't let them die. Call down lightning or something."

"I can't."

"Why?" Sandy asked before Valerie could.

Jeff sighed. This was going to be difficult to explain; he'd tried before, but hadn't quite gotten through to them. He barely understood himself. "God loves them. When they die, they will go to heaven. You should be happy for them. I don't understand why God allows evil to succeed sometimes. All I know is we should trust Him anyway. That glorifies Him. Perhaps God wants to take them home because He misses them."

More shots rang out.

"These people are not afraid to die," Jeff continued. "Their trust in Him to the point of death glorifies Him. Look. They all have smiles on their faces. They are at the peak of their joy, ready to meet their God. In a way, I envy them. They will go to heaven now. They don't even have an ounce of revenge or fear on their faces."

When it was all over, not a single Christian was standing, except for Jeff's family. The Lord still had work for them to do.

Despite his confident explanations, Jeff almost relished in the next command from God—kill the rest however he wanted to. The new converts might not want revenge, but a part of Jeff did. However, he knew God would right all wrongs in the end. Vengeance was God's. In the final judgment after death, everyone would get what they deserved. So, he refrained from any evil intent, and simply executed them efficiently with fire from heaven. Now the whole town was dead. Everyone had been a believer or an unbeliever, one group shot, the other incinerated.

It almost seemed futile. He wondered why he should work so hard if God was just going to let them die quickly anyway. But the Lord reminded Jeff that they were with Him now, and he felt a little jealous again. Jeff was tired and desired to go to heaven too. It would be refreshing to rest after all his labor. No, it hadn't been a waste of time. Their souls had been saved. Now it was time to move on.

God directed Jeff next to every town in Edmonton's surrounding area, starting with Devon and Calmar. The combined efforts of every mission group in Lawrence's Complex could never been as successful as Jeff's group now. Jeff could remember days when they'd not be able to convince a single person to trust in Jesus. He was almost tempted to criticize the preachers who'd preceded him, but God reminded Jeff that He hadn't poured out His Spirit so massively ever before.

Over the next few months, God expanded Jeff's ministry in concentric circles. They covered greater and greater areas, expanding across provincial boundaries, and didn't stop until they'd overlapped with other mission groups. Now God told Jeff that his work was finished and it was time for his own family's deaths to glorify Him.

Jeff didn't think he was going to like what he was about to hear.

Chapter 24

"I don't like it," Jeff said to himself, as he sat alone in a lawn chair on the patio.

Nick had flown them to their home in Star City, and it was past midnight. Sandy and the others had fallen asleep rather easily, but not Jeff. He was still waiting for God to explain what He meant about dying to glorify Him. He had worried so much he couldn't sleep.

Jeff prayed for further revelation, but received no answer. Since they came back, God had not talked audibly to Jeff. It felt rather strange, not hearing His voice. Jeff had gotten used to it. "I don't like it," he said again. "Please tell me what you meant."

But there was no answer.

Jeff felt a little ashamed. He knew a true believer shouldn't be afraid of death. On the contrary, he should welcome it. Death ushered in a change of status, leaving the physical body and receiving a new spiritual body. He would go to be with the Lord, in heaven. Paradise. Forever. He should look forward to it. Most of the time he did. Jeff didn't think he could have done ministry the way he had if afraid of death. He'd faced it every day since he became a Christian, and so did his family. He was sure they felt the same way. They lived everyday as lambs waiting to be slaughtered. It was a great adventure.

So he pondered what his problem was, wondering if his faith was drying up. He knew the Bible says God is not pleased with anyone who shrinks back in fear.

Understanding suddenly came to him. Jeff wasn't a coward as far as dying was concerned. He was a coward about suffering. The Lord hadn't told him how he would die. Up until now, most dangerous situations they'd faced held the possibility of instant death—being shot by possessed humans. But he was most worried about dying slowly, in agony.

Thoughts of the cross came to mind. His Lord had died a slow, painful death for his sins. The least he could do is be willing to suffer if God asked him to. But Jeff wished God would somehow deaden his pain receptors; then he would do it gladly. However, it wasn't likely to happen. Compared to how Stephanie had suffered and died though, he felt like such a wimp. But Stephanie had been a willing warrior with years of experience. Jeff didn't think he could personally bear something like his daughter's experience or see his family suffer some similar fate.

Nevertheless, he was ready to obey no matter what, and he felt confident his family would express the same sentiments. That, perhaps more than anything, really bothered him. Since the beginning of history, God's people had always suffered unjustly in the hands of evil, and God had allowed it. Jeff knew he wasn't anyone special to be somehow exempt. Even before the Son of God had been tortured to death, He had warned His followers to expect the same. The servant wasn't any better than the master. Still, if he could ask for one small favor, he would ask for a quick death. Jeff didn't think he'd make a good slow death martyr.

"Don't you know I love you and your family, Jeff?" God said.

It was good to hear it again. It had seemed like such a long time. "Yes, Lord."

"Don't you know I will not allow my children to be tempted beyond what they can bear?"

Jeff was silent, eagerly waiting to hear more.

"You and your family will die quickly and painlessly."

Jeff felt relieved, as the weight of uncertainty lifted off his back, and he began to think more clearly. "Tell me more about tomorrow. When and where will we go? What's going to happen?"

"I will not tell you."

Jeff knew better than to insist. God told him things little bits at a time. He would be overwhelmed otherwise. Not only that, but Jeff knew he would not be living by faith if he understood everything, and God wanted Jeff to trust Him implicitly.

"Go back inside and rest."

"Yes, Lord," Jeff said and went inside. The lights were off and it took several seconds to adjust before he could walk around obstacles and silently tiptoe upstairs. He didn't want to wake anybody else. They didn't know what was going to happen tomorrow and he wanted to give them a good night's sleep.

* * *

The next morning, Jeff was the last out of bed. He heard everybody downstairs, clanking dishes and making breakfast. He knelt at the foot of his bed. "Lord, reveal to me your will. What would you have us do this day."

"Since you left the complex, you have been faithful to do all I have commanded you, as have many others. My witness and warning has been taken to every corner of the earth and many have responded, but there are still a few I desire to have. I am coming back very soon and want to take these ones with me when I arrive. Therefore, I am sending you to the whole world to give one last warning for people to turn from evil and come to me."

"But I can't reach the whole world in one day. It took us months to evangelize a relatively small area. Surely, the whole world would take years!"

"I will supply the means."

"Very well. When will we go."

"When you leave your house, you will go."

Jeff nodded his head and said, "Your will be done." Then he went downstairs, sat at the kitchen table, and told his family everything, from the quick and painless death to the worldwide witness.

"We can do it for God," Nick said. "The next thought we have will be in paradise, and we'll all be together. I can tell you firsthand it's glorious."

Jeff was proud of Nick's courage, but glancing at Valerie and Sandy, he noticed they seemed rather glum. This was supposed to be a joyous time! They were going to see their Lord! Perhaps the adults could learn something from Nick here. Jeff could understand, though. He was nervous too.

He compared the way he felt now with the way he'd felt when he'd first married Valerie. He knew he loved Valerie, was ready for marriage, was looking forward to it with confidence, and yet, he had been nervous. Just human nature, he supposed—that old sinful and insecure human nature which frequently gets nervous over things it shouldn't. Soon the new creation, the new inner man, the real Jeff, would be totally free from the old nature nuisance. Until then, he would crush its fears with his will, and appropriate the courage and faith to complete the task he'd been called to do.

Jeff looked down at the dinner table. The traditional bacon and eggs covered his plate. "I guess I should've waited until we finished breakfast."

There were several seconds of silence before Valerie spoke. "Nonsense. It's just a shock. We need a few seconds to adjust." Valerie nodded her head. "There I think I'm ready."

"Me too," Nick said.

Sandy smiled and took a huge bite of toast.

"That's the spirit!" Jeff said and shoved some egg into his mouth. His head suddenly felt a little dizzy and his arms went tingly-numb. The Spirit of the Lord fell upon him and Jeff started praising God. Everybody joined in. This wasn't going to be so bad after all.

When they were done, Jeff threw his dishes onto the floor. "I've always wanted to do that," he said. Since they weren't coming back, he didn't see any reason why he shouldn't.

Nick asked where they were going, but Jeff simply directed him to the door. The moment they stepped outside, they found themselves in an entirely foreign location, none of the surroundings of Star City.

"Where are we, dad?" Nick asked.

"I don't know."

They were facing a large fence with barbed wire tracing the top. Inside the fence was a large brown building. A short distance alongside the fence, a human walked with a dog, back and forth, guarding the entrance. Further down, the building itself was guarded by several demons. They no longer bore any resemblance to Balazons, but appeared as grotesque monsters.

The dog started barking and the man turned around. "Hey, what are you doing here? This is a restricted area."

"Tell him I sent you ."

"God has sent me," Jeff said. "Please let me in."

The man snarled. "Very well. If you're so foolish as to come here, enter and be welcome."

Jeff didn't know what to make of the man's sinister remark, but it didn't matter. There was no turning back; everybody knew they weren't coming out alive.

The man led them to the building's entrance and told the demon guard what Jeff had said. The dark slimy bulk heaved as he laughed and looked at Jeff. "So, you've brought the whole family to die. Or do you think your God is going to save you?" Huge razor teeth and glowing red eyes returned Jeff's stare.

Jeff was silent. In this instance, whether it intended to or not, the demon was speaking truthfully. The evil spirit led Jeff inside, down a hallway, into a small room, and closed the door. "What is so urgent you felt it necessary to disturb the master? He is very busy ruling the world."

"You mean destroying it."

The demon laughed again. "We've had puny men come here who thought they had heard from God. They all died the same slow deaths you will die."

Jeff felt as if a knife cut him in the chest. His faith started to waver, but he pushed back his fears. "I want to talk to your master, Satan."

The demon cocked his head. "What do you want with him?"

"That doesn't concern you."

"He is too busy. You will either tell me what you want or I will kill you."

"I don't know, but I will know when I speak to him. He may be displeased if you don't let us talk to him."

The inhuman creature's bleeding cracked lips curled up in a snarl, yellowish slime oozing out. "He is busy right now. Wait here." The creature left the room.

"Open the door and go down the hall. At the end you will see a VRT broadcast in the making. I want you to interrupt the speaker and preach the message about my son Jesus Christ. Impress upon everybody that my coming is very near."

Jeff told everybody what God had said.

"Well go on," Valerie insisted. "There's no time to waste."

Jeff tried the door and it opened. He was surprised because he thought the demon would've locked it. Actually, the door *had* probably been locked. How foolish. God could easily open it.

Jeff led his group down the hall as ordered. At the end, they turned left into a wide studio space. Satan was sitting at a desk and talking into a camera. The devil was a hideous monstrosity, at least 3 or 4 times the size of a large man, with the face and body of a dragon, and large reptile wings folded behind his back. He dripped slimy ooze and had scales for skin like some ancient dinosaur.

"...all over the world," Satan finished his sentence. "We must act quickly if we are to save the earth." Jeff hadn't heard much of the speech, but soon caught the gist of it. "Our enemies are planning an assault. Christ is coming to try to take control of the earth. You must rally your forces, all your nuclear and conventional weapons, and hit Him with everything. We will fight with you as well. If you have to destroy this entire world, do so willingly. Anything is better than being enslaved by Him. We can yet win."

Jeff knew the truth. Satan wouldn't win, even though he was determined to try. He would use whatever means he could, but it would be to no avail. This broadcast must be beaming into every VRT in the world, and this was also the opportunity God had given him.

"You guys cover me!" Jeff said and ran for the camera. The others followed, taking up positions behind Jeff but in front of Satan. The human cameramen and studio technicians were momentarily startled, and so was the devil.

"People of earth," Jeff said as he stared into the camera, "don't listen to this liar."

Satan snarled, "Kill these fools!" Immediately, several humans and demons ran at them.

"Back!" Sandy said as she raised her arms and would-be attackers flew across the room. Satan shouted for the transmission to be cut, but the human cameramen and essential technicians had temporarily lost control of their bodies; God was forcing them to continue.

Satan snarled again and pointed in Jeff's direction. Instantly, columns of fire leapt from the devil's scaly claws like a flame thrower.

Valerie and Nick held out their hands and the flames bounced off. Then they commanded everyone to be still, instantly paralyzing all except technicians and cameramen.

Jeff glanced around the room, especially noting Satan's angry expression. The devil was struggling to get free, but couldn't move; even his voice was silenced.

"Fellow humans," Jeff said as he looked into the camera again. "Satan is not going to win, but the one true God has sent me to warn you one last time of this fact. Soon, very soon now, God's Son will be coming back to execute final judgment upon the earth. If you do not want to be banished to hell forever, along with Satan and his demons, you must repent and believe on the Lord Jesus Christ. If you do not, He will not spare you at His coming. Do not doubt He has the power to do it. He can do it as easily as He has paralyzed the evil ones in this room."

Jeff panned his hands over the room. The camera followed, and revealed immobile demons and humans alike. "Do not worry about your life on earth, for soon it will be gone, one way or another. The devil's cohorts may kill you if you choose God, but they cannot destroy your soul. Do not be deceived any longer. If you do not turn to Him now, you will not get another chance."

Jeff heard a noise behind him and glanced at a human who was moving. Apparently, Jeff had said most of what God had wanted him to, for the paralysis was lifting. Soon, another human could move, but the demons were still immobile.

One human grabbed a handgun from a desk drawer, ran over to Sandy, and shot her in the head. Jeff felt as if the bullet had entered his own skull. He breathed in stiffly as his friend fell to the floor. "That's my family being shot," he said loudly, as he turned once again to the camera. "But I'm not concerned for their safety because I know God will raise them from the dead and they will be with Him forever in heaven. You can have this assurance too."

Jeff paused, as he sensed the Holy Spirit pushing back demonic forces all over the world. Millions of minds were being partially set free. However, in this moment of decision for the people, he could also feel the Holy Spirit mourning, as Jeff sensed many people were hopelessly lost and needed a special miracle in order to repent and believe in Jesus.

Jeff felt a hand on his shoulder and turned to see his son come alongside him. "I feel it too, dad. God tells me this is why I came back. I can help them." Nick closed his eyes and began to glow, the glow quickly increasing in intensity to become dazzling light. Then Nick broke into seemingly millions of marble sized bits of brilliant light, and the tiny globes shot out of the studio in every direction.

Jeff turned back to the camera. "Some of you need special aid to respond. My son is coming to help you win the battle for your minds. The rest of you, if you want to live forever in heaven when you die, repent of your sins now and invite Jesus into your heart as your Lord and savior." Jeff paused to let the words sink in.

"With sincerity, pray after me and you will be saved." Before leading the viewers in a model prayer, the Holy Spirit convicted Jeff to add something. "Mere words won't save you, but a true prayer of faith and repentance will, for God knows the condition of your heart."

Another shot rang out and Jeff heard a loud thud behind him.

Then Jeff heard footsteps quickly approaching him from behind, and he quickened his pace. "Lord Jesus, I repent of all my sins and of all my evil and for following Satan in this world. I put my faith and trust in you, and your death on the cross as payment in full for all my sins. I ask you to come into my heart by the power of your Holy Spirit and to wash me clean of all my wickedness. I thank you for loving me enough to die for me, and for showing me mercy even in this last hour. Help me to change my life, and live for you in what little time I have left on this earth. By faith, I receive you now as both savior and Lord, and I look forward to a life with you beyond this world."

Jeff felt someone directly behind him, but he kept his focus on the camera. "Don't fear those who can only destroy the body. Fear Him who can cast both body and soul into hell." Then he felt cold steel against the back of his neck. "Though you die, you will live."

Jeff only heard the first part of the shot with his physical ears.

* * *

He heard the last part while hovering over his body in spirit form. Jeff watched in horror as he saw his own brains being shot through the front of his face and splattering all over the camera lens. Satan was released and started to shout something, but Jeff became distracted by the turmoil around him.

He was surrounded by a circle of angels, who were fighting demons trying to attack him. One angel, standing with Jeff inside the circle, said, "We must go. Satan doesn't like us in his territory. Especially after the way you defeated him and glorified God."

Jeff looked below and saw Satan staring at him in anger, daggers for eyes. "Can he see us?"

"Yes."

Satan leapt off the ground and transformed in the air, becoming huge, towering over all of them, shinning with a beautiful radiance and wearing robes of purest white. Apparently, no humans on the physical plane could see him anymore because they wondered where he had disappeared to.

Jeff was shocked.

"Not what you were expecting, Jeff?" Satan said. "Perhaps this would be more to your liking." He suddenly transformed into the traditional depiction— red, with horns, tail, and a pitchfork. "Some humans think I actually look like this." He laughed and thrust his pitchfork through Jeff's angelic circle of protection, throwing them aside like flies.

The angel beside Jeff drew his sword and stood between him and Satan.

"You don't actually believe you can defeat me, do you?" Satan asked.

The angel stood there, staring the devil straight in his eyes. Satan laughed again, raised his giant pitchfork, and thrust with all his might, enough to cut through both angel and Jeff. But before it reached its target, it was parried by another sword, as huge as Satan's pitchfork.

"Michael!" the angel cried out with relief. Satan thrust again with wild fury at the Archangel Michael.

"Come," Jeff's angel said. "We must escape while we can."

The angel led him upwards through a tunnel of light. They were ascending quickly, but Jeff glanced down, the two large combatants now tiny toy figures.

Soon, Jeff found himself outside the gates of an immense and beautiful city. The city was surrounded by a high wall composed of solid gold, and a bright light was spilling over the walls, which were shining with white brilliance.

"What's that light?" he asked.

"That's God himself, illuminating all of heaven.

Jeff was ecstatic with joy and expectancy. "Can I go see Him?"

"No. You are to wait out here with the rest." The angel pointed to the left, a huge open space where thousands upon thousands of people waited, sitting upon white horses with wings, swords drawn.

The angel led Jeff to his horse near the front where he met Sandy and the rest of his family. Only Nick was missing. After a brief reunion the angel said, "These people are your peers, resurrected humans. They are all waiting for the last martyrs to be killed. Then the king Himself, Jesus Christ, will mount His horse and lead the procession to earth, conquer it, and start His millennial reign."

Jeff saw the horse the angel was referring to. It was larger than any others and adorned with beautiful jewels. Jeff mounted his own horse as a different angel came up to them with another person.

"There's only two left," the second angel said.

"Good," Jeff's angel said. "Excuse me. I have some final preparations to make."

"Wait a minute," Jeff said. "Do you mean we're only waiting for two more before we go?"

"Yes."

"But there are hundreds of horses without riders. What about them?"

"Not all the saints are to accompany us to earth. There will still be some alive when we get there. Those horses will be filled then."

"And what about this thing." Jeff pulled out the long sword strapped to the side of his horse. "Am I supposed to fight with this?"

"No. It's symbolic. Christ Himself will single-handedly sweep aside His enemies and take control of the earth. You're just along for the ride."

"Oh," Jeff said. The angel excused himself again and went away.

Jeff nervously talked with his family and several others around him. He was surprised, as he thought nervousness was only a human emotion. It should be different here. Then he realized he felt more anticipation than anything. Jeff couldn't wait to see his Lord face to face.

He realized he couldn't really call them his family anymore, either. Valerie, and Stephanie didn't look quite female anymore. There were some similarities to their former human bodies, but they had a kind of neutral look about them, same with Sandy. When he questioned them about this, they commented he too looked different. They were all children now, with God as their Father.

"Why isn't Nick here yet?" Jeff asked but none of his family could answer until an angel came up and explained it to him.

"God gave Nick the ability to simultaneously enter millions of minds and suffer for them in love," the angel said. "He has helped inspire millions to trust in Christ for salvation. Would you all like to see what is happening over earth right now?"

"Yes!" Jeff said and all his family shouted an affirmative.

"We're not allowed to leave heaven yet," the angel said. "But you can open a channel in your spirit and witness what is happening, sort of like tuning your mind into an old earth TV signal. You're new and don't know yet how to use all of your abilities. Here, let me show you."

The angel merged part of his essence into each of them and showed them how to remote view in the spirit. Jeff had his eyes closed and was concentrating, but he felt as though he was floating over the earth without a body.

Jeff witnessed Nick hovering several miles above their old home state of Louisiana, shining like the sun, sword drawn and staring down a blockade headed by Satan and billions of demons.

"We're not afraid of you anymore, Satan!" Nick said. Spirits of dead people were rising from the earth and gathering around Nick, smiling and shouting for joy, likewise shining radiant like the sun.

"When the last one dies and joins us, we're going to show you we've learned who it is we should rebel and fight against."

Satan laughed. "You talk so confidently, like you think you know so much. My demon, Stro-kar, has really done a number on your head. You're outnumbered and out powered. I warned you not to take this assignment. Now I'm going to make you pay big time!"

Jeff was awed as millions of lights from all over the earth continued to flow to Nick's gathering spot, forming into likenesses of people, with swords drawn and ready to battle at Nick's signal.

Jeff could witness what was happening both in outer space and on the earth at the same time. The spirits were being violently liberated from their physical bodies, as Satan's human followers were killing them in gruesome fashion, but all over the earth, while in flesh form, the new Christians were simultaneously singing songs of praise and thanksgiving to God's graciousness and forgiveness.

Jeff focused in on a downtown street in Nashville, Tennessee and witnessed a young woman being brutally gangraped by thirteen men, but she was full of joy and sang the same song that reverberated throughout all the newly redeemed from earth, full of faith and confidence at her soon joyous welcome into heaven.

She sang, "Amazing grace! How sweet the sound that saved a wretch like me! I once was lost, but now am found. Was blind, but now I see!"

The brutal, unfeeling animals that appeared human then slit her throat and her spirit rose to join Nick's group.

Jeff focused next on a battle scarred street in Moscow, Russia. A gang of Satanic thugs was beating a man to death as he continued the worldwide chorus.

"Twas grace that taught my heart to fear. And grace my fears relieved. How precious did that grace appear, the hour I first believed!"

The man took one final blow to the head with a baseball bat before his spirit also joined the rest.

A middle aged man in London, England was being held down by several thugs while his limbs were being sawed off with hacksaws by four demon possessed men.

"When we've been there ten thousand years, bright shining as the sun! We've no less days to sing God's praise, than when we'd first begun!"

A man in Beijing, China was chained to a fence and being torn apart by vicious dogs that beast-men had unleashed on him.

Then the worldwide chorus changed to a new song, *How Great Thou Art*.

"O Lord my God! When I in awesome wonder, consider all the worlds Thy hands have made. I see the stars. I hear the rolling thunder. Thy power throughout the universe displayed!"

A young woman in Tehran, Iran had just had her arms handcuffed behind her back to a telephone pole. Then she was doused with gasoline and set on fire.

"And when I think that God, His Son not sparing, sent Him to die, I scarce can take it in. That on the cross, my burden gladly bearing, He bled and died to take away my sin.

"Then sings my soul, my Savior God, to Thee: How great Thou art, how great Thou art! Then sings my soul, my Savior God, to Thee: How great Thou art, how great Thou art!"

A man in Vancouver, Canada had just been chained to the workbench in a lumber mill and was being sawed in half.

"When Christ shall come with shout of acclamation, and take me home, what joy shall fill my heart! Then I shall bow in humble adoration, and there proclaim, my God, how great Thou art!"

Soon, the last of the lights joined the group, and Jeff instinctively knew the exact number by Nick's side, an amazing

11,872,312 spirits made perfect in death.

Jeff opened his eyes and was back in heaven again. "We need to help them or something!" he said to the angel beside him. "How are they going to get through that blockade?"

"Don't worry, Jeff," the angel said. "God knows what He is doing."

Jeff watched as a large mass of glowing white energy rose from above the walls of the city of heaven. It flashed brightly and shot off in the direction of earth.

"There, see," the angel said. "Help is on the way."

Jeff went into his mind again just in time to witness the white energy mass from heaven splash into the newly redeemed spirits hovering above the earth, dazzling them with brilliance and power. They charged the demonic blockade, Nick taking up personal sword battle with Satan himself. The rest of the lights pushed a hole through billions of black figures. When the last light had pushed through, Nick thrust Satan aside and said, "You're not worth my effort anymore. The Lord will deal with you."

Satan roared with rage, and Nick calmly past through the opening, none of the black figures even bothering to try and stop him.

Jeff opened his eyes and next witnessed Nick leading the mass of lights towards heaven, singing a new song he had never heard before, in a language he had never heard but understood nevertheless.

Nick approached his family and embraced them all one by one. When he got to Stephanie, he said, "You were right, Steph. There's no way I could have done that if I had known for sure whether or not we had preexisted as fallen angels. I understand now how even God's mysteriousness is good as the grappling and struggle makes us stronger and able to do the things He requires of us. That was the hardest thing I've ever had to do, and I'm glad things turned out well for so many, but I also know I just couldn't do it again."

"You'll never have to," Stephanie said. "We should merge and share memory of it so I can understand better."

"I did pretty much the same as you did for me," Nick said. "Except the Lord gave me the ability to do it simultaneously in the minds of millions at one time. I'd love to merge and share it. Then I can also learn what you know about preexistence. Before my mission, you seemed to imply that the Lord had revealed the truth to you on this matter."

"We'll share later. It looks like we're almost ready to go."

The last two spirits arrived and took their mount. The gates of the city opened, and Jeff saw a part of the city light moving. His anticipation increased. Any moment now he would see His face.

A figure appeared at the entrance, bathed in white light. Jeff marveled at how the light expanded, enveloping Nick, who closed his eyes and seemed to start having a conversation with the light surrounding him. "Please forgive them Lord," he was saying. "Yes, I know they're Your enemies, but I have it on good authority one should love their enemies and forgive them…I agree there are limits and You have a right to define them…but I was your enemy too…yes, I changed with Your help, and I understand why most choose not to…you're right, I agree they've sinned against You and You have every right to do as You please with your wayward creation…if you say so, I trust the lake of fire is just and necessary but…"

Suddenly, the light enveloped Jeff as well, blinding him from seeing people, angels, or the city. He closed his eyes and powerfully sensed the presence of God all around him.

"What's happening? Where are you, Lord?"

"You also have burning questions in your spirit."

"I don't understand what you mean," Jeff said, but realized the Lord was right. God knew him better than he knew himself. He had repressed it, perhaps thinking it not proper to question. But he had questions about God's ways, just as sure as Nick did.

"Ask me, and I shall answer."

Jeff paused. "I'd like to know why, if You could have won this battle at any time, did you put us through all of this? Why did you allow evil in the first place?Why did so many have to suffer and die?"

The scene changed.

Jeff saw the beginning of time, when God decided He wanted to have the companionship of intelligent creatures who could, of their own free will, love and worship Him. He created the angels. Jeff felt as if he were in a VRT room, for everything was happening around him as if he were right there. He witnessed God create three powerful and beautiful Archangels— Lucifer, Michael, and Gabriel—and give them each authority over one-third of the angelic host.

God then initiated the Big Bang, which started the physical world into existence. He showed the angels how to mold matter into galaxies, stars and planets, and they all worked together for many eons to perfect the vision God had in His mind of what kind of universe He wanted. Next, He showed them how to form living cells and how to fit the cells together to make complex living organisms, telling them that He would also one day create many different intelligent physical creatures. He, along with His spiritual helpers, would serve them by comprising the Kingdom of God and supplying all their needs and governing their affairs.

But Lucifer became enamored with his beauty and power and rebelled against God, galled at the idea of becoming a servant to lower sentient physical creatures. He questioned the Lord's sovereign right to be King over all creation, to decide what is right and wrong, what should be done, or to demand obedience.

He decided he didn't want to submit to God or His laws, but claimed complete moral independence. Lucifer became Satan, the devil, and succeeded in turning the angels in his charge against their Creator also, following a new path, a new philosophy of living called evil.

Then a great war ensued, lasting millions of years and devastating most of the partially finished universe. God's faithful angels eventually succeeded in capturing all of Satan's followers and the Lord pronounced judgment upon them. He created hell and was about to cast the devil and his angels into it when Satan accused God of being unjust and cruel, raising doubt in the remaining holy angels' minds about the correctness of His ways, and His sovereign right as Creator to do whatever He deemed proper. The Lord didn't want His remaining faithful to fear Him or to question His character, so He proposed a challenge to Satan.

God recreated the surface of planet Earth, a casualty of the war which had seen most of the dinosaurs abruptly destroyed. He made intelligent creatures called man and woman, named them Adam and Eve, and set them in a beautiful garden named Eden. The test was this: if the devil could cause all humans to follow the path of evil, then the Lord agreed to abdicate His throne and let Satan rule the universe, but if even one mere limited human being could love God and be perfectly faithful to Him in all things, it would prove He is worthy of such devotion and the Lord would judge the devil and his angels.

Adam and Eve failed, but the Lord promised One would be born who would defeat Satan. Throughout the ages, the devil succeeded in turning many away from their Creator, but there was always a small remnant that tried their best to remain faithful to Him. However, because of inherent imperfections due to the fall of man, humans needed another Adam to accomplish what the first could not—live a perfect life and never sin.

One day, a member of the Godhead took on human form as the man named Jesus, who obeyed the Lord completely under all trials and temptations, and because of His sacrificial life and death, God won. On the cross, Jesus also chose to bear all of God's wrath for rebellious humans, thereby winning the right to forgive whoever He wanted and grant them eternal life. In this way, He showed His worthiness to be King by demonstrating His great love for His creatures—suffering for them, bearing their sin, shame, and punishment. The devil knew he was defeated but continued to fight on, hatred driving him to try to drag as many down to hell with him as he could.

After Jesus' triumphant resurrection, God could have ended the test and started rebuilding His Kingdom, but He allowed human history to be played out completely, to stand as a testimony for all time of the utter hopelessness of evil. The pain and heartache of human history would be an eternal example for all God's creatures to come that His way was better than any other. Not a single person's suffering went without notice or eternal purpose and meaning; each life proved God's side of the issue, and the Lord's servants were rewarded thousands of times over in the next life. Their suffering also served another purpose: it perfected their characters so they would be fitting rulers with God in His new Kingdom.

Now the scene changed to a vision of the future.

Jeff saw a new universe governed by God and His perfect government made up of resurrected humans and angels. The trials and temptations humans had faced in their lifetimes gave them a perfect and complete understanding of why good was better than evil; consequently, they were able to rule justly in the new order. God gave His saints powerful new spiritual bodies like the angels', and gave them authority over everything He had made. Together, they completed the cosmos, filling it with innumerable life forms, covering every planet in every galaxy. God's Kingdom kept growing and growing until the physical universe could no longer hold it. Then the Lord widened all of creation and His kingdom continued to grow. There was no end.

Abruptly, the spectacular vision ended.

"But you haven't shown me where the spirits came from that lived the human experience," Jeff said. "Is Nick right? Did all humans preexist as fallen spirits before coming to earth, and you've now simply removed memory of it from our consciousness?"

"Ask Nick. I've explained this mystery to him."

Again, God stood at the gate of the heavenly city, bathed in white light. This time Jeff could see His face.

He was beautiful, was all Jeff could think.

* * *

Author's challenge: Have you thought about the really big questions in life, questions like is there a God? Have you wondered if there is a purpose to life, and if so, what it might be? Have you asked yourself, if there is a God and He is good, why is there so much suffering and evil in the world? How can a loving God torture most of His creation in hell forever? How can I be sure I'm going to heaven? If you are searching for answers and you can just *sense* some things are not quite right in your belief system and/or the belief systems of the world, please visit:

www.theunveilingbook.com/MinistryPage.html

for a deeper understanding of the spiritual message(s) behind *The Unveiling*. I will show you how my work answers these deep questions of life, and is not only a metaphor for what is happening on the earth right now, but is a prophecy for the immediate future as well as a prophecy for the next 1000 years!